In Like a Lion

Laurie Scott

In Like a Lion

Laurie Scott

Cressy Lakeside

Editor: Peter Blendell
Copy Editor: Jessica Posgate
Designer: Kathy Fowler (Printcraft)
Cover Design: Laurie Scott
Printer: Marquis Printing

Library and Archives Canada Cataloguing in Publication

ISBN 978-1-7751492-0-0

Printed and bound in Canada

Cressy Lakeside Books

Cressy Lakeside

For Bev

In Like a Lion

PROLOGUE

Sunlight flickers through leaves as the blue Nissan Pathfinder travels along a street lined with tall maple trees. Lily's destination comes into view and she touches the brakes. To her right, a flash of chrome catches her eye. She glances at the silver car parked at the side of the street, then her attention shifts to the circular driveway just ahead. Her stomach lurches. Some of her anger has dissipated, but the gut-punched ache remains. She turns into the driveway, parks in front of the house and walks swiftly to the door. She'll speak her mind and be done with it.

He hasn't answered her calls, but he's there. She feels it. The door is unlocked and she barges in, entering the foyer. "Brent!" she shouts. She crosses the living room and enters the doorway to the kitchen, unprepared for the sight that awaits her. Brent is lying beside the counter in a puddle of blood.

Lily dashes into the room and kneels at his side. He's facing away from her in a semi-prone position and his eyes are closed. Gripping his shoulder, she speaks again, the anger that was in her voice seconds ago gone. "Brent!" There is no response. She slides her hands over his chest and rolls him onto his back. As his body turns, she sees the deep slash across his throat. He's gone. Dead. Murdered! She freezes, panic overtaking rational thought. Then, quickly, her feet are moving toward the phone on the other side of the room. Midway she halts. This is a crime scene. She shouldn't touch anything. She sees the blood she's just tracked across the floor. It looks fresh and the room is still charged with the shock of whatever just happened here. Her eyes dart to the countertop. Brent's favourite chef's knife, the Miyabi Birchwood nine- inch slicer is lying there, its blade smeared with blood. The four-hundred-dollar knife he had praised for its sharpness and craftsmanship has taken his life.

A sense of impending danger sends her bolting to the front door. She needs to get to her phone and call the police, but first she must get away from this house and whoever may still be lurking here. She runs to her car. When she tries to open the door, the handle won't budge. She has no memory of locking it. She fumbles for the key in her right pocket. It`s not there. Frantically, she pats down her pants pockets, front and back, noticing for the first time how much blood is on her hands and her white capris. She's rooted to the spot, unable to collect her thoughts – until a sliver of coherence penetrates her terror. She remembers now. The fob was in her hand when she entered the house. She runs back into the kitchen and scans the countertops. No key. Then, with horrible clarity, she realizes where it is. Kneeling again beside Brent, she tries to roll him onto his side. Dead bodies are heavy. She struggles, finally moving to his other side and pulling on his arm. As she snatches the key fob she hears a sound. A door? Then, the click of shoes on hardwood. Someone is in the living room and heading her way.

Scrambling to her feet, Lily stumbles over the body, falls face first into the edge of the countertop and sends a bar chair clattering to the floor. Pain shoots through her cheek as bone meets granite and, in the same instant, the intruder appears in the doorway. Female, blonde, aging cover-girl good looks; the face from a photo now seared into her memory. Her name is Melissa and she is – was – Brent's fiancée. The recognition delivers another stab of pain. Lily is staring wordlessly at her when the woman turns on her heel and streaks back through the living room.

Lily runs after her, following her out the door that opens to the side driveway. As Melissa bursts outside, she screams for help. Before Lily can reach her, she throws herself into her car, locks the doors and lays on the horn. In the frantic seconds that follow Lily has one clear thought: she must make the 911 call before Melissa does. She races along the side of the house toward her own vehicle. But she's taken only a few steps when the hedge bordering the driveway trembles and a gorilla of a man comes crashing through it.

Melissa's shrill voice replaces the blare of the horn. "Stop her, Drew! She killed Brent!"

Lily has almost reached her Pathfinder when rough arms capture her from behind. Before she can object, she's pinned on the ground. Melissa is there, sobbing, her ear pressed to her phone. Lily is hollering, trying to explain. The man tells her to shut up, save it for the police, and clamps a hand over her mouth. Melissa completes her call and steps closer. She stands over Lily and their eyes meet. She is calmer now, her relief evident. A subtle shift in the arch of her eyebrows and the set of her mouth transforms her face and, for an instant, Lily glimpses the smug expression.

Melissa's eyes harden as she turns away and a siren wails in the distance.

CHAPTER

1

March 1

In like a lion, out like a lamb. Any time March roared in on a winter storm, Lily could count on her mother to quote this old saying. From her memory those words came to her once again. The freezing rain that had begun overnight had turned into snow just after breakfast. It came down thicker and harder now, pelting the hospital window in ferocious gusts of wind. Lily followed the traffic on Queen's Boulevard three stories below and watched it fade into a blurry white curtain a block to the north. A few pedestrians hurried toward the parking lot across the street, heads down, clutching their upturned collars. Two of them paused to embrace, their gestures conveying a kind of warmth that made Lily ache for the company of friends who had all but vanished from her life.

The rustle of nylon turned her from the window, her leg irons rattling as her feet shifted. A nurse stood just inside the doorway, holding a puffy red jacket.

"Lily's sister wanted me to give her this." The nurse was looking at Beryl, the correctional officer, who leaned her two hundred seventy pounds against the wall, arms crossed and looking thoroughly bored.

Lily brightened. "My sister is here?" She realized that Meredith, who lived in Toronto, must have travelled the two hours to Kitchener before the bad weather moved in.

The nurse had taken a few steps when Beryl's thundering voice brought her to a stop.

"Give it here," she scolded, snatching the jacket. She cast a scathing glance in Lily's direction. "Your sister arrived last night, but she can't visit you here. Regulations." Beryl searched the pockets and squeezed the quilted nylon panels. She withdrew a folded piece of paper and a package of Milk Duds. "You know the rules, Mullaly," she added unnecessarily, tossing the jacket onto the bed. She shot the nurse an unpleasant look for good measure.

The nurse ignored Beryl's sour expression. "Your sister and her husband went back to the hotel when the storm started moving in, but they'll see you tomorrow after you're settled back in at the… institution." Grand Valley Institution for Women. Located just south of Kitchener, Ontario, it had replaced P4W, the Kingston prison for women, in 1996. It was hailed as being modern and progressive, but like any place of incarceration, it had its problems. The loneliness, desperation and conflict were inescapable.

Lily was a writer, made her living stringing words together, but she was at a loss for them now. "Thanks," she mumbled.

The attending physician walked briskly through the door and the nurse gave Lily a sympathetic smile before leaving the room.

"Sorry to keep you waiting. Still feeling okay?" Dr. Osborne asked. She slid a chair away from the wall and touched Lily on the shoulder. "Have a seat."

Lily wished she could prolong her stay. She'd spent two nights here, a peaceful interlude in an existence that had become unbearable. The staff were accepting, even friendly, though she was certain they had plenty to say about her in their whispered judgements and speculations.

"I'm doing better. Just a mild headache," Lily said as she sat down.

The doctor stood behind her and lifted a section of Lily's dark brown hair to inspect her stitches, then focussed a pen light on her pupils. "Looking good. *But,* that was a nasty concussion. You'll need to take it easy. No marathons for a while, okay?" She smiled.

"And no more fighting," Beryl added with a grunt, as she stuffed the note she'd just read back into the pocket of the jacket.

"It was not a fight," Lily said quietly. "I was assaulted."

Dr. Osborne turned to Beryl. "Could you not speak, please?" She held her gaze until Beryl pursed her thin lips and looked away.

The doctor shifted her attention back to Lily. "Your people have all of this information." She meant the prison staff. She handed Lily a plastic sleeve containing two capsules. "Ibuprofen. If you start to feel sick or the headaches get worse, let someone know right away."

Lily had no idea how Dr. Osborne felt about her personally, but she respected her professionalism. She'd given Lily the same quality of care that any other patient would have received and her friendly manner felt genuine.

There was a shuffling of feet in the hall and another uniformed correctional officer entered the room. "Are we ready? The snow is picking up," He was a decade older than his female counterpart, early fifties perhaps, slightly built and reeking of cigarettes.

Dr. Osborne signed a form and handed it to Beryl. She held open the red jacket. "You're going to need this, Lily."

"Thank you," Lily said, sliding her arms into the sleeves. "You've been very kind."

"And you've been a good patient. Take care."

Beryl's expression remained neutral, but she wasted no time snapping handcuffs on Lily's wrists. The prison did not customarily use restraints when transporting women, particularly minimum security inmates. It was considered degrading and unnecessary, but Lily Mullaly was not part of the usual roster of drug mules and petty crime offenders. Murderers warranted more stringent precautions. The fantasy of escape crossed her mind. She could easily outrun this mountain of a woman but, hobbled as she was, actual running was not an option. In any case, for a rule-following, law-abiding citizen like Lily, the idea was ludicrous.

"All set, Rick," Beryl said as they approached the door.

Farther down the hall, curious faces turned to steal glimpses of the departing group.

Beryl tugged her roughly toward an orderly who was approaching with a wheelchair. Lily seated herself in the chair and the group moved off toward the elevator. They waited in awkward silence, interrupted only by Rick's gravelly cough. Finally the orderly said, "It's turning into quite a blizzard out there. I hope it's over before my shift ends."

"When's that?" Beryl asked.

"Five o'clock."

"You could be stuck here overnight." Beryl chuckled at the orderly's pained expression. "Don't worry. It'll pass."

"Hope you're right. Reminds me of the ice storm of ninety-eight. It was my first day on the job in Kingston and I had to work a double shift."

Lily remembered the storm. It had begun on a Monday in early January. Freezing rain for five days. Eastern Ontario was paralyzed by the ice. Huge branches cracked and crashed to the ground, fragile as matchsticks, as she stared out the living room window of her childhood home on the Thousand Islands Parkway. She had an exceptional memory and keen powers of observation, skills that served her well in her vocation.

Memories of the ice storm occupied her thoughts while the others chatted on about the weather. Beryl's bellowing laugh snapped Lily back to the present. This friendly exchange with the orderly was in stark contrast to the hostility she obviously felt for Lily. Although Lily had her small share of sympathetic supporters, Beryl was not among them. She believed this inmate to be guilty as charged in the murder of a man who was a legend to Canadian hockey fans. A former NHL forward, the victim had been a handsome, gifted man whose death had elevated him to even greater heights of hero worship.

The elevator arrived and the orderly pulled the wheelchair backward into position. Rick drew his arm across his moist forehead and Lily noticed how pale he looked. He turned to stand directly in front of her and she studied his frame. His legs appeared to sprout directly from his waist. Beryl towered over him, more muscular than doughy, with a no-nonsense haircut and a stern face to match.

As the elevator doors opened and they proceeded toward the

exit, Rick burped softly.

"You alright?" Beryl asked. "You've been kinda quiet, bud."

"Yeah, just a little under the weather. Whoa, look at that." Rick was first to catch a view of the exit where the wind-driven snow was piling beneath the portico outside St. Mary's Hospital. "Good thing we don't have far to go."

"Well, come on then, let's get this freak show on the road!" Beryl's cavernous voice filled the hallway, drawing a scowl from a man in scrubs as he brushed by them.

Lily shuffled from the wheelchair to the rear doors of the van. With Rick's help, she settled into a seat behind the grate that separated her compartment from the front. Beryl plopped onto the front passenger seat while Rick strapped Lily in.

"There's a note in my jacket pocket," she said. "Could you get it for me?"

Instead, Rick removed a key from the hook on his belt. "You don't need those in here," he whispered and he removed the handcuffs. He secured the doors and waded through snow along the side of the van. Up front Beryl held the Milk Duds near the metal grate and, glancing back at Lily, uttered a long "mmmm" before returning them to her pocket.

"It's indigestion, I think," Rick said as he climbed into his seat and started the engine.

"What?"

Rick thumped his fist against his chest and burped. "Sorry. You got any Rolaids or something?"

"Not me. Iron gut."

The van eased toward the street. Traffic was inching along through heavily falling snow. "Crap," Rick grumbled. "We'll be crawling all the way."

Lily slipped her hands into the pockets of her jacket and found the folded note she'd been waiting to open. It was from her daughter, Jemma, and it had been printed from a message sent via Meredith's email. At fourteen, Jemma was already a stunner with long gold hair and green eyes. Lily's only child was becoming a woman, growing up without her. She read the note twice, smiling over the part about "our favourite tooth-rotting indulgence". The package of Milk Duds that Jemma had asked Meredith to deliver was a tangible expression of love.

Lily closed her eyes, leaned back against the headrest and pictured her daughter's face, struggling to hold a smile the last time they'd said goodbye. The four and a half hour trips from the Thousand Islands Parkway to the prison were infrequent. Those visits were precious, but they were soul-wrenching, and the prospect of a long future apart was devastating.

The down jacket was thick and warm. Lily had purchased it many years before from Land's End and handed it down to her sister when she'd grown tired of it. The red exterior was stitched in large horizontal sections. It was reversible, the other side being navy blue with a smooth finish. Lily realized Meredith must have seen the forecast and scoured her closet for the warmest thing she could find.

There was a vertical chest pocket on the inside of the jacket. Lily felt beneath the thin flap for the zipper. As she shoved the note deep into the pocket, her fingers brushed against another papery texture. To her surprise, she withdrew a twenty-dollar bill. The hidden pocket had escaped Beryl's notice. Lily would be required to have the money added to her prison account, but she'd hand it over to a different officer in Beryl's presence, if only to draw attention to her oversight. A tiny pleasure. And she'd demand her Milk Duds back while she was at it.

Grand Valley had been designed to be a kinder, gentler type of prison, but overcrowding had compromised that vision. Bungalows within the compound allowed for the placement of inmates in cooperative living arrangements, but with no available space left, Lily had been assigned to a small cell. That suited her well enough. She had access to common areas and, in the privacy of her own space, the relative peace she needed to read, write and wait. Wait for her appeal.

A false sense of spring had teased Kitchener in the last days of February, but winter was returning with a vengeance. The van slowed almost to a stop and Rick leaned forward, squinting, as another blast of snow obliterated the landscape. "This is nuts. I can't even read the street signs."

"The GPS will get us there. Just head south." Beryl fiddled with the radio and tuned into a local program. The van accelerated into a short, sideways slide before fishtailing around the corner.

"I think we should circle back around and stay put for a while." Rick's raspy voice disintegrated into a rattling cough.

Beryl scowled. "No way do I wanna hang around that hospital all day. Just take it slow and stop being such a pussy."

The announcer's voice filled the van, as Beryl cranked up the volume. *"–and another collision at the intersection of Weber St. South and Union St. East, so if you're headed that way you'll want to take a detour to avoid getting tangled up there. Police are advising the public to stay off the roads. The freezing rain that fell last night has left slippery conditions under the snow and this has already resulted in several accidents."*

The van was creeping down one of the avenues that led south off Queen's Boulevard. Since turning, they'd met only one car. It had materialized suddenly in a dense veil of snow. Lily could still make out the telephone poles as they drifted by the side window, roughly defining the edge of the street. The houses beyond were only vague shapes with muted colours. She heard the low rumble of an engine somewhere behind them.

"Flashing red straight ahead," Beryl was saying. "Make a right."

The GPS confirmed it with a ding-dong chime. Rick tried to ease to a stop, but the van kept moving, the anti-lock brakes stuttering their staccato groan as he cranked the wheel to the right. The rumbling sound grew louder and suddenly, it was upon them. A dark, massive shape filled the passenger side window, slamming into them with startling force. The jolt accelerated the van's sideways slide and a second later, it came to a crashing stop against an unseen obstacle. Lily's head banged against the window during the impact. In the same instant, airbags deployed up front, punching Beryl hard in the face and clouding the air with white dust-like particles.

Beryl screamed and her hands flew to her nose.

"Are you okay?" Rick coughed violently.

"What the hell!" Beryl scrambled to release her seat belt. "My door is freakin' blocked. Idiot!" she screeched at the unseen driver of what appeared to be an old dump truck. It had come to rest, nose first against the van, crushing in the side and pinning the front passenger door. The driver's side of the van had slammed into the steel pole that supported the flashing light at the three-way junction, indenting the door frame and shattering its window.

"Can't open my door," Rick gasped. His breathing was laboured and wheezy. He tried moving the van, first in reverse, then forward, but the tires spun in place. "I smell gasoline," he said, flicking off the ignition. He turned to check on Lily and saw that her head was drooped forward. Blood trickled down the side of her face. "Crap!" He released his seatbelt, wrestled the deflated air bag out of his way and punched out the remnants of crumbling glass from the side window. With much effort, he forced his body through the narrow opening between the steel pole and the window frame.

"Get me out of here!" Beryl wailed. There was no way she could squeeze through the same tiny space. Air bag powder reached her lungs and she began to cough and spit.

Lily touched her fingers to the side of her forehead, dimly registering pain as she tuned into the unfolding chaos. A man wearing a scruffy canvas jacket and a grubby cap appeared at the window as Rick wrapped his arms around the pole, pulled his legs through the opening and dropped into the snow.

"Oh, man, I'm sorry! Geez, are you alright? I had no control on that ice. I was goin' slow, but the weight of my load nailed ya hard." The man, apparently the driver of the dump truck, helped Rick to his feet.

"I think I'm gonna be sick," Rick panted, steadying himself with one hand on the van as he began moving around to the back end.

Beryl stuck her head out the driver's window. "Get that ugly-ass truck off of us!" she hollered at the driver. "We've got leaking gas and I'm friggin' stuck!"

"I'm stalled, lady. We'd better wait for the cops. I'm callin' now," the man said, pulling a cellphone from his pocket.

"The police won't get here anytime soon!" Beryl yelled. "Get a tire iron or something and break the damn windshield. Now!" The driver continued to press the phone to his ear as he sauntered away.

"Don't you walk away from me!" Beryl thrust her left arm out the window and whipped the box of Milk Duds at him, hitting him squarely in the back.

The driver turned and plucked the package from the snow. He whipped it back in the direction of Beryl's face and it skittered off the roof as she quickly withdrew her head.

Beryl gave the horn a long blast and screamed into the wind. "Idiot! Asshole!"

Rick had made his way to the back of the van and was opening the cabin door. "Come on, get out," he said. "We're sitting ducks if another vehicle comes skidding into this intersection." He grasped Lily's arm as she hunched over and hopped out. But her shackled feet hit ice and down she went, pulling Rick with her. Lily stood up carefully, bracing herself against the van, but Rick remained on the ground. He was gulping air. "Something's wrong." He moved his hands to his chest. "Can't move."

Lily knelt beside him, fresh shock rippling through her. "I think you might be having a heart attack, Rick. I've got to get you off the road, but I need to get these leg irons off first," she said. She was taking the key from the hook on his belt as she spoke. Precious seconds passed while she fumbled with the downward facing locks. At last she freed herself and dragged Rick backwards off the street onto what she assumed was someone's front yard. She saw that the street they'd been travelling on ended in a T-junction at the flashing light.

With Rick in a sitting position, leaning against her legs, Lily removed her jacket. She draped it loosely around him and pulled the hood up over his head. Rick closed his eyes and mumbled unintelligibly. She was easing him onto his back in the snow when a middle-aged couple wearing parkas approached.

"We heard a crash and then a car horn!" the woman exclaimed. "We live in that house over there," she added, jabbing her finger at a white wall of swirling snow. "What can we do to help?"

"You can call an ambulance. Tell them it's his heart, I think, but I'm not sure," Lily replied. "And warn them about the ice in the intersection."

"Right away," the woman said, and hurried off.

The wind tore at Lily's thin turtleneck sweater and whipped her hair wildly about her face. She shivered as she turned her attention back to Rick, lowering her ear to his face. "He's still breathing," she said to the man kneeling beside them.

A younger man who Lily guessed was either the couple's son or a neighbour arrived and peered at the van. The driver of the dump truck was striking the windshield with a heavy-looking wrench. Beryl was yelling.

The older man said, "Joe, come here. Help me carry this guy inside. We'll take care of him until the ambulance gets here. I know CPR. And you," he added, glancing at Lily's face, "come with us and have that gash looked after."

The men lifted Rick off the ground. Lily shook her jacket and put it back on. For a moment, she felt lightheaded and saw only fuzz before her eyes, but it dissolved and as the scene around her came into focus, it seemed to play out in slow motion. Every detail was clear. The truck driver, whacking the crumbling windshield. Beryl's head poking out the side window, taking in the action with a look of sheer horror. Rick being carried away. Beryl screaming, "What did you do to him? Shit, shit, shit!" as she struggled to haul herself through the opening in the windshield. The truck driver standing there dumbfounded.

"Mullaly, don't you move!" Beryl snarled and the spell was broken.

Lily looked at her unshackled feet and something akin to electricity surged through her. It erupted through her skin in a flash of exhilaration and fear and heat, diffusing in the rush of cold air against her face. She took a slow backward step, her eyes on Beryl.

"Stop her!" Beryl ordered the truck driver as she wriggled onto the hood of the van. "She's escaping custody, damn it!"

The man looked at Lily without any apparent recognition.

"Are you deaf? Get her!"

This earned Beryl a dark frown.

Lily took another backward step and a triangle of yellow poking up through the snow caught her eye. The Milk Duds. She scooped it up and her eyes shot back to Beryl, who was withdrawing her legs from the van's cabin. The truck driver's voice gave her a physical jolt, slamming into her chest with the force of a punch. "Run! Go, girl!"

Lily's mind raced. This was crazy. What kind of chance did she have if she fled? Where would she go and what would she do when she got there? She'd have the cover of the storm, but it would be a harsh companion. She'd need to find shelter, a near to impossible challenge. Then what? Still, an opportunity – a gift wrapped in snow – had just been offered. She couldn't refuse.

Her mouth curled into a wry smile. "Sorry, Beryl. Got to run, now. Thanks for the lift." Beryl swung her legs free and their eyes locked. Lily waved the package of Milk Duds at her and the sound she made slid smoothly into a lull in the wind. "Mmmm." Then she turned and vanished into the storm.

CHAPTER

2

Dean James sipped his Million Dollar Legs martini at the Royal York's Library Bar as he waited for his *linguini cioppini* to arrive. The foul weather settling over Toronto had forced him into a holding pattern at the hotel. Gazing out the window at the heavy snowfall, he shook his head and muttered to himself, "Unbelievable." Yesterday he'd felt the warm sun on his shoulders as he stood in his Connecticut driveway loading luggage in a taxi. He wondered if this was typical Toronto weather. His last visit here had been just before the wedding, and he didn't dwell on the memory. It held too much regret and guilt. The waiter arrived with a steaming bowl. Dean had just speared a scallop when a figure stopped in front of the table.

"Seafood any good here?"

Dean stood quickly, extended his hand and grinned broadly. "Spencer! I thought we'd agreed to cancel lunch and meet later."

"Well, I changed my mind. I knew you'd be going stir-crazy, so I braved the storm."

Spencer seated himself as the waiter reappeared to take his order. "I'll have what he's having," he said, "but make it a Guinness, instead of that red concoction he's got there." He turned his attention back to Dean and smiled. "Glad you beat the storm. How was your flight?"

"Quick, uneventful. I haven't been here in years."

"New York's been hogging your attention."

"Well, it'll be great to finally work with you."

Dean had established his reputation as a singer-musician and a burgeoning composer in the New York musical theatre scene and had met the director, Spencer McKenzie, on a few occasions over the years.

"The honour is mine," Spencer said. "Everyone is confident that *Thin Air* will be a huge hit here in Toronto and once that happens, it'll be on to Broadway for sure. You and Georgia are already respected in the business, but this is a quantum leap. Music and lyrics by James and Wilder. The best new songwriters in the business."

Dean's face felt hot. His tendency to blush was genetic – a gift from his father, and one he'd return if he could. "I sure hope we can live up to your expectations."

"Have you ever been a part of the audition and development process before?"

"Only to the extent that was necessary to launch the workshop in New York. We had a small budget."

"Open call will be a marathon, but we'll weed through it as quickly as possible."

"Any good prospects for the lead?" Dean asked.

"A dozen names come to mind, but that doesn't mean someone off our radar might turn up. For the role of the young Valerie, we'll have to choose actors who pair convincingly with the person we choose to play her older self. We'll use three on rotation."

The waiter returned and placed a second bowl and a glass of beer on the table.

Spencer nodded his thanks. "Assuming flights are back on schedule, Georgia will be arriving tomorrow afternoon. We're having a little reception at Michael's place in a few days and there'll be some people there that I'd like you to meet. Oh, and the apartment will be ready for you and Georgia on Tuesday."

"Excellent."

"When exactly *were* you last in Toronto? Were you here to perform?"

An image of Lily immediately popped into Dean's head. Sapphire blue eyes sparkling as she laughed. Long dark hair, graceful nose, sculpted cheekbones and straight, white teeth. He sighed and forced the memory aside. "No, just a social occasion. Fifteen years ago."

Spencer detected something like mild irritation and led the conversation back to the subject of the production. They sat at their window table watching the snow descend as they finished their meal and enjoyed a leisurely round of coffee.

"Promised my wife the afternoon," Spencer said, checking his watch. "If you're bored, you can always go for a walk."

"In this weather?"

Spencer laughed. "Your hotel lobby is connected to PATH. It's the largest underground shopping complex in the world. There's more than thirty kilometres of pedestrian walkways for you to explore."

"Well, how can I say no to something as incredible as that?

At the door of the Royal York Hotel, Spencer departed with a promise to meet at the studio in the morning. Dean said goodbye and strolled across lobby. It blended seamlessly into tasteful shops that led down to the PATH. Soon he found himself underground, oblivious to the storm that raged in a parallel universe overhead, oblivious to the slippery roads and swirling snow and havoc on that other plane, and unaware that Lily was caught up in the chaos, moving through the same storm. His path and Lily's would soon converge. For now, Dean walked alone, unknowing, biding his time while he waited for the next exciting chapter of his life to begin.

For most of her adult life, Lily had started her mornings with a 3K run. That routine had been interrupted on the day of her arrest. She'd been granted bail on the condition that she would live in her parents' home under house arrest while awaiting trial. She and Jemma had moved into the basement suite, a large comfortable space with a walkout to a back yard that sloped to the St. Lawrence River. There, she'd resumed her fitness regime, circling the property, pounding up and down the stairway to the river and putting the treadmill to regular use. Following her conviction, she'd kept in shape by running around the huge prison compound and working out on the equipment in the gym. It was as though she'd been preparing for this moment: to run, not out of routine, but with great urgency, on the streets of Kitchener.

In some places, the snow was knee deep, and in others the wind had blown it to bare ground. Lily steered around drifts, and followed tire tracks when she could, falling into a steady if not smooth pace. She'd been moving instinctively in a northeast direction with the wind at her back when she finally slowed to a walk. Her strong, well-conditioned body, boosted by the rocket fuel of adrenaline, had quickly carried her far from the accident scene.

She needed to make a plan. Soon, news of her escape would be broadcast along with a description of her appearance and, eventually, she would be noticed. From somewhere to the west, Lily heard the distant whine of sirens. For the first time since she'd left the van, she touched her fingers to her temple and felt the bulge of a goose egg near the hairline. Two knocks to the head in just three days! Had it knocked the sense right out of her? She scooped up some snow and rubbed the blood from her face, then removed her jacket, and turned it inside out to the navy blue side. Unfolding the neck of her black turtleneck sweater, she pulled it up over her mouth. By the time she'd secured the hood, little of her face was exposed.

Lily visualized the layout of Kitchener. The Grand River meandered along the eastern border of the city and the busy 401 Highway crossed it to the south. She remembered that Victoria Street also crossed the river to the northeast and calculated that it might be ten kilometres away. Following that route would take her toward Guelph where she might be able to find shelter in a farmer's barn. She'd also need to get to a phone. Calls could be monitored. Family would be watched. She knew who she'd call, but that was all. She pulled her jacket sleeves over her bare hands and set off. She was wearing running shoes and although she wasn't terribly uncomfortable at this stage, she could feel the icy touch of snow against her skin where it had collected inside her pant legs.

On she travelled, running, slogging, slipping, wading. When a solitary figure suddenly materialized in front of her, she had no time to execute her disappearing act. It was a man, walking into the wind, snow plastered on his glasses.

"Wild, eh?" he said, wiping at his lenses with a gloved finger and laughing as he passed by, not giving her a second glance.

"Sure is," Lily hollered into the wind.

Another siren sounded in the distance and the accident scene flashed through her mind. Had the storm not interceded, she'd probably have arrived back at the prison by now. This made her think of Rayne, who had recently dropped like a bomb into her life.

Lily is seated at a table in the prison library. This is her third session working with a shy native inmate who is struggling with a learning disability. Scuffing sounds approach and Lily sees a correctional officer with a woman who is young, perhaps twenty, coming her way. She has long, dishwater blonde hair with a single, wide streak of blue at the front. Her shoelaces are loosely strung, allowing her sneakers to clop against the floor and she's chewing a wad of gum. They come to a stop at the table.

"Rayne, this is Lily. She's helping some of the women with their writing skills," the officer says.

Rayne snaps her gum, her hard grey eyes wandering over the space around them.

"Lily, Rayne has just arrived and is enrolling in the GED class so she can get her high school diploma while she's here. She'd also like to join the writing group you're teaching."

"Maybe," Rayne pipes up. She has not yet made eye contact with Lily.

"I'll do whatever I can to help," Lily says.

"Whatever." Rayne rolls her eyes to the ceiling.

To her dismay, the snowfall had begun to lighten and visibility was improving. Arriving at a corner, Lily turned onto a recently ploughed street. Less snow meant making better time and preserving strength. She had slowed to a brisk walk when, at the intersection ahead, a Crown Victoria suddenly moved into view from the left and pulled to a stop. Its colours identified it as belonging to the Waterloo Regional Police, the force that serviced the cities of Waterloo, Kitchener and Cambridge.

She couldn't turn and run. That would give her away, and she would be easily cornered. No doubt the police were aware of her escape by now and were watching for a woman in a bright red jacket and, in spite of the colour switch, she would be scrutinized.

The cruiser signalled right and rounded the corner, creeping toward her. Lily adopted what she hoped would pass for a nonchalant, male gait, and eyed the homes coming into view. The second one was an older brick house with an enclosed side porch. The police car was still inching toward her, when she turned and strode up the driveway. She hoped the door of that porch would open when she turned the handle. With a little luck, the occupants of the house might not even notice her. Heart thundering, she willed herself to move calmly. Maybe the adventure would end here, mere minutes after her dramatic escape had started it.

A car was parked in the driveway and as she moved alongside it, Lily noticed tracks. Recent footprints, already filling in with fresh snow led to the door. Just maybe this would work. She heard the crunch of tires coming to a stop on the snow behind her and felt the penetrating stare of eyes on her back as she mounted the porch steps and closed her hand on the doorknob. *Please, please, please.*

Commander Robert Gaynor's eyes momentarily left the computer screen as he motioned for Sergeant Moretti to enter his office. "Looked outside lately, Carla?" he asked, pointing at the window to her right.

"Yes, it's nasty," Moretti replied. "The storm was supposed to pass north of the Thousand Islands, but we've caught the edge of it."

Gaynor swivelled his chair around to face her. "Well, Kitchener's worse. They're getting the brunt of it. They'll probably nab her as the snow tapers off, though. Or maybe she'll give herself up. That weather would be enough to turn anyone around."

"I'm not so sure. Apparently, she's in great shape and she's motivated. Still claims she's innocent. I think she was desperate when she decided to run."

"Think there's any chance she's telling the truth?"

Moretti shrugged. "Seems unlikely. The evidence against her was overwhelming. How did she end up at the hospital, by the way?"

"Knocked out cold in a fight with another inmate just outside the main building."

"No security cameras?"

"None in that area and no one saw what happened. She claimed the other woman was threatening her and they argued. Says the last thing she remembered was being yanked around. Looks like she was pushed into a concrete wall. The other inmate claimed Lily took the first swing."

"I read one of her books a while back," Moretti said. "I like stories about real life drama. True crime, survival stories, that kind of thing. And now she's the subject of a huge drama of her own."

Gaynor shook his head. The murder had shocked everyone in the community. "I know the parents a little, Jeff and Emma Mullaly. They live on the Parkway. Good people, three adult children, all very respectable. Lily was co-editor of that magazine, *Canadian Voice*, and lived in Toronto for a time, but she moved back here to the Thousand Islands area a few years ago. A shame the way things turned out."

"What's the plan?"

"The Waterloo Police and the OPP in Cambridge will be searching for her. They probably won't need us, but if she's not picked up right away, we need to be on top of things. She may try to call a family member or a friend. That means surveillance of phones, cars and people. Any contact is likely to happen very soon. Her sister is at a hotel in Kitchener right now, but I've spoken to the parents and they're getting in touch."

"The father's a lawyer, right?"

The commander nodded. "Jeff Mullaly and I have had some professional contact over the years and we were in Kinsmen Club together at one time. He's been retired for a year or two, but before that he had a law practice in Kingston. Two younger siblings, Mark and…" He glanced at the folder, "Meredith. Both live and work in Toronto. Addresses and other information are in here. Of course, Mark and Meredith are not in our jurisdiction, but if they make an appearance, we'll be watching. I'd like you to speak with Jeff and Emma Mullaly this afternoon about Lily turning herself in. And put together a list of friends she might try to contact."

Sergeant Moretti opened the folder and examined a photo. "No husband in the picture?"

"Far as I know, there never was. There's a daughter, though. Thirteen or fourteen now. Lives with the grandparents. Alright then," the commander said, rising from his chair, "let's hope this all blows over soon." He gazed out his office window. "And the snow as well."

The porch door swung open and Lily stepped inside, closing it without a backward glance. A bamboo blind covered the window to her right where the porch joined the house. Moving behind it, she flattened her back against the brick wall and cautiously peeked through a narrow crack. The Crown Victoria was still idling there, the pale face of an officer visible through the gusting snow. She glanced at the back of the long porch, hoping to spot a rear exit, but the other two sides offered only windows above the knee wall. She looked back toward the street in time to see the cruiser pull slowly forward and move out of sight.

Lily took stock of her surroundings. The porch appeared to serve as a winter mudroom. Its rustic interior was littered with mittens and hats and boots of various sizes. Two hockey sticks were propped up in a corner and a sports duffel bag sat nearby. The wicker furniture that occupied the centre of the room was strewn with colourful pieces of outerwear. Small clumps of snow near the entrance attested to the recent passage of feet.

A heavy door with a glass panel in the upper half was directly to Lily's right. She could hear faint sounds of a cartoon coming from inside. She peeked through the glass and spied a large, unoccupied kitchen. Beyond that, the flickering light of a television was visible. The chance to grab a few scraps of clothing was too good to pass up.

Near her feet she spotted a black glove. Adult size, suede, with a Sherpa fleece lining. There was no mate in sight and no time to be fussy. The green woollen mitten next to it would have to do. A purple scarf dangled from a coat tree and Lily crossed the porch to get it, ducking as she passed in front of the kitchen door. She added a burgundy toque and a baseball cap to the collection. The boots all looked too small, but she snatched a rolled up ball of socks from a jumbled collection of footwear on the floor.

Turning to leave, Lily heard a voice coming from inside the house. Hastily, she stuffed everything she was holding down the front of her jacket and stood out of sight, beside the kitchen door.

The muffled voice came closer. "I'm not driving anyone anywhere in this weather." Mother talking.

"But it's not fair," a younger voice whined. "Jason gets to be with his friends and I'm stuck here."

"He left before the storm got so bad."

"But look, Mom, it's not so bad now."

"Go watch TV with your sister."

The young voice became defiant. "I can walk there. It's only, like, four blocks." The door knob twitched accompanied by a series of thuds.

"It's way too far and stop kicking the door, young man."

The thudding stopped, but the handle turned and the door opened a crack, exposing a small pink hand.

"I said no!" The sharp reprimand of an exasperated mother gave Lily a jolt.

The door slammed and the voice moved away, sulking now. "I'm going to ask Dad. He'll let me go."

"Knock yourself out."

Sounds of someone moving about the kitchen continued for a few seconds and then it grew silent. Lily ducked back across the room and slipped outside. Once she'd cleared the property, she shoved the extra hats under her hood. The cap would help to keep the snow out of her eyes. She tore two long strands of yarn from the scarf and used them to tie her pant legs snugly around her ankles. Her close brush with the police had been unnerving, but she knew a full-scale search was unlikely. At this point, weather-related emergencies would take priority.

At the next corner, taller buildings loomed ahead and Lily realized she was coming into a business district. She was still apprehensive about being spotted, but traffic had almost vanished. The street took her past some shops, all of which were closed. On the next block, there was more of the same until she arrived at a brightly lit convenience store. *Lucky Variety*. An Asian man stood inside at the door. Lily remembered the twenty-dollar bill in her pocket. The storm was gathering steam again, so this might be her last chance to pick up food and water and change for a pay phone. It was time to pull out an accent. Something to help obscure her identity. Québécois.

Lily and her brother, Mark, had a talent for accents and voices. They were born mimics and many a family gathering had been enlivened with their imitations of celebrities, quirky people they knew and characters they'd invented – an Irish barmaid, a Russian farmer and so on. Their impressions were sometimes unflattering or politically incorrect, but too much fun for anyone to point it out.

As Lily entered the store, the clerk said, "Sorry, just closing up."

"I 'ave jus' to get a little. Give me two minute, please?" Lily asked sweetly.

"Okay, sure. Comment allez-vous?" the clerk said as he eyed her curious ensemble.

Lily veiled her surprise. *Not only does this guy not have a trace of an Asian accent, but he speaks high school French and wants to practise, too.* "Comme ci comme ça," she replied.

The clerk's gaze travelled to the purple yarn wrapped around her ankles, as Lily removed her green mitten and black glove.

"My car, it is ah… stop in de snow, tree block away. I 'ad to put on what I find in de car and walk 'ome." She laughed.

"Got far to go?" the clerk asked.

"No, no. I get dere soon," Lily walked to the cooler and took a bottle of water. A sign at the coffee stand advertised a special: *Any* *size coffee and muffin $1.79.* She poured an extra-large coffee and added sugar and a generous dose of cream, then picked up a large carrot muffin and a handful of napkins. Her eyes darted across the shelves.

"C'est froid," the clerk called out to her back.

"Oui, oui." Lily flinched. She had a basic knowledge of French, but wasn't prepared to expand on her replies. She grabbed a snack size bag of peanuts.

"D'ou venez-vous?" the clerk persisted.

Lily hesitated as the words sank in. *Where are you from?* "Mo-ray-al." At the counter, she added a Slim Jim and a mini flashlight to her pile.

A small TV hung on the wall behind the cash register. Images of the storm filled the screen and a voice described road conditions.

"Quelle… qu'avez vous, ah… what did you do to your head?" the clerk asked.

"Oh…" Lily's hand instinctively flew to the lump. She guessed she must have missed some blood when she'd wiped her face. "I fall on de ice an 'it my 'ead on de… de…"

"Pavement? Sidewalk?"

"Yes, de walk. But it is okay, yes? Ve-hry small. No pain."

The clerk began to scan her purchases.

The voice on the television rose over the beeps. *"There's a lane closure on the Contestoga Parkway near King Street East where a three car pile-up has blocked traffic. It is estimated that…"*

"That's fourteen twenty-five, ma'am," the clerk announced.

As Lily handed him the twenty, a new picture filled the screen and she found herself staring up at her own face.

"Ontario Provincial Police are alerting the public that an inmate from Grand Valley Institution for Women has escaped custody while en route from St. Mary's Hospital at around eleven o'clock this morning. Lillian Mullaly was serving a twenty-year sentence for the second degree murder of former NHL hockey player, Brent Baines who…"

Lily was suddenly desperate to divert the clerk's attention and she interrupted loudly. "Could I 'ave loonies in my change and one bag more please?"

"Sure."

"–five eight, one hundred thirty-eight pounds. She has brown hair and blue eyes and was wearing a red jacket and blue jeans when she fled the scene."

The clerk handed her another plastic bag and turned toward the TV. Lily reached for the bag and purposely tipped over a display rack of gel pens sitting next to it.

"Oh, I am so sorree!" Lily exclaimed. "De bag, it catch de pen. I 'elp you fix it."

The clerk turned to the mess on the counter. "No worries." He began putting the pens back in their slots, but turned to glance at the screen. "Isn't she that writer who killed her boyfriend, you know Baines? Played for the Habs?"

"Never 'eard of 'er," Lily mumbled. "Merci beaucoup."

"Au revoir," said the clerk cheerfully as he followed her to the door and turned the sign to the *Closed* side.

"C'est mon jour de chance," Lily mumbled to no one as she peeled back the tab on her coffee. *My lucky day.*

CHAPTER

3

From the kitchen window, Emma watched the snow descend on the St. Lawrence River. "Here I am, sipping hot tea, and Lily's out there somewhere, cold and hungry and scared."

Jeff put the last of the lunch plates in the dishwasher and turned to his wife. "You know Lily. She's strong and she's smart and wherever she is, it's by her own choice." He lowered his voice. "And don't say anything that might upset Jemma."

"I can totally hear you," Jemma's voice floated in from the family room.

"Your grandpa's right, sweetie. I'm just a worrywart."

Jemma appeared in the doorway and cast a solemn look in their direction.

"Why don't you let us hear one of the songs you've been working on with your voice coach?" Jeff suggested.

"I don't feel like singing."

"Know what she told me?"

Jemma plopped down on a kitchen chair.

"She said you have more raw talent than anyone she's ever worked with."

"She's paid well to say stuff like that. She probably gushes to all the families."

"No way," Emma said. "Your mother is going to be so amazed when she hears you sing."

"You haven't told her, have you?" Jemma asked.

"Of course not."

"Because I still want it to be a surprise when she comes home."

Lily had given her daughter the guitar she wanted for her twelfth birthday and by the end of the first week, Jemma had mastered several chords. She'd studied songs and followed video tutorials for hours, becoming quite accomplished in a few months' time. For her thirteenth birthday, Lily had upgraded her to an expensive Gibson guitar.

Following Lily's conviction, Jemma's grandparents had offered to arrange for advanced guitar lessons, something they hoped would distract her from the despair they were all feeling. After a few days of gloomy despondence, Jemma had asked if she might have voice lessons instead. The soft ballads she'd crooned had been impressive, but no one had foreseen the powerhouse of sound or the incredible musical instincts that were now surfacing. She'd been practising behind closed doors in the basement, sifting through her grandparents' CD collection, listening intently to artists from various eras and mimicking the vocals. Her voice coach had been astonished and was grooming her new client for a debut that Jemma optimistically predicted her mother would attend.

"What's going to happen if they catch her?" Jemma asked.

"Nothing terrible, but she'll go back to prison, of course," Jeff said.

"I was thinking that maybe her case will get some attention because of all this, you know? You still think there's a good chance she'll get out soon, right?"

"I do, Jemma, but not this way. And maybe not *real* soon."

"What if she calls and needs our help? You'd help, right?"

Jeff sighed. "Let's just wait and see what happens, okay?"

Jemma's expression darkened.

"We'd have to talk things over with your mum." Jeff looked at Emma, silently communicating his concern.

With a sigh, Jemma turned and disappeared into the family room, but in seconds she was back.

"Mum's picture is on TV," she announced breathlessly, "and there's a cop car in the driveway."

The snowfall had almost obscured the deserted parkette, but Lily spotted it as she crossed the intersection. She waded to the bench, brushed snow off one end and sat down. Her feet were cold and her scalp was starting to feel tender and achy around her stitches. She squeezed all of her purchases into her pockets. Then she removed her shoes and stripped off her damp socks, replacing them with the thick grey ones she'd taken – borrowed – from the messy porch. She would repay the donors generously in the end, whatever the end would be. Before putting her shoes back on, she pulled the plastic bags over her feet and adjusted her pant legs, securing them with the yarn ties. Finally, with renewed determination, she set off for Victoria Street.

Back in the rhythm of her run, her mind wandered once again to the prison. Until Rayne, there hadn't been any serious antagonists to add to her misery. Lily had passed her days with quiet dignity and, in time, she'd been accepted, even treated with some deference. But when Rayne showed up, everything had changed.

Six women are seated with Lily around a table. Their assignment is to write a personal narrative about an event in their lives that triggered a specific emotion. Anger, fear and love are among the titles selected. Across the top of Rayne's page JOY is scrawled in capital letters followed by three exclamation marks. She has made a point of talking distractedly throughout Lily's explanation of the exercise to Michelle, a mousy young woman claimed by Rayne as her new best friend.

Not quite ten minutes have passed and Rayne speaks without lifting her eyes from her paper. "Hey, lady, how do you spell pulverized?" It's a power game. She's forcing Lily to confront the rudeness or be a doormat.

"Rayne, I know your name and I use it when I speak to you. I'd appreciate it if you'd show me the same respect." Lily's reply sounds unruffled, but beneath the surface something uneasy is stirring and Rayne is sniffing it out.

"I wasn't disrespecting you, I just couldn't remember your damn name," Rayne is slouched in her seat, examining her nails.

"Fine. I'm Lily. Now that I've refreshed your memory, perhaps we can get off to a better start."

"Whatever. How do you spell pulverized? Wait a minute, I just remembered." Rayne sits up, grabs her pencil and loudly recites, "U-R-A B-I-T-C-H."

A couple of the women giggle. Lily ignores her and the room goes silent again. She knows the score. To Rayne, she represents an authority figure, but one without any actual power. An irresistible target.

A minute passes and Rayne suddenly throws down her pencil and shoves her paper across the table at Lily. "Done!"

Lily scans the half page of scribbles. Rayne has written a short account of the sheer joy she felt when she confronted a rival for her boyfriend's affections and beat her to a bloody pulp. She knows Rayne was going for shock value, but she offers no reaction when their eyes meet. "How about writing a longer account of a different experience."

"Nope. That's all I wanna do," Rayne says and she leans into Michelle, drapes one arm over her shoulders and reads what she's writing.

Michelle stiffens slightly, but says nothing. Lily waits, but Rayne continues to glue herself to her friend and is now whispering in her ear. Another challenge.

"Rayne, how about giving Michelle some space so she can focus on what she's writing."

Rayne erupts. "I'm not stopping her from writing! Am I stopping you from writing, Michelle?"

Michelle has always been on good terms with Lily, but she's avoiding eye contact now. She resumes her writing and meekly says, "No."

"See? I don't know why you have such a problem." She glares at Lily, her arm still slung over Michelle's shoulders. "Why are we doing this stupid shit anyway?"

Lily sighs. "Because literacy is a part of the GED test that you'll need to pass in order to get your high school equivalency certificate. I can help you edit and improve your writing and it's also a good way for us to get to know each other better."

The writing has come to a standstill and all eyes are on Rayne now. "All this stuff you're making us write is bullshit and it's nobody's business but ours."

"None of you have to share anything you feel is private. I was asked to help and we're all here voluntarily. Why waste this opportunity?"

One of the women speaks up. "My son would be real happy if I got my GED. I dropped out, but I told 'im I want 'im to stay in school, don't do like I did."

Rayne quickly shuts her down. "Oh, my God. What a load of crap! If you get a diploma, you'll still be stuck in the same old shitty jobs you've always had and anyone who doesn't believe that is just stupid."

The room falls quiet, then Lily says, "Why do you have so much anger?"

"You're not my fucking therapist, lady, so fuck off." Rayne crosses her arms and sneers. More giggles, louder now.

"I simply want to give you a chance to voice whatever is bothering you, so we can move on." Lily waits. "Maybe we should all just talk today. Any thoughts from any of you?"

No one dares to set themselves up for Rayne's ridicule. There is a long silence, then someone farts loudly and the group bursts into hysterics. Rayne fist bumps the perpetrator.

"That still ain't as stinky as this piece of shit," says one, crumpling her paper into a ball. More hooting follows.

Lily is dismayed by how quickly Rayne is coercing the loyalty of her fellow inmates. But she understands the bully/followers dynamic. It's safer for the women to side with Rayne than to stand in her crosshairs. Earning the acceptance of a bully tends to foster a gang mentality, and Lily is watching that reality take root now. In a rougher institution it could have played out differently for a newcomer like Rayne, but so far she has not been challenged here.

The laughter settles and Lily says, "Anyone have something a little different to share?"

Rayne yawns loudly, stands and shoves her chair aside. "This is bullshit. Come on, Michelle." She eyes the others. "You guys can hang with us if you want." She shuffles off with Michelle in tow.

The four remaining women hesitate. "I can't write no more today," one of them says.

They all follow Rayne, without a thank you or a goodbye. Lily sits, motionless, absorbing the sound of their fading voices, then gathers up the papers and pencils that have been left behind. One of the women had crossed out her title, Anger, and printed the word, Rage, in its place. Lily reads the two paragraphs she'd managed to write. It could have been the opening of a great story. But she doubts any of them will be back.

The driving snow played tricks on Lily's eyes and she had to blink and shift her gaze to shake off the hypnotic effect. She was reminding herself to stay alert when her feet caught some ice and did a little jig before shooting out from under her. She landed hard, taking most of the weight on her left hand. As she sat holding her wrist, momentarily defeated, a snowmobile roared onto the scene.

Lily struggled to her feet but there was nowhere to take immediate cover. The machine puttered to a stop. The driver raised the visor on his helmet and looked Lily up and down.

"Are you alright?" he asked. "Need some help?"

From her bank of mastered accents, Lily pulled a Scottish one. She thought it wise to stick with the English language this time. "Well, I was doing just fine until I found that patch of ice." Lily launched into a story about her car getting stuck in the snow and how her cellphone was dead so she'd set out on foot.

"I'm actually enjoying this weather," the man said. "The last good snow of the season, I'm sure. Anyhow, I've, ah, already rescued a few stranded motorists. I'd be happy to give you a lift."

Lily knew snowmobiles were generally not allowed to travel more than short distances on public roads, but guessed their presence was tolerated on days like this. With the help of the snowmobile, she could make good time getting out of the city. "Are you sure?" she asked. "I live clear up by the river on Victoria."

"That must be close to, ah... seven kilometres. You were going to walk the whole way?"

"Yes, but I didn't factor in the severity of the weather," Lily responded, the lilting Scottish brogue rolling off her tongue.

"I'll take you there." The man smiled. "My name's Gordon, by the way."

"And I'm Fiona," said Lily.

"Now, where by the river do you mean? That whole area is industrial."

"Well, actually, it's just over the river." Lily didn't know if there were any houses there at all.

"You mean, ah… Breslau?" Gordon asked.

"Yes, Breslau." Lily had never heard of the place.

"Hop on. We'll use the back streets until we get to the bridge. The roads are practically deserted, but it's not exactly, ah, legal ground for snowmobiles. Not that anyone cares today."

As they moved toward Victoria Street, the snowfall grew heavier and Gordon reduced his speed. Lily began to worry about the bridge. It occurred to her that the police could have checkpoints set up at roads leading out of Kitchener. But they were in the midst of a snowstorm that was paralyzing the city. Surely that was taking priority. They travelled on slowly through the driving snow until the blurred shapes of buildings disappeared. Lily squinted, recognized guardrail on their right and realized they must be crossing the river. Moments later, Gordon made a right turn, crossed another small bridge and entered the outskirts of a residential community. He slowed to a near stop and turned his head. "Okay, where to?" he shouted.

"Straight ahead. I'll tell you when to stop," Lily hollered back. She selected a house at random and gave Gordon a pat on the arm. "Here," she said.

They came to a stop and Lily stepped off, conscious of the chill that had invaded her legs. She thanked Gordon effusively and then waved goodbye as he turned his machine around and disappeared into the white haze. When the sound of the engine faded away, she walked swiftly back in the direction from which they'd come, her limbs warming a little with each step.

CHAPTER

4

Lily washed down an Ibuprofen capsule with some water. She used the purple scarf as a tensor bandage to wrap her sprained wrist, then withdrew the squished carrot muffin from her pocket and ate it as she made her way back to the main road. The food revived her somewhat and by the time she reached Victoria Street, which continued east as Highway 7, she felt ready to run. A few strides brought her alongside another sign: *Guelph 19*. For a moment, her confidence wavered, but she kept moving.

As her headache receded and her leg muscles stretched, Lily picked up speed. Her feet found the shallow spots in her path as her eyes searched warily for ice. Nineteen kilometres! Was it even possible in these conditions? She decided that she'd need to make it all the way to Guelph while she had the cover of the storm in order to find a public phone. The snow was whipping at her back and with no buildings in sight, it was difficult to orient herself to her surroundings. She stayed close to the left side of the road, using the ridge of ploughed snow as a guide.

As Lily ran, she wondered how her family must be feeling. Sick with worry, she supposed. If only she hadn't agreed to write that damn book about Brent Baines and his disastrous sailing trip. The famous hockey player at the end of his career, thrust back into the spotlight by a duel with death in the middle of the Atlantic. It was the kind of white knuckle drama the public craved and the kind of writing for which Lily was becoming known. She, too, had been swept up in his story and swept away by his charms.

Brent Baines is ushered into the living room of the cottage at Loon Lake by Lily's publisher, Sue Emerson. They've had a preliminary meeting in Sue's Toronto office, but today Lily will interview him and discuss the outline for the book. She rises from the sofa and greets him warmly. In contrast to their earlier meeting, she's dressed casually in jeans, white T-shirt and a crew neck sweater that matches her swimming-pool-blue eyes. Brent takes it all in and gives her a winsome smile.

He sets a large envelope and a flash drive on the coffee table. "I brought a few pictures I thought we might use."

"Great," Lily says and she watches him arrange his lean frame in the chair across from her.

Sue has already disappeared as Lily begins questioning Brent about his childhood and family. She laughs as he relates lighthearted stories and she admires his features as she listens. The sandy mop of hair. The dark blue eyes, clear and intelligent. The laugh lines that appear when he grins.

Lily was jarred out of her thoughts by the grating sound of a plough straight ahead. She jumped over the bank and immediately sank to her hips in the ditch. Pitching herself backwards, she buried herself in the snow. By the time the plough passed, she'd been absorbed into the white landscape. As the noise faded, she re-emerged and struggled back to the road, muttering curses as she brushed herself off. At least she finally had a smooth surface under her feet. She set off again, walking and deep in thought.

It's afternoon. They've had lunch on the deck, watched a family of mallards drift by the dock, peeled off their sweaters and warmed to each other considerably. They're back in the living room, sitting side by side on the sofa, examining photos that Brent has spread out on the coffee table. He hands Lily a picture of two small boys and tells her that's him at age three with his brother, age four. Brent's thigh is warm against hers as he reaches for another photo. His hand brushes her knuckles and she's struck by his soft skin and tapered fingers ending in neatly trimmed nails.

"This was taken by a tourist when I was rescued and brought ashore on Guadeloupe," he says solemnly as Lily examines the next photo.

Brent looks painfully thin in his faded, grubby shorts. His scruffy beard and tangled hair add an element of wildness. His ribs are showing and his skin is marked with open sores. She glances up at his clean-shaven face. His tan has faded, but sun-bleached streaks are still visible in the long strands of hair. He's slender, but no longer skeletal. Brent seems to read her mind.

"The healing power of the body is amazing," he says. "I lost thirty-seven pounds, but I've gained most of it back. And the salt water sores healed well," he adds, pointing to a faint blotch on his forearm. "It's hard to believe that was only three months ago."

"Yes, amazing," Lily says. "While I was researching sailing disasters, I discovered several accounts that parallel many of your experiences. Steven Callahan's, for example."

"Speaking of pictures..." Sue has entered the room and is moving toward them, one hand behind her back. She brings it forward with a flourish, displaying a magazine opened to a full-page ad. It features a very fit Brent, a decade younger, wearing snug trunk briefs. "Remember when this graced Toronto billboards?"

Groaning, Brent says, "Geez, where did you find that?"

"I have my connections. I think it belongs in the book, don't you?"

"No, I..."

"What? You should be proud. I mean, look at those muscles, especially that six pack."

Brent looks away. "I lost a lot of that tone when I was in the life raft. The body raids muscle tissue for fuel when it's starving."

Lily takes the magazine from Sue and lays it on the coffee table. "How about we negotiate that one later?"

"Readers would love it," Sue sings as she leaves them.

Brent and Lily are left smiling self-consciously at each other until Lily breaks eye contact and plucks another photo from the table. It's a family portrait of the two brothers with their parents. Something about it seems off, but her thoughts have already shifted when she meets his eyes again.

"I can't imagine how devastating it must have been to lose your brother," she says. "I want to treat that relationship truthfully in the book. It may be painful, but it's something we'll need to discuss."

Brent shrugs. "We had our differences in the past, but we'd become closer since then and this trip was really a healing time for us. Um, you were commenting on someone named Callahan. Is that a name I should know?"

"No. He wrote a book called Adrift about his seventy-six days lost at sea, but it's been out of print for years. I did some research and stumbled onto his story."

"I get the feeling you don't do much stumbling," Brent says. "What are the similarities?"

"Well, the cause of the sinking, for one. Something rams the boat and there's a mad dash for the life raft and whatever supplies he can grab. Actually, I found several accounts of whales bumping or sinking sailboats and another of a boat running into a partially submerged cargo container."

Brent smiles. "You do your homework."

Lily gulped some more water before coaxing herself back into a trot. A dark patch of trees near the side of the road came into view and beyond that, she could make out the shape of a barn. It was tempting to investigate, but she knew she couldn't stop yet. Her feet carried her on and her mind travelled its own course.

"This is incredible," Lily says. "I had no idea you were an accomplished photographer." She's staring at a large framed photograph displayed on the living room wall in Brent's Oakville home. The lower legs of a hockey player have been captured in the foreground. They're angled away from the lens and shooting stars of ice are spraying up from the skates. A frozen pond stretches to a line of bare trees, set against the backdrop of a brimstone sunset. It's hand-numbered and signed in pencil on the white border: "Fire and Ice" Brent Baines 1/50

"Thanks," Brent says. "It's just a hobby, but I'm starting to sell a few in galleries. That one sold out. Kids playing pond hockey. A lucky shot."

"I'm impressed." Lily moves to a large window that opens to a view of the pool.

"My father bought this place after the divorce when I was fifteen," Brent says. "Mom was quite bitter about us moving in with him. She thought we were taking his side."

"Were you?"

"No, but with Dad so involved in hockey, it seemed natural to follow him. Our mother was rather… stern, and although Dad pushed us hard, at least he had a sense of humour. Ben didn't bother much with Mom after they split, but I tried to spend time with her every week before my career took me away."

"We'll treat the divorce as sensitively as possible in the book," Lily says.

Brent nods. "I was living here with my father when he died last year."

"I read that it was sudden… a stroke."

"Yes. Dad was older than my mother – forty-six when I was born. When that last knee injury ended my career, coming back here felt like the right thing to do. Dad was showing signs of dementia and I didn't think he should live on his own anymore. But now that it's just me here, I may sell the place. I find it lonely sometimes."

"Because of the memories?"

"I guess. It would be different if I wasn't alone."

Lily scoffs. "You appear to have plenty of companionship, judging by the number of women who've been pictured on your arm over the years."

"That's mostly for publicity, but yes, I've had a few… entanglements."

"And you have a son. What about his mother?"

Brent turns to look out the window. "Okay, I promised we'd talk about this, but it's complicated. For now, let's just say that BJ was not… planned. I love him and I wouldn't change things now, but ten years ago I wasn't ready for marriage or parenthood. Stacey and I had been dating for a few months and I was about to pull the plug when she told me she was pregnant. The pill had conveniently stopped working for her."

"She was trying to corner you into marriage?"

"It didn't work, but she got a piece of me anyway. She moved back to Niagara-on-the-Lake to have the baby. In exchange for hefty child support payments, I get to see him from time to time." Brent turns to face Lily. "Things are different now. I want shared custody of BJ. And I want to be in a real relationship."

Lily swallows. Brent is standing very close. The intensity of his gaze unnerves her. The magazine ad flickers across her thoughts. She turns again to the view beyond the window. "There was a photo of you with your arm around a woman at the airport the day you came home and she was identified in the story as your girlfriend."

"There was a girlfriend," Brent said, "but my time alone on the ocean made me see what I was missing and it wasn't her. So, I told... the woman in question... it was over. I don't think I've ever truly been in love, but now my heart is opening to something I've never felt before."

They're not quite touching, but Lily can feel heat radiating from his body. Her cheeks are burning as she turns to face him. "I can't get involved with you," she says quietly. Brent draws her close and she raises her arms to push him away. She kisses him instead.

The snowfall eased up. Minutes later the faint whine of a snowmobile rose and faded somewhere to the south. Headlights glowed in the distance and Lily hid behind a thick row of cedars near the road. A half-ton came into view, followed by an OPP cruiser. When they disappeared, she took up her journey again. By then, she'd passed a garden centre, a gas bar and some other buildings that had been indistinct through the snowfall. As the snow tapered off, she saw stretching before her only white countryside, smudged with the dark shapes of trees. Her brain relayed this information to the rest of her body and her legs and lungs protested, unwilling to carry her that distance and beyond.

She came to a halt and collapsed on a snowbank, its dense form cushioning her like an icy bean bag chair. She let herself sob until the penetrating cold overcame her exhaustion, forcing her back to her feet. Her pulse was tapping at the stitches in her scalp, a sharp reminder of her last encounter with Rayne.

"A big shot writer like you must have lots of money to throw around." Rayne has stepped in behind Lily who has just left the prison commissary with a bag of snacks.

Lily frowns. "I don't have 'lots of money'. And what I do have is rapidly disappearing into the pockets of my defense team."

Relationships and food are the main sources of contention here. Women in minimum and medium security live in groups in bungalows within the compound. They plan and cook their own meals, and squabbles over the consumption of food are regular occurrences. Treats from the commissary are commodities, available to some more than others, depending on the amount of money in the inmates' accounts.

Lily moves away toward the exit, but Rayne is still trailing after her.

"You wanna fit in around here, you gotta share," Rayne says to her back.

Lily stops at the door and turns. "I've tried to be nice to you. I gave you a chance to talk it out with me privately when your little entourage wasn't around and you've given me nothing but grief, and now you've poisoned just about everyone against me. Why should I 'share' anything with you?" She pushes open the door and steps outside. Rayne follows.

"Let me put it this way. You send something my way once in a while and maybe we won't beat the shit out of you."

Lily wheels around, seething, and brings her face close to Rayne's. "This isn't a playground and you're not going to bully me into handing over my lunch money. So, let me advise you to steer clear of me. If you ever so much as touch a hair on anyone's head, including my own, I will serve your ass up to the warden so fast, you won't have time to blow your friends a goodbye kiss on your way to Isolation."

"Ooh, so you do have a temper. Is this how you felt when you murdered that guy? Huh? Not so lucky now, are ya? At least I won't be stuck here for the rest of my life. I'll be free and you'll still be here, rotting in prison."

"Better than rotting in hell," Lily says, turning away. She walks along the side of the building. "I should feel sorry for you. You're pathetic."

"You are dead!" Rayne screeches and she launches herself at Lily and grabs her by the collar, jerking her around. The memory ends there, swallowed in blackness.

Lily knew her choice of words had been reckless the second they were out. You don't insult someone convicted of battery and expect to walk away. But, as it turned out, the consequence had led to this unexpected break. A chance. To do exactly what, she had yet to figure out. With fresh resolve, she moved on, jogging again.

The storm continued its attack-and-retreat pattern. The road passed steadily beneath her feet and finally the scenery began to change. There was an intersection, then a few signs. One said *Guelph Township Road 3.* Minutes later she noticed a pale orange glow in the darkening sky. The lights of Guelph!

Finally, Lily saw the big blue sign. *Guelph.* Her legs felt every one of those nineteen kilometres, but she'd made it. Soon she was looking at car dealerships and other businesses typical of the kind that spring up on the outlying edges of cities. She passed a brewery, a mini-mall and some industrial and office buildings. Not surprisingly, there were no pay phones in sight. In this age of cellphones, they were nearly obsolete. That problem would have to wait until morning. She paused at the intersection and scanned the street ahead. The scene seemed to stretch on without end. Turning north, away from the main drag, would take her just outside the city limits where she'd be more likely to find shelter at a residence with outbuildings.

With this in mind, Lily changed course and was soon back in a rural landscape. She could only walk now and her pace was slowing. Coming upon a farm, she approached the barn, but a motion detector light and the squeak of a door sent her stumbling back to the road. She was becoming discouraged and a little panicky.

She ate a handful of Milk Duds, slowly dissolving them in her mouth as she travelled farther away from the city limits. A few houses appeared and she watched for sheds and detached garages. She tried a couple of doors, only to find them locked. Her toes had finally pushed through the plastic bags on her feet and her socks were wicking back cold moisture. Lily kept moving, producing body heat, but the chill was sinking into her bones. It wasn't the kind of intense, bitter cold that stung the skin, but it was damp and pervasive. Stopping to rest before finding shelter was not an option. Hypothermia would set in.

Except for a few rogue flakes straggling after the storm clouds, the snow had stopped. A brisk wind continued to skim over the fields sending ghostly streams across her path. Plodding along, bone tired in the darkness, she spotted a light flickering through some trees. As she drew closer, she could see that it was coming from an upstairs window of a house that was set behind tall spruce trees. The driveway had been cleared. The house was large and handsome, even in the dim light. Shades of beige filled the night sky, a reflection of light from the city, and against this backdrop, just beyond the house, another shape loomed. Cautiously, she moved in its direction. It was an outbuilding, red and barn-like in shape, but decoratively trimmed with white shutters. A low stoop on the left side fronted a single door. Lily tried the knob and found it locked. Her fingers traced the ledges above the door and window. No key.

Not ready to be defeated, she trudged along the left side of the building, searching for another way in. Her path was blocked by the featureless wall of a small addition, a shed of some sort. She made her way around it to the opposite side. There, she discovered a large slab door with a thumb latch handle.

A hard tug created a small opening. She cleared away some of the snow and when she tried again, the door budged enough to allow her to squeeze through. It was cold and completely dark inside, but Lily knew she was out of options. This would be her refuge for the night. She pulled the small flashlight from her pocket and shone it around the room. The walls and floor were rough, greyed wood. There were two mullioned windows on either side of the door with crude tables positioned in front. Bags of fertilizer were stashed underneath. The light passed over rakes and shovels, clippers and saws, pails and jugs. The wall opposite the door had a row of pegs on which some clothing was hung – a raincoat, a straw hat, a pair of white painter overalls, and a pink and grey flannel shirt. Nothing in here would keep her warm, but it would keep her alive.

Lily shone her light on the wall that connected the shed to the larger building. This was clearly a potting shed. Dozens of pots were stacked on the floor and on wall-mounted shelves. To the right of the shelves was a door. She approached it hopefully. "Open Sesame," she whispered as her hand closed around the door knob, but it did not obey.

Leaning against the door, she fumbled for her last gel cap and popped it in her mouth, drinking all that was left of her water. She thought about her parents' property. They kept a key for the boathouse under a rock and a spare key for their home under a can of insect spray in the boathouse. She checked the coco mat at her feet and the ledge above the door. Then her attention shifted to the large flower pots on the floor and she inspected those too. Rising up again, she found herself eye level to a shelf of smaller clay pots. She lifted the first stack of three and peered inside. There was nothing there, but as she was returning them to the shelf, she heard a soft scraping sound. And there was the key, resting between the bottom and middle pot. Balancing the flashlight in her bandaged hand, she tried the key in the lock. The smooth click was a magical sound.

It was several degrees warmer in the main building. Keeping her pool of light low, Lily moved about the space, quickly identifying the positions of three windows, a third door and a small two-piece washroom. The overall space was quite large, perhaps fifteen hundred square feet, with a loft covering the back third. The area adjoining the potting shed served as a workshop. Heavy posts and beams supported the loft above it. Lily guessed the building had once been a stable. The place was now drywalled and presumably, insulated.

Moving into the front part of the room, she noticed a glowing red jewel of light. Closer inspection revealed a wood stove, a dying ember still visible through its door. Faint residual heat emanated from its surface. Two recliners, some lawn chairs and a few side tables were grouped nearby. On one wall was a bar fridge and a bank of old kitchen cabinets with a small countertop, sink and microwave oven. The words *man cave* came to mind.

She checked the cupboards and found some plates and cups, a bowl of sugar, a box of tea, and a nearly full package of shortbread cookies. She checked the taps, but the waterlines had been drained for the winter. The bar fridge was unplugged and empty, but there was a kettle of water on the counter. Lily refilled her bottle, shoved a handful of cookies into her pocket and returned to the area that had first caught her attention.

A set of steep stairs in the workshop stretched up to the loft. Remembering the flannel shirt and overalls, she went back into the potting shed to fetch them. She was rapidly losing body heat and needed dry clothing. She also grabbed a pail with a lid and picked up a roll of toilet paper from the washroom.

Shivering, she climbed the stairs to the loft and surveyed her surroundings. The open space had no railing – it was likely the former hayloft. Stacked in rows against the back wall were many cardboard boxes. A pulley was suspended from the ceiling above the edge of the loft floor and a large cargo net hanging close by suggested it had been used to hoist things up from the lower level.

Lily directed her light over the boxes. All were labelled in thick black marker. She guessed that the ones with Lake scrawled at the top contained items used at a cottage. According to their labels, these boxes contained such things as towels, life vests, inflatables and… blankets. She grinned. The blanket box might as well have said *Jackpot.* She removed it from the stack, opened it and withdrew two comforters enclosed in plastic bags. As she moved her light around, she noticed two stuffed duffle bags hanging on the wall. She let them down off their nails, loosened the drawstrings and reached inside. Sleeping bags. *Jackpot.*

Lily studied the stacks of boxes. They were three deep to the wall. Rearranging them, she created a small den behind the outermost row, just wide enough for her bedding. She left a narrow crack between two of the boxes, angling them a little wider on the outer side to give her a partial view of the man cave. Her plan was to leave at dawn, but her body had been pushed to the extreme and she was considering the idea that she could hide here for another day. Lay low and get her strength back.

She found some flattened cardboard boxes and spread them out in a thick layer on the plank floor of her den. Over this, she laid both sleeping bags and the two comforters. Her teeth were chattering, and when she unzipped her jacket, she discovered it was wet inside and out. The combination of melting snow and her own sweat had finally defeated the puffy down. She unwound the scarf from her sprained wrist and gingerly flexed the joint. It was tender but functional. Shaking, she stripped off her clothing. She put on the flannel shirt, plucking off bits of dried leaves, and pulled on the overalls. Near the head of her bed, she laid out the contents of her jacket pockets. At the foot of her den she arranged her wet clothing and her pail, then crawled into the top sleeping bag, curled up on her side and pulled the comforters snugly around her.

Lily lay there trembling as the events of the day tumbled through her brain. Her great escape, her long journey, her incredible luck. What challenges remained were a problem for another day, but at that moment she felt greatly relieved and profoundly exhausted. Slowly, her nest filled with warmth. The wind blasted icy crystals of snow against a window somewhere above her head, its roaring breath buffeting the building. Timbers protested with creaks and groans. Lily took comfort in the thought that her footprints outside had probably already vanished. She let the tension melt away and, completely spent, sank into deep sleep.

CHAPTER

5

March 2

Only a dream, tugging Lily back to consciousness, intruded on her rest. She'd been trying to run, but the gravity pulled so intensely on her feet, she could barely lift them. Her first waking thought was that she needed to use her pail. Rolling onto her back, she became aware of dim light entering the loft. It was coming from a window under the peak of the hip roof directly above her head. As she struggled to her feet, the soreness in her muscles was immediately apparent and she knew the worst was yet to come. Although her excellent physical conditioning had enabled her to make it from Kitchener to Guelph, the magnitude of this journey was exacting its price. Wincing, she slowly straightened until she could brace her hands on the window sill.

In the blue light of predawn, Lily could see only fields stretching to the tree line on the horizon. Clouds still blanketed the sky, but the snowfall had stopped. The wind had lost most of its bluster but wisps of snow still trailed across the pale landscape. Her cold feet prompted her to hurry and soon she was tucked back in her bed, in deepening slumber.

The clanking of the wood stove's door startled Lily wide awake. Someone was building a fire. Propping herself up on her elbow, she peered through the crack between the boxes. A grey-haired man moved across her line of vision. There were more clunks and rattles and soon, the smell of burning wood and the sound of crackling flames. She heard the man loudly blow his nose. This was followed by the creak and thud of a door opening and closing. Then silence.

When it became apparent that she was alone, Lily ate two of her cookies and half of the Slim Jim. They took the edge off her hunger, but it wasn't the kind of warm meal her body craved. Several minutes later the man returned to the workshop, threw more wood on the fire and left. Lily lay back and waited. The building was filling with warmth and she pushed off the two comforters. Shortly, the door opened again and she heard a woman's voice.

"There's nothing like a real wood fire," the woman said, and Lily caught her profile. She had short auburn hair and appeared to be in her mid- to late fifties.

The man was standing at the front window. "Here come Millie and Dave," he said. He walked out of Lily's visual range and she heard a metallic tinkle.

"What are you doing?" the woman asked.

"I'm getting the spare key. Dave and Millie can check the house while we're gone."

"Put it back. I like Millie, but she's nosey and I don't want her snooping around in our house. You know we should step out of the stone age and get an alarm system."

The man sighed and walked back in the direction of the cupboard.

His wife opened the door and hollered, "We're out here, come on in." The sound of excited barking filled the room and Lily became aware of the presence of a small dog, a yappy poodle mix of some kind.

"Jinx! Hush!" the woman scolded.

The yapping continued and soon a man's voice, presumably Dave's, said, "Howdy, neighbours. We were out for our walk and saw your smoke. Thought we'd drop in and see how you survived the storm."

"Well, come in and have some coffee. We're staying put today, so it would be nice to have some company," the woman replied.

"Sounds good to me."

Jinx grumbled and uttered a final, half-hearted woof.

Through the exchange that followed, Lily learned that the hosts' names were Ed and Karen. After some brief conversation, Karen went into the house and soon returned with a pot of coffee and a tray.

"Coffee cake. Baked it yesterday," Karen said.

"Oh, you spoil us!" Millie exclaimed.

The conversation buzzed on with much discussion of the previous day's storm. How Millie had left work almost as soon as she got there, how Ed had spent the whole day working on one of his duck carvings. No mention was made of an escaped prisoner in Kitchener.

"How are Kate and Flynn doing?" Millie asked.

"Kate's in Toronto, living with Ed's mother for a while. She's doing better on the new meds, but not ready to go back to work yet. And Flynn is fine. He and Nancy are thinking about moving to the suburbs," Karen said.

"Actually," Ed added, "we're meeting Flynn in Miami. They're bringing the boys down for March Break and we're all staying at my mother's condo there."

"Oh, how nice for you!" Millie said.

"Karen and I will stay on for the rest of the month and then take our time driving back."

"If you need someone to look in on the house while you're gone, we'd be happy to," Dave said.

"Thanks, but it'll be fine. We'll have the lights on timers and the furnace on low. Anyhow, we've got one of GP's finest living right next door," Ed laughed. "If you notice any trespassers, Dave, feel free to open fire."

Lily quickly deciphered. *GP…Guelph Police. The neighbour is a cop.*

Millie persisted. "Really, we wouldn't mind at all. It would give you peace of mind…"

"All we really need is someone to collect our newspapers and mail," Karen said, cutting her off. "Would you do that?"

"Of course."

"Who's looking after Jinx?" Dave asked.

"We're dropping him off at my mother's place in Toronto," Ed said. "Kate will be there too, so he'll have lots of attention."

Karen picked Jinx up off the floor and kissed him on the top of his head. "Oh, mommy's going to miss her widdo baby," she cooed. "You are da best boy. Yesh, you are."

Ed groaned. "Embarrassing how she babies that mutt."

Dave chuckled. "When are you leaving?"

"Day after tomorrow."

"I've got tons to do before then," Karen complained. "I have to clean out the refrigerator and pay some bills and I haven't finished packing yet."

The morning wore on and eventually Millie and Dave departed to another chorus of barking from Jinx. "See you in April," Karen called after them.

Jinx wandered around, sniffing the floor directly beneath the loft. Lily caught glimpses of him through the gaps in the floor boards. She'd been propping herself up with her left arm and her sprained wrist was beginning to throb. As she quietly lowered her body, her hand brushed the plastic bag next to her head and the half-eaten Slim Jim rolled off and tumbled through a gap, landing with a soft plop on the floor below. Lily leaned forward in time to see Jinx wolfing down the pepperoni as he gazed upward to the heaven from which this manna had fallen. Her breath caught in her throat.

There was a clattering of plates and then Karen's voice. "Coming in soon? I'm going to make some lunch."

"You go ahead and eat. I want to put another coat of Tung oil on this Merganser."

"It's looking good, hon. Butternut?"

There was a soft plodding sound and as it grew closer, Lily realized Jinx was making his way up the loft stairs. She cringed and cursed under her breath. All her effort to get this far was about to be undone by a careless mistake.

"Jinx!" Karen was moving quickly toward the dog. "You little rascal!" Her feet ascended the stairs and her voice rang out from the top. "Bad boy! You can't be up here! You could fall, sweetie." Her voice trailed off again as she retreated to the workshop below. "That's so strange! He's never done that before."

"Crazy mutt," Ed grumbled. Lily heard some shuffling near the base of the stairs. "There. That should block him. Pain in the ass."

"Okay," Karen said. "I'm going in now. You be a good boy, Jinxy." Lily peeked through her barricade and watched Jinx jump up on a recliner as Karen left the building.

The sound of a radio filled the workshop with music. Ed moved around, making stirring and tapping noises and humming happily. "Are you going to be Daddy's widdo helper?" Jinx wiggled in the chair and wagged his tail as Ed leaned down to scratch behind his ears. "Well, Daddy has a treat for you."

Jinx barked enthusiastically.

"Here you go, shweetie pie." Ed offered a chunk of coffee cake and the dog quickly devoured it. "Him's a good boy. Yesh, him is." Jinx responded with the canine equivalent of a grin.

Lily couldn't suppress a smile. Secretly, Ed was a big softie and Jinx knew it.

A few minutes later Karen swept into the workshop, bringing a rush of cool air with her. "I know you and you're going to get so caught up in your projects, you'll forget all about your lunch, so I brought us Kate's Moroccan soup and some chicken sandwiches. And a fresh kettle of water."

"I was just cleaning up," Ed said.

An enticing aroma wafted up to Lily's hiding place.

She lay back listening to snippets of conversation as mealtime progressed.

The song on the radio faded out and the news cut in. The previous day's storm was the lead story. After a few minutes, the topic segued to Lily's escape.

"Police suspect that she found cover in Kitchener or was able to contact someone who came to her aid. They're urging anyone who may have seen her to come forward."

"Where the hell could she go in a storm like that?" Karen asked.

"Beats me, but she wouldn't have gotten far. They'll find her. Kate's read her books, hasn't she?"

"Yes. She's a big fan. I'm curious now. Maybe I'll borrow one for our trip."

There were excited yips and then Karen's voice again. "I'm going to take Jinx for a little walk. Bring the dishes in when you come, okay?"

"Yes, dear. I won't be long."

Ed puttered around for a few minutes, then turned off the lights and the radio and left. Rising stiffly to her knees, Lily looked out over her barricade of boxes. The plates of food still sat on the counter. So much for Ed's memory. It was tempting to grab a sandwich, but not worth the risk. Soon she would have an entire house to herself. Thanks to Karen, she knew where the key was hidden. There would be food, a bath, a phone, a computer!

Sun broke through the cloud cover and Lily listened to the sounds of melting snow dripping and sliding from the roof throughout the afternoon. She stood at the loft window, gazing out at the landscape. Fields of pale gold-white shimmered in the light of the setting sun and fingers of violet sky stretched overhead. It was hardly conceivable that a mere day had passed since she'd staggered into Guelph on the tail of a blizzard. She winced as she knelt and crawled back inside the sleeping bag. The soreness had peaked. *All I can do is wait,* she told herself. As her mother, the queen of quotes, had often reminded her, *Patience is bitter, but its fruit is sweet.*

CHAPTER

6

March 3

When Lily finally awoke to darkness, her stomach was growling. She made her way down the loft stairs, every step delivering fresh torture to her legs. In the narrow beam of her little flashlight, the workshop clock informed her that it was two twenty-seven. She moved the doggy barricade, a folding card table, out of the way and followed the pool of light to the countertop where the remains of the day's food beckoned. Five pieces of quartered sandwiches were covered loosely with plastic wrap. Surely the disappearance of two would go unnoticed. Soon she was back in the loft with her stale sandwiches, a slice of coffee cake and a mug of hot tea. She leaned back against the loft wall wrapped in a comforter and blissfully consumed her meal.

The sun rose and climbed high, but no one entered the workshop. Passive heating from the window above her head was warming the loft and the white world before her eyes was rapidly melting. A long day stretched out before her. She'd eaten her small stash of food, but she could endure a little more hunger. There were cookies in the cupboard and in one more day she'd be in the house.

Lily knew her family must be in anguish. She was especially concerned about her daughter. The emotional roller coaster of puberty had coincided with the very public turmoil of Lily's arrest. As if Jemma hadn't been through enough already, now she had to worry about her missing mother, last seen running into a raging blizzard.

There was something else too – a festering concern that weighed heavily on her conscience. She'd lied to Jemma and it was a whopper. The lie had been all about anger and self-pity in the beginning, but it was selfishness that kept it going. At her insistence, her family had gone along. As time went by, they'd urged her to do the right thing, but Lily made excuses, *Not yet. Not now. Jemma's mine. That SOB will want joint custody and hurt me all over again.* And then her world had caved in. The arrest, the trial, prison. And so, the subject was dropped. No need to put poor Lily through more pain than she was already experiencing.

As much as she tried to block Dean from her life, Lily recognized him every day in Jemma's face. They were alike in so many ways. Fine, golden hair that gleamed strawberry blonde in sunlight. Emerald eyes and long dimples that creased her cheeks when she laughed. It would have been so much easier if Jemma looked more like her. Yet Lily could not imagine seeing her any other way or loving her more than she did.

The relationship with Dean had been brief and would've had the substance of a dream had Jemma not given it permanence. Like cliché fireworks in the night sky, it had flared brilliantly for a few glorious moments before its twinkling ashes surrendered to gravity. The whirlwind courtship, the impulsive marriage, the aborted honeymoon in the paradise of St. Kitts.

It had been a low-key ceremony, but the excitement and the ordeal of travelling had worn them down. The first night at the resort had been tender, if not passionate. The next day Dean had proudly paraded Lily around, chatting with other vacationing couples. They'd wandered through shops, picking up souvenirs and absorbing the local colour. Time alone was not to be had that day.

In fact, Dean had kept those first few days quite full with boat tours and snorkelling and socializing. That was fine, but there were moments when Lily wanted to simply spend some quiet, one-on-one time with Dean. To stroll hand in hand down the beach. To kiss under a starry sky. Dean had acquiesced to some of these suggestions, but his strolling was more like a brisk walk and his kissing was more of a chaste peck. And before long Lily would find herself back amid the throng, music and conversation flowing around her.

By the fourth night she'd grown concerned. Their brief intimacy felt forced. Dean had stood on the balcony in his boxers for some time, gazing out at the sea, and when Lily finally called him to bed, he'd slipped beneath the covers and stretched out on his back. She'd snuggled close and Dean had responded with some perfunctory caressing, then yawned and told her he was feeling wiped. He'd kissed her, cryptically murmured, "Tomorrow," and rolled away. And tomorrow had come all too soon.

They're lunching at the resort's outdoor cafe. Dean is leafing through a brochure and Lily is finishing her salad and contemplating the length of time that's passed since he last told her that he loves her. Sixty-four hours, give or take a few minutes. Unless she counted the "Me, too" he'd offered the night before.

Their solitude is interrupted by the gleeful arrival of three men who seat themselves at the next table. Two of them are wearing vibrant shirts and have accessorized with the colourful drinks they've picked up at the bar. The third is considerably more subdued and is neatly outfitted in light tan shorts, a crisp white shirt and sandals that are same chestnut shade as his hair. He politely nods and smiles at Lily and Dean as he sets his bottle of Carib beer on the table. Before long it's apparent that the two men in the loud shirts are a couple and one of them is celebrating his thirtieth birthday. The third is a newly single friend.

"Don't be silly, Vince," the yellow-shirted birthday boy is saying. "Why should you feel like a third wheel?"

"Let me put it this way, then," Vince says, "you're great company, but I could use some down time on the beach with a good book today."

"Oh… well, we'll try not to take that personally, honey, but if you need some space, you've got it," says the man in purple.

Lily leans across the table and whispers to Dean. "Sweetie, I'm going to go to the rest room and then we can be on our way." She rises and as she turns to leave, her purse catches the edge of her water glass and sends it tumbling to the concrete where it shatters and scatters between the two tables.

"Ooh!" purple shirt squeals. His hand flies to his chest, fingers splayed dramatically.

"Oh, no," Lily wails. "I'm so sorry. What a klutz I am."

Vince is already on his feet, gingerly picking up some of the larger fragments and placing them on her table. Even in her state of embarrassment, Lily notices his clean-shaven, good looks and warm brown eyes. "Not to worry," he says, smiling at her, reassuringly. "I've done much worse." Charming, too.

Dean, who has been mutely observing the scene, suddenly snaps into action and signals a waiter. "Better not handle that glass," he says. He extends his hand to Vince. "Thanks. And hello. I'm Dean and the klutz is Lily."

"The clumsy wife," Lily adds.

They engage in friendly chat until the waiter arrives with a broom.

"I'll be right back," Lily says, sidestepping the shards of glass. "So sorry," she apologizes to the waiter.

"Get me a rum punch on your way back, would you please, Lil?" Dean calls after her.

Lily is a little surprised, but she nods as she leaves. Dean rarely drinks, especially this early in the day, but she knows the rum punch and the tropical paradise will soon end and they should enjoy it now. She orders one for herself as well.

As Lily waits at the bar, she watches her husband across the patio. He's nodding and grinning, occasionally running the fingers of one hand through his blonde locks. It's a habit she finds endearing. His father does it, too, and she idly wonders if it's a genetic quirk. She remembers Dean's excitement as they talked about the children they would have some day and she thinks about the traits they might inherit. He'll be a wonderful dad, she tells herself and she smiles as she catches his eye.

Gordon Dolan leaned forward in his chair and stared at the image on the television. "Huh." He pushed the pause button on the remote and the picture froze.

"What?" asked his wife.

"I'm not sure, but those eyes… " He studied the face staring back at him. "You know the day of the storm, that woman I gave a ride to?"

"Which one?"

"The one I took to Breslau. I only got a quick look at her, you know? Just her eyes, really. But I, ah… I remember thinking how pretty they were. Real clear blue with long, dark lashes."

"Oh, really. You failed to mention that little detail."

"Seriously, she looked a lot like that."

"That's the woman who escaped from Grand Valley."

"I know, but… it couldn't be. I mean, she had a Scottish accent. And I took her straight to her house." He pushed the pause button again and the news resumed. "Plus, her jacket was blue, not red." Another image of Lily, this one a clip from an old interview, played across the screen.

Gordon squinted and shook his head. "Still, those eyes…"

"What if she fell into the river, or met up with a serial killer or something?" Emma's agitation was expressing itself in the clacking of dishes and the slamming of cupboard doors.

"Mum, sit down, you're going to wreck my kitchen," Mark said.

"Think anyone would notice?" Emma responded, surveying the cluttered countertops.

Jeff patted the bar stool beside him. "Come here, dear. Our girl is okay. She'll get through to us when she can."

Emma threw the dishcloth back into the sink and sat down beside her husband. "I need to believe that."

Mark sighed. "We're agreed then? When Lily gets in touch, we do everything we can to help her. Whatever happens, it's her call. If the cops ask, we know nothing."

"Absolutely," Emma said. "No more prison time. No more waiting for useless appeals. I've got a feeling about this and we're not going to give up until her name is cleared."

"I wish I knew exactly how that's going to happen," Mark said.

The queen of quotes wagged her finger. "Don't worry about the horse being blind, just load the wagon."

Jeff slid his hand over Emma's. "I suspect the police know where we are right now, and they'll probably keep an eye on you and Meredith, too, Mark."

"I've warned her about that. You know we can't have these kinds of conversations on the phone, right? Or the computer."

"Exactly," Jeff agreed. "Just be sure you understand the seriousness of this choice. If we're caught helping Lily there will be criminal charges."

"I know, Dad. If we do it right, we'll be okay. Once she makes contact, we'll come up with a plan, use codes, get some disposable phones."

"Aren't we being a little paranoid?" Emma asked. "It seems a bit much to assume everything we say and do will be so closely monitored."

"Maybe so," Mark said. "But I don't want to screw everything up by being careless, do you?"

"It just seems a little double-oh-seven."

"I'm serious, Mum. If Lily calls using one of her special accents, for example, don't burst out with, 'Oh, Lily, honey, is that you?'" Mark said, raising the pitch of his voice to mimic his mother.

Emma reached across the bar and punched him on the arm. "I don't sound like that! But I get your point."

The door to the workshop creaked open and Lily kept perfectly still as she listened intently to the movements below her. Footsteps. A plastic bag. Plates. Someone was cleaning up yesterday's mess. The footsteps retreated, the door closed and the lock clicked. She pulled the blankets to her chin and stared up at the rafters. It was mid-afternoon. She was sore and an odour of mildew and stale sweat clung to her. The idea of a warm bath had never been so appealing. The hours dragged by and the cold gloom of night settled over her. Sleep would not come.

Her thoughts wandered to the nagging questions about Brent's murder. His girlfriend, Melissa, was almost certainly the who. The how and the why were fairly obvious too. But the answers to these questions didn't fit together perfectly. Only the Lily-as-killer pieces to the puzzle seemed to work in the eyes of the jury. And one of the pieces had been that first voicemail.

Lily is furious. She's finally stopped crying and dry-heaving over the bathroom sink in her hotel room and now she's staring into the mirror at her face, pink with emotion. "You fool," she chides, then one last, involuntary sob erupts. She splashes cold water over her face, pats it dry and steps into the bedroom. She surveys the scene for a few moments. The desk, her notes, her laptop, the bed – the bed she had so recently shared with Brent. An image from the video that Melissa's daughter, Kristie, had shown her minutes ago crowds its way into the scene and shuddering, she springs into action. She pulls her suitcase from the closet and begins pitching things inside. Her anger sizzles as she stuffs folders and loose material into her briefcase and slams it onto the bed. Kristie. What is she? Sixteen, seventeen? Having sex with Brent. Her mother's fiancé.

She thinks about calling Sue. Instead she grabs the phone beside the bed and stabs in Brent's number. It goes to voicemail and Lily explodes in a verbal rant that is so unlike her, she hardly recognizes her own voice.

"You son-of-a-bitch! I cannot believe I was taken in by your slimy lies, your righteous image and your spectacularly deceitful portrayal of a genuine, decent human being. I know you're there so don't try to avoid me. I'm on my way to see you and you're going to look me in the eye and admit the truth. And then it's over – you, me, the book, everything!"

Lily slams down the phone, grabs her bags and goes to the lobby. The receptionist observes as she fumbles and fumes her way through the checkout process.

"Are you alright, ma'am?" he asks tentatively.

"Men are cheating lowlifes," Lily mutters.

"Okaaay..." the young man drawls. He will much later, in court, characterize her demeanour as "ready to castrate me."

"Well, not all men, just the ones who date me." She zips up her purse and collects her bags.

"I hope things work out for you."

"I'll be fine, but he will suffer."

She's on the Gardiner Expressway when her cellphone rings. She glances at the caller ID. K. Applebaum. Kristie. How the hell did she get this number? She lets it go to voicemail.

Arriving at Oakville, she exits the 403 and turns south onto Dorval Drive. She's only gone a short distance when she turns again onto a residential street, but she isn't heading in the direction of Brent's house. She's beginning to lose her stomach for this and decides it might be better to deliver her message on the phone. She has four words for him: I know about Kristie. She pulls over and enters Brent's number. Again, he doesn't answer. Her frustration peaks and tears spring to her eyes.

"What the hell? You're still unavailable to take my call? Pick up the damn phone," she yells and it all comes out in a sniffling wail. So much for regaining her composure. She hammers her fist against the steering wheel and tries to think. A man walking a dog throws her a disapproving look as he points to a No Parking sign in front of her car.

Lily nods and pulls away. She drives numbly, making random turns until finally, on a quiet street, she parks and opens her window. She glances at the phone, kills the engine and slumps down in her seat. Several minutes tick by, then wearily, she picks up the phone and listens to the last message.

"It's Kristie. Okay, so listen. I know you're really super mad, but you never let me finish. I need to talk to you, so don't go after Brent right now. You need to back off until my mother has a chance to see him. I didn't think you'd go all ape-shit like that, so just chill and… call me back. Please."

Lily tosses the phone on the car seat and sits staring straight ahead. Could it be that Kristie is just now realizing the gravity of what she's done? Nothing Brent can say is going to fix this. She'll have to write the whole thing off as a gigantic error in judgement, a painful life lesson. Her publishers can find themselves a new writer if they really want to pursue the project. She should just turn around and go home. She hasn't seen Jemma in almost a week.

Then she decides. She'll follow through with this thing. Get some closure. She starts the engine and glances at the rearview mirror. A woman, well into her senior years, is standing at the end of a driveway, hands on hips, a scowl etched on her face. Lily scowls back as she throws the car into gear. Busybody. And then she does something completely uncharacteristic. She sticks her arm out the window and flips her the bird. Because she is royally pissed off. At cheaters, at liars, at promiscuous teenagers and self-serving predatory superstars. At the world.

CHAPTER

7

March 4

Lily awakened as the first traces of dawn appeared in the window above her head. She shoved apart two of the boxes on the top layer of her barricade, giving her a view of the driveway through the front window. The dream she'd just had about Brent was still on her mind as she waited, watching for the car to leave. She'd known something was wrong in the conversation they'd had the last time she'd seen him alive.

Brent reaches across the table and takes Lily's hand in his. "You're the best thing that ever happened to me and I don't want to mess it up, but I need to tell you something and you're not going to like it."

Lily withdraws her hand, sits back in her chair and folds her arms. "What?"

Brent looks down at the table. "This probably isn't the best time."

"Too late. What is it?"

"For one thing, it's the book. I don't think it's such a good idea anymore. Now that you and I are involved… I don't know, I just… I'm not feeling comfortable telling this story."

Lily looks puzzled.

"You know, sharing it with the world. It doesn't feel right."

She leans forward. "Are you kidding? This is a story that needs to be told. And I've got precious time invested in this. Why would you want to stop now?"

"I didn't think it through." Brent pauses and searches Lily's eyes. "It was a difficult experience and underneath the public persona, I'm a very private kind of guy."

Lily returns her hand to his. "Listen, I know you've been struggling to talk about your experiences. You have these emotional blocks and I've had to push to get you to go back there in your mind. But it will be alright. I'll help you get through it."

Brent kisses her hand. "I love you," he whispers against her fingers.

"I can't let myself say that right now because I haven't let myself love anyone in a very long time. Someday I'll tell you the whole sad story. But you know how much you mean to me and… I'm getting there." Lily waits expectantly. "And another thing?"

"What?" Brent asks.

"You said, 'For one thing, it's the book.' What else?"

"Yeah, um… there are some other… things I wanted to discuss, but this isn't the place for it." He glances around the restaurant. "When I see you this weekend, we'll talk. I promise." Brent smiles and squeezes her hand.

It was almost noon when Lily heard the sounds she'd been waiting for. A garage door motor. A vehicle idling, then pulling away. She scrambled out of her hiding place and down the stairs as quickly as her body would allow. She peered out the window in time to see a Lexus SUV moving up the long driveway toward the road. Two adults occupied the front seats and the little ginger head bouncing up and down in the back was sure to be Jinx. They were on their way at last.

She decided not to enter the house right away. People routinely forgot things and returned to get them or do them. The house key was easy to find. After removing it from the top of the cupboard, Lily turned on the radio, wrapped herself in a blanket and sat in a recliner, watching the driveway. At around four o'clock, a car pulled up beside the mail box and Millie got out and opened the flap. When she left, Lily decided enough time had elapsed. She put on her now-dry clothes and went to work, restoring everything she'd handled to its original order. Finally, she stepped outside and locked the workshop door behind her. Dashing across the driveway to the back of the house, she hardly noticed her sore muscles. Beneath her feet, frozen puddles crunched and tinkled as they collapsed into dirty water that seeped into her shoes. Lily didn't care. Things were about to get much better.

In a common room at Grand Valley Institution for Women, a large group of inmates were clustered around a television, watching an expanded version of a news program about Lily's escape.

"Run, Lily, run!" squealed one of them.

"I can't believe she actually did it!" exclaimed another.

"Shut up, I wanna hear this," someone said.

The anchorman introduced the next clip and Lily came to life in front of them in the form of archival footage. She was being interviewed about her recent book. Laughing, articulate, confident and sincere, she breezed her way through the discussion.

"Holy shit, she was a big deal, wasn't she?"

From the back of the group, Rayne, recently returned from Isolation, piped up. "They'll get her. She won't last long." The women seemed not to hear her as the broadcast continued. "She can't hide forever." Silence. "I mean she killed a guy, for God Sake. They're not gonna let her–"

"Shut up!"

The segment wrapped up with a clip from a post-trial interview. *"No, I never considered a guilty plea, not for a second. Whoever killed Brent Baines must answer to the law, but that wasn't me. My family knows it. My friends know it. And someday, the rest of the world will know it, too."* The shot tightened to a close-up of her blue eyes and then faded to black.

The room erupted in hoots and hollers and one of the older women yelled, "You tell 'em, baby!"

"She was helping me with my reading," announced the young

woman Lily had been tutoring when Rayne arrived. "She was really nice and respectful and I believe everything she just said."

Rayne, who had been leaning against the wall, arms folded, scowled at the emotional display in front of her. No one paid her any attention when she turned and slipped out the door.

Commander Gaynor greeted his visitor with a polite handshake. "Jeff."

"Commander."

Gaynor's eyes held a serious expression behind the facade of his smile. When they were seated, he said, "You have something to tell me?"

"Not what you're hoping, I'm sure." Jeff fished a small black object from his pocket and placed it on the desktop in front of them. "First of all, I thought you might want to have this little eavesdropping device back. I was going to toss it but, you know, this is our tax dollars at work. Found it after the little chat I had with your sergeants in my home office."

Gaynor looked unfazed. "We had a warrant, Jeff."

"That was fast."

"We figured your daughter would make contact sooner than later."

"Well, if this trick had worked for you, you'd realize that we have no idea where she is."

"Would you admit it if you did?"

In answer, Jeff offered him a half smile.

"I know you were a lawyer, but do I need to remind you that assisting any person in escaping from lawful custody is an indictable offense?"

Jeff leaned forward and looked him squarely in the eyes. "She didn't do it, Bob. Tell me, what would you do if it were your wife or sister or daughter? If you knew that she'd been falsely accused, wrongly convicted and confined to prison?"

"I don't have a sister," Bob replied. "And my ex? You can have her. And throw away the key." He sighed. "I do have an eighteen-year-old daughter who's causing me to rip my hair out right now," he said, patting his balding head, "but that's not the point. I have a job to do and right now it happens to involve finding your daughter."

"I understand. Look, I know you probably have phones and computers and people under surveillance and just so you know, those will be dead ends for you. If Lily ever contacts us, she'll never be so obvious." He leaned back in his chair. "Anyway, that's not why I'm here."

"Why *are* you here?"

"You and I have known each other for a while now," Jeff said.

"True, but I might remind you that you didn't even know I was divorced."

"Sorry… okay, we aren't exactly close, but we've liked and respected each other in the past and have mutual friends who wouldn't hesitate to vouch for either one of us."

"You're right about that."

Jeff got to the point. "I need a favour. Do you know any of the powers that be with the Halton Regional Police Service?"

"Not well. I've met the superintendent of 2 District in Oakville and I have a good friend who used to work with him. Why?"

"I'm going to appoint myself as Lily's counsel with my son, Mark, as my assistant. I need quick access to the original case files and to the investigators who were on the scene at the time of her arrest."

"Her legal representatives have probably seen everything there is to see."

"I'm not so sure. Mark and I want to dissect this case, piece by piece. The wheels of justice turn far too slowly and waiting politely for things to follow due course is not working for any of us. Your position, your influence – that could open the door for me."

Gaynor stood, indicating the interview was at an end. "I'll see what I can do," he said.

Jeff rose and shook his hand. "Thanks, Bob. That would be most appreciated." He moved toward the door.

"I'd resign and then I'd do whatever it took," Gaynor said.

Jeff turned. "Pardon me?"

Gaynor smiled. "If it were my daughter."

Lily perused the contents of the refrigerator with delight. Karen hadn't found time to clean it out after all. The pantry and the freezer were well stocked, too.

A nice hot meal was in order, but first she wanted to acquaint herself with the layout of the large two-story home. Family photos, including several of Kate and Flynn, were scattered throughout the rooms. A fair-haired preteen Kate in riding clothes, sitting atop a horse. Flynn, in cap and gown, standing between his parents. Kate, smiling and elegant in a wedding gown, her upswept hair now honey brown.

Upstairs, after checking out the master suite and a back staircase, she quickly determined which bedrooms had belonged to Kate and Flynn. Kate's closet and dresser drawers contained a few items of clothing, which Lily assumed she still used when visiting.

Another bedroom appeared to be a guest room with en suite. A basket containing a selection of sample size toiletries sat on a stand just inside the bathroom. She seized a toothbrush in a wrapper with a triumphant "Yes!"

Lily opened the last door and found herself in an oversized bathroom, dominated by a jacuzzi set into a windowed nook overlooking the driveway and gardens below. She caught her reflection in the mirror above the double sinks. She guessed she'd lost at least five pounds since leaving the hospital. Her hair looked greasy and matted and her face was smudged with dirt. She moved closer to inspect the scabby area near her hairline and was surprised to see a yellowish bruise extending to the corner of her eyebrow. Touching the stitches at the back of her head, she noticed that the soreness there was almost gone.

After stripping off her clothes, Lily stepped into the shower and stood beneath the spray, soaking in its heat as she scrubbed her hair with shampoo that smelled like fresh strawberries. Twenty minutes later she stood in Kate's bedroom, zipping up a pair of jeans. They were loose and a bit long, but they would do. A green sweat shirt and fuzzy slippers completed the outfit.

Downstairs she found the thermostat and nudged it up a few degrees, then headed to the kitchen. Darkness was beginning to set in and she wanted to prepare her food while she still had some daylight. Her stomach rumbled. There was a container labelled *Kate's Moroccan soup* in the refrigerator. She poured what was left of it into an oversized mug and heated two pieces of naan bread in the toaster.

When the soup was hot, Lily loaded everything on a tray and headed for the main floor office. She was halfway across the family room when the lights flicked on. Startled, she nearly spilled the soup as she jerked around to see who was there. It took her a heart-thumping three seconds to remember that Ed had mentioned some of the lights would be on timers. She hurried into the office and closed the curtains. On the desk she found bills addressed to Edwin Young. Nice to know whose house she was borrowing.

The first delicious spoon of soup made her moan out loud. Between mouthfuls she fired up the desktop PC, pleased that the embedded password opened the home page automatically. She planned to make contact with her family through her trusted friend and publisher, Sue Emerson, but fearing Sue's computer may be monitored, she'd devised a bit of subterfuge.

Lily had written an outline for a new novel, a work of fiction for a change, before signing on to write the Brent Baines book. She was counting on Sue's memory of her novel's protagonist, Sam Swain, to make a connection. She created a new email account that incorporated that name and then, fingers flying over the familiar territory of the keyboard, tapped out the message.

Dear Ms. Emerson,

Just a quick note to thank you for the amazing support you've provided since our initial meeting. I've taken your advice and have found the perfect retreat where I can work, undisturbed. It's isolated, but the accommodations are comfortable and I have everything I need. I'm feeling quite optimistic about the revisions we discussed. When you can, please pass along my heartfelt thanks to the rest of the team and let them know that things are proceeding well. I'll be in touch soon.

Best regards,
Sam Swain

Lily took a deep breath and clicked *Send.* She trusted that Sue would easily decode her message: Thank you for believing in me; I'm in a good, safe place; discreetly inform my family that I'm okay; more contact will follow.

She put the computer in sleep mode and went into the den. The light was on in this room, too, but the blinds were closed. She drew the curtains as well, then turned on the TV, clicked through the channels, and found a local news station. At the top of the hour, the day's leading stories unfolded. Lily was number three on the list. Her escape "continued to baffle authorities" according to a field reporter doing interviews. Apparently, several people had come forward, claiming to have seen her on the day of the storm. An older man wearing a John Deere cap and a nearly toothless smile looked directly into the camera.

"Well, I seen her an' I know it was her. She was wearin' a red jacket and had that long, dark hair and them bright blue eyes. Why, they just gave me chills. It was over there at the Tim Horton's on the south end and this girl walks up to me and says, 'Mister, can ya help me out? I need a lift.' Well, I don't have no car, eh, an' so I says, 'There's a cop out there in the parking lot. He'll getcha home' an' she just took right off like a shot. Gone."

Lily chuckled. She didn't recognize the next witness without his bulky snowmobile suit and helmet at first. Gordon Dolan faced the reporter, one hand tucked casually in his jeans pocket, the other gesturing as he spoke.

"I'm not one hundred percent sure it was her. She was all bundled up, so I could just see part of her face. But, ah, when I saw her on the news, it sure looked like her, even though she didn't quite match the description, as far as clothing goes and, ah… I remember thinking her feet must be

cold. She was wearing running shoes, the kind with the mesh. She had a Scottish accent, so I thought at first it couldn't be her but, ah, yesterday I went to the house where she told me she lived – I took her clear up here to Breslau that day – and the thing is, that wasn't her house at all."

He was pointing down a street that Lily recognized as the one turning into Breslau and, here, some footage of the house was inserted.

"Oh, and she told me her name was Fiona. And, ah… when I asked around the neighbourhood, no one knew her. Personally, if it was her, I think she was headed for Guelph, though I can't imagine she made it – unless someone picked her up. That was one hell of a storm."

Lily groaned as the camera panned from his face to the road sign behind him, slowly bringing into sharp focus the words, *Guelph 19*. When the news ended, she decided to raid the refrigerator. Settling on an apple and a chunk of cheese, she headed back to the den. As she was passing by the kitchen window she noticed the beam of a flashlight moving down the driveway. Quickly, she rushed up the back staircase and peeked out the dark window that overlooked the driveway. In the light spilling from the kitchen directly below, she recognized Dave, the neighbour. The cop. She followed his progress, moving silently from room to room as he made a complete circuit of the house, stopping near windows to peer inside. He shone his light around the snow near his feet, but Lily knew her own footprints wouldn't stand out against the jumble of tracks at the back of the house. At last he left the property and walked briskly down the road in the direction of his own house. Lily hadn't expected him to be so vigilant in his neighbourly duties. This could get tricky.

"I am… completely… exhausted," Georgia said, kicking off her shoes before plopping down on the sofa. "All I want to do for the next hour is watch some mindless TV. Any chips in there?" She grabbed the remote and began scrolling through the channels.

Dean appeared in the kitchen doorway and tossed her a bag. "Doritos."

Georgia continued to click the remote. "Where's reality TV when you need it?" The sound of a cork popping reached her ears. "Do I hear wine? Bring it on."

Moments later, Dean delivered her a glass of white wine, then picked up her shoes and jacket and headed for the hall closet.

"You know, you'd make someone a good little wife," Georgia teased, crossing her feet on the coffee table as she nestled deeper into the cushions.

"I'd be offended by that if you hadn't run circles around me all day."

"We both did great."

"Yes, but you're so much better with the words. You know how to get the ideas across. And you can oppose something without sounding… oppositional."

Georgia murmured, "Thanks, hon," as her attention shifted to the news program she had just clicked on, but Dean was back in the kitchen, out of earshot.

Lily's picture flashed into view as a woman seated at the news desk recapped the story.

"Hey, did you know there was an escaped killer on the loose?" Georgia asked loudly.

"What?"

"Some woman from a prison in Kitchener. Killed a hockey player in a lover's spat. Did you hear about that?"

"No, and I don't follow hockey either," Dean said as he returned to the living room with a glass of clear soda in his hand.

Georgia clicked the remote a few times. "Brent Baines. I vaguely remember hearing that he'd been murdered. The story wouldn't have had as much coverage in the US, but I imagine it was a big deal here in Canada." She settled on a rerun of *Just for Laughs.* "Feel like some comedy?"

Dean joined her on the sofa. "That would be much preferable to the news. I sure don't need to add an escaped killer to my list of concerns."

By sunrise, Lily was seated in the sunroom, coffee and toast in hand, with a view of Dave and Millie's house. Their side door was

CHAPTER

8

March 5

visible through a gap in the row of pines bordering the large yard. She contemplated her situation as the sky grew brighter. The safest thing would be to move on as soon as possible. Sue would probably be able to come and get her. She needed to erase every sign of her presence here. Computer activity could be found and linked to Sue. And the nosey neighbours were a problem.

At last, a figure emerged from the house next door. Lily watched Dave, who was dressed in uniform, get into his truck and drive off in the direction of the city. Shortly after, Millie descended the steps and headed the same way in her car. Lily moved quickly to the opposite side of the house where she peered through the blinds at the empty driveway, before deciding she could move about freely.

She spent the morning checking email, doing searches and reading material related to her case. There were several postings concerning her escape. Many of them expressed sympathy and in some cases, gleeful admiration.

At noon Lily pulled together a meal. She managed to overcook the chicken, undercook the rice, and wilt the peas, but she wolfed it down with relish. Mid-afternoon found her back at the computer. There was a reply from Sue Emerson. A thrill ricocheted around her stomach as she opened the email.

Dear Sam,

We're so pleased to know that you've been successful in dealing with the problems you were experiencing. There was concern among the editorial staff when we didn't hear from you immediately following our last meeting. We feel that you're on the right track with your new ideas and are happy that you've found an environment in which you can write comfortably and productively.

Dylan Cassidy would like to speak with you regarding the art work for the book jacket. Please contact him directly. We are available to give you feedback and assistance at any time. I'll be sure to share your comments with the rest of the team when I see them today. We look forward to meeting with you soon.

Susan Emerson

Lily smiled as she reread the email. A thread of comfort had stretched through cyberspace to connect her with her old familiar world. Sue and her husband owned Emerson Books Limited. Dylan Cassidy was Sue's brother, who also resided in Toronto, and whom Lily had met on several occasions. She recalled that he lived in The Beaches. Lily wasn't well acquainted with Dylan, but trusted Sue's judgement in designating him as a contact.

The Toronto phone directory sat on a shelf above the desk and Lily had little difficulty finding Dylan's name on a street in The Beaches. When she called the number, a woman's voice answered on the second ring with a tentative, "Hello?"

"Hi... were you expecting a call from Sam..."

"Lily!" Sue's voice came at her in a rush. "I've been so worried. Where are you?"

"I'm fine. I'm in Guelph. Can you call me back at this number? I don't want a big charge to draw attention to this phone bill."

"Sure," Sue said and, within a minute, re-established the connection from her end.

"I know you're calling from Dylan's, but is it safe?" Lily asked.

"I'm alone. Dylan's in Mexico. The police have already questioned me, but in case they're watching, I've been very careful."

"I was counting on that. Were you able to contact my family?"

"I talked to Mark. Discreetly."

Lily told Sue about her experiences following the crash on the day of the storm.

"You utterly amaze me!" Sue said when Lily finished. "Okay, what do you want to do next?"

"Sue, I can't go back. I want to clear my name and I'm going to need help."

"I'm here for you, Lily. We need to get you out of Guelph."

"Okay, but the Young's neighbours might be around. It would be best to pick me up after dark. Down the road. And maybe you shouldn't use your own car. Can we do this tomorrow or even tonight?"

"I'll use Dylan's car." Sue said. "Give me a day. I'm going to buy one of those prepaid phones. I'll make a plan and call tomorrow afternoon."

"Okay. Let the phone ring once and hang up, then call right back so I know it's you." Lily paused. "Sue, this could get you in all kinds of trouble and I'm sorry I had to ask. Once I get out of here, no one has to know you were involved."

Sue laughed. "If I get caught and have to spend a few months in the slammer, so what? It'll make a great story and we'll sell a lot of books."

Lily didn't find the remark quite as amusing as it was intended to be, but she knew Sue was just trying to alleviate her concern. "Tomorrow then. Thanks, Sue."

After the call ended she settled into a chair in the living room, watching the road through the front window. It had begun to rain and patches of snow that remained in the low areas of the yard were melting into large puddles. Her thoughts drifted to her trial. She had testified – against the advice of her defense team. Everything she'd tried to explain had been twisted by the prosecutor.

Lily's hands are clenched in her lap. Her nemesis, Barrett Pierce, paces in front of the witness stand and begins a new line of questioning. "I'm given to understand that you're highly intelligent and have a good memory," he says.

Lily listens warily.

He holds up a magazine for all to see. "This feature about you in Canadian Voice *magazine was published just prior to the release of your last book." He opens it to the page he's marked. "It says, and I quote, 'Mullaly's sharp intellect, her unerring attention to detail and her keen powers of observation are the tools she uses to unravel the truth about her subjects and their often questionable claims. Her memory is impressive. Names, dates and facts from her extensive research were recalled without hesitation during our interview.'"*

"Objection," comes a call from Jack Waverly at the defense table. "Irrelevant."

"I'll show otherwise, Your Honour," the prosecutor says.

"Overruled," says the judge. "Get to the point."

Pierce looks at Lily. "You're a regular savant, aren't you?"

"Of course not," Lily says. "I just make a point of noticing the world around me and yes, I have a good memory, but certainly not an eidetic memory." A presentiment of what is coming fills her with dread. She's responding truthfully, but with mounting reluctance.

The prosecutor gives her a smug smile. "You claimed to have seen a silver car parked outside Brent Baines' house on the day of his murder." He had dared to use air quotes as he pronounced the words, silver car.

"Objection, Your Honour! Prejudicial!" Waverly barks.

"Sustained. Consider yourself warned, Mr. Pierce."

"Yes, Your Honour. Ms. Mullaly, please describe the vehicle that you claim to have seen outside that house."

Lily frowns. "It wasn't exactly outside his house, it was…"

"I've asked you to describe the vehicle, not its location."

"It was a silver compact car. A sedan, I think, but I'm not sure."

"Make and model?"

"I don't remember. I mean I didn't notice."

"License number?"

"I don't know."

"Spoiler? Stickers? Tinted windows?"

Lily sighs. "I don't know."

Pierce shakes his head. "You mean to tell me that in spite of your superior powers of observation, you can't tell us anything about this so-called compact car except its colour and maybe, only maybe, that it was a sedan?"

"I was focussed on… I was upset and…"

"Well, yes, we've established that you were very upset indeed, but with that photographic memory of yours, wouldn't you be able to see it all in your mind's eye?"

Waverly was on his feet. "Objection, Your Honour. Mr. Pierce is not qualified to know what she can or cannot see in her mind's eye."

"Sustained. Bring this line of questioning to a close, Mr. Pierce."

"Certainly, Your Honour. Ms. Mullaly, the description you gave police of the mysterious car was vague, to say the least, and you didn't even offer this information until the day after your arrest. Did you, in fact, fabricate this detail when you learned that on the day Brent Baines was murdered, Kristie Applebaum had been driving a silver Chevrolet Cruze?"

"Absolutely not. And I just told you that I don't have a photographic memory! You're leading everyone to believe…"

The judge intervenes. "Ms. Mullaly, I caution you to answer only the questions that are asked.

Lily's tone is defensive. "Photographic, eidetic, same thing. He's misleading…"

"Your counsel will have its turn."

The prosecutor flashes Lily a grin and clasps his hands behind his back. "Let's get back to your rather imprecise description of this car. Would you say this could describe the car Kristie Applebaum was driving on the day she came to see you at your hotel – the same day Brent Baines was killed?"

"I don't know. I didn't see her driving the car."

"You are now aware that Kristie sometimes drove a Chevrolet Cruze that is registered to her father, Matthew Applebaum, correct?"

"Yes."

"And were you shown a photograph of that car?"

"Yes, but that was after I recalled seeing the car near the crime scene."

Pierce brings his fingers to his temples as though trying to solve a difficult math problem. Annoyed, Lily waits for the prosecutor to move through the next step in his choreography of poses.

He extends his arms outward in a dramatic shrug. "What you're saying is, it could have been Kristie's car that you saw, but maybe it wasn't; probably it was a sedan, but maybe it wasn't. If it turns out that Kristie and her car have an alibi, that leaves the possibilities wide open. You've cast a pretty wide net of suspicion, haven't you?"

"Was that a question?" Lily asks flatly.

Pierce chuckles. "No, ma'am, but this is. If the car in question was not Kristie's, would you say that it was just a huge coincidence that something matching its description was parked at Brent Baines' house moments before you arrived and found him dead?" His voice drips with sarcasm.

Lily glances at Waverly, expecting him to object, but only silence hangs in the air. She shifts her gaze to the jury. "If it was not Kristie's car, then yes, it would be, in my opinion, some kind of coincidence, but I have no means to determine to what degree it would statically qualify as 'huge'. And once again, to clarify, the car was not 'at' Brent's house," she says, adding little air quotes as an afterthought.

A soft titter ripples through the court room. Pierce maintains his smirk, but his neck reddens. "You're a smart one, Ms. Mullaly," he drawls, "but you will not outsmart this court."

At five thirty Dave's truck slowed down near the top of the driveway and inched by until it had cleared the property. Lily moved to the sunroom and watched as he parked and entered his house. It was closer to six o'clock by the time Millie arrived home, grocery bags in each hand.

Lily went into the kitchen, retrieved a tuna sandwich that she'd made earlier and took it into the den. Flipping through the channels, she caught a glimpse of her own face. The image changed to a reporter, microphone in hand as he questioned various people, who had interacted with her on the day of her escape.

The nurse who had been with Lily when she was discharged spoke first. *"Understandably, she was not feeling great, but I thought she was very nice. I just can't imagine she could hurt anyone."*

Lily recognized Dr. Osborne as she hurried along a hospital

walkway. The reporter kept pace. *"Dr. Osborne, can you tell us about the time you spent with your patient, Lily Mullaly?"* he asked.

"That would be inappropriate," she answered, avoiding eye contact with the camera.

"Well, can you just tell us what your impression of her was?"

Dr. Osborne came to a stop and faced the reporter. *"All I will say is that she seemed to be a decent person. If she's been wrongly convicted, as she claims, then I wish her well in finding the justice she deserves."*

A man introduced as Al was identified as the driver of the dump truck that had struck the corrections vehicle. He was wearing the same grubby work jacket and appeared to be at his job site.

"That guard, the... big gargoyle," he said spreading his arms to indicate a large girth, "she was cursin' and screamin' at me the whole time she was tryin' to break out of that van. I broke the windshield, but she was so rude, I shoulda left her in there. Meanwhile, the Mullaly woman pulled the other guard off the road and she was tryin' to revive him. She stayed right with him until those other people came along and took over. And then she ran. And I told her to go for it, too, by God. I hope they never find 'er."

A middle-aged couple appeared next, explaining that they were the ones who had discovered the accident. *"She was hurt, too,"* the man said, *"and had blood running down the side of her face, but she was only concerned about the guard, and, by the way, we didn't realize at first who any of them were. She wasn't shackled and the snow was so thick we couldn't see the vehicle clearly. Anyway, she'd taken off her own coat and wrapped it around him and I believe she would've stayed right there with him if we hadn't come along."*

Rick's wife was in the next shot, speaking directly to the camera. *"I don't care what she's been convicted of. When my husband had that heart attack she tried to help him. Now does that sound like a killer to you? Rick's doing much better now and if you're listening, Lily, thank you from both of us!"*

The setting changed to a parking lot where the reporter was hot on the heels of the unmistakable form of Beryl. *"Ms. Sweeney... Beryl Sweeney? What do you have to say about Lily Mullaly's escape from your custody?"*

Beryl continued to walk briskly away from the camera.

"Is it true that she rescued your partner who was driving the van?"

"No comment," Beryl said gruffly.

"How did she manage to get away?"

"I can't talk to you," she grumbled.

"How did you feel about her, personally?"

"Get that (bleeped) thing out of my face!" Beryl said, giving the reporter's microphone a shove as she arrived at her SUV. She got in and slammed the door.

Lily was relieved to learn that Rick had survived and pleased to note that some of the comments were in her favour. Perhaps all the media attention would do some good.

CHAPTER

9

March 6

Instantly awake, Lily looked at the luminous face of the bedside clock. Throwing off the covers, she practically bounced out of bed and made her way through the darkness to the kitchen. She made coffee and toast by the dim glow of a night light.

Once in the sunroom, she wrapped herself in a throw and settled into a wide wicker chair to wait for dawn. When the morning light finally crept in, stretching its cool pink fingers across the fields and through the gaps in the pines, a tranquil world was revealed, glistening from the recent deluge of rain and almost fully emerged from its shroud of snow. A few small mounds lingered in the shadows of trees and in slushy puddles scattered here and there. Lily knew that if she could smell the air, it would carry the kiss of spring.

She moved into the office to check for emails from Sue and read the news. The morning dragged. At noon she poured a can of hot chili over baked fries, casting frequent glances at the phone. "A watched pot never boils," she said, repeating one of her mother's chestnuts.

Finally, she decided to take a bath. Tossing the pajamas she'd been wearing into Kate's laundry hamper, she headed for the jet tub down the hall. She felt suddenly exposed, walking naked through a stranger's house and when she stepped into the bathroom, she self-consciously closed and locked the door.

While her legs were recovering well, a new stiffness had revealed itself in her neck, spreading from just below her right ear into her shoulder. A good hydra massage would do it good. When the jacuzzi was ready, she pinned up her hair and eased herself into the warm embrace of the water. She pressed the button and twelve nozzles sprang to life, shooting out a pounding stream of water that massaged her body from every side. She leaned back with a contented sigh, allowing the jets to knead the soles of the feet that had served her so well.

The water pulsed against her shoulders and neck. She dozed lightly, inhaling the warm, scented air, soothed by the deep whir of the tub's motor. It was a rumbling white noise that lulled her into a state of semi-conscious awareness. And it was a loud noise, sufficient to mask the slam of a car door in the driveway below and to swallow the sound of footsteps entering the house.

Hands in pockets, Ryan Cross stood in the kitchen of the Baines house, casually inspecting the floor. "The new tile looks great. Good job, Leo," he said to the man leaning his back against the counter.

In his grubby jeans and plaid flannel shirt, there was a handsome ruggedness about Leo, but with a little cleaning up, he would have looked equally at home in a business suit like Ryan's. Flashing a white smile, he opened the refrigerator, took out two cans of beer and sat them on the kitchen table. "It's a shame the entire floor had to go, but I couldn't match the tile."

"It needed updating anyway," Ryan said, as he pulled out a chair and sat down. "There's something else I need to talk to you about, Leo, and it's rather... delicate."

Leo popped open one of the cans and seated himself across from Ryan. "Something I've done – or haven't done – to your satisfaction?"

"No, nothing like that. You've done a great job getting the house ready for the closing. It's about what's been in the news the last few days. You know, the woman who killed Brent. It got me thinking again about something that came out at her trial. Do you remember hearing about a letter that she claimed Brent had written, disclosing some dark secrets?"

"Vaguely."

"Supposedly, he was going to give it to her or use it somehow to purge his conscience. She said it was some kind of confession and worried that he might have been thinking about killing himself. Most people assumed she just fabricated the story to throw suspicion elsewhere."

Leo smirked. "Didn't she claim he'd been banging his soon-to-be stepdaughter?"

"Right. Anyhow, the police never found this letter but I don't think they looked very hard."

"You think it's still here?"

Ryan shrugged. "There's been a lot of speculation about the facts in her case lately. If she's innocent, maybe she was telling the truth."

"You weren't just Brent's attorney. You were his cousin. Wouldn't he have told you if he were facing legal or personal problems?"

"I thought so, but we weren't as close as you might think." Ryan looked down at his hands clasped together on the table. "If there is a letter, I'm afraid of what might be in it. Do I have your word that this conversation will be just between us?"

"Absolutely."

The room went silent for a few moments before Ryan spoke again. "Something happened shortly before Brent left to go on that sailing trip with his brother. I was here one evening when Brent's girlfriend was out of town and he had some of his buddies over and there were these… women."

"Prostitutes?"

"No, more like groupies. Anyhow, we'd all had a few drinks and one thing led to another. A couple of them seemed young – I thought eighteen or nineteen at the time, but possibly even younger."

"And you were… with one of them?"

Ryan's heavy sigh was answer enough.

Leo gave a low whistle. "Did you look for this letter once the police released the house?"

Ryan nodded. "Yes, and I decided there was nothing to find. But now I'm not so sure. He may have gone to some trouble to hide it. Anyhow, the thing is, I have a wife and two kids and…"

"If Brent was planning to tell all, you don't want to get dragged down with him. I understand."

"I don't know if this so-called letter is a short confession or a detailed account of every regrettable act in his past. It could be part of a journal for all we know. I sowed some wild oats when I was young. Brent and I both did. But after I got married, I never strayed, not until that night. Huge mistake. If this gets out, it could ruin me."

"I doubt there's anything about you in this confession or whatever, if it even exists," Leo said.

"I'm thinking about Brent's reputation, too."

Leo scoffed. "He's dead and gone. Who cares?"

"His son will someday. And his mother. She's my aunt, after all," Ryan said. He finally opened his beer and took a long swig.

"You want me to search for this thing?"

"As you get things ready for the estate sale, I want you to check everything – books, furniture, even behind baseboards. It would be terrible if it were left behind for the new owners to find. There's a bonus in it for you. Five thousand if you find it and hand it over to me. But no one else is to know about it, ever."

"Deal." Leo extended his hand across the table and they shook on it. "Now I have some news for you. I'm getting married."

"No way!"

"She's the woman I met on that internet dating site a couple of years ago. We'd broken up, but we're back together now. I just turned forty so I figured it was about time I took the plunge."

"Well, congratulations! Here's to you," Ryan said, bumping his can against Leo's. "Okay, details."

"Her name is Hannah. She lives and works in Newmarket, so we aren't spending much time together at the moment."

"Have you set a date?"

"Not yet. Anyway, I know you had something in mind for me after this job ends, but I thought I'd better let you know that I'll be moving on, probably looking for work in Newmarket when I'm done here. And I wanted to say thanks. This caretaker job came at a time when I really needed it."

"You're welcome," Ryan said. "It was perfect timing for me, too."

"I've agreed to stay here full time and I understand why you don't want guests at the house, but would it be alright if Hannah stays with me on her days off? It would only be a night or two a week and she could help out with some of the work while she's here. I can vouch for her honesty."

Ryan hesitated. "Well, you are engaged, so it wouldn't be fair for me to ask you not to see her. Just don't allow anyone else in the house."

"No socializing here, as agreed."

"And I don't think it would be a good idea to tell Hannah about the letter. You can continue to look for it without her knowing, right?"

"Sure. My lips are sealed."

Ryan twirled his key ring. "I'm running late, as usual." He moved toward the door. "Thanks for the beer. I hope to meet Hannah soon. And give her my congratulations."

The door closed with a thud. Moments later a car engine roared to life.

As Leo stood at the front window watching the black sports car disappear from view, a pair of arms slipped around his waist.

"Seriously? He drives a Crossfire?"

Leo chuckled and turned to face the woman who'd just embraced him. He tucked a strand of blonde hair behind her ear. "Mr. Cross just said it would be alright if you stayed here from time to time."

"So I heard."

"You were listening?"

"Of course." She laughed. "You know for five thousand dollars, I could write that letter from Brent myself. It would talk about nothing *but* that orgy and how Ryan got it on with an under-aged girl. Then we'll tell him we made a copy. Make him sweat."

Leo laughed. "You're wicked."

"I'm just fantasizing. Something about him reminds me of my ex, so it's hard to hide my contempt."

"I hope you never feel that way about me," Leo said.

She pulled him close. "Never," she breathed against his chest.

It was the barking of a dog, sharp and excited, that jarred Lily wide awake. She instinctively hit the power button to kill the jets and sprang to her feet, sloshing water over the sides of the tub. Then she stood, frozen and indecisive, dripping and listening. The yipping continued, but faded into more distant parts of the house. Lily turned, heart knocking, and peered through the clear glass above the privacy shutters to the driveway below. A white Mercedes was parked there and someone clad in jeans and visible only from the waist down stood at the open rear door, leaning into the interior.

Frantic thoughts immobilized Lily as she tried to formulate a plan of action. Finally, she made her move. As quietly as possible she stepped out of the tub and wrapped herself in a towel. Her best option, she decided, was to silently make her way to the bedroom, slip on some clothes and try to sneak out of the house when the coast was clear.

Lily stepped lightly across the room, straining to hear voices or movement. There was not a sound. She released the lock on the handle, drew in a deep breath and opened the door.

The shock nearly dropped her to the floor. Standing an arm's length away, in the middle of the doorway, was an elderly woman holding a marble rolling pin above her head. Their eyes met, each of them staring, dumbfounded, at the other. Lily opened her mouth, but no sound came out. The woman held her gaze for a moment, then calmly spoke. "Lily Mullaly."

Lily clutched her towel tightly with both hands. "I won't hurt you!" she blurted.

The older woman cracked a hint of a smile. "I'm the one with the weapon."

Lily thought it best not to point out that she could easily disarm her.

"Promise you won't run?"

"I promise."

"Good, because this thing weighs a ton," the woman said and she dropped her arm heavily to her side.

There was a sound of footsteps and a voice called up the stairs. "Gram? Where are you?"

"Come here, Kate. Come see what I found," the woman hollered back. Then she smiled at Lily. "Don't worry, dear. You're among friends. We were just talking about you."

A tall woman wearing fashionably ripped jeans and a T-shirt that displayed the phrase, **You lost me at hello**, rounded the corner and Lily fell speechless again. Every muscle in her body from her forehead to her toes was tensed. Kate stopped abruptly in her tracks. "What the–"

"It's Lily Mullaly!" her grandmother declared in the same tone an adult might use when pointing out Santa Claus to a small child.

Kate clapped a hand over her mouth, her eyes wide behind tortoise framed glasses.

Lily found her voice. "I'm sorry. I kind of broke in and helped myself to things, but I had every intention of paying it back."

Kate lowered her hands, but stood there, slack jawed.

"I was desperate and hungry and cold and I was just a day away from moving on."

Kate stepped closer. "Lily Mullaly. I'm… I can't believe this." She slowly shook her head. "Gram and I have been following your story in the news. And we've been rooting for you. And you're *here*!"

Lily leaned against the door frame and a fat tear streaked down her face. "Sorry, my knees just turned to rubber. I wasn't expecting anything but trouble."

"Oh, honey, now don't you worry," the older woman said and she dropped the rolling pin to the floor and wrapped Lily in her arms. "We are going to look after you."

Lily stood woodenly, gripping her towel, as this complete stranger patted her on the back. Finally, she was released.

"Lily, I'm Clair Young and this is my granddaughter, Kate. My son, Edwin, owns this house."

"You could get in serious trouble by helping me, Clair," Lily said.

"I think it would be best if I just move on right away."

"You'll do no such thing," Clair countered. "Because, first of all, we're not going to get caught. And secondly, I would have absolutely no regrets if we did."

Kate exhaled a long "Wow" and announced, "I'm going to make some tea. Lily, we'll leave you to put on some clothes. Come down to the kitchen when you're ready."

Lily gave her a sheepish look. "About that. I've been wearing your clothes and using your room."

Kate laughed. "Be my guest." She turned to leave, then looked back. "I can't believe it! Lily Mullaly!"

Lily got dressed. She was still trying to compute what had just happened and wasn't sure what to make of it. A terrible moment had just been transformed into something astonishingly wonderful… she hoped. The older woman, Clair, seemed to be a bit of a kook and the granddaughter, at this point, was simply unfathomable.

Lily joined the others at the kitchen table and Kate poured tea into three mugs, then she and Clair sat, eyes riveted to Lily. Jinx planted his butt on the floor beside the table, likewise transfixed.

"Guess we took you by surprise," Kate finally said.

"Dare I say you were somewhat unprepared for me, as well."

Clair laughed. "I didn't know what to think when I heard that tub running upstairs."

"She's eighty years old, but do you think she'd wait for me or call the police first? Nooo. Up the stairs she goes with that damn rolling pin, like that would've scared anyone," Kate said.

"Well, now, aren't you glad I did just that? Poor Lily could have been on her way back to prison right now".

"I reluctantly concede that point, Gram." Kate took a sip of tea and smiled at Lily. "If not for Jinx, we wouldn't have found you. My folks dropped him off at Gram's house on their way to Florida and he's been whimpering and staring out the windows since they left, so we decided to come back here. Stay a couple of days, show him that his human parents are not here and get some of his toys."

"And clean out the refrigerator, too, since Karen didn't get to it." Clair levelled her gaze at Lily. "What's your story, dear?"

Lily gave her rapt audience of two a play by play of her dramatic escape, referring to Sue only as "a friend" when she got to that part of the story. They peppered her with questions and marvelled at her account. *You came all the way from Kitchener on foot? In that blizzard?* Jinx had waddled off to search the house for other signs of life, returning periodically to beg for bits of cookies.

By this time, Lily knew that Clair and Kate sincerely wanted to help her, but she was reluctant to draw them into her schemes. "I appreciate your willingness to come to my rescue, but I don't think you understand the seriousness of my situation. If you could just drop me off somewhere, no one will ever know that you had a hand in my escape. You can forget that you ever saw me.

"I'm fully aware of the implications of helping you," Clair insisted. "I haven't lived this long without learning a thing or two about the law and human nature and knowing right from wrong. I will do as my conscience dictates and it's telling me that helping you is the right thing. And not just my conscience. I believe that fate has set you on our path for a reason. Now, I think the best plan would be for you to stay at my place."

"I totally agree with Gram," Kate added. "Anyway, I don't care about rules and conventionalities. The way my life has been going the past few months, I don't give a..."

In the midst of Kate's rant, the phone rang once.

"If that's my friend, she'll call right back," Lily said. Following a short delay, the phone rang again and she rushed across the room to pick it up. Lily proceeded to fill Sue in on the recent turn of events and after some discussion with Clair and Kate they agreed to put the rescue mission on hold.

Clair sat in the background, bright-eyed and looking very pleased while Kate pawed through a grocery bag. Lily finally put the phone back in its stand and returned, smiling, to the table.

"Lily, I haven't had anything this exciting happen to me in I don't know when," Clair sighed. "Kate's going to fix us some dinner. She's quite the chef."

"Unlike me, I'm afraid," Lily said.

Kate disappeared into the walk-in pantry and Clair lowered her voice. "She suffers from depression, bipolar they're calling it now.

She's feeling much better, though. There's an imbalance of the chemicals in her brain, but she's not crazy or anything."

Kate re-emerged with some spice bottles in her hands. "I'm not deaf, either, Gram." She glanced at Lily. "I have a mental illness with a physiological cause. It's still misunderstood, but that's beyond my control so I've let it go." Kate was clearly attractive, but her face was pale and tired and there was puffiness around her eyes.

"When did it start?" Lily asked.

"In hindsight, I guess there were signs when I was in my late teens, but it didn't become obvious until about four years ago, when I was twenty-eight. It wrecked my marriage, but at least we had no kids to mess up. You have a child, don't you?"

Lily felt a twinge of guilt. "Yes, a daughter."

Clair took the opportunity to fish for details. "There was practically no mention of her in the media during your trial."

"I tried to keep her out of it."

"And her father?" Clair gently prodded.

Lily averted her eyes and stared silently out the window at the fading light. "That's a subject I'd rather not discuss."

Kate began chopping something on a cutting board. In the next instant, two faces passed by the large kitchen window and looked directly into Lily's eyes as they continued in the direction of the side door. Millie and Dave. Lily flew off her chair and disappeared into the next room to the sound of two knocks, followed quickly by the squeak of the door.

Kate was right behind her. "I don't know what they're doing here," she whispered.

"Yoo-hoo," Millie's voice chimed. "Clair! We thought that was your car."

"Hello Millie and… Dick."

"Dave."

"Oh, yes, of course, Dave. How nice to see you again."

"Goodness, where did Kate go so fast? That was her at the sink, right?"

Lily and Kate stood motionless, just around the corner.

"You'll have to excuse Kate. She hasn't been well. Very depressed, as I'm sure you've heard, but on the mend. However, she's just not up to socializing right now."

"Oh, what a shame. We'd love to see her," Millie said.

"The other girl, the dark haired one sitting at the table. Who was that?" Dave asked.

"A friend of Li… Kate. Lynn is her name. They have a special relationship, very close if you know what I mean," Clair said, lowering her voice.

"Oh." Millie looked stunned, but she recovered quickly. "What brings you here?"

Clair went through the explanation, to which Millie responded with another string of questions and unsolicited tidbits of news, while standing just inside the door.

Dave finally said, "Well, I see that you've started getting supper ready, so we'll be on our way."

They said their goodbyes and Clair locked the door behind them. She'd barely turned away when it rattled against the frame. The knob twitched.

"What now?" Lily heard Clair grumble.

The door creaked and Millie's voice penetrated the room. "Clair, would the three of you join us for dinner tomorrow? It would do Kate good, don't you think?"

Kate let out a sigh and whispered to Lily, "I'm going in." And with that, she rounded the corner and entered the kitchen.

"Kate! There you are!" Millie exclaimed.

"Hi," she replied, her voice glum. "I'm sorry. I didn't mean to be rude. I'm just not up for being around anyone right now."

"Except your friend," Dave observed and his eyes darted to the dark room behind Kate. "Is she feeling antisocial, too?"

Kate ignored the insensitive remark. "We're leaving for Toronto tomorrow afternoon, so dinner is out, but thank you for asking."

Millie crossed the room. "Well, I'm going to give you a big hug before we go," she said swallowing Kate in her arms. Kate gave her a stiff pat on the back and shrugged her gently away.

"How about we bring over some fresh cinnamon rolls in the morning and at least have coffee together?"

Clair had had enough. "Your kindness is much appreciated, but you must hear what we're saying. Kate needs peace and quiet and the things that comfort her right now. She is following medical advice. You shouldn't take this personally, but it would be best if you give her some space. I hope you'll understand and not press the issue."

A look of dismay fell on Millie's face. "Of course."

Tears sprang to Kate's eyes and she covered her face with her hands. "I'm so sorry. Please don't be upset with us."

"We're not," Dave mumbled, taking his wife by the arm. "Please excuse us for barging in like this. You know we're right next door if you need anything." He led his wife back to the door.

"Thank you, Dan," Clair said.

"Dave."

"Right. Thank you for understanding." Once again Clair locked the deadbolt, watched through the window as Millie and Dave walked away and then turned to look at her granddaughter, who was still rooted to the spot.

"Gram, did you just tell the neighbours I'm gay?"

CHAPTER

10

The Beef Richelieu with Madeira sauce was delicious.

"Are you a professional chef?" Lily asked, finally setting down her fork.

"No, before I went on leave seven months ago, I was a radio personality. I hosted an early morning show in Hamilton called *Coffee with Kate.*"

"Oh, she was good," Clair enthused. "Giving her views on current events, chatting with callers, interviewing guests. People said they could hear her smiling."

"What I was good at was hiding my depression. People had no idea how hopeless I really felt at times."

"Kate's living with me now," Clair said. "Just like years ago when she was studying Broadcast Journalism."

"Yes, then I got a great job break, married a wonderful guy and screwed it up anyway."

"It wasn't your fault, dear," Clair said, patting her hand.

Jinx woofed. Lily slipped him a piece of meat and gave him a stern look. "You almost blew my cover in the loft, poodle boy."

Clair cast the dog a critical look. "He's a Cavapoo. A mix of poodle and Cavalier King Charles Spaniel. But not very regal, I'm afraid."

Kate threw back her head and Lily could hear the round, musical notes of laughter that must have floated over the air waves to her listeners. She began collecting their plates. "I don't think Dave and Millie will be back, but just in case, you need to stay away from the kitchen window. It's lucky they didn't get a good look at you."

"I hope they didn't. What if they see my mug on the news tonight and make the connection?"

"You'll be much safer at my little house in Toronto," Clair said.

Kate froze. "They might come back for a second look. I think we should clear out of here tonight."

It didn't take long to make a decision. Thirty-five minutes later, dishes were done, garbage was tossed and everything destined for Toronto was loaded. Kate was at the wheel and Jinx was snuggled next to Lily in the back seat.

"Hopefully, they won't see us sneaking away," Kate said, casting her eyes to the right toward Dave and Millie's house. She turned left at the end of the driveway and drove in the direction of the Guelph.

Lily shifted in her seat, staring back at the Young property as it shrank from view. Her stiff neck protested and she turned to face the road ahead. Everything looked peaceful and non-threatening in the warm light that fanned out in front of the car. Low, dirty ridges of snow edged the sides of the road, remnants of the banks heaped up by the ploughs only five days before.

"I can't believe how lucky I was to find my way here," Lily said. "That house gave me everything I needed, including the two of you. How likely is that?"

Clair chuckled. "Oh, my dear, that was not luck. There are powers all around us that we don't understand. This experience that you're having is part of a journey that, for whatever reason, you must make. Kate and I are part of the fabric of that experience. The three of us have been brought together for a reason."

"You could be right. It's all pretty incredible."

"You must let me do a reading for you. We'll consult the Tarot cards."

"You're a fascinating person, Clair." Lily studied her profile in the near darkness of the car. She smiled, remembering her first glimpse of this delicate silver-haired woman, a rolling pin wobbling over her head. She seemed neither elderly nor delicate now. She moved with a spring in her step and had a quick, witty tongue.

Clair placed a thumb behind her ear and leaned closer. "Can you see my earring?"

Lily examined the circular design with the small dangling star. "I noticed them earlier."

Clair touched the silver stud. "The moon. It's the unconscious mind. The light of the moon is reflected and it both illuminates and disguises the landscape of our lives. It warns us of chaos, fear and confusion. But it can also reveal astonishing breakthroughs, powerful magic and intuition. It tells us that things are not always as they seem."

Her fingers moved to the suspended star. "The star is all about hope and inspiration. It tells us to have faith, both in the power that lies within ourselves, and in power greater than our own." She looked into Lily's eyes. "There are symbols all around us. Archetypes that have existed in the consciousness of our culture for millennia. They appear when we need them."

"That's really interesting," Lily said, "but I don't put much stock in fortune telling and things like that."

"Tarot cards are not about fortune telling," Kate piped up. "I think of it more as a therapeutic way to examine the experiences one is having. It opens us up to different ways of looking at problems and opportunities and relationships. That doesn't mean it will magically fix all our troubles, but it can help us navigate."

Clair nodded. "My way, when I read for someone, is to ask questions and suggest ideas to help the person explore the concern they have. But sometimes, I also get impressions, psychic flashes or mysterious little nudges, that lead me to interpret the cards a certain way."

"Hmm."

"My dear, you're willing to consider the possibility that a force beyond our understanding has guided you here. Is it such a stretch to consider that some other-dimensional intelligence could influence you in an untold number of ways?"

"Guess not," Lily admitted. "It's just that I'm so accustomed to thinking in mundane terms and to seeking logical, scientific explanations for everything."

"Well, stick with us and everything will be clear as mud," Kate laughed.

Soon they were driving into the twinkling lights of Guelph. Landmarks that Lily had struggled past on foot slipped quickly by.

"Tell me about your family," Lily said.

"Have you seen the 'Be Young at Heart' ads?" Kate asked. "My parents own that chain of stores. Young Sports. My brother, Flynn, has taken over the Toronto store. He's married with two sons."

"Ed is a good man," Clair said, "but quite conservative, considering who raised him. He's not given to pondering life's deeper mysteries or taking huge risks or say, harbouring fugitives."

"Do you have any other children, Clair?"

"I have a daughter, Celeste, who's married and lives in Ottawa with her husband and three daughters," Claire replied. "I won't be seeing them until Easter, so I don't expect we'll need to hide you from any visitors. And my dear husband, Bill, passed away three years ago."

"Oh, I'm so sorry."

"I know that before your arrest, you lived near your parents along the St. Lawrence River in the Thousand Islands region," Kate said. "What about the rest of your family?"

"My younger siblings, Mark and Meredith, are twins and they both live in Toronto. Mark works in the gaming industry. Computer genius, divorced, no kids. Meredith and her husband are both filmmakers and they're expecting their first child in April. My father is a retired lawyer and my mother is an artist."

"Lovely," Clair said.

"Interesting, isn't it?" Lily mused. "When you think about how chance meetings and decisions can change our fate. If my parents hadn't met while boating on the St. Lawrence one day, we – their offspring – wouldn't exist, and there would be a chain reaction in so many different directions for so many people. The ripple effect would be never-ending."

Clair looked back and smiled. "There are no coincidences."

Jinx snored softly next to Lily and a comfortable silence descended on the car. It sped on through the night, in darkness that was interrupted periodically by a wash of passing headlights. It had been a long and exciting day. Lily's eyes closed as she sank into quiet retrospection. Luck. Coincidence. Fate. Had fate been at work when she'd married Dean?

It's day six of the honeymoon and Dean is sitting on a deck chair, ankles crossed, looking bored or distracted. Lily hands him a club soda. He mumbles a thank you.

"You're quiet. Anything wrong?" she asks.

"Just a low-grade headache."

"Maybe you should take a Tylenol and have a nap." She runs her hand alongside his knee. and notices how the fine, pale hair gleams in the sun. "Your tan is starting to catch up with mine."

"I'll never catch up with you, Lil." Dean gives her a weak smile. "Why not use that voucher you have for the spa this afternoon? You deserve a nice long massage and a manicure and whatever else you women do to look beautiful."

Lily was roused from her near doze by a burst of laughter from Clair. Her loud "Ha ha!" punctuated the air in a throaty, singing gust of sound that comforted Lily as much as it startled her. She wondered what had tickled Clair this time and smiled to herself. Only hours ago, these two remarkable women had slipped into her life and already they'd become fixtures. And this got her thinking about fixtures. About people who come and go in life and others who stay. Did Jemma make Dean a fixture? Denying that for so many years couldn't erase him. He was right there in the sparkle of her eyes and the blush of her cheek. Dean was a fixture and he didn't even know it.

Lily is feeling refreshed as she returns from the spa to the room where she'd left Dean two hours earlier. It's empty, the bed still neatly made. She steps out onto the balcony. A nagging little voice in her head frets about his headache, his distant gaze, his preoccupation with unshared thoughts. She studies the pool area and the clusters of furniture scattered below. And then she sees them. They're beyond the pool in the shade of a tree. He's sitting next to Mr. Charming, the hunky guy they'd met during the shattered glass incident. Vince. Their facial expressions are unreadable from this distance, but the body language is clear.

Dean gestures emphatically, then leans forward and lowers his face into the cradle of his hands. Vince is attentive, head tilted to one side.

Lily watches for a few more minutes, alternately fearing that Dean is unhappy about something, and convincing herself that they are simply swapping interesting stories. Vince leans in toward Dean and for perhaps five seconds, places his hand on his shoulder. Dean nods. And for all of Lily's gifts of perception, she still doesn't get it. She sighs and trades the balcony for the bed.

"Still awake back there?" Clair asked. "You're awfully quiet."

"Thinking."

"Well, you certainly have a lot to think about."

Aborting her attempted nap, Lily glances at the bedside clock. Thirty-five minutes have elapsed. She returns to the balcony and looks at the spot where Dean and Vince had been talking, but they're gone now. Her eyes come to rest on an elderly couple sitting, silent and glum, under a palapa and she feels something clench in the pit of her stomach. Immediately below her, a young couple stops mid-stroll. She laughs. He whispers something in her ear and she melts into his arms. Irritated, Lily turns away.

She goes to the lobby and looks for something to read in the borrow/swap bookcase. Not a love story. Something weighty; something true. She selects an Ann Rule paperback, The Stranger Beside Me. *How appropriate. She goes back to the room. Nothing like a good tale about a serial killer to pass the time.*

It's six forty-two when Dean finally slides his card key in the door and steps inside. Lily, seated in a wide rattan chair at the opposite side of the room, somberly closes her book.

"Before you say anything, I'm sorry. I'm not wearing a watch and I totally lost track of time."

Lily waited a couple of beats. "How's the headache?"

"Fine. The Tylenol got rid of it. I went for a long walk on the beach. I figured you'd be a while and..." Dean's voice trailed off with another, "Sorry."

"Alone?"

"Huh?"

"You walked alone?"

Dean avoids Lily's eyes as he pulls off his sandals. "No, I picked up two beautiful babes along the way and we had a threesome under the palm trees."

Lily doesn't laugh, just stares down at the book in her lap.

Dean comes over to her and kneels on the floor at her feet. "Look, I know I've been moody, lately. Honey, you deserve so much more. I'm afraid that I'm just not good enough for you."

Lily cups his cheek. "I don't know where your head is right now. But I love the Dean James that I married. I love everything about you. I've just been feeling..." She wants to say neglected, marooned in a tropical paradise, but it seems harsh, so she edits, "distance."

Dean is on his feet, pulling Lily up with him. "Let's go out for dinner and then dance the night away," he says and his cheeks are slashed with the dimples Lily finds so adorable. He pulls her close and they hold each other as sounds of night life in St. Kitts rise and drift in through the open balcony doors.

"Almost there," Clair announced, as the car turned down another street. They'd been driving through Toronto for several minutes and were making their way into a residential area. Lily noted the stately older homes and the tall trees. The car cruised slowly by a Tudor, wide and immaculate, then a massive Victorian, windows gleaming with gold light.

She sat up straight and peered through the windshield. "Are we in Rosedale?"

"Very perceptive, my dear," Clair replied.

Anyone familiar with Toronto didn't have to be all that perceptive to recognize Rosedale. It's one of Toronto's oldest and most affluent neighbourhoods. Built among three ravines that are preserved as parkland, its beautiful meandering streets boast gracious refinement. Except for the spectacle of modern cars, Lily imagined the view would be largely unchanged from the way it appeared over a century ago.

The car slowed and pulled into a long driveway tucked behind a wall of wrought iron and stone and tangled vines that, in summer, would no doubt be festooned in luscious greens. The scene gave way to a sprawling, stone neo-Georgian house surrounded by a beautifully landscaped lawn.

Kate pressed a button on the dashboard and ahead of them, the door of a beautiful carriage house began to rise. "Home, sweet home."

"You're kidding," Lily croaked. "This is your *little* house in Toronto?"

Clair laughed and clapped her hands together. "And you thought you were going to be confined to some tiny bungalow?" She caught herself quickly. "Not that there's anything wrong with bungalows. But I do love the expression on your face right now."

"You're full of surprises, Clair," Lily chuckled. "Are the servants going to be lined up to greet their returning mistress?"

"Now wouldn't that be a hoot! But no dear, nothing like that. Other than my housekeeper who comes in twice a week and a few others who show up when they're needed, we girls are on our own."

The inside of the house was as grand as Lily had imagined. Clair and Kate showed her through the first floor, encouraging her to make herself at home. When they came to a door that opened to a huge, dark space, Clair flicked a switch and light flooded in, revealing a large indoor pool and spa, complete with hot tub, sauna, shower stall and glassed-in mini gym.

"I use it most days," Clair informed her. "Keeps me limber."

Lily took it all in. "Incredible."

Clair looked pleased. "When the young ones come to visit, they head straight for the pool."

"Let me show you to your room," Kate said.

With its cozy chairs, its soft greys and blue accents, and large, bright windows, the guest room was tastefully luxurious.

"I'll bring you some fresh clothes, but you're a size smaller than I am, so as soon as we can, I'll get you some things that fit."

"Oh, don't– " Lily started.

"No protests," Kate said. "I know you're worried about being a burden, but you're not. And don't be concerned about the state of my health either. I see it in your eyes whenever you look at me. I'm actually feeling quite well. If I seem quiet sometimes or look like crap it's not an indication that anything's wrong or that being here is wrong. Okay?"

Lily wrapped her arms around Kate and squeezed. "I wouldn't say I'm a *whole* size smaller, but thanks."

Kate laughed. "At *least* one size."

By the time Lily joined them in the living room, three armchairs had been pulled close to the gas fireplace and there was a bottle of wine, three glasses, a plate of artisan cheeses and a thick candle arranged on the coffee table. A pair of eyes belonging to Jinx hovered just above the edge, intently focussed on the cheese.

Clair picked up the bottle of wine. "This *Chateau Margaux* is a very nice thirty-seven-year-old Bordeaux from my late husband's collection. Based on some clues you dropped, I'm going to say you're the same age."

"You're dead on," Lily said, then winced at her choice of words, given the still-fresh reference to the departed Mr. Young.

If Clair noticed, she gave no indication. "I think we need to honour this day of coming together with a special toast."

"This wine sounds too expensive for my humble tastes."

"I cannot imagine a more appropriate occasion to partake of this fine wine." Clair poured three glasses and passed one to Lily. "Would you offer the toast, my dear?"

Lily raised her glass. "Here's to the three of us, brought together this day by the mysterious and wondrous workings of fate."

They clinked glasses and Lily took a sip. "This is very nice."

"Well, 1958 was a very good year for *Chateau Margaux*," Kate said, straight-faced but with one arched eyebrow.

Lily rolled her eyes and took a bite of the aged gouda. "Is this from the year of my birth, as well?"

"No, no, it's aged, not *ancient!*"

Clair cackled. "Oh, Kate, it's so good to see that sense of humour again. Lily's not old enough for that comment to sting, but bless you for not directing it at me."

Grinning, Lily lifted her glass. "Just out of curiosity, how much is a bottle of this very fine stuff worth?"

Clair wiped her mouth with her napkin as Lily took a generous swig. "Oh, it's not one of the most valuable vintages in the collection. Three, maybe four hundred, tops."

Lily quickly brought the glass under mouth until she could safely swallow. "Dollars?" she sputtered.

Kate giggled and Clair smiled, but she looked thoughtfully at Lily. "You must think I'm ridiculously self-indulgent."

"No, no, I–"

"Gram is smart with her money and gives generously to worthy causes," Kate said.

Clair gazed at her surroundings. "Well, I'm not about to give it all away and take a vow of poverty, but I *am* conscious of what it takes to keep a big place like this going, just so I can rattle around in here with a lot of memories."

"It must be lonely for you," Lily said.

"Oh, I miss my dear Bill, of course, but I'm rarely lonely. I have the company of friends and family and more than enough interests to keep me busy."

Time flowed and at length, Clair rose to her feet. "If you girls will excuse me, I'm rather tired."

Lily stood and embraced her. "Thank you, Clair. I could never express how grateful I am for what you and Kate are doing, but I hope you know how I feel."

"You're a blessing for us, too. Sleep well, honey." With that, Clair turned and left the room. When Lily sat down again, Jinx was making smacking noises and crumbs of cheese clung suspiciously to his chin hair. Kate sighed and moved the plate away from the edge of the table.

Lily finished off her wine and glanced at Kate's empty glass. "Alcohol doesn't affect your illness?"

"Not in small amounts. I partake on occasion and pay attention to getting proper sleep and nutrition."

Lily rubbed her eyes. "Speaking of sleep, it must be past eleven."

"It's twelve forty-two, my friend," Kate laughed softly, checking her watch.

"No!"

"We could both use some rest."

Lily and Kate carried the cheese and wine into the kitchen. Jinx was underfoot as they moved from sink to refrigerator to dishwater, finally scoring a cracker when they were done. He padded up the stairs behind them and followed Lily to her door.

"Lucky you. Looks like you're the new favourite in the house," Kate said.

"I'm certainly lucky. Thank you."

Kate smiled. "It was meant to be."

CHAPTER 11

March 7

An enticing aroma was wafting into the guest room when Lily awoke. By the time she arrived downstairs, Kate was pulling a baking sheet from the oven.

"Morning, Kate."

"Good morning," Kate replied over her shoulder. "Cranberry scones." She piled some on a plate and placed them on the breakfast bar. "Pour yourself some coffee."

Jinx, who had been at Kate's heels, bounced over to Lily and she knelt to stroke his head.

"Smells delicious! How long have you been up?"

"Long enough to throw this together."

"Did you get enough sleep?"

"I'm completely refreshed."

Lily seated herself at the bar where Kate was stirring her coffee. She wore a white T-shirt that featured a quote printed in red: I cook with wine. Sometimes I even add it to the food. Her brown eyes looked brighter today, her skin a little pinker, and her short, highlighted hair was freshly washed and styled.

"You look great," Lily said.

Kate grimaced. "Well, a little better every day. How do you feel?"

"Except for this stiff neck, my aches and pains are pretty much gone."

A voice floated into the room. "Oh, I do love it when Kate bakes!"

Clair was wearing a bright, floral-patterned top.

"Well, aren't you a vision of spring this morning, Gram," said Kate.

"Let's have breakfast in the solarium," Clair said, nodding toward the room off the back of the kitchen.

The solarium was spacious and bright and abundant with green plants. A squirrel scrambled up a tree outside one of the glass walls, sending Jinx into a flurry of barking.

"My little grand-dog seems to be adjusting now," Clair observed.

Kate smiled. "And he's taken quite a shine to Lily."

"He only loves me for the treats I slip him," Lily said, and upon hearing the magic word, Jinx abandoned his harassment of the squirrel and scampered over for a share of her scone.

"We have to spell t-r-e-a-t around here," Clair laughed, gazing outside. "Oh, look!" She motioned for them to follow her to one of the glass walls that bordered a flower bed. She gleefully pointed to the soil. "Daffodils."

Lily spotted the tiny green nubs that had broken through the moist dirt and her heart did a little skip. That the earth could perform this miracle so soon after it had been ravaged with ice and snow was hard to fathom.

Crime scene photos covered the table where Mark was seated in a private room at 2 District. He studied the image of the gray cotton hoodie with dark blood stains splattered across the front. The report indicated that Lily's DNA had been present in microscopic skin cells found on the inside. But DNA from Brent, Melissa and two undetermined sources had also been found. Touch DNA, the experts called it, transferred by individuals who had worn or handled the garment or had come into contact with Brent while he was wearing it.

Lily had admitted wearing the hoodie, but insisted it had been three days before the murder when she'd found the air conditioning in the house too cool. Melissa had also confessed that she'd worn it, claiming that she'd slipped it on outside by the pool a few days before she left for Asia. But the police had found it in Lily's vehicle. That had put her squarely in their sights.

Mark turned his attention to a photo of the weapon, a chef's knife that had been removed from a block on the kitchen counter. The handle had been wiped clean, but a fingerprint from Lily had been found on the heel of the blade.

He reread the timeline of events from the tenth of July that police had pieced together. It fit neatly with the theory developed by prosecutors. They argued that Lily had arrived at Brent's house much earlier than 5:35 PM as she'd stated, early enough to argue with Brent and kill him. Bruising on Lily`s cheekbone implied that the argument had turned physical. Brent's blood alcohol content at the time of his death was 0.18, indicating that he'd been extremely intoxicated. They painted a scenario for the jury that neatly dovetailed with the evidence.

She's wearing the hoodie. Maybe she was cold; maybe she anticipated the blood. They argue; perhaps they scuffle. Brent punches her in the face. She grabs a knife, either threatens him with it or lashes out in anger. Brent tries to grab the knife and in one vicious swipe, she slashes his lower neck, cutting his carotid artery. He drops to the floor. She panics and runs to her vehicle, tracking blood behind her. She takes off the bloodstained jacket, rolls it up in a ball and tosses it onto the floor of the car. But she realizes she needs to get rid of evidence so she runs back into the house, wipes down the handle of the knife and is about to clean up her bloody shoe prints when Melissa Applebaum arrives and discovers her at the scene.

Lily's version of events suggested other scenarios. Lily could have arrived shortly after the murder and before Melissa. Or Melissa could have arrived first, her vehicle tucked out of sight in the side driveway. If Kristie was involved, she could have been there before or at the same time as her mother. Her whereabouts at that time were unknown. She claimed to have been out driving around after she dropped off her friend, Natalie, at her Etobicoke home. She'd placed a call to Lily from that location at 4:27, putting her several minutes closer to Oakville than Lily.

The drive from Lily's hotel in Toronto to Brent's house in Oakville would have taken about forty minutes. That should have put Lily there at around five o'clock. She'd accounted for the delay by claiming that she'd pulled over somewhere to think.

Melissa's trip from her house to Brent's should have taken under thirty minutes, but she said she'd stopped in Etobicoke to look for Kristie at her ex-husband's apartment and then had driven along some of the streets where her daughter's friends lived. She stated that she'd spotted Kristie in her vehicle at around 5 PM and had stopped to speak with her for about fifteen minutes. It would have taken twenty to thirty minutes to drive from Etobicoke to Brent's house, depending on traffic.

Mark noted that a surveillance camera had recorded Kristie leaving Lily's hotel in her father's silver Chevy Cruz sedan at 3:36 PM on the day of the murder. The driver of the vehicle was her friend, Natalie VanHorne. He circled her name. He would start there.

Beryl had never learned to move delicately through the world. As a child, she had bulldozed her way, imposing her will on the playground, taking control of games and intimidating anyone who dared to oppose her. Always taller and bigger-boned than the other kids in the neighbourhood, her physical presence had bolstered the air of authority that permeated her bearing.

Puberty had not been kind. She'd grown taller, heavier, moodier. But she'd had friends, the same girls who'd played on every team in every high school sport and she'd relished her occasional roles as captain. She was even popular with some of the boys but, to her dismay, only as their buddy. Whenever an opportunity for leadership presented itself, Beryl was on it. She organized, controlled, bossed and pressured. Some called her gutsy. Others called her brash.

Naturally, she'd been drawn to professions that granted her authority. She'd considered the military, but the long climb to power involved too much subservience and regimentation. A career in law enforcement had appealed to her. She'd imagined herself decked out in the uniform of the OPP or, better yet, the RCMP, but she hadn't made it past the rigorous recruitment process. She'd finally enrolled in a program to train as a correctional officer and had found an open door with Corrections Canada.

The social aspects of her job weren't all that satisfying, though. She'd had to work hard to expand her circle of friends, joining a rod and gun club and a curling league, organizing regular poker nights and recently, signing up with an internet dating site.

At an inch over six feet and with an appearance some would call "butchy", she'd found that men who were tall enough, burly enough and tough enough to date her were in critically short supply. She'd been smitten with a man she'd met on the job back in January. He was big, six four, broad and muscular, with the unlikely name of Twig and a belly big enough to land him in what Beryl thought of as a pursuable category. But she'd discovered Twig's taste in women leaned toward petite blondes and slender babes with pretty blue eyes – like Lily Mullaly, who'd become his current obsession and favourite topic of conversation. In any case, Beryl simply wasn't skilled in the art of flirtation.

She'd had a week to obsess about it and had come to a decision. The incessant coverage of Lily's escape was intolerable and with her recent suspension, she'd had plenty of time to think. The events of March the first were being reviewed and investigated. There were questions concerning the decision to leave the hospital in white-out conditions and about her conduct before, during and after the accident. And this was not the first incident.

Beryl finished her last set of bench presses, towelled off her face and checked the clock. It was almost time for the news. As much as she hated hearing about it, she needed to stay on top of the latest developments. So far, the police hadn't found a single shred of evidence as to where Lily could be hiding. But she was going to show them. She'd show everyone.

Her bag was packed and soon she'd be on her way to her brother's apartment in Toronto. She'd done her research and discovered that both of Lily's siblings lived in the same city. It seemed to her that Lily was most likely hiding there and that Mark or Meredith would be the key to finding her. The police had limited resources and by now, the search would be winding down. Beryl smiled. She had all the time in the world. She'd be the hero in this story.

Following breakfast, Sue had called and made arrangements to talk on Skype. As her face appeared on the computer screen at the appointed time, Lily felt a tingle of excitement.

"Hey, you! You look good," said the face.

"Better than a week ago, that's for sure," Lily replied. "Where are you?"

"In a hotel room. And we've taken every precaution getting here."

"We?"

"I'm not alone," Sue said and as she moved aside, Jemma's face appeared on the screen.

Lily could only cover her mouth and utter a little sobbing choke.

"I'm glad you're safe, Mum," Jemma said. "I miss you so much."

"I miss you, too, sweetie."

"Look who else is here."

Two faces filled the screen and the tears Lily had been trying to hold back streamed down her cheeks.

"Hi sweetheart," Jeff said. "Wish we could be there, but it's still too risky."

"Honey, how are you holding up?" Emma asked.

Lily regained her composure. "I'm fine. I'm more concerned about you."

"You had us worried for a while, but we don't blame you. Your case is getting a lot of attention and it's making everyone take a harder look at the facts," Jeff said.

Emma leaned so close to the webcam Lily could see only skin. "Now listen, honey. You stay put. Don't go digging around the way you do when you're researching for your books. Your dad is taking over your defence and Mark is helping him."

"Really? But that puts them both in a terrible position. If it's ever discovered that they knew my whereabouts, there will be serious consequences."

"The family has talked it over and we're aware of the dangers, but for now at least you won't be going back to that prison," Jeff said. "We'll talk about turning yourself in at the appropriate time, but meanwhile Mark has taken some time off work. He's looking at the case files. We'll come up with a suitable explanation for your whereabouts when the time comes."

"I don't think I could bear being locked up again. Fortunately, I have all the right people helping me. And on that note, I want you to meet my new friends."

Lily angled the computer toward Clair and Kate and a flurry of conversation followed. As the visit drew to its conclusion, Sue appeared on the screen again. "It wouldn't be wise for us to be making regular calls, but we'll keep in touch when it's needed. However, Mark is going to pay you a visit tomorrow. He has some clothes and some cash for you. Not a lot. Around four hundred. Any large withdrawals from your parents' account might look suspicious, but this will help with whatever expenses come up for now."

"She doesn't need money here," Clair hollered from the sidelines.

"The plan is already in motion," Sue said. "He'll be taking precautions to avoid being tailed."

Lily nodded. "Thanks, Sue."

"We're being very careful, honey," Emma said, sticking her head back in frame. "We have secret codes and everything."

"Oh, Mum, I'm so sorry you and Dad got dragged into this mess."

"You know we wouldn't have it any other way. And when your innocence is proven, who's going to have the nerve to come after us? You know what they say. It's easier to beg forgiveness than to ask permission."

Lily laughed. "I knew we couldn't end this conversation without one of Emma's adages."

Goodbyes were said and the screen went blank.

"You have a wonderful family," Kate said. "And Jemma is a

beautiful young woman. Now I have something very serious to ask you."

"What?"

"Dinner. Baked fish or chicken?"

Lily's sober expression slid into a grin. "Chicken, but only if you allow me to help."

Carla Moretti tapped on Commander Gaynor's door and poked her head into his office. "The Mullaly case. Lily's parents withdrew several hundred in cash from their bank yesterday. A phone call to their daughter, Meredith, indicated they were going to visit her for a couple of days. I've alerted Toronto."

"Could be it's exactly what it looks like. Just a visit. But keep me posted."

"Will do," Moretti replied. She paused. "The media is certainly hanging on to this one. You sure you don't want more surveillance?"

Gaynor looked over the top of his glasses at her. "The family is fully aware of our watchful eye. Even if they know where Lily is, they'd never tip their hand."

"There's talk in the press of reopening the investigation."

"I hope she gets a fair shake when she's found, but as her father said, the wheels of justice turn very slowly." Gaynor looked to the window where the branches of a forsythia bush danced in the wind and scraped against the glass. They looked stark and sterile, but their tiny buds would soon swell in the warmth of the sun. "It's nice to see the light coming back. Let's hope for an early spring."

CHAPTER

12

Hot steam rose from the water and dampened Lily's face as she dumped potatoes from the pot into the colander. "I've been thinking," she said.

"Yes, I can see the smoke billowing out from your ears," Kate teased.

"Very funny. But seriously, I need to get out there and find some answers. I can't just sit around here, inhaling your delicious food and twiddling my thumbs."

"Didn't you promise your mother you wouldn't go 'digging around'?"

"Nope, I didn't. I was thinking if I could disguise myself well enough…"

Kate stopped tossing the salad and stared at Lily. "That would be too dangerous."

"Not if I could steer clear of people who know my face."

"Hellooo. All of Canada must know your face by now."

Lily emptied the potatoes into a bowl and reached for the butter.

"It was just a thought."

"Well, unthink it," Kate said as she headed for the dining room with a stack of plates and cutlery. When she returned to the kitchen, Lily was in a state of distress.

"I don't understand," she said lifting a spoon from the bowl. "My mashed potatoes are the texture of glue!"

Clair entered the room and came over to peer into the bowl with Kate, whose eyes wandered to the food processor beside the sink.

"Did you use this?" she asked pointing to the appliance.

Lily nodded.

"On high?"

"Yes. And I think I added too much milk. Leave it to me to ruin dinner."

Kate cracked a smile. "I'll bet it tastes good, anyway." She dipped her finger in the bowl and brought a slimy glob to her mouth, then winced. "Perhaps a little heavy on the salt."

Clair let loose one of her cackling "ha-ha's" and walked over to the pantry. She held up a box of Stove Top Stuffing. "For just such occasions as this," she announced.

Soon all three of them were laughing as they scraped potatoes into the garbage and pulled the rest of the meal together. They sat down to eat at the dining room table.

Lily took a bite of a homemade roll. "Oh! Wow. What's in here, crack?"

Kate giggled. "I got the recipe from my ex-husband's great granny just before she died. I practically had to beat it out of her."

Lily high-fived her. "Good move."

"Gram," Kate said, "guess what Lily's considering."

"A second roll?"

"No, hunting down Brent Baines' killer."

Clair didn't look surprised. "We need to do that Tarot reading so we can explore your options."

A little paw tapped Lily's leg and she looked down at Jinx. "Want some potatoes? They're *really good*."

Jinx cocked his head to one side and Lily slipped him a piece of chicken.

"By the way," Clair said, "I've cancelled Ivy for tomorrow. My housekeeper. Oh, and those neighbours of Ed's, Millie and Dick?

"Dave," Kate corrected with a sigh.

"They called while you girls were busy in the kitchen. It seems Millie came around this morning to snoop, or to use her word, 'apologize'. Well, imagine her surprise when she saw that we'd left already. Everything's okay, though. I think I've put that issue to rest."

"Like you did when you explained my 'special friend' to them? I'll bet that news travelled fast."

"Change of subject," Clair said. "Are you convinced that it was Melissa Applebaum who killed Brent, Lily?"

"Kristie is another possibility or even her father, but I didn't see either one of them at the scene. That silver car I saw parked on the street could have been his, though."

"Melissa and Kristie had alibis?"

"They were each other's alibi. Melissa claimed to be in Etobicoke until around five fifteen, arguing with Kristie over a credit card charge. It's not likely Melissa would have driven the twenty minutes straight to Brent's after that and knifed him without some kind of dialogue first. It's more likely they both lied about meeting in Etobicoke."

"And Kristie's father?"

"With his girlfriend, according to him. They were at his home when the police called that evening."

"What do you think happened?" Kate asked.

Between mouthfuls, Lily continued. "Well, Melissa had been out of the country for about three weeks. She's a buyer for some big retailer. I didn't know anything about her when Brent and I were working together, and had no idea that day that the... poop was about to hit the fan."

"It's okay, dear, you can say *shit*," Clair said, smiling.

"I prefer *poop*," Lily replied, spearing a morsel of chicken.

Kate laughed. "My chicken can't be *that* bad."

Lily grinned and chewed before continuing. "I'd been interviewing one of Brent's former teammates that afternoon and when I got back to my hotel, Kristie was waiting for me. I didn't know who she was, but apparently she knew about me and I assume she'd figured out that Brent and I had begun a relationship. She showed me a photo of her mother and Brent looking very cozy and then proceeded to tell me that not only was Brent engaged to her mother, who'd arrived from Thailand the night before, but that she – Kristie – was involved with him as well. She was only seventeen at the time. Kristie and her mother had a rather volatile relationship and she had convinced herself that Brent was going to break it off with her mother and be with her… if she could take me out of the equation."

"Wasn't there a sex video that she showed you, too?" Kate probed.

"Yes," Lily sighed. "On her tablet. It was sickening. I can only guess that she'd originally recorded it on a hidden camera so she'd have some kind of proof or leverage. He may have been nearly twenty years older, but she had it bad for him. It was time-stamped June 22nd, after I'd met Brent, but before I let the relationship go beyond a professional one."

"You were in love with him?" Kate asked.

"I didn't know how I felt. It was exciting and new and I was daring to think that we might spend our lives together, but then things moved too fast and I put the brakes on. As for the video, I couldn't watch much of it. I just lost it and hustled her out the door."

Clair made a *tsk tsk* sound and Lily noticed that both she and Kate had stopped eating.

"Here's a scenario." Lily said. "After seeing me, Kristie and her friend, Natalie, drive to Melissa's place and she tells her mother about me *and* about her own relationship with Brent. They have words, and Kristie leaves with her friend, who's waiting in the car. Melissa then leaves in her own car, bound for Oakville to confront Brent. Of course, when questioned later, Melissa denied any knowledge of her daughter's romps with Brent, and Kristie claimed nothing had ever happened with him.

"According to the surveillance video, I left the hotel at four eighteen. In Oakville, I drove around and then parked for a while, trying to decide what to do. I finally went to his house. It's in an upscale neighbourhood with big, deep lots and mature trees. The house is set well back from the street, tucked behind blue spruces and tall bushes. There's a circular driveway at the front, but one arm of it connects to a long side driveway that runs along the house to a garage. A high hedge separates the entire property from neighbours on both sides. It would be simple for someone to come and go without being noticed." Lily put down her fork and dabbed her mouth with her napkin.

"Melissa beats me there by at least half an hour. She doesn't know I'm on my way. She confronts Brent and they argue. He's probably been drinking all day. Kristie had been there that morning and, whatever was said, he must have known his house of cards was about to crash. At some point Melissa puts on Brent's grey hoodie then for some reason she grabs the knife from the block on the counter and goes after him. Maybe he'd become physically aggressive with her or maybe she was just out of her mind with rage.

"After she kills him she wipes down the knife handle and drops it on the counter, then removes the hoodie and starts to leave. But she notices a car pull up out front. She sees me through the window and realizes who I am. She's parked out of sight in the side driveway, but she knows there's a good chance I could hear or see her car leaving, so she slips out the side door and waits for me to enter the house. Then she plants the hoodie in my car and gives me time to find the body so she can appear to catch me in the act."

Kate nodded. "And then you both ran outside and that neighbour tackled you."

"Or, if Kristie did it, her mother could have followed her there, found her standing over Brent's body and sent her running while she cleaned up the evidence," Clair suggested.

Lily had twisted her napkin into a rope. "Tell me something. How is it that you're both so sure it wasn't me?"

Clair smiled. "To be perfectly honest, dear, I wasn't – until I laid eyes on you. You were standing there, dripping wet, clutching that little towel around you. I looked into your eyes and felt your purity."

"And it was the voice we hear in your writing," Kate added. "Through your books, we felt in a way like we knew you."

"That," Clair said, "and the fact that we know someone who knew Brent."

"What?" Lily exclaimed, jerking to attention.

"Friends of the Baines family who were aware of some of his problems."

"Problems?" Lily shot to her feet, mouth open. "Let me get this straight. You know someone who has information about Brent that affected your opinion of the case against me? Why didn't you mention this sooner?"

"Well, my dear, it's only been..." Clair checked her watch, "twenty-seven hours. All things in good time."

"I guess we're done," Kate said, looking at their half-eaten meal. "Peach crisp, anyone?"

Lily shook her head and she was not even thinking about peach crisp, but about the bizarre turn the conversation had so casually taken. Clair was unlike anyone she'd ever met. She stared at the eccentric older woman. "Who are these people who knew Brent?"

"Grant and Fran Davenport. My husband was a media proprietor with interests in television, radio and publication, and the Davenports were shareholders in one of his companies. We socialized with them from time to time. Fran and I started a Bridge club and oh, what fun we had! We'd all take turns..."

"Clair! What was their connection to Brent?"

"Patience now, dear, I'll get it out."

"Sorry."

"They used to live in Oakville and back then their son, Jack, played hockey on the same teams as the Baines brothers. I don't think he saw much of Ben after they grew up, but he and Brent remained friends, even after Brent made it to the big leagues."

"Jack knew Brent at the time of his murder?" Lily asked, still stunned by the news.

"The whole family did," Clair answered. "They seemed to know all about his girlfriend. "That reminds me," Kate said, "I got to know Fran's daughter when I was living here with Gram and Grandpa in my university days and she made an interesting comment once. There had been some reference in the press to Brent's Adonis-like appeal to female fans and Hilary said, 'If only they knew that under that skin beats the heart of a poisonous snake.' A little bitter, don't you think?"

Lily's mind instantly produced a full colour image of Brent's body, the live one, the one in the magazine. The Adonis bit was obvious. The snake part, she was anxious to hear more about. "And?"

"She wouldn't elaborate."

"What did the family say about Melissa?"

Clair picked up the story. "They thought she was a selfish bitch and a gold digger. Brent told Jack she was pressuring him to let her move in and to set a wedding date, but he was in no hurry. They'd become engaged two weeks before he and Ben left on their big sailing adventure, but he didn't talk about her in the news reports about his rescue and that upset her."

"Why didn't he just break it off with her?" Lily asked.

"I don't know. Relationships don't always end so neatly. Sometimes they sputter to a finish."

"And another thing. Brent had loaned her a lot of money in their early days together and he told her he wanted it repaid, as they'd originally agreed. She didn't react well," Kate said.

"Did Melissa believe she'd get any of Brent's money if he died?" Lily asked.

"I don't know, but Brent left everything to his son. If they'd married, she probably would have been entitled to some of it anyway."

Clair looked thoughtfully at her granddaughter. "Peach crisp, you say?"

"Clair!" Lily raised her hands in exasperation.

"Oh, let me have my little fun, Lily. Okay, we think Brent and Melissa were already on shaky ground and you became the tipping point in that relationship. We're not certain Melissa knew about Kristie's involvement with Brent, but either way, there's a motive."

Lily resumed her strangulation of the napkin. "I need to get Dad to talk to the Davenports, but I can't have anyone making a connection between you and my family."

"They'd talk to me," Kate said. "I could tell them that I'm making a career change, maybe writing something for a magazine. They know that before *Coffee with Kate*, I did a few pieces for CBC Radio."

Lily brightened. "How about if we got Sue involved? Would the Davenports believe that your grandfather owned shares in Emerson

Books and that because of that connection you've been tapped to pick up the Brent Baines story?"

Kate grinned. "I believe I have a new career. Now, can I interest anyone in some peach crisp?"

Soft notes from an acoustic guitar drifted through the chic loft as Dean threaded his way into the open space of the former warehouse where other guests stood chatting. He moved in the direction of the music. Not far into the room, he spotted Spencer engrossed in conversation with Lyndon, the head choreographer. He caught the words "tempo" and "deplorable" as he ambled toward them.

"Dean, my man!" Spencer welcomed him. "Someone has been asking to meet you. Excuse us," he apologized to Lyndon, as he steered Dean away. "Thank you for rescuing me," he mumbled into his glass. It was apparent from his demeanour that it was not his first of the evening. "I didn't come here to top shock all night."

"You mean, 'Talk shop'," Dean said, smiling.

"Right." Spencer was moving Dean in the direction of the bar. "Our backers are here tonight with their… various… sinifi… cant others. See that stout guy over there with that hottie in the little black dress? Can you believe that's his wife? C'mere."

Dean grasped Spencer's arm. "Maybe let me do the talking? You're slurring a bit and I know you wouldn't want anything to undermine their confidence in you."

"I am? Okay, tell you what. I'll introduce you and then I'll 'scuse myself and get another drink."

Dean raised his eyebrows.

Spencer laughed and downed the last of his Scotch. "Lighten up! You're way too sur… too serious."

Dean allowed himself, somewhat apprehensively, to be towed to the sixtyish man standing near the bar with his fortyish wife. Spencer introduced them as Micky and Minnie Struthers, but the man quickly corrected him. "It's Winnie, actually. And Mick."

Spencer apologized and headed in the direction of the bar, leaving them in momentary silence.

"I understand you're American," Winnie said.

"Yes, I bring greetings from my people," Dean replied.

This made Winnie giggle. "Sorry, I'm a little nervous in the presence of such great talent." Her eyes travelled down and back up his body, drinking in his physique.

Dean blushed. "Not sure I deserve such a generous compliment, but thank you."

"We have every confidence that your music is going to be a phenomenal success," Winnie said.

"And every hope that Mackenzie will be able to pull it all together," Mick added.

"He's a respected director and he works extremely hard. He won't disappoint you."

The conversation that ensued was pleasant, though stilted, and the music was competing for Dean's attention. A resonant tenor voice was now singing along with the guitar.

"Shall we head over that way?" Mick asked, following his eyes to the far end of the room.

"Sure, if you don't mind."

A baby grand stood next to an expansive bank of windows in one corner of the room. The guitarist sat on a stool next to the piano. His fingers glided effortlessly across the strings, and his voice had a mellow, fluid quality that made Dean's skin tingle.

"That's Travis Wright," someone whispered into Dean's ear.

Dean turned to see Michael, their host and the producer of *Thin Air*, standing just behind him.

"Ever heard of the band, The Wright Stuff?"

"No, but I like what I hear."

"They're a cover band, mainly, but Travis has written some of his own stuff. He's starting to make a name for himself."

"Friend of yours?"

"Yes. He's a guest, but I asked him to bring his guitar and serenade us for a while. I'd like the two of you to meet. I think you'll find you have a lot in common," Michael said with a wink.

Dean turned his attention back to Travis. Slender, attractive, early thirties. Black jeans and a silky gold shirt. Short hair, dyed platinum and gelled to messy perfection. He sang with his eyes closed and

Dean wondered what colour they were. *You're disconnecting with your audience, he thought. Look up.*

The song came to a soulful close and there was a ripple of applause. Michael called out to Travis. "Time for a break. Come and meet Dean."

Travis laid his guitar on the piano bench and as he approached, he extended his hand. "Hi, Dean. I'm so honoured to meet you. I'm a big fan."

"Really?" Dean laughed. "I don't get that a lot. I'm now officially a fan of your music, though." He realized the eyes he was staring into were the colour of maple syrup.

"Thanks. Coming from you I'm... well, honoured. And also repetitive. And a little nervous. Michael let me listen to the score from *Thin Air* and I was blown away."

"What I was hoping," Michael said, "was that the two of you might team up tonight..." He paused, coyly, "and thrill us with some tunes. An impromptu jam session, if you will."

Dean looked at Travis and grinned. "I'm game if you are."

"Sure! Let's give it a shot."

Michael motioned to someone and another guitar and stool materialized.

"Very spontaneous, Michael," Dean chuckled. "Pre-tuned, I suppose?"

Michael shrugged.

"You start and I'll join in if I can," Travis offered.

Dean picked up the guitar and strummed softly. Then he began to sing and the space around him vibrated with the soulful sound of his voice. Recognizing the familiar song as *I Don't Want to Miss a Thing*, Travis joined in on his guitar and halfway through the verse, with a nod from Dean, he took over the vocal. At the chorus, Dean reclaimed the melody and Travis launched into a higher part, singing harmony. Their duet was intuitive and magical.

When the song ended, the other guests clapped and whistled enthusiastically. Michael beamed. Dean and Travis bumped knuckles. Someone at the back of the knot of bodies gathered around them yelled, "You guys practised!" It was Georgia.

"They'd never even met!" Michael hollered back. "It's called talent."

"Come up here and join us, Georgia." Dean looked at Travis and chuckled, "My songwriting partner."

"Maybe later," she replied, but she was cozied up to a man of the tall, dark and handsome variety, and Dean doubted anything would pry her away.

A relaxed atmosphere permeated the room as the evening wore on and the alcohol flowed freely. Dean moved easily from guitar to piano, improvising with Travis. It was shortly after one in the morning when they finally called it a night. Several guests had left and a few more were saying their goodbyes to Michael and his partner, Derek. Spencer was snoring softly on a sofa, head back and mouth agape. Georgia and the hunk were nowhere in sight.

Dean turned to Travis who was putting his guitar in its case. "This was fun. Maybe we can do it again sometime." As Travis stood, they shook hands.

Travis wrapped his free arm around Dean and drew him into a hug. Then he broke away and looked him in the eye. "I feel so..." He searched for the words.

"Honoured?" Dean asked and they both laughed.

"I'm glad you enjoyed it, because I've been thinking the whole time we were playing and... okay, you can say no, but I'm going to ask anyway."

"Go ahead."

"I have a gig at Phil's Room on the fifteenth. It's a restaurant and live music venue connected to the Chandler Hotel. It's not huge, seats around two hundred, but they have some pretty big names there from time to time and local artists like me, too." Travis hesitated. "We couldn't pay you anything, but, I mean, since you had such a good time tonight, I'd love it if you'd join us on stage for a bit."

"I'd enjoy that, actually. I don't want to horn in on your spotlight, but sure, I'd do a set with you. Would that work?"

Travis looked like he was about to hug him again, but he picked up his guitar case instead and squealed, "Hell, yeah!"

"Shall we get together first and actually rehearse this time?"

"Definitely."

A hand reached between them, holding a business card. "I knew you boys would hit it off," Michael said. "I've written Dean's number on the back."

Travis took the card and headed for the door. "I'll be in touch," he said, walking backwards. "Thanks. Thanks so much. Had a great time." He bumped into a lingering guest and nearly knocked over another with his guitar case as he turned.

Michael was grinning like a Cheshire cat. "Lovely and talented, isn't he? A tad clumsy, though."

"Yes, indeed."

"So, ask."

"Is he?"

"Well… there *is* a girlfriend – or a friend who is a girl. So, possibly not. I just thought you'd enjoy each other musically," Michael laughed. "I heard him perform a few weeks ago and invited him to audition for a part in *Thin Air*. No promises, just an opportunity."

"Good idea." Dean yawned. "Well, Michael, great party." He gave Michael's shoulder a squeeze, thanked him and left to collect his jacket.

"Hey, wait for me," said a familiar voice. Georgia had fallen into step behind him.

"Thought you'd left already," Dean remarked. "What about your… date?"

"Married, wet and gone – in that order."

"Wet?"

"I threw my drink at him after Derek clued me in that the sleaze bag has a wife. Had to wait till I got him on the patio so it wouldn't splash all over these beautiful mahogany floors."

"Very considerate of you."

"You wouldn't believe how he came on to me. Since my divorce, all I've met is jerks."

"Sorry," Dean said as he held her overcoat for her. "Your Prince Charming is out there somewhere."

"I know, but unfortunately he's waiting for a prince, too." Georgia linked her arm through his and they stepped outside into the chilly darkness of early morning.

CHAPTER 13

March 8

Beryl couldn't believe her luck. Mark and Meredith lived just four blocks apart, not far from Sir Winston Churchill Park. She'd chosen Mark as her first target and, a little over an hour into her stakeout, there he was, backing out of his driveway in his red Ford Fusion. She waited for him to drive to the end of the block before she pulled away from the curb in her black Chevy Tahoe.

Once he hit Bathurst Street he sped up, zipping in and out of traffic. Beryl managed to keep him in her sights and wasn't far behind when he reached the traffic circle on Spadina. Then he did a strange thing. He made a complete revolution of the circle so that Beryl ended up directly behind him. When he began a second revolution, she realized he would notice if she stayed on his bumper so she reluctantly turned east, watching in her rearview mirror as Mark exited south on Spadina.

Cursing, Beryl turned south at the next corner and at the end of the block, she spotted the red Ford passing through the intersection just ahead. Drumming her fingers against the steering wheel, she waited for the light to turn green and then screeched onto College Street, blasting her horn at the Toyota that changed lanes in front of her. "Stupid Asians!' she griped, drawing a dirty look from the Caucasian driver as she pulled around him.

Ahead of her, in the distance, the red car made a right turn. Swerving dangerously close to a cyclist, Beryl moved into the turn lane and waited in frustrated silence for the traffic to press forward. After some manoeuvring, she was once again on Mark's tail.

Several blocks and turns later, Mark pulled into a parking lot. Beryl followed, swinging into a parking space as Mark made his way on foot to the crosswalk, wearing a backpack and rolling a suitcase behind him. She walked briskly in his direction, watching his red cap bob as he made his way down the block. Suddenly he stopped.

In profile, Mark appeared to be standing at the edge of the sidewalk, gazing at traffic. In the next moment, a streetcar squealed into view and braked in front of him. Beryl accelerated to a lumbering sprint and climbed onboard just before it pulled away. Breathing hard, her eyes searched the passengers for Mark and found him staring straight at her from the third row. She quickly refocussed on a spot behind him, straightened her jacket and made her way to one of the vacant seats.

After several stops, Mark finally disembarked. He walked another block with Beryl hot on his trail before hailing an orange cab. By the time she flagged down a cab of her own, his had rounded the corner and melted into a flowing sea of colourful traffic.

"Where to now?" the driver asked after a fruitless chase that ended several blocks north. That's when Beryl realized she had no idea where she'd left the Tahoe.

"Did you have any trouble getting here? Anyone following you?" Lily asked as Mark released her from his hug.

"Yes and yes. A cop – some Amazon in plainclothes – was on my tail from the moment I left home. Practically sat on my lap on the streetcar. But don't worry. I gave her the slip."

Jinx came charging into the hall, yapping furiously. Mark knelt down and reached into his pocket. "I heard all about you, fleabag. Couldn't wait to meet you." Jinx eagerly snatched the rawhide bone from Mark's fingers and trotted happily off.

"So, you *are* being watched."

"Well, you're still all over the news, so the police must be feeling the pressure." Mark slipped off his shoes and picked up the backpack. "This is from Sue."

"First, let me introduce you to my friends," Lily said. "Or was it just the dog you couldn't wait to meet?" She led him into the kitchen. "Mark, this is Clair and her granddaughter, Kate."

"I was told you were wonderful, but no one mentioned gorgeous," Mark said, grinning.

"I like you already," Clair said and she hugged him. The instant kinship she felt for him made the idea of a handshake too formal.

Kate crossed the room, drying her hands with a dish towel.

"You can't be the only person in this room that I don't hug," Mark said and he wrapped his arms around her. As he stepped back, his eyes dropped to the message on her T-shirt. SARCASM. BECAUSE BEATING THE CRAP OUT OF PEOPLE IS ILLEGAL. "Sneeringly droll," he laughed. "I like that in a woman."

He opened his jacket to reveal the print on his own T-shirt. I REFUSE TO ENGAGE IN A BATTLE OF WITS WITH AN UNARMED PERSON.

Kate laughed. "We may be joined at the brain." Her eyes lingered on his face. "You look a lot like Lily."

Mark nodded. "I know. More than I look like Meredith, who's my actual twin. And who's not so, you know, *old*."

Lily grabbed the damp dish towel from Kate and held it at opposite corners, spinning it between her hands. "Remember this, little bro?"

"Don't you dare!"

"I used to torture him as a kid," Lily said. "Which, since I was eight years older, wasn't very nice, I guess."

"I had my revenge," Mark laughed, his blue eyes twinkling. "Lam."

Lily glared at him.

"Her initials are L.A.M. so, apparently, our father used to call her his 'little lamb' when she was too young to object. I save it for special occasions."

"And it's rather appropriate right now since she's on the lam from the law," Kate said.

Lily started to walk to the sink, then turned and snapped Mark with the towel, making him yelp. "That's for old time's sake. But I guess I should be nice to you since you're part of my defense team now." She turned to the others. "My father isn't a defense attorney. He dealt mainly with litigation in the business sector. After my arrest, I chose someone with a good track record in criminal defense to represent me but, as it turned out, I might as well have hired a plumber. I feel like I finally have a chance with Dad and Mark in my corner."

Mark unzipped the backpack at his feet, pulled out a cardboard box and set it on the counter. "This is all your research for the Brent Baines book. Sue said she was hoping you'd continue with the project so that when this is all over, the entire story can be told. Including your escape. She says this book would shoot sales through the roof."

Lily opened the lid and looked at the collection of folders and envelopes inside. "I won't be able to focus on the book right now, but thank Sue for me." She withdrew a flash drive from the box. "I think I should take another look at this stuff, though."

The late afternoon sun cast a warm rectangle of light on the library floor where Lily was examining the papers and photographs scattered on the carpet. She looked up when Kate and Clair entered the room.

Clair looked at the sheets of paper fanned out around her. "Is it true that you remember almost everything you see and do and read?"

"No," Lily replied emphatically. "That nonsense was circulated during my trial. There are a handful of people in the world who have a syndrome called hyperthymesia and somehow, they can remember practically every day of their lives in detail. It's as if they remember a day from a decade ago like you or I remember yesterday. Scientists think this kind of Super Memory may be a type of synaesthesia – in this case, cross wiring between parts of the brain that process vision and memory."

"You sound like a walking encyclopedia," Kate said.

"I'm just interested in a lot of unusual subjects and I remember the things that are important or get my attention." Lily eyed the plastic bag in Kate's hand. "Enough about me. What have you been up to?"

"Shopping for your disguise, since you seem determined to defy common sense." From the bag, Kate withdrew a blonde wig styled in a short, asymmetric cut. "Cute, don't you think?"

Lily picked up the wig and twirled it. "Stunning, in a drag queen kind of way."

"And these." Kate handed her a pair of tortoise shell glasses. "Like mine, but with plain glass." She handed her two small plastic cases. "And two sets of non-prescription, brown contact lenses to hide your blue eyes."

Clair bent down and picked up one of the larger photographs. "Brent must have been about twelve when this family portrait was taken. The boys don't look much alike, do they?"

Kate inspected the photo. "Brent has a fair complexion like his father and Ben is darker like his mother. And Ben has coarser features. Even then, Brent was well on his way to becoming a babe magnet."

Lily plopped the stack of file folders she'd reassembled on the library table and sat down on the sofa. She sighed.

"What?" Kate asked.

"You just reminded me of one of my many flaws. Falling for attractive men. Guess I'm shallow that way."

Kate chuckled. "There's nothing wrong with being attracted to attractive men."

"There is if it's to the exclusion of more important characteristics."

Clair descended on the sofa. "Was Jemma's father one of those 'babe magnets'?"

"Not now," Lily replied, closing her eyes.

"And, what are some of these other perceived flaws?"

"For one thing, I'm not very domestic. There was never an aroma of fresh baked cookies in the air when Jemma came home after school. Gourmet meals? Forget it."

"That's small potatoes," Kate said. "Oh, no reference to last night's meal intended." She was grinning.

"I did spend lots of quality time with Jemma, but I haven't had time for much else. Like baking cookies and… dating." Lily was silent for a moment. "Also, I'm self-serving and unforgiving."

"That, I can't believe."

Lily took the photograph from Clair's hand and studied it. "It'll be interesting to hear what the Davenports have to say about this family."

"They didn't answer when I called, so I sent an email," Clair said.

Kate picked up a more recent photo of Brent. "Nice eyes. Blue, but not as blue as yours."

"In reality, blue eyes aren't even blue," Lily said. "Neither blue nor green pigments are even present. The pigmentation of the iris varies from light brown to black, depending on the concentration of melanin in the…"

"Keep it simple," Kate said.

"Eye colour is an expression of structure and varies, depending on the lighting. It's similar to the phenomenon that makes the sky look blue. The idea that blue eye colour is a simple recessive trait is incorrect." Abruptly, Lily sat up straight, staring at the photo. "I just realized what it is about this picture that's been bothering me!"

Kate and Clair leaned in close to take a look.

"The eyes," Lily said. "Father and mother and Brent all have blue eyes. Ben has brown eyes. It's possible for two blue-eyed parents to produce a brown-eyed child, *but* it's not very common. It has to do with whether or not certain genes are what scientists call 'broken'. The right combination of 'turned on' genes is needed to produce pigment."

"It's possible, but unlikely, that Ben would have brown eyes."

"Right. *And* check out the hair. Everyone has straight hair, except Ben. His hair is curly – in every photograph. Since the gene for curly hair is dominant, neither one of Ben's parents could have carried it. They couldn't have passed curly hair on to Ben. So, in all likelihood..."

Kate nodded. "Either Ben was adopted or his daddy was not the biological father."

"Strange. Brent never mentioned that," Lily said.

"Perhaps he didn't know," Clair suggested. "It wouldn't be the first time a parent has kept that kind of information from a child."

At this, an image of Jemma flooded into Lily's head on a wave of guilt, drowning her other thoughts. Wearily, she sighed. "I think it's time I faced some bad decisions I made a long time ago. If you're right about there being no coincidences, then you two are the ones I should talk to. If I can."

"How about we do that Tarot reading tonight and just let the conversation develop naturally?"

Lily wasn't thrilled with the idea, but considering the secrets she was about to spill, staring at cards would be easier than making eye contact. "Sure," she said. "Is there a special place in this house set aside for these occult activities?"

"Yes," Clair whispered and she leaned in close. "It's called the kitchen table."

With a giggle, Kate stood and walked toward the door. "I'm going to start dinner."

"Want some help?" Lily asked.

"No," Kate answered a little too quickly. "Thanks, but I've got it covered. We're having *Coquille Saint Jacque Marseillaise* followed by *Salmon en Croute* with champagne cream sauce and julienned vegetables, and for dessert, strawberry *crème fraiche* crepes. A very French menu tonight."

"You're making me salivate!" Lily wailed.

"Speaking of salivation, I should check on Jinx," Clair said, following Kate to the door. She turned to Lily. "Keep an open mind. The Tarot may surprise you."

Natalie VanHorne looked distinctly uncomfortable. Her eyes remained on the window as the waitress set a plate of poutine in front of her. Mark accepted his cheeseburger with a polite, "Thank you," and turned his attention to the girl who sat across from him in the booth.

"This is your second year at Brock University?" he asked.

She nodded.

"Do you like it here in St. Catharines?"

"Yeah. I was glad to ditch Toronto."

"Did you stay in touch with Kristie after you left?" Mark asked, leading her gently back to the subject of their conversation.

"No, I didn't see her again until the trial."

"But you were good friends at one time, right?"

"I guess. She lived next door with her dad, so we spent a lot of time together. She was a year younger, but anyway..." Natalie stopped talking and watched the gooey cheese dangle above her pile of fries as she rotated her fork.

"Did you two talk around the time of the trial?"

"Not much. I was only there for a few days. My parents never liked her and they didn't want me to have anything more to do with her." She hesitated. "But she did call me just before the trial."

Mark kept his voice casual. "I assume she wanted to make sure you were going to say what she expected when you testified."

Natalie finally took a bite of her poutine and glanced around the mostly empty diner. "Something like that. Of course she was all, like, 'I miss you so much. We need to get together and hang out,' and stuff like that."

"You don't really like her all that much anymore, do you?"

"You know what it's like when you're too close to something to see it for what it is? Like when you're going out with a guy and you think he's so great and then you break up and suddenly you can see what an ass he was?"

Mark laughed. "I know exactly what you mean. When I was in high school I fell in love...with a car. A 1974 Mustang convertible that belonged to the widow next door. I got it in my head that she should sell it to me. I didn't see the time or the money it was going to take to fix it up. I spent my entire savings on that old clunker, but I couldn't afford to keep it running. It wasn't until I sold it – at a loss – that I realized what a monumental waste of time it had been."

Natalie met his eyes and offered him a faint smile. "Kristie was my Mustang. She was pretty and popular and fun, but she was way more trouble than she was worth."

"What kind of trouble?"

"Just stuff like, she'd tell her dad she was going somewhere with me when she was really meeting up with some guy. I was expected to cover for her. Or partying too much. Drinking and stuff. But I heard she got scared and cleaned up her act.

"Because of the murder?"

"Yeah. And the trial. You know, she looked and acted a lot older than she was. Like, she thought she was so mature, but really, under the makeup and all the talk, she was really childish."

Mark nodded and let a few seconds pass. "Natalie, I really appreciate your willingness to talk with me and I think you've been truthful so far. I need to ask you some tough questions."

Natalie stared at her plate. "I told the police already that I was with Kristie that day. I drove her home from her mother's house in her dad's car. I'd had my license longer and was more confident on busier streets. When we got home, I got out and she took off."

"Did she ever tell you anything about what she or her mother did after that?"

"Just that she drove around. And when she heard later that night that Brent had been killed, she came over, screaming and crying 'cause she was all, like, shocked."

"Did it seem normal to you?"

"Well, yeah."

Mark studied Natalie's face and she shifted nervously. "Why did Kristie go to Lily's hotel that afternoon? Why not just call her if she had her phone number?"

"She went there to tell her that Brent was engaged to her mother and to back off."

"Why not let her mother handle it?"

"Maybe she hadn't planned at first for her mother to find out about the relationship."

"What relationship, Natalie? Lily's or her own?"

Natalie's fork was shaking, and she put it down. "I thought this was all over with." She sniffed and Mark noticed her eyes were filling with tears. "I don't want to say anything that's going to mess things up. I don't care so much about protecting Kristie anymore, but I really don't believe she had anything to do with the murder. I just… I don't want to get in trouble."

Mark leaned forward. "My sister is in much more trouble than you will ever see in your life and I'm trying to help her by uncovering the facts in this case. I'm not trying to throw Kristie or her mother under the bus. I just want to find out what's true and what's not. Isn't that fair?"

Natalie nodded. "What will happen to me?"

"Nothing terrible. Probably nothing at all if you come forward voluntarily. And it'll be off your conscience."

Natalie wiped her eyes with her serviette. "We went to Lily's hotel so Kristie could show her a video to prove that she was Brent's lover. She was obsessed with him and when she found out about him and Lily, she went nuts."

The words were out. This information could provide motive for both Kristie and Melissa. Natalie continued. "I don't know how she thought this was going to help her hang on to Brent. I guess she figured if she couldn't have him, nobody would. Maybe in her screwy way of thinking, she imagined him coming back to her after Lily dumped him. I told her it was crazy."

"Then you drove Kristie to her mother's house, right?"

Natalie nodded.

"Did she tell her mother everything?"

"She said she did. Not about the video, though. Just that she'd had a thing with Brent and that he'd been seeing Lily. Her mother had arrived from Thailand late the night before and she was supposed to see Brent that day. Kristie and her mom had a blowout fight. I was waiting in the car when Kristie came running out and told me to get her the hell out of there. And then she started getting all freaked out about what she'd done.

Mark didn't let his excitement show. Melissa and Kristie had both lied to the court, claiming that Kristie had come only to visit her mother.

"What about the video?" he asked. "Kristie denied showing Lily a video and said she didn't even own a tablet or a camcorder."

"She used her dad's camcorder and transferred the video to her tablet – the one Brent gave her. Probably to, like, ease his conscience. Or keep her from talking."

Mark he kept his voice casual. "Do you know what happened to it?"

"She gave it to me for safekeeping. After she deleted the video. That would have been disgusting. And later, she told me I could keep it. I should have realized it was a bribe."

"You still have it?" Mark reached across the table and squeezed Natalie's hand. "There's a chance the video can still be retrieved, but that space on the hard drive may have been overwritten by now. Have you used the tablet much?"

"Actually, no. I got an iPad for my birthday not long after that. I should've given it back to Kristie I guess, but..." Natalie rubbed her eyes. "I don't know. We'd moved away and by then I'd put Kristie behind me."

"I'm going to need to borrow the tablet, okay?"

Natalie gave him a defeated sigh. "I know."

After the dishes were done, and with the aroma of dinner lingering in the air, Lily took a seat between Clair and Kate at the round table in the breakfast nook. A soft stillness had settled around them. Even Jinx seemed attuned to the shift in mood, quietly sprawled on his bed. Or perhaps he was feeling the effects of the strawberry crèpe he'd managed to seize from the coffee table during dessert by the fireplace.

"Ordinarily I wouldn't sit in, but I'm too invested," Kate said, setting three glasses of *baco noir* on the table. "I won't participate, though."

Clair slowly shuffled the cards as she spoke. "Of the seventy-eight cards in the deck, fifty-six belong to the Minor Acana. They concern what's happening in your everyday life. The other twenty-two are Major Arcana that relate to matters of a higher purpose. There are many ways to spread and interpret these cards. My way of reading them is to ask for input and suggest meanings."

"Unlike reading tea leaves or using crystal balls," Lily said.

"Right." Clair passed the deck to Lily. "But I do allow the images to inspire me. Shuffle the deck for a while, dear. As you transfer your energy to it, think about the question you're asking. Phrase it in a way that requires something more than a yes or no answer."

She sat back and watched Lily handle the deck. "I think we all have flashes of intuition at times, but some of us are more attuned to it than others. You're Capricorn, aren't you?"

"Did you intuit that?"

Kate spoke up. "No, she didn't. I found that out when I Googled you. Sorry, I'll say no more."

Lily chuckled. "Do you dabble in Astrology, Clair?"

"Well, it has associations with Tarot, so yes, to the extent that I see it as part of the symbolism and meaning embedded in the cards." Clair noticed Lily's dubious expression. "It's possible this is nothing more than a framework for a conversation. Then again, maybe there's more to it than that."

"What about palm reading?" Lily asked.

"Oh, that's nonsense."

Lily could not suppress the smile that twitched at the corner of her mouth.

The shuffling ritual was concluded and Clair took the deck from Lily. "What is your question?"

Crossing her arms, Lily focussed on the bare table. "How should I handle the issue of my daughter's father?"

"That's rather vague, but we'll get more specific as we go." Clair spread ten cards face up in a pattern that formed a cross and a column and examined the arrangement thoughtfully. "Hmm," she murmured. "Lots of Cups and Swords. Cups rule the realms of emotions and love and swords concern the mind. Four Major Arcana cards. Let's begin with the Justice card. Its position in the spread indicates that it represents the root of the problem. It's the reason you're asking the question. Has there been unfairness, dishonesty, or a lack of accountability on your part or on someone else's part that is at the core of this issue?"

Lily sat up straight. Her eyes travelled to the card with the robed figure holding a sword and a set of scales. She swallowed. "I, uh…

yes. It was on my part and his – Jemma's father – but mostly mine. I've been unfair to everyone concerned." She bit her lower lip.

"Let's see how this fits together." Clair moved her finger to another card. "The Two of Swords. This card shows that you find yourself in an unhappy situation through fear or reluctance. But it's telling you this can be changed if you're prepared to face up to it." She looked at Lily, who remained mute. "And this next one – the Eight of Swords. It's what opposes you. Being held captive by your own fears. Those swords represent your thoughts, and your thoughts have become your prison. But you aren't truly trapped. This card is asking you to acknowledge the truth, to have the courage to set yourself free."

"Both of those women are blindfolded," Lily remarked, comparing the two cards. "That says it all." She finally met Clair's eyes. "Jemma doesn't know who her father is. When she was old enough to ask about him, I told her that I'd wanted a child so much I'd used a sperm bank. She thinks I was too focussed on my career to look for a husband."

Kate made a little wow sound under her breath, then whispered, "Sorry."

"It gets worse," Lily said. "Dean – that's her father's name – doesn't know about Jemma. I was crazy about him. He was charming and handsome and talented. We'd only been together for two months when he asked me to marry him. A week later it was done. City hall wedding, only our families present. No one else knew. We wanted to come back from the honeymoon and flash the ring. You know – 'Surprise! Look what we did!'"

"And then what?" Kate asked, leaning in. She'd forgotten about her pledge of silence.

"Well, Dean's grandparents had gifted us with a two-week honeymoon at their time share in St. Kitts and we left right after the ceremony. It felt strange – wrong – somehow, but I chalked it up to fatigue. I'll spare you the details, but a week into the honeymoon, Dean told me he didn't want to be married to me anymore."

Kate slammed both hands onto the table. "No!"

"Yes. He said he was very sorry for all the trouble, but he'd made a huge mistake and by the way, he was gay." Lily looked down at her ringless fingers. "He was contrite and broken, really, but I wouldn't listen. I was livid. And devastated. I told him I never wanted to speak to him again and took the next flight home."

"Ah," Clair sighed, "so these are the deceptions pointed to by Justice."

"Yes, and I used his deception to justify my own."

"Did he ever contact you?" Kate asked.

"No. His mother called to apologize on his behalf and, I suppose, to try to gain some insight from me. The news that their only child was gay and leaving his wife a week into his marriage didn't sit well with their conservative religious views, so I imagine she was struggling with it, too. I thanked her for the call, but told her I wanted to put everything behind me and get on with my life.

"When I found out I was pregnant I was shocked, but elated. I had a profound sense that it was my destiny to be this child's mother. I should have told Dean, but I was bitter and I wanted the baby all to myself. I saw him as an unwitting sperm donor, not the father. Mum tried to talk to me about it sometimes, but I kept stalling. Then, two summers ago I was arrested and the subject was never raised again."

Kate looked puzzled. "How is it possible that Dean hasn't heard anything about you in all these years?"

Lily smiled. "For one thing, I doubt that he Googles everyone like you do. And he's American, so things happening up here aren't likely to filter down to him. He probably hasn't heard of my books, wouldn't even be looking for them. To be safe, I've tried to keep any mention of Jemma out of print and in the few that exist I've shaved a year off her age."

"How did you and Dean meet?" Kate asked.

"My mother is from Saranac Lake. That's in the Adirondacks, only a two hour drive from my parent's home. My grandparents were still living there at the time and they were friends with Dean's grandparents. It was probably a set up, but that August they invited me to come for a visit when Dean happened to be there and they introduced us. I'd just finished my MA in Journalism and moved back home."

"And it was love at first sight?"

"Almost," Lily said. "We hit it off and decided to stay on at Saranac Lake for a while. He worked on some music he was planning to record and played weekends at nightspots in Lake Placid. I waited tables and fired off resumes to newspaper and magazine publishers."

"You know it's only a matter of time, don't you?" Clair asked gently.

"Yes, and I dread the fallout."

"Ah, your fears." Clair tapped a card that showed an image of a cloaked figure looking at three cups toppled on the ground. Behind him, two cups stood upright. "The Five of Cups. You are concentrating on what you have to lose," she said, pointing to the spilled cups, "and not on what you will retain and eventually multiply."

"And let me guess – the Three of Swords?" Lily asked, motioning to the card that showed three swords piercing a large red heart.

"That's in your past," Clair answered. "What do you think that represents?"

"A broken heart. Disappointment, deception, emotional upheaval."

"In your case, I would say that one is obvious."

Lily frowned. "I don't like the looks of this one."

Clair followed her eyes to the card. "The near future. That's Death, but it's almost never about physical death. It speaks of an ending, in which something has to die before something else can begin to grow."

"As in, my relationship with Jemma has to die before her relationship with her father can begin."

"I don't think so. It may involve losing face, but not losing your daughter. I feel that it means the deception must die. It's about rebirth and renewal. Letting go of old patterns of behaviour and thought." Clair spoke gently. "How will you do that? Look at this Major Arcana card." She handed it to her.

Lily studied the image of the maiden prising open the jaws of a lion. "I don't know. Suicide?"

Kate snickered.

"Look deeper, dear. The girl's face, how does it look?"

Lily gazed at the illustration. "Serene."

"Yes. She is taming the lion, not with force, but with love. The Strength card is about the need for confidence, courage and perseverance. It symbolizes understanding your own inner beasts and conquering them. The message of this card is that your task may be easier than it looks."

"I'm a coward," Lily stated flatly. "I never wanted to hurt Jemma. But every time I looked at her, I saw Dean. It was as though he had a stronger claim on her. That made me tighten my grip."

"You're human and you've made mistakes. But I think you owe Dean the right to be a father," Kate said. She looked at her grandmother. "Sorry. I'm not supposed to make judgements."

Clair pointed to a card. "The six of cups, the power of the past. This could represent the strong feelings you have about Jemma, or nostalgic memories. But I think it suggests that someone from your past will make a reappearance. Dean, perhaps. Is that something you might set in motion?"

Lily nodded. "It will mean putting my hands into the jaws of the lion."

Clair gazed thoughtfully at her. "I wish I could see this more clearly. I was not blessed with my mother's highly developed gift of clairvoyance. She made her living as a psychic and a medium."

"Why am I not surprised?" Lily looked back at the spread. "Do you suppose this card could represent Dean?"

Clair smiled. "When the King of Wands represents a person, it describes someone who is enthusiastic and vibrant, someone who has enormous charm."

"That sounds like Dean."

"The King of Wands enjoys family life and is an excellent father figure. Once he finds his soul mate, he's committed. But otherwise, he may promise more than he can deliver. He is creative and puts a great deal of energy into his interests."

"Like his music. It's probably his career now."

"You have no idea what's happened to him all these years? At *all*?" Kate asked, incredulous.

"None. That would mean acknowledging his existence."

"Your family didn't investigate?"

"They'd been warned. And I think, on a subconscious level, they were content to have Dean out of the picture, too. We're a close knit family."

"Ohhh," Kate said, squeezing her eyes tightly shut. "*Puleeeaze* let me Google him."

Lily sighed, but she was smiling. "We'll do it together. Tomorrow." She turned to Clair. "And what does this King of Wands want to tell me?"

"I think he's just telling you that you need to open your heart and your mind to understand his behaviour," Clair said. "And now, let's talk about outcome."

Clair's eyes move to a card at the top of the spread, depicting a man hanging upside down.

"The Hanged Man. There is a karmic lesson in this one. If you follow the decision you've made to unite your daughter with her father, you'll gain a new perspective. It often indicates a time of waiting and of some sort of sacrifice you must make for a greater purpose. For a while, you may feel as though you have no control, suspended between chapters in your life, but in time you will gain enlightenment and wisdom."

Lily sat in silence for a few moments and then she said, "That's beautiful, Clair."

Clair beamed. "Why don't we do a short reading about the other matter, investigating the murder? A simple three card draw."

"Okay, let's do it."

While Lily shuffled and Clair laid out the cards, Kate refilled her glass. Clair was ignoring her wine and Lily had taken only a few sips.

"This one is the Chariot," Clair said as she examined the first of three cards. She inhaled deeply, clearly enjoying the moment. "When a challenge seems insurmountable, this card offers encouragement because it's letting you know that you have what it takes to overcome obstacles. The white horse and the black horse represent positive and negative energies, powers that you will balance and control. But you must pay close attention to the road before you. Be prepared before you rush into anything."

"Do my homework before I set out," Lily offered.

"Exactly! And you *will* set out. Horses often represent literal travel. You'll need confidence. Hmm," Clair murmured. "This next one is puzzling." She was staring at the Four of Pentacles. It depicted a man holding four large coins. "This card often has a dual message. It's about having a sense of financial security. It could also warn about being reluctant to take risks or spend money. Perhaps it's assuring you that you'll have financial help at your disposal, but I think it suggests something more." She closed her eyes in deep concentration and lapsed into silence.

This gave Lily a tickle of amusement and she tried to convey it with a sideways glance at Kate, who was already draining her glass. Kate gave Lily a thumbs up and flashed a smile that reflected less amusement than pleasant wine buzz.

Finally, Clair came out of her trance and refocussed on the card. "This is about someone else who is concerned with the crime. It involves money. As the miser card, it shows the effects of greed and selfishness. There is a fear of losing all that has been gained. And great danger."

Lily brought her glass to her mouth. "That's sobering."

Kate claimed Clair's untouched wine and took a long swallow.

"The final card," Clair said, her serious tone lingering. "The High Priestess, who sits before the mysterious and the divine. She speaks in a whisper to your unconscious mind. She tells you to trust your intuition. But..." Clair closed her eyes again. "I think the message here is that we need to communicate with someone who has entered other realms." She opened her eyes, placed her hand softly over Lily's and gave her a somber look. "I think we should consult my mother."

Lily pulled her hand away with a start. "Oh, no, I'm sorry, Clair. I'm okay with Tarot cards, but not a séance. That's too morbid. You've done so much for me and I appreciate it, but..." She looked to Kate for support, but Kate was leaning heavily on the table, her cheek propped on one hand and a crooked beatific grin plastered on her face. Lily's eyes shot back to Clair, who wore a patient smile. "Really, I don't want to offend you, but I must refuse any kind of macabre communication with the dead. It just–"

Clair finally cut off her rambling protests. "Oh, my dear," she said gently, "my mother is not *dead*. She's alive and well at a retirement home in Forest Hill."

CHAPTER

14

March 9

When Lily opened her eyes and threw off her covers, she was stunned to see that the trees outside the bedroom window were covered in snow. By the time she made her way to the kitchen, the grey clouds were unleashing a fresh crop of swirling flakes. Clair, a pair of narrow reading glasses perched on her nose, sat at the breakfast bar.

"Snow," Lily muttered in greeting.

"And a sunny good morning to you, too," Clair replied with a smile.

Lily looked around. "Is Kate in the solarium?"

"No, dear, I expect she'll sleep all morning. These little setbacks are not unusual."

"Must've been the wine and the late night. My fault."

"Don't be concerned. You've been so good for her. Now, Mother said she could do a reading for you tomorrow, but it will have to be after the talent show."

"Talent show?"

"Yes, it's an annual event for residents at the retirement home and other seniors in the community."

"Oh, of course, she should see the show first."

"Actually, she's *in* the show." Clair wrote something on her calendar.

"You're joking. Exactly how old *is* she, anyway?"

"Ninety-nine. She turns one hundred in September. Big party planned."

"And what will she be performing at this show?"

"She'll be lip syncing *I Will Survive* by Gloria Gaynor. It's one of her favourites."

"I suspect you and your mother are a lot alike," Lily chuckled.

"I'll come pick you up right after Mother performs and we'll meet her in her suite."

Lily poured herself some coffee and walked into the solarium where she gazed out at the gardens, now shrouded in white.

Clair followed with a tray of warm croissants, butter and jam. "Is all that snow getting you down?"

"A little."

"That's what March is like. It's a tug-of-war, with spring trying to wrench winter from its grasp."

"I can't see those daffodil shoots anymore."

"The new growth is still there, dear, just under the snow. Soon it will flourish."

Lily sat down on one of the red leather chairs near Clair and buttered a croissant.

Clair watched as she laid the knife back on the tray. "How was it that your fingerprints ended up on the murder weapon?"

Lily's hand froze halfway to her mouth. "Having second thoughts?"

"Not at all. I simply don't recall the details."

"There was one print on the base of the blade. I'd made dinner there a few nights before and I obviously touched it when I was putting it away."

Clair looked askance at Lily. "Honestly?"

"You don't believe me?"

"You made dinner?"

"Oh, Clair!" Lily wagged her finger. "I do *sometimes* cook edible meals."

They fell into silence and Lily settled back into her chair, a warm mug of coffee pressed between her palms.

"Lily, did you ever undergo hypnosis to see if you could recall any details about the silver car you saw at the murder scene?"

"No," Lily replied slowly. "Where are you going with this? You're not about to tell me you're a licenced hypnotist, are you?"

"No, no," Clair said, with the wave of her hand.

Lily took a sip of her coffee.

"But I did take a course in hypnosis as a tool for doing past life regressions."

The coffee took a wrong turn in Lily's throat and her swallow turned into a cough. She put the mug down. "You're serious, aren't you?"

"Of course I am. Now, I was wondering if perhaps we could try taking you back to that day and…"

"Have you done this before?"

"Well, with members of the class. And once to help a friend stop smoking."

"And do you believe in this reincarnation business?" Lily asked.

Clair shrugged. "I don't know and I won't pretend to. I believe in those other dimensions I talked about and I believe our consciousness goes on in some form. Past life regression is just one of the subjects I explored. And that was some years ago." She held Lily's eyes. "When you get to be my age, you may find yourself thinking more deeply about these things."

"At the moment, my head is too crowded with the problems of the here and now."

"Of course it is, dear. I was merely offering a suggestion."

Lily watched Clair's hands, spotted with age, pick up a plate and return it to the tray, and she felt a rush of warmth for all the kindness this remarkable woman had showered on her. "Let me do that," she said, rising quickly to her feet. She loaded everything on the tray and headed for the kitchen. At the doorway, she turned and looked back at Clair. "What the hell, hypnotise me."

"Now?" Clair asked brightly.

"Now."

Clair cackled, "Ha, ha! This will be fun. Let's go into the living room."

Lily smiled. She doubted she could be hypnotised by a professional, much less Clair, but she knew how much it would please her friend. Clair closed the drapes and invited Lily to sit in a recliner. Then she sat on a chair next to her, told her to close her eyes, and began talking to her in soft, soothing tones.

After a minute or so of this, Lily giggled and, eyes still closed, she said, "Sorry, Clair, but I don't think I'm hypnotisable."

"You need to relax," Clair said. "Let's start over and this time, try not to be so skeptical. Just give yourself up to it. Meditate and let my voice guide you. Trust me."

Lily allowed herself to sink into a calm, relaxed state as Clair's words seeped into her mind. She felt warm and safe, drifting, floating, as she followed Clair's voice.

Clair took her back to the fateful day in Oakville. She was in her car, driving down Brent's street. She saw the sun flashing through green leaves, sprinklers on a lawn, a squirrel scampering in the ditch.

"You're almost at the house, Lily. Now look to the right. What do you see?"

"A silver car parked at the side of the street."

"Describe the vehicle. Look at its shape."

"It's small, probably a compact. Clean, newish. There's a thick row of bushes and trees in the background."

"Look at the rear of the car. Do you see any words or symbols?"

Lily concentrated. "No."

"I want you to look at the license plate now. What colours do you see?"

"White, I think, not sure."

"Focus on it, Lily. Imagine that you're looking through binoculars at the plate." Clair paused. "The numbers are coming into focus. What do you see?"

Lily was silent for several seconds. "Nothing," she mumbled.

"Alright, let your eyes travel up to the back window. What's there?"

"Dark interior, silhouettes, maybe headrests."

"Now you're driving by the vehicle. You turn your head. Slow down time and take a long look."

The scene played slowly by in Lily's mind. "I see shiny chrome on the wheels, silver, and then... there's a triangle of fabric caught near the bottom of the rear passenger door."

"Good. Now describe everything about this fabric that you see, Lily."

"It's dark, maybe black or navy. It's the size of a piece of toast cut in half diagonally and it's doubled over like... the cuff of a sleeve."

"What else?"

"I see a small movement and..." She paused and frowned. "I think the engine is running."

"Focus on that movement. What is it?"

"I don't know. I just see something shadowy from the corner of my eye."

"Okay. Now you're passing the car. Look back at the front of it. What's there?"

"I don't see the front. I'm looking at the driveway to Brent's house."

"Do you see any vehicles or people there?"

"No."

Clair took Lily step by step through the murder scene, but no new memories emerged until she found herself pinned down on the driveway by the neighbour.

"There's a scratch on his inner arm – just above his watchband," Lily said. "It looks fresh."

"What's happening when you notice this scratch?"

"He's wrestling me to the ground. I'm on my back and we're both yelling."

"What else is happening?"

"Melissa's looking down at us. She's calm. I hear a siren. The police arrive quickly. Must've been in the area. She runs over to them and starts to cry."

Clair gently brought Lily out of her trance state.

"Amazing. I did remember some new details," Lily said. "The car was definitely a sedan. But I don't think I was truly hypnotised."

"I had you dancing like a chicken at one point," Clair insisted.

"Nice try, Clair." Lily laughed. "Seriously, though, the cuff in the car door? That's new. And the scratch on the neighbour's arm. Maybe that happened when he came through the hedge, but what if..."

Clair was already speculating. "Is it possible Melissa and this neighbour were having an affair?"

"Drew Fowler – that's the neighbour – was a witness at the trial and he testified that he'd encountered Melissa on three occasions, all casual, drinks around the pool sort of thing."

"Was he single? Rich? Good looking?"

"Married, no kids. Judging by his house, I'd say he was well off. As for looks, freakishly muscular men might appeal to some. Certainly not my type. I can't imagine a scenario in which he would help Melissa kill Brent."

"Perhaps Drew was there when she confronted Brent and things got out of hand. *Or* she called him for help. It seems rather convenient that he was on the scene so quickly."

"Supposedly, he was trimming the hedge. I wonder if police ever checked to see if there was any communication between those two in the months before the murder."

"Well, I'm calling this a breakthrough!" Clair said and she drew open the drapes just as the sun broke through the clouds.

By late afternoon much of the snow had melted. Lily pulled a terrycloth robe on over her swimsuit and tugged open a sliding door that led from the pool wing to the back gardens. She breathed in the fresh air as she rubbed a towel over her wet hair.

"Thought I might find you in here."

Lily turned to see Kate padding barefoot toward her.

"How's the neck?"

"Tolerably sore. How are you feeling?"

"Better," Kate said, averting her gaze to the scene outside.

Lily noted that Kate's hair had been freshly washed and left damp. Lines from the bed sheets still creased her cheeks and her eyelids looked puffy. The message printed on her wrinkled T-shirt declared, I HATE BEING BIPOLAR. IT'S AWESOME!

"I thought I'd come down and start planning dinner," Kate said.

"Not today. Clair wants Thai food tonight so she's ordering in. And you need to take it easy. I offered to cook, but she shot me down."

Kate smiled. "I'm okay, really. There was a time when working up the will to even take a shower seemed hopeless, but here I stand, fresh and clean."

"Guess I should keep the heat inside," Lily said, closing the door.

"About Mark," Kate said, leaning against the wall. "I, um… I feel like there's some chemistry between us, but…" She bit her lower lip. "I mean, I'm not even sure he's that interested in me, but before he left, he asked if we could see each other again." She paused and focussed on the floor. "I'm not a safe bet for anyone right now – I'm not sure I'll ever trust myself to make another relationship work, so…"

"Welcome to the club," Lily interjected.

"Okay, I know you have issues, but mine are different. They're organic, deep. I could be going along just fine for awhile and the illness will pop up like some horrible Jack-in-the-Box, or it might creep in slowly like mould. You haven't seen it. I'd like to think the medication has it under control, but it's too soon for me to take on any kind of major life change."

"I'm sorry. I didn't mean to trivialize your illness. Look, to my knowledge Mark's not involved with anyone at the moment, but he is a serial dater. If he asks you out, tell him how you feel."

"Is he interested in settling down?" Kate asked quietly.

"I think he's tiring of the single life. He's been happily divorced for three years now and the bad memories are far enough in the past.

"It's not that I don't find him attractive. I do. Very much. But I don't even know that I ever want to be a mother and Mark would probably want children. Even if I decided to get pregnant, I'm afraid of how my body would handle the hormonal changes."

"These are heavy questions. But you don't have to have all the answers right now. As you continue to get better things will become clearer."

Kate nodded. "Let's hope. Soooo… as long as I'm not going to be busy in the kitchen, shall we do that internet search for Dean James?"

"I promised, didn't I? Let me put on some dry clothes."

A few minutes later, they were seated in front of the computer, Kate's fingers resting lightly on the keyboard.

"I can't believe you never once tried to search for Dean. I'd be dying of curiosity," she said. "We could start with his name and add something."

"I can't imagine him not having some connection to music. Try that."

Kate typed the words. "Ready?"

"As I'll ever be," Lily said, and she felt her pulse flutter.

In the next instant the screen filled with row after row of results, all highlighting *Dean James.*

"Look!" Kate squeaked.

Lily sat bolt upright. "Maybe it's not the same one."

Kate clicked on one of the entries and several photos appeared. "That's him?"

Lily nodded.

Kate read some of the captions. "Dean James and Georgia Wilder attend Tonys. Broadway producer, David Hudson, with composer, Dean James. He's famous! Sort of."

Lily leaned in closer and stared at the pictures of Dean, older and more handsome than ever. The man in these photos was a stranger to her now and yet, through the mirror of Jemma's face, he was entirely familiar. Images of a living, breathing Dean played in her head like a film clip. Suddenly, their short time together felt like yesterday.

"Let me refine the search," Kate suggested. "Maybe we can see what he's up to now."

A new set of results appeared.

"Thin Air" is slated to open in Toronto in December. With music by Dean James and Georgia Wilder, this production will be the first major...

"Toronto!" Kate opened the page and began reading in earnest. "Lily, he's here in Toronto. Right now!"

Together, they unravelled the details of the *Thin Air* production and gleaned information about Dean's career. Lily leaned back in her chair and covered her face with her hands. She was trembling.

Kate wrapped an arm around her shoulder. "You know what Gram is going to say when she finds out Dean is here?"

"There are no coincidences."

"You got it. This is your cue."

The group gathered in the studio had just wrapped up the last audition of the day. Spencer studied the headshots spread out in front of him on the table. "I'd still like to see Tess. I think she'd be fabulous in the role of Valerie. Have you been able to find her yet?"

"I've got someone working on it," Michael replied. "Word is she's somewhere in Europe, but her contact information has changed and she's parted ways with her agent." He sighed. "She's as hard to find as that Mullaly woman."

Nearby, still seated on the piano bench, Dean whipped his head in their direction. "What Mullaly woman?"

"Don't you ever watch the news?" Michael asked. "It's been a top story for days."

Georgia rolled her eyes. "Dean is more of a cave dweller once we get home. Locks himself up in the den with his music and occasionally comes out to hunt food in the kitchen."

Dean continued to stare at Michael. "Who is she?"

"She's a convicted killer who escaped custody in Kitchener during that blizzard. No one can find her."

"Oh," Dean said. He stood up and pulled a coin from his pocket. "I'm starving, Georgia. Heads, we get take out. Tails, you cook."

"Tails we eat at the pub."

"See you guys in the morning then," Spencer said.

Dean flipped the coin. "The pub it is."

As they stepped out onto the street, Georgia threw him a sideways glance. "You went quiet all of a sudden."

"Sorry, just lost in thought. Mullaly. I used to know someone by that name."

"Who was your Mullaly?"

"Oh, someone I… met years ago. She was from Ontario, actually."

They walked in silence. There was an easy closeness between them. Their professional collaboration had proven to be a formula for success and their friendship had deepened with time. Still, Dean had his secrets.

Finally, he spoke. "This escaped convict. What's the back story there?"

"Can't let that go, can ya?" Georgia said, smiling up at him.

"Just curious now."

"She was convicted of the murder of a famous hockey player. Remember, I asked you the other night if you'd ever heard of him. Brent Baines."

"Right. And?"

"Apparently she's a writer from the Thousand Islands region. Around our age. Pretty, long dark hair, blue eyes."

Dean's feet had stopped moving. "What's her first name?"

Georgia turned and noticed his odd expression.

"Lily," she said. She watched his face go slack as his eyes closed. "She's not the Mullaly you knew, is she?"

Dean nodded. "I think so."

"Wh… What?" Georgia stammered. "Who is she to you?"

"She was my wife."

The ringing of the phone drew Emma into the family room where she found Jeff dozing in his recliner. The MacBook on his lap had gone into sleep mode, too. She glanced at the call display and caught her breath. Dean James. Could it be the same one? After all these years? She was still staring numbly at the phone, when her husband opened his eyes.

"Are you going to get that?"

"It's Dean, Dean James," Emma whispered as though at that very moment the police had their ears pressed to the door. "What do I say?"

"Don't answer. We'll try calling him back from the Bat Phone." Jeff had named their recently acquired disposable phone.

When the ringing stopped, Emma checked voicemail, but there was no message. She copied the number in the caller ID on a note pad. "Let's go somewhere else so the p-i-g-s don't hear us," she said. "They could have this place bugged or pick up our phone signal."

"Good thing they can't spell," Jeff said. "Em, we can't tell Dean too much."

"We won't." Emma scooped up the car keys from the hall table. "Let's go."

Jinx raced to the open dishwasher and began licking the remnants of red curry sauce from the plates Lily was loading as Clair entered the kitchen.

"Fran answered my email," she said. "She and Grant are in Florida right now."

"Oh." Lily sounded deflated.

"However," Clair continued. "Their son, Jack, is right here in Toronto and he says he would be delighted to talk to Kate about Brent."

"Even better!" Kate exclaimed."

"I told him that Kate has signed a contract to write the Brent Baines story. Oh, and they're all thrilled for you, dear," Clair said, patting Kate's shoulder. "He's agreed to meet with you and Sue at his place two days from now."

"Thanks for this," Lily said. "I fear you'll tire of me and all my drama soon."

"Honey, as long as you can stand us, you can stay in our lives forever," Clair said. "You're family now."

CHAPTER

15

March 10

Beryl was certain Mark Mullaly had been up to something on the first day of her surveillance, but since then her patience had been tested. On the chance that he'd noticed the Tahoe following him two days before, she'd switched to the little nondescript car she'd borrowed from her brother.

On this, the third morning, she'd followed Mark to Oakville and watched him walk into the Halton Regional Police headquarters. She had no idea what he was up to, but knew Lily certainly wouldn't be hiding there. After a couple of hours of waiting, she'd given up and driven back to Toronto to watch Meredith's house. By early afternoon, her strategy had paid off. A Beck's Taxi pulled up in front and immediately a young woman carrying a tote bag emerged from the house. She appeared to be in an advanced stage of pregnancy. Beryl looked at the photo on the screen of her phone and compared it to the woman. Shoulder length wavy hair the colour of a wheat field, fine features, late twenties. It was definitely Meredith.

Beryl tailed the taxi as it travelled east. It was entirely possible that Meredith was merely on some mundane errand. Nonetheless, the anticipation excited her. She was in her secret agent mode. Special Agent Beryl Sweeney. It had a ring to it. She adjusted her dark glasses and smiled as the taxi led her into Rosedale.

Kate cruised slowly along the paved road in Mount Pleasant Cemetery, scanning the evergreens to her right. She came to a stop as a figure stepped out from behind a tree and approached the car.

"Kate?" asked the woman, moving toward the open window.

"Hi Meredith."

Meredith moved around to the passenger side of the vehicle. "Thanks for coming to my rescue," she said, lowering her pregnant form onto the seat. "Those prepaid phones are coming in handy."

"Fortunately, I was home. Gram and Lily are visiting my great grandmother."

"I almost blew it. I foolishly thought I could take a single cab to your place."

"When did you realize you were being followed?"

"We were already in Rosedale, so I told the driver to keep going north and when we reached the maze of roads in the cemetery, I asked him to lose the car that was on our tail. When it was out of sight, I threw him the fare, jumped out and ducked behind those trees, which wasn't easy, given my present girth. If the guy ever caught up to the taxi, it was probably a while before he realized I wasn't in it."

"He?"

"It looked like a man in dark glasses. A cop, but – interesting choice of vehicle."

"That concerns me," Kate said. "It's been ten days and they're still watching."

Meredith ran a hand over her belly.

"When are you due?"

"The ninth of April – and it can't get here soon enough.

Kate scanned Moore Avenue before leaving the cemetery. "Keep an eye out for that cop, just in case."

Meredith sat silently for a few moments, stealing glances at Kate while perusing the traffic. "I'm so glad you found my sister."

"Me, too," Kate said.

"When do you expect her back?"

"In time for dinner. Will you stay and eat with us?"

"Sure, and I can help you in the kitchen."

"Ah…" Kate hesitated.

"Let me guess," Meredith groaned. "You've sampled some of Lily's cooking and now you're afraid of mine."

Kate laughed. "You can help. It's just that I was only planning on making pasta, *Bucatini all'Amatricianna*, but…"

"Made with *guanciale*?"

Kate grinned. "Yes, cured pork jowl. Am I in the presence of a fellow foodie?"

"Yes, and I love pasta."

"Then pasta it shall be. But nothing too spicy that might upset the baby. Do you know the gender yet?"

"Yep, but it's a secret. I'm afraid my husband is going to blab, though. Speaking of husbands, you were married once, right?"

"Mm hmm. How'd you know?"

"Mark told me," Meredith said, continuing to focus on Kate.

"Mark? He talked about me?"

"Yes." A trace of a smile bloomed on Meredith's face as she turned away.

Kate made a left turn and glanced in the rearview mirror. "It's nice that Mark lives so close by. To *you*, I mean."

Meredith's smile grew. "Yes. It's fortunate."

"And Mark lives alone?"

"He does. And no, there's no girlfriend in the picture at the moment." Meredith rolled her head toward Kate. "You look a little flushed. Are you okay?"

After changing out of her costume, a silver sequined top, a short black skirt and knee high red leather boots, Abby emerged from the bedroom of her suite. She'd won the People's Choice Award and had received a huge bouquet of flowers that now sat in a vase on a side table. She motioned for Lily to sit at the end of the sofa near her chair.

Clair stood. "I'm going to remove my energy from the room and do some reading." She went into the bedroom, leaving Lily to look into the eyes of the old woman sitting across from her. They were the same clear amber as Clair's.

Lily was wearing the wig and the brown contact lenses that Kate had bought for her and she'd insisted on being introduced by her middle name, Alice.

Abby sat back, closed her eyes and became very still. Two minutes passed without a sound and Lily was beginning to wonder if she'd have to check for a pulse when Abby opened her eyes and began to speak.

"Well, many things are flooding into my mind," she began. "First of all, I'm feeling a pain, a tightness here in my neck and it's going into my shoulder. Have you been having a problem with your neck?"

Lily's jaw dropped as she watched Abby run her hand along the right side of her own neck. "Yes! It's been sore for over a week."

"Well, I want you to focus on the colour green throughout the reading. You see, I'm a psychic healer, too, and green is a healing colour."

Lily's initial surprise was diminished by the notion that concentrating on a colour could heal *anything*, but she followed the instructions and pictured a large field of green.

"Now, I'm seeing great upheaval in your life. Things are not as they should be and you want to make it right." Abby paused, her brow furrowing. "Are there legal problems in your life or some conflict with the law?"

"Yes," Lily replied, quietly stunned, but unwilling to expand on her answer. She'd heard about "cold readings" in which mediums employ highly probable guesses by analyzing the appearance, speech and mannerisms of their subjects.

"I'm feeling that there is much love and admiration from those close to you. They will help you in the task that lies ahead, but... you mustn't rely only on them to solve this problem. You must take the reins and step into the arena yourself."

An image of the Chariot card from the Tarot reading flashed before Lily's eyes.

"I see a lion. You will need to balance courage with strength and wisdom as you follow this path."

"Okay."

"Someone comes to you from the other side with a great deal of love and affection. Your parents are still living, aren't they?"

"Yes," Lily said. That wasn't a stretch. Her parents were only in their sixties.

"I'm getting an M and a B. Something short. B… e..."

The name slipped out. "Brent?"

Abby was quiet for a moment. "And who would he be?"

"Someone I was involved with, professionally and… romantically."

Abby's next words took her by surprise. "No, this is an older person. I'm seeing a bell."

Lily thought. "I don't know who that could be."

"Bill? Belle? Something like that?"

"Don't think so."

"There is an older family member who has passed. A grandfather or an uncle?"

Lily felt a twinge of excitement. Was this a lucky guess? "My grandfather. His name was Marcus."

"He's the M. Did he live near a body of water and spend time on boats?"

"Yes. He had a cruise boat and ran tours of the Thousand Islands." Her eyes widened as the realization sank in. "The boat was called *Island Belle*."

"Ah ha!" Abby trumpeted. "I see him standing on the deck and the wind is blowing through his hair. He loved the water and was sad when he had to give it up. But now he is free and can go back to the places that brought him joy. He wants you to know that he is very proud of the person you have become." Abby paused, then was off on another tangent. "You have a child?"

"Yes."

"A daughter?"

"Yes."

"Hmm. Your daughter is quite brilliant, but she is something of a loner. She likes people, but she doesn't find satisfaction in friends her own age. She is mature for her years. And I see her busy, always doing."

"That's her," Lily said.

"Yes, and she idolizes you. But her age… I think she's coming into a new awareness. Whatever these things are that you are dealing with at the present time, they affect her greatly. She will never lose her love for you, but you may need to have faith that the dark clouds that come your way will part. Think silver linings."

The mention of silver brought colours to mind and Lily focussed again on green.

"Now who is it that has the D name?"

"Dean."

"And Dean is close to you?"

"He was, years ago."

"Yes, there has been a separation. Has he passed?"

"He was my husband, and he's alive."

Abby frowned. "He is your daughter's father?"

"Yes."

"He is disconnected and yet… that's not what is in his heart."

Lily felt a tear streak down her face.

"Now, your daughter – she bears a strong resemblance to her father."

"Yes, she does," Lily said. "There's very little of me in her at all."

"Oh, but you are only looking at the outside. She has your brilliance and your spirit. Your destinies are bound together."

Sniffling, Lily blurted out the truth. "She… and her father. They don't know about each other. I never told Dean I was pregnant. That little omission snowballed into a huge deception. And I made my family share the burden of that guilt."

"But you've decided that you must fix that and you will."

Lily nodded.

"Now this other B name you mentioned," Abby said closing her eyes.

"Brent."

"Yes. I'm not getting much on him, except a sense of regret." She paused and went silent for several seconds. "This Brent, he is in the spirit world?"

"Yes," Lily said, swallowing.

"And hmm… yet another B. Is there a B connection between you?"

"I don't think there's a connection, but his brother's name is Ben."

"Yes, yes. Now I don't know what this means, but Brent wants to show you his brother."

"Ben also died. In an accident a few months before Brent… passed away."

Abby was frowning. "I'm sorry dear, things are coming to me in a jumble. That's how I receive information, in fragments. I'm getting Bs and boats, different kinds of boats, and water. And papers, documents… and violence. Does this mean anything to you?"

"Yes." She resisted telling Abby about the boating disaster and the murder.

"Whatever this concerns, it is not over yet. There is a house. A family home?"

"There was a family home that Brent inherited."

"Was he a painter?"

"No."

"An art collector?"

"Don't think so."

"I see beautiful works of art on walls. Landscapes, pretty paintings." Abby rested her head on the back of her soft chair and sighed. "There is something about this house that is important." She rubbed her brow. "Secrets. And people, those who knew him. You must talk to them." Her eyes closed.

Lily could see that Abby was tiring. "You've had a long day. We should probably end this session."

"Well, now, just a moment, dear. Before we do, let me clear these thoughts and see if anything new comes through." Her eyelids fluttered and a slight smile came to her face. "You'll be going on a cruise. I see you leaning on the railing of a large ship and looking out over the water. Lots of people around, and laughter." She became silent again.

Lily shifted forward to the edge of the sofa. This reading was quickly going off the rails. "Abby, you're amazing. I was so impressed when you zeroed in right away on my sore neck."

"That's gone now."

Lily turned her head from side to side and felt nothing but the faint shadow of the discomfort that had been there a few minutes ago. "It *is* gone! How is this possible?" She stood up, nonplussed, and rolled her head in every direction.

A look of amusement crossed Abby's face.

Lily bent down and took Abby's hands in her own. "Thank you, Abby. This has been one of the most interesting experiences I've ever had."

Abby met her eyes and smiled warmly. "You are most welcome, dear. I hope it has helped you. Whoever you are under that wig."

By the time dinner was over, Lily had filled everyone in on her reading with Abby and her thoughts about Dean. A serious mood had settled over the group as they sipped tea around the fireplace. Jinx lay belly up on the floor next to Kate.

"I'm relieved that you're the one to bring this up, Lily," Meredith said. "No one knew how to talk to you about it."

Lily stared into her mug.

Meredith took a deep breath. "I was even younger than Jemma when you married Dean, so I didn't really understand everything that happened but now, I… well I can't imagine keeping our child from Eric, even if we were divorced." She gave Lily's arm a squeeze. "Sorry, Lil. I shouldn't judge. Your experience was different than mine."

"I get it," Lily said, her eyes still riveted to her tea. "We found him, Mere. On the internet. He's here in Toronto."

"I know," Meredith said. "He called Mum and Dad yesterday."

"What?" Lily gasped, turning to stare at Meredith. "What did he say?"

"That he'd just found out about your situation. He knew absolutely nothing about your current life until yesterday."

"He doesn't know about Jemma, does he?"

"No, but Mum practically told him we knew where you were. He believes wholeheartedly in your innocence."

"Wow," Lily mumbled, her eyes wide.

"*And* he said he needs to see you."

"Why?"

"I assume he wants to talk about the past. Neither one of you had very good closure."

"Alright, I know this needs to happen, but how?"

"We get you and Jemma together first so you can have a long talk. Then, we arrange to meet Dean so you can deliver the good news."

"Sure. Congratulations, Dean, you are the father of a bouncing… teenage girl."

"Then someone takes Jemma to meet him at a safe, yet-to-be-determined location."

Lily sighed. "Let's do this. We'll decide on the times and places before you leave."

"Good. I'll contact Dean and set it up." Meredith glanced at her watch. "I have to call a cab soon and text Eric that I'm leaving 'Aunt Ruby's'. That's our code for you."

Lily smirked. "Isn't Ruby your cat?"

"It is, but the cops don't know that." Meredith rose awkwardly from the sofa. "I'll be right back. I need to get my bag."

"The ubiquitous bag," Lily moaned.

When Meredith returned she was reaching into a large suede tote. She extracted a small plastic bag and handed it to Kate. "This is for you. From Mark."

"Mark?" Kate's face reddened as she accepted the bag. She peered inside and withdrew a yellow T-shirt. Pinching the shoulders, she held it up at arm's length and laughed, then turned it for the others to read. If life gives you MELONS then you may be dyslexic. She looked shyly at Meredith. "Why the gift?"

"Ask him next time you see him."

Meredith's grin made Kate avert her eyes and busy herself folding the shirt.

Lily changed the subject. "What else have you got in there, sis?"

"Oh, the usual. Wallet, sunglasses, makeup, phone, pens…" She rifled through her bag. "Water, instant oatmeal, um… my Kobo reader. You know, stuff."

Lily laughed. "Can't wait to see what happens when you have to juggle a diaper bag as well."

"No problem." Meredith settled back into the sofa and resumed drinking her tea. "Don't know why everyone has to make fun of my big purse. It's most useful." Turning to Clair, she said, "Know what I'm thinking? Your mother would make a fascinating subject for our next film. I totally believe in psychic phenomenon."

"Of course you do," Lily said dryly, "but I have to admit, most of what Abby told me was spot on."

Clair looked delighted. "What a wonderful tribute that would be to Mother."

Meredith had more news. "Jemma is at my place." Mum and Dad left her with me after you talked to them on Skype."

Lily perked up. "Really?"

"It's March Break and they arranged for her to have extra time off school. Actually, she hasn't been at school all month. Soon you'll get to see her and have that long talk."

"Her teachers are okay with the extended break?"

"Lil, she could miss the rest of the year and still be at the head of the class," Meredith laughed. "Depending on how things go with Dean, she may be here even longer."

Lily lowered her eyes. "Will they ever forgive me?"

"Yes, they will. Will you ever forgive yourself?"

CHAPTER

16

March 11

Clair sat at the kitchen table, listening, as Kate and Lily reviewed the questions they'd drawn up for the Davenport interview. "I have an idea," she announced. "Lily, remember how one of the staff at Forest Hill mistook you for Kate when we were leaving the lobby yesterday?"

"Sure, I waved hello and then practically sprinted to the parking lot."

"What if we were to style you to look even more like her? If you're going to be out in public, you need a better disguise. From a distance, the neighbours will see you as Kate."

"Oh!" Kate cried. "I like it. I could cut and colour your hair just like mine."

"Hold on," Lily said, "I haven't had hair that short since I was twelve. Do you even know how to cut hair?"

"Well, I watch my own stylist cut mine all the time. How hard can it be?"

Lily raised an eyebrow.

"Hey, you can't just waltz into a salon, can you?"

"Aside from the hair and eye colour, the two of you have similar features," Clair said. "Same face shape and spacing of the eyes, same mouth, straight nose, nice teeth. Stand up, girls."

Lily and Kate stood side by side, facing Clair.

"I know, I know. I'm heavier by at least fifteen pounds," Kate said.

"Hardly noticeable on your tall frames." Clair's eyes scanned their figures. "And your overall builds are…"

Lily made a show of adjusting her breasts and shoving out her chest and Kate giggled.

"Kate, you could use a little padding, ironically, in the region of the word, MELONS," Clair said, pointing to the slogan on the front of the T-shirt Mark had given her. And you're about an inch taller."

In the moment of silence that followed, Kate eyed Lily's hair.

"Okay, okay." Lily shrugged. "I hope I don't regret this."

"It's all there," Mark said when his father picked up. He'd been able to retrieve the infamous sex video from Natalie's tablet. "Fifteen minutes and forty-two seconds from the time lover boy entered the frame until the camera is turned off."

"Good job. Beyond the few seconds that, ah, Ruby saw, what else have you got?" They were avoiding real names and getting more mileage out of Meredith's cat.

"Just under nine minutes is actual intercourse. Then there's about three minutes of talking, some of it inaudible. Before he leaves the room, he tells her she's a great girl, but they can't be doing this anymore and it will never happen again. The last few seconds show our Lolita pulling on a baggy shirt and turning off the camera.

"How does Lolita come across?" Jeff asked.

"It will blow her little Miss Innocent act out of the water."

"This will establish motive for the girlfriend and possibly, Lolita, too. Anything else that was deleted?"

"Some kids getting high at a party. A drinking game. Don't worry, I've got it all."

"Thanks," Jeff said. "You're a genius."

"Good of you to notice," Mark chuckled. "I have several hours of surveillance video to scan. You have any idea how many cameras there are between... that house and the highway? A lot of it was preserved, but I don't know how much was ever viewed."

"I'll be there tomorrow to start pouring through the case files," Jeff said. "Your mother says she can live without me for a few days, so have your guest room ready."

A giddy Kate led Lily toward the solarium. "Okay, Gram. Close your eyes." After cutting Lily's hair, she'd coloured it a light shade of honey brown before adding blonde highlights. She'd even lightened and shaped her eyebrows and applied makeup to match her own. The brown contact lenses and glasses with tortoise shell frames completed the new look.

Kate deposited Lily in front of Clair's chair. "Ready."

Clair opened her eyes and gasped. "Oh, my dear, you've done a marvellous job. You're twins!"

Lily ran her fingers through her short, layered cut. "I was a nervous wreck when those scissors appeared, but I have to say, it looks good."

After greeting Kate and being introduced to Sue, Jack ushered the women into his living room where they chatted politely for a few minutes. Then Kate turned on her voice recorder.

"Let me say something up front," Jack said. "Brent was a buddy, but I don't have any kind of blind allegiance to him. I'll be open with you on the condition that I can approve anything you quote before it goes to print."

"Fair enough. Thanks, Jack. Now, let's begin with how you came to know Brent."

"I met him and his brother, Ben, in Oakville when we were around ten, in Atoms. Actually, Brent was a year younger but he played on our team and we became friends that year. His dad was very involved with hockey. His mother, not so much. She ran the house, fed us, kept us in line, made sure we minded our manners. She wasn't what I'd call a joyful or affectionate woman."

Kate nodded. "What was their relationship like as brothers?"

"Well, 'the Baines boys,' as they were called, were the star players right up to Midget. Brent was his father's golden child and although Ben was good, he could never measure up to his brother so there was jealousy, I think. He used to push Brent around a lot when they were kids. By the time I met them, Brent was much more skilled on the ice and that didn't help things. Ben was mean, always looking for a fight. Brent was more cool-headed. Plus, Ben must have felt inferior to Brent in the looks department and I'm sure he resented the constant comparisons."

"You say 'up to Midget'. What happened after that?"

"Ben got mixed up with the wrong crowd. His game suffered and finally he just gave it up."

"What about their physical differences. Do you happen to know if Ben was adopted or had a different father?"

Jack looked surprised. "Not to my knowledge. Brent looks like his father, that's for sure. I guess you'd have to ask his mother, Marie."

"Marie is still alive?"

"Very much so. We saw her at Ben's memorial. She's only sixty something. She moved to Kleinburg a few years ago and is probably still there. If you want to talk to her, I suggest you don't call first. Just show up. And don't expect to be invited in for tea."

"Duly warned. So what happened to Ben after he dropped out of hockey?"

"His father finally laid down the law and Ben managed to finish high school," Jack said. "He was actually pretty smart, just disengaged. Ben wanted Ray to fork over the money he'd put aside for his college education so he could take off and see the world, but dear old Dad cut him off. So, he worked construction. Eventually he bought a small house, fixed it up and flipped it for a nice profit. From there he invested in bigger properties and went on to get his realtor's license. He became relatively successful."

"Define 'relatively successful.'"

"Successful enough to afford a modest house and a nice sailboat" Jack said. "He was passionate about sailing. Then one day, maybe four or five years ago, he just sold everything and took off."

"Did Brent ever say why, or where he went?"

"No, but I had the impression he was tired of Oakville and tired of real estate."

"Obviously, Brent and Ben were getting along better by the time they set off on that Atlantic crossing. How did their relationship evolve in their adult years?"

"That's an interesting question. I know Brent made an effort to bond with him when we were all still in our twenties. He even invited him along when a group of us spent a week in Vegas, but Ben was an ass the whole time.

"How?"

"Being generally obnoxious. And constantly hitting on women. Without much success, I might add. I don't think they spent much time together after that."

"What can you tell me about Brent's relationship with Melissa?"

"It's no secret that Brent liked to play the field so I was a little surprised when he got engaged to her."

"Any theories?"

"I think that in a weak moment he caved in to some pressure from her. Maybe he figured it was time to settle down. But after the accident, things changed."

Kate was hanging on every word. "You saw him after he was rescued?"

"Oh, yes. After he'd recovered a bit."

"And did he call off the engagement?"

"No, but he told me they were having problems. And then Lily Mullaly came along and he was completely smitten. Melissa was out of the country for most of that time. Apparently, he didn't even pick her up at the airport. He must have made some excuse, so he didn't have to face her until the next day when he planned to dump her."

"What about Kristie?" Kate asked. "Did he ever admit to fooling around with her?"

"No, but once, when I dropped in on Brent, she was there. Brent said she came over to use the pool sometimes. I shrugged it off. I mean, what kind of sane person would mess around with his fiancée's kid? Still, why was Kristie there without her mother, parading around in that tiny bikini? She had this sensual energy. She brought out a tray of Long Island Iced Teas. Said hers was just 'iced tea' and gave me a wink." Jack shook his head. "And speaking of drinks, that's when I realized Brent was boozing again."

"Brent had a drinking problem?"

"Actually, he never touched alcohol when he was playing. He knew he couldn't handle the stuff. But when he busted his knee the first time, he got discouraged and he drank. He got past it, though. He worked hard to get back on the ice and he did, for a while. The day I saw him with Kristie, he was half in the bag, but I figured hey, it's his life. He's not in the NHL anymore. Cut him some slack. I think he was prone to addictions."

"Such as?"

"I've heard about people who have a sex addiction and if there really is such a thing, I think Brent fit the bill. It's amazing that most of it stayed out of the press – all those women, I mean. And gambling – something else that didn't come out at the trial."

"Tell us about that."

"Horses, tables, high-risk investments," Jack said, ticking them off on his fingers. "You name it, he'd bet on it. It wasn't so bad in the early years, but toward the end, he was in deep. His career was over and the money was running out. He'd loaned Melissa something like sixty grand and when he told her he wanted it repaid, she threw a fit, said that since they were getting married, it shouldn't matter. She kept hounding him to set a date. And to get her name on the insurance policy and will."

"And they never lived together?"

"No. Melissa wanted to move in after Brent was rescued, but he kept stalling. She had to know he was having second thoughts."

"Did she realize the extent of his financial problems?" Kate asked.

"I don't know."

"Okay, what about his ex-girlfriend, Stacey, and his son? Did Brent ever talk about them?"

"Not much. Stacey married some jerk and moved to Grimsby.

Brent hated him. His lawyer could tell you more. Everything has been held in trust for the boy. Too bad Brent never had the chance to become more of a father to him. He had some problems to work out, but the future looked bright."

"How so?"

"In addition to the book deal, Brent was counting on a new career. After his rescue, he was interviewed on various news programs and caught the attention of some network execs. He was well spoken, good looking and famous, and the story of his survival at sea had reached a large audience. Brent had always hoped to work as a sports analyst or something along that line when he retired and when I last saw him he told me he was about to begin discussions with TSN. But after he met Lily, he seemed troubled. He wouldn't say exactly what was going on, but he indicated that he had some serious problems to deal with."

Kate nodded. "Melissa and Kristie."

"He must have known it was about to come to light. And maybe he did some soul searching and wanted to come clean about his past."

Kate nodded. "Is there anything else you'd like to add or is there anyone you think I should talk to besides Brent's mother?"

Jack thought for a moment. "The only person that comes to mind is a guy named Buzz. Brent hadn't known him very long, but they'd become friends."

"Buzz who?"

"Don't know. He was Ben's sailing buddy. He was at the memorial service and there was a picture of him with Ben in the slide show. When Ben's death hit the news, he contacted Brent and he stayed in the area for a while."

Kate turned off the voice recorder and stood up. "I'm so grateful for your help," she said. "I won't keep you any longer, but if you think of anything else, let me know."

They walked to the front entrance together and Jack grasped the door handle, then hesitated and released it. "Well, there's one more thing, but I want it off the record and I don't want my parents to hear this."

"Of course."

"Um… I guess you noticed I haven't been all that sympathetic toward Brent," he said.

"I was a bit surprised, given your long friendship," Kate replied.

"Well, I was talking to my sister, Hilary, after I found out you were coming and, at her husband's urging, she confided in me. They hoped it would encourage me to speak openly about Brent." Jack hesitated and stared at the floor. "When Hilary was very young, Brent always enjoyed making her laugh, and later, when she was in her teens, it got a bit more flirtatious. She had a big crush on him. Like most girls her age, I guess. I thought it was all pretty innocent. He was five years older and had a girlfriend. One Saturday when Hilary was eighteen and I was enrolled at U of T, Brent paid us a surprise visit. Hilary was the only one home that afternoon so Brent invited her out for a drive in his new Corvette. They ended up in some conservation area, making out. When things started to heat up, she tried to politely discourage him."

Kate grimaced. "He raped her?"

"I don't consider what happened consensual. He told her that he'd broken up with his girlfriend and wanted to start a relationship with her. That's pretty heady stuff for a girl not quite out of high school. He was a superstar and a trusted family friend. But she was confused and intimidated. She said no, but he kept up the pressure – until she finally just gave in.

Sue, who'd been listening quietly, was seething. "She was probably scared senseless."

"And ashamed," Jack added. "After he dropped her off she never heard from him again. And he'd never actually broken up with his girlfriend. Other than her husband, Hilary hasn't told a soul until now." He shook his head. "If only I'd known."

Kate squeezed Jack's hand. "It's good that Hilary has confided in you now."

"Maybe you can talk to her sometime," Jack said.

They parted with promises to stay in touch.

Kate opened the door of her Prius and slid behind the wheel. "I feel like such a fraud."

Sue gave her a questioning look.

"Jack is such a nice guy and here I am, extracting information from him under false pretences," Kate said, yanking the seat belt across her torso.

Sue chuckled. "You have a pure heart, Kate Young. But on that subject, I have a thought."

"What?"

"You know, when I told Jack I'd read some pieces you'd written, that was true. I checked you out and your work is exceptionally good. So... when the time comes, how would you feel about co-authoring this book with Lily? Assuming she's officially cleared and none of us get thrown in jail. We'll want to get this book to press quickly."

"Oh, Sue, this is Lily's story, not mine."

"Think about it. You could piece together what Lily has started. She could write about her involvement with Brent and everything that followed." Sue's eyes sparkled. "*You* are a part of this story, too, you know."

For a few moments, Kate stared straight ahead without expression. Finally, she said, "Do you honestly like my writing?"

"I do. Very much," Sue assured her.

"Do you know that I have trouble coping with life at times? I can't guarantee that I'll handle responsibilities and deadlines to your satisfaction. I'm doing pretty well now, but I wouldn't want to jeopardize anything."

"Your health would always come first. If we make this official, you won't have to lie to get interviews. We'll just omit the co- in co-writing. Say yes."

"Only if Lily is totally in favour." Kate smiled. "Meanwhile, let's do some interviews."

CHAPTER 17

March 12

The town of Kleinburg was a mere half hour from Rosedale. Kate and Sue landed there the following morning for what they hoped would be their next interview. They'd found an address for Marie Baines – a small, well-kept bungalow on a pretty side street.

Sue pressed the doorbell. A shadowy face appeared behind leaded glass, then the door jerked open and a slender woman stood before them, unsmiling and mute. Her dark, grey-streaked hair was gathered into a knot at the back of her head and the neatly pressed white blouse she wore was buttoned snugly at the throat.

"Hello," Sue said warmly. "Are you Marie Baines?"

"Yes," the woman replied warily. "And you would be…?"

"I'm Sue Emerson, publisher of Emerson Books and this is Kate Young, one of our biographers. Mrs. Baines, we're proceeding with our plans to publish the book that was being written with your son's cooperation almost two years ago and we'd like to talk with you about some of the material we've gathered."

Marie looked neither surprised, nor pleased. "Taking advantage of the recent publicity?"

"It's true there's been a resurgence of interest in the case involving Brent's tragic death, and let me say how sorry I am for your loss. I met with him on a few occasions and I liked him very much. It's also true that we've been planning to follow through with this book all along and we…"

"I'm not interested," Marie interrupted.

"We want to do this book justice by interviewing the people who knew him best and who would like to honour his legacy. And with Kate, we have a writer of the highest caliber to pick up the story," Sue continued in her honeyed tone.

Marie gave Kate a stony glance as Sue continued.

"Until recently, she hosted a popular radio program in Hamilton – *Coffee with Kate.*"

"Doesn't ring a bell," Marie said. "Look, I'm not interested in participating in any endeavour that puts money in the purses of vultures taking advantage of my son's life and death. He should be left to rest in peace."

"I understand your concern. I want you to know that, in recognition of Brent's cooperation and contribution to this book, a portion of the proceeds will go to his son's trust fund."

"I hardly see the boy anymore," Marie said, and a shadow of something like sadness or pain flickered across her face.

"Look at it this way," Kate said. "The story is going to be told anyway, but this is an opportunity for you to make sure we get it right. To help the world see the best parts of him."

Marie's hand was still clutching the door knob. She clenched her jaw and dropped her gaze for a moment. "Brent spoke well of you and your husband, Mrs. Emerson," Marie said, "and he said he was pleased with the book deal."

"We would do everything we could to ensure that your role as his mother was represented fairly," Kate said.

"Our family had its problems," Marie said. "You can be fair, but it won't be a pretty picture. Just know that I loved my boys and I tried my best with them."

"We'd be sure to convey that." Kate held her breath.

Marie seemed to vacillate, her eyes still fixed on the stone landing beneath their feet. Finally, she collected herself and took a step back, retreating from the doorway. "No, I can't," she said. "I'm sorry."

Sue persisted. "Please, if you would just think about it. Let me give you my card," she said, reaching into her pocket. She pressed the card into Marie's hand. "If you change your mind, please give me a call – and thank you, Marie, for listening."

"Thanks for your time," Kate added, smiling.

Marie nodded and began to close the door. Sue and Kate descended the steps and walked toward the curb.

"Wait," Marie called softly. They turned to see Marie still holding the door. "Simone might talk to you," she said.

"Simone?"

"My sister, Simone. I guess I could give you her number."

The stakeout near Meredith's house had yielded some interesting information for Beryl. First of all, Meredith, who had taken her on a wild goose chase two days earlier, had not returned until late that evening. Secondly, the following afternoon, a teenage girl had emerged from the house, retrieved something from the car in the driveway and gone back inside. Beryl wondered if she might be Lily's daughter. Photos of the rest of the family had been easy enough to find on the internet, but there was no information on the child. Assuming she was right about the girl, this was another indication that Lily was hiding close by.

Beryl was parked near the house once again, oblivious to the man approaching her borrowed car until the tapping on the glass next to her head caused her to jump. She lowered the window and a blast of cool air invaded the warm interior of the vehicle.

"Exactly what are you doing here?" a gruff voice demanded.

Beryl eyed her interrogator. An older man, wispy grey hair, newspaper tucked under his arm. "This is a police matter, no need to be concerned," she mumbled.

"You got ID? You've been parked up and down this street for three days. Looks to me like you're stalking somebody or staking out some property."

"Undercover investigation. I'm sorry if I alarmed you," Beryl said. She turned the key in the ignition and the old four-cylinder engine rattled to life.

The man glared at her. "I have your plate number and if I ever see you anywhere around here again, I'll call it in."

Beryl pulled away from the curb, her face burning. She'd been careless. Different tactics were needed. She'd been toying with an idea and now it was time to set it in motion.

Leo remained focussed on the TV as his fiancée came bustling into the kitchen. She dropped her sunglasses, cap and car keys on the counter.

"Don't I even get a hello, or a little kiss?" she pouted, crossing into the family room to perch on the arm of his recliner.

"Quiet! I want to hear this," He turned up the volume and continued to listen to the update on the search for Lily Mullaly.

"It's the same old news. They can't find that woman so they dig up her history and go on forever about it." After several seconds, she huffed and clicked the remote. The screen went black.

Leo's face reddened and he grabbed the remote. "Don't ever do that to me! There's nothing I hate worse than a controlling woman." He scowled, but seeing the stunned hurt in his lover's eyes, he reined in his temper. "Sorry," he mumbled. "I'm just tired and hungry. And I'm very happy to see you." He pulled her off the arm of his chair onto his lap and gave her a lingering kiss.

"Are you sure this is what you want? Me for the rest of your life?" she asked meekly, tracing the line of his strong jaw with her finger.

"You're the only one for me," he said and smooched his way along the side of her face, his tongue slipping playfully into her ear.

She giggled, rolled off his lap and moved toward the kitchen. "Let me make you some lunch." She opened the refrigerator and removed some containers. "Muscle man next door passed me in his car just as I was pulling in, but I pretended not to see him. He may be rich, but he's creepy."

"Drew Fowler?"

"Yeah, the Incredible Hulk."

"The Incredible Asshole. Thinks he's God's gift."

Leo came into the kitchen. "He's talked to me, or should I say, talked down to me, a couple of times. We don't plan on making any friends here, so just keep avoiding him." He slid onto a bar chair. "Cross wants me to replace the damaged brick interlock out back now that the snow's gone. Maybe you could start on the attic. There's a bunch of boxes up there. Probably nothing, but we need to sort through every one of them, piece by piece.

Although they were sisters, Simone bore little resemblance to the woman Kate and Sue had spoken with earlier. She was shorter, fleshier and a decade younger. She answered the door with the remnant of a sandwich in her hand, her mouth full as she waved them inside.

"Thanks for agreeing to speak to us on such short notice," Kate said, stepping into the hallway.

"Sorry," Simone laughed after she swallowed. "Just polishing off lunch." She brushed some crumbs from her chest, where a bit of mustard had dropped onto her pink sweatshirt. "Let's go into my office," she said, indicating a room to their right. "I work from home, so don't mind the mess."

"What kind of work do you do?" Sue asked.

"Oh, a little graphic art, some web design. We're semi-retired."

Two side-by-side work stations occupied one wall. The rest of the room was furnished with storage cabinets, bookshelves, a console table and a leather chair. Folders, stacks of paper, and a few mugs were scattered on various surfaces.

Kate's attention was drawn to a large framed photograph above the table. "This is lovely," she said, moving closer to read the title penciled on the bottom edge of the mat. "Setting Sail."

"It's one of mine," Simone said. "I used to be a photographer.

Well, I still am I guess, but only as a hobby these days. That shot was taken from Ben's boat several years ago."

"Did Brent's interest in photography come from you?" Sue asked.

"I'll take credit for that," Simone chuckled. "He liked my work and I encouraged him to give it a try, gave him some pointers. But one has to have an eye for it, and he did. Frankly, I was surprised."

"I haven't seen his work, but Lily said it was excellent." The words were out of Sue's mouth before she could censor them.

Simone gave her a penetrating look.

"Not that I knew her that well," Sue said, amending her careless admission. "The editor she was working with passed the comment along."

"Yes, well, it still stings when I hear that woman's name. I can't believe they haven't caught her yet." Simone tucked a lock of dyed rosy-red hair behind her ear and invited them to sit.

"Personally, I think someone is hiding her," Kate said. "We'll all be happy to see Brent's killer captured and locked up."

Sue's eyes widened slightly as she made eye contact with Kate.

"Amen!" Simone piped.

"I promised we'd keep this short, so let's begin," Kate said. "I think you're in the best position to ensure that I get the facts about Brent's early life straight, and I want you to know that I won't quote anything you say without your consent."

"You can quote me all you like. Just spell my name right," Simone said and her rumbling laugh filled the room.

"Let's start with Brent's parents – a little family background."

Simone launched into the story, her hands moving in animated concert with her perky narration. "Ray was quite a bit older when he and Marie got together, but he desperately wanted children. His previous marriage had been childless – so imagine his disappointment when it seemed Marie couldn't conceive. They finally decided to adopt."

"Ah!" Kate smiled. "That would explain the lack of resemblance between the brothers. Were they both adopted?"

"Oh, no," Simone said. "Within three months of adopting Ben, Marie was pregnant with Brent. It often happens that way, you know. A baby comes into the marriage and it jump starts the ovaries. Ray doted on those boys. He had them in skates when they were barely walking."

"And Marie? Was she as… enthusiastic?"

"Well, Marie is a good soul, but quite a perfectionist and I think two babies so close together overwhelmed her. And Ben was never an easy child. Tried her patience. And when they told him he was adopted – let's see, he would have been around eight – that didn't help matters. The whole business was kept quiet, you know. His parents didn't want him to be treated differently. But Ben took every punishment as an act of discrimination. He resented the closeness between Brent and their father. It never seemed to occur to him that it was his own truculent behaviour that got him into trouble."

"Even when he was older?"

"He always blamed someone else. I actually bailed him out of jail once. He'd been arrested for assault, but in the end, the charges were dropped."

"Were you and Ben close?"

"Not really. I went out on his sailboat a few times, saw him at family gatherings, that's about it. And then when he found his biological family, he pulled away from everyone."

Kate leaned forward. "What do you know about them?"

"Well! Ben tracked his mother down to Windsor and went to see her. He found out he'd been put up for adoption as a newborn, along with a two-year-old brother who'd been in foster care. The boys had the same father, but he deserted the family before Ben was born. Ben wasn't able to locate him. He was disappointed in whoever his mother turned out to be. But the older brother had tracked her down, too, and that's how Ben found him. He was married and living in Chicago."

"Was that around the time Ben left Oakville?" Kate asked.

"Yes – in fact that's why he left. He moved to Chicago so he could be near his 'real' brother."

"Do you know the brother's name?"

"Uh huh, and so does all of Chicago. Richard Hogan. He and his wife, Nicole, were sent to prison for running a Ponzi scheme. They bilked clients out of something like twenty-seven million. More than half was never recovered. It was after the arrest that Ben came back to Oakville and started to make amends with Brent."

Kate glanced at Sue and conveyed a *wow* with her eyes. "Do you think Ben was involved in the Ponzi scheme?"

"No idea. I think he hightailed it out of there when the police showed up. Ben was pretty taken with Richard and Nicole's lifestyle. He'd met some of their boater friends and was doing some sailing on Lake Michigan, but whatever else he was up to I don't know," Simone said with a shrug.

"What else can you tell me about the case?"

"Not much. I didn't follow the trial, but I know they were convicted. I think Richard's doing his time at Menard."

"Did you see Ben after he returned from the States?" Kate asked.

"Just once. He didn't seem interested in reconnecting with any of us other than Brent."

"And you learned about the Ponzi scheme from Ben?"

Simone sighed. "No, he didn't share any of that. Actually, Marie was contacted by the police who were trying to locate Ben. He was wanted in Chicago for questioning regarding Richard's little operation, so it all came out then. He went back there for a few days and then returned to Oakville. I guess he got things sorted out."

"Is it true that, as a child, Ben bullied Brent?"

"Well, some of that was just normal friction, you know, boys being boys. When they got a bit older, they played on the same teams. The Baines boys, people called them."

"But didn't Ben later drop out of hockey?" Kate asked.

"True. I think Ben resented Brent's success and popularity. Eventually he quit the game and, as Brent's fame grew, Ben came to hate hockey. Or so he said. He hated ice, he hated snow and he hated winter. Sailing became his main interest and he couldn't wait each year to get his boat in the water." Simone chuckled. "That boy lived for summer."

Kate proceeded gently with her next question. "What can you tell me about the ocean crossing he and Brent attempted together?"

"It was so tragic. They were finally getting to be real friends and they were excited about this trip. I was a little surprised because after their father died, there'd been some contention over the will."

"Over the division of his assets?"

"Um-hm. You see, Ray didn't have a whole lot of money left when he died. Ben got only a pittance and the house was left to Brent. Ray's will had been updated just a few years before his death. Ben claimed that his father had been in the early stages of Alzheimer's and was mentally incompetent at the time. He even accused Brent of dipping into his father's account. But it never went to court, so I guess they settled it.

"Then Ben decided to buy a thirty-eight-foot ketch he'd found online. He wanted to fulfill his dream to sail across the Atlantic. This boat was in Portugal, so the plan was for them to fly there and sail it to Barbados by way of the Canary Islands. I don't think Brent's girlfriend was too thrilled about it, but he went anyway. They left in November and spent a month or so preparing for the trip. They expected to reach Barbados by mid- to late January."

Kate glanced at her notes. "They had emergency equipment – the SSB radio, a GPS, satellite phone, survival packs, but I guess with the boat sinking so fast there wasn't time to gather everything and get a message to anyone."

"Well, exactly, and you know they'd been having trouble with the phone so no one worried too much when they didn't hear from them right away. That's a big ocean and there was no sign of Brent until he was picked up by that fishing boat off Guadeloupe." Simone shook her head. "Poor Ben died when he went back into the cabin for that second survival pack. It happened so quickly. It was all Brent could do to get himself out of there and cut the line before the ketch pulled the raft down with it. It must have been terrible for him to watch that boat sink in the darkness with his only brother on it."

"And that was just the beginning of his struggle," Kate said.

Simone nodded. "No one picked up the signal from that radio beacon thing before the batteries died."

"The EPIRB. Emergency Position Indicating Radio Beacon. I had to look it up."

"Yes, and the raft had a canopy, but that didn't keep him very dry and that built-in solar desalinator didn't produce much water. If it weren't for the rain water he collected he would have died."

"I understand he ate raw fish, too."

"Oh, yes. The fish started following his raft to get at the barnacles that started to build up on the bottom and he was able to spear a few, but he was skin and bones by the time he made it to Guadeloupe."

"It's amazing that he survived," Kate said. "Now, um… can you tell me anything about a possible gambling problem that Brent may have had in recent years?"

Simone shook her head. "Not that I know of. I mean, he lost some money in investment schemes several years ago, but so did a lot of people. My son, Ryan, is Brent's attorney and the executor of his will. You could ask him. He's handling the estate. I'll give you his number if you like."

"That would be great! Just a couple more questions. What can you tell me about Brent's relationship with his son, BJ, and BJ's mother?"

Simone chuckled. "Well, Brent was quite a playboy in those days and more than a few young ladies tried to snag him, but he was a slippery one. Stacey tried to trap Brent into marrying her and he stepped away from that whole situation. But as time went by, he started seeing BJ more often and I know he grew to love him. He was petitioning for joint custody. I think Stacey might have been okay with it, but that husband of hers, Tom Newell, he's a scumbag if you ask me. Obsessively jealous, greedy. Quick to take the child support, but didn't want Brent in the picture otherwise. Yeah, Stacey and Brent were on pretty good terms by then, but Tom didn't like it."

"I don't suppose you'd have a phone number for Stacey, would you?"

"I do," Simone said. "I've called a few times on Marie's behalf. She's not good with self-advocacy."

"Do you think Stacey would talk to us?" Sue asked.

"Well… she'd be more inclined to if her husband's not there. He works for a heating and cooling company in Grimsby. Stacey is likely at home right now because she's a school secretary and she'd be off for March Break." Simone paused for a moment. "Tell you what. I have a pretty good connection with her and I think I could convince her to talk to you. I'll give her a call this afternoon and get back to you."

"That would be wonderful!" Kate said as she stood to leave. "One last question. Ben had a friend named Buzz. Ever heard of him?"

"Buzz... No, sorry."

"Well, you've been tremendously helpful. Thank you so much."

Simone led them to the front door and bid them a cheerful goodbye.

Sue groaned as they settled into their car seats. "I can't believe I slipped up like that – calling Lily by her first name like I talk to her all the time."

"You covered it well," Kate assured her.

"I don't know. I think I'm a liability for you. And you!" she said, giving Kate's arm a swat. "With your 'Personally, I think someone is hiding her' remark. I about had a heart attack!"

Kate heard herself laugh and it occurred to her that laughter was such a peculiar, primitive thing – a spontaneous, odd burst of sounds triggered by some deeply embedded impulse in our emotional circuitry. She imagined that alien visitors of a more highly evolved sort would perceive it as not entirely different from the shrieking of an ape. She'd been producing quite a lot of these sounds in recent days and it felt wonderful.

CHAPTER 18

March 13

Rain drizzled, dampening the view, dampening spirits. Jemma's forehead rested against the cold pane. Beyond the window, pools of water had collected in the slimy patches of dark brown leaves that lay beneath dead stalks of last season's perennials.

"Pretty ugly out there," Meredith said, coming up beside her.

"Pretty – ugly. There's an oxymoron for you," Jemma replied.

"Well, in that case, a few of the guys I dated before I met Eric were oxymorons. How 'bout a movie this afternoon?"

"Sure, Mere. And popcorn."

Meredith smiled. Jemma had recently dropped the use of Aunt and Uncle when speaking to her mother's siblings. Now, they were simply Mark and Mere. "Are you going to sing for us while you're here this week?"

Jemma thumped her head against the window pane. "Maybe. I've been hoping Mum would be there when I perform for the first time. My voice coach wants to set something up – a public thing. But maybe I'm making too big a deal out of it."

"I totally understand, but if you decide to give us a sneak preview, it'll still be a wonderful surprise for her." Meredith eased herself into one of the club chairs near the window and put her feet up on the ottoman. "I'm so tired of this big belly."

"But it'll be totally worth it, right?"

"Absolutely!"

Jemma sat in the opposite chair, hugging her knees to her chin. She gazed silently at the grey scene beyond the window for a few moments before shifting her eyes back to her aunt. "Why did my mother want a baby when she was so young? What was the big rush?"

Meredith's eyes flew open. "What would make you ask such a thing?"

"Well… it's like she had no intention of finding a man. She hardly ever goes on dates and when she does, it never lasts. Maybe she's secretly gay or frigid or something."

For a few maddening seconds, Meredith was speechless. This conversation could take her quickly into the web of lies that stretched uncomfortably between them. "I don't believe that's the case," she said at last.

"Well, what is it then?"

"Oh, Jemma, I'm really not comfortable talking about your mother's… private life."

"It's not like I don't know everything that was said at the trial. It's all on the internet, including the stuff about her relationship with Brent Baines. I just don't understand it."

Meredith wasn't often at a loss for words, but this was one of those times.

Jemma stared at the fine wet drops misting the window and dribbling down the glass. "I mean, I'm lucky to have her, but I feel like the other half of me is missing. All I know about my father is that he's a healthy, well-educated man of English-Irish descent who, apparently, felt compelled to make donations to a sperm bank."

As she listened, Meredith thought about how much Jemma reminded her of Lily. Like her mother, she could shut herself off from social contact for long stretches. She also had Lily's gift for language, and learning came effortlessly to her.

"Have any of the kids at school given you a rough time about your mother?" Meredith asked.

"No one I care about. And know what? Since the escape, everyone seems to be pulling for her. Did you see that group chanting 'Run, Lily, run!' on TV?"

"Yeah, but she has enemies out there, too, so we have to be careful."

Ruby the cat wandered into the room and eyed the seating arrangements. She jumped up on Meredith's outstretched legs and settled in against her belly.

"When do I get to see her, anyway?" Jemma asked.

"Soon," Meredith said, stroking Ruby's ginger-red coat. "Tomorrow, we shop till we drop, then probably the day after that. Some arrangements have to be made."

"Why is it so complicated?"

Jemma's interrogation was interrupted by the doorbell. Ruby sprang from her cozy nest and ran for cover, leaving claw marks in Meredith's thigh.

"God damn!" Meredith exclaimed. "That had better not be missionaries trying to save my soul again!" Pushing herself slowly to her feet, she rubbed her gouged leg and made her way to the front entrance. A man and a woman, both attired in slacks and rain coats were waiting at the door. A uniformed officer stood behind them. Meredith guessed there was another one posted at the back of the house. As she opened the door, the woman held up a police badge.

"Meredith Larson?" she asked.

Meredith nodded curtly.

"I'm Detective Alvarez and this is Detective Krueger."

"As in Freddie from *Nightmare on Elm Street?*'

"As in we have a warrant to search your property," he said dryly, his face all business. He held the court order up for Meredith's inspection.

"My sister's not here," Meredith said. "But see for yourselves." She moved aside.

Jemma appeared in the living room doorway and watched soberly as the detectives entered the hallway.

"You're Jemma, right?" Alvarez asked. "Please remain in here with Sergeant Callahan," she said, gesturing toward the uniformed officer.

Meredith and Jemma sat wordlessly on the sofa under the watchful eye of Callahan who positioned himself in the doorway. Minutes ticked by in heavy silence. A light creak from the door to the basement sent the sergeant charging into the hallway, only to be met by Ruby who hissed loudly, swatted his leg and then rocketed away.

Jemma giggled.

Finally, Alvarez and Krueger reappeared in the living room.

"All clear," Krueger said to Callahan, who took this as his cue to leave.

"Sorry for the intrusion. We'd like to ask you a few questions before we leave," Alvarez said. "Nothing formal." She turned to Jemma. "You and I can talk here while Detective Krueger speaks with your aunt."

Jemma glanced at Meredith.

Meredith winked at her. "You don't have to say anything."

Jemma tucked her legs beside her on the sofa and played with the lace on her slipper. Alvarez sat on a chair next to her and smiled as Meredith led Krueger out of the room. "This must be a very difficult time for you," she said.

Jemma remained impassive, avoiding her gaze.

"Jemma, your mother needs to turn herself in if she is to get the help she needs. As you must know, her case is getting a lot of attention and there are people who are ready to hear what she has to say. People who can help her." She paused, leaning forward to rest her forearms on her knees. "Do you know where your mother is?"

"No."

"Do you have any information as to whether or not your mother is safe or hiding somewhere?"

"No."

Alvarez sighed. "Are you and your mother very close?"

"Yes."

"And you'd do anything to protect her, wouldn't you?"

"Like lie for her? Do you honestly expect me to answer that question like I'm a six-year-old? Obviously, if I'm lying I'm not going to tell you I'm lying. But if you're hoping for a big revelation, listen closely. My mother is missing and I have no idea where she is. This is very upsetting for me, and my aunt has brought me here to try and be of some comfort. However, the sudden appearance of the police and this subsequent grilling has caused me further distress and I feel that this entire procedure has been carried out in a highly insensitive manner."

The detective sat in stunned silence for a moment, then stood. "You're right, some of the things we do are intrusive and indelicate. It's an unpleasant, but necessary part of the investigation process." She moved toward the hall, then turned and gave Jemma a curious, appraising look. "Thank you for sharing your thoughts."

Once the police had left, Meredith sank again into her club chair.

"I didn't squeal," Jemma announced.

Meredith grinned. "I knew you wouldn't."

"Wait till Eric hears about this. He'll be pissed."

"Language! If your mother asks when she hears that mouth of yours, you didn't learn it from us."

"You talk like that all the time. Anyway, I'm not a child anymore, you know."

"Well, technically..." Meredith began to say. She threw up her hands. "No, I guess you're not."

"Hey," Jemma said, pointing at the window. "A sun shower."

Meredith craned her neck to look up at the sky. The clouds overhead were flowing to the east, thinning and ripping apart to reveal a widening patch of blue. Fat drops of rain splattered against the window, glistening gold in the sudden awakening of light. "Maybe we'll see a rainbow."

The bright sunlight streaming in through the glass wall in the pool wing was irresistible. Lily climbed out of the hot tub and dried herself off, then rolled a chaise lounge into the sunny area and stretched her nude body over its length. She had the place to herself for a while. Kate had left for a medical appointment earlier and Clair was taking a nap.

The details from Kate's interviews sifted through her mind. Brent's dangerous obsessions, his high-risk investments and gambling problems. The pieces of the puzzle were beginning to click into place. The book and the prospect of a career in television had been opportunities to sidestep an impending financial collapse and to recapture the spotlight. But amid all this promise, Brent had still managed to sabotage himself with Kristie. There's no way the corporate world would touch him in the face of such a public scandal. And no way his about-to-be-jilted fiancée would let it go, either.

Something intuitive, something beyond her cautious nature, had warned Lily to step back from her growing intimacy with Brent. He'd been troubled in their last days together and that mysterious, nagging something else had begun to reveal itself in their final conversation.

His voice is just above a whisper on the phone. "I'm not the honourable guy you think I am. I've done some dumb, selfish things and I want you to know that I'm going to do whatever I can to make it right. You can still write the book if you like, but I don't think you're going to want me in your life after that."

Lily tries to suppress her alarm. "What on earth could be so bad? Is it something you did in your youth? Women in your past? What?"

"That, and more."

"Why can't we talk about this face to face?"

"I don't think I could look you in the eye right now."

Lily's voice rises. "Are you going to share this information with me now?"

"No, not on the phone, but… I've written everything down just in case…"

"What do you mean 'just in case'? Should I be worried?"

"No, no, I've hidden it here. Bad things could happen if it falls into the wrong hands. It's all in writing. There are some things I needed to explain… share… in case… I just… I thought it might be easier if you read the whole story instead of…" He sighs. "But I know I need to talk to you, too."

Lily's thoughts are skittering wildly as she tries to imagine what concerns Brent so much that he'd have to record it in a… what? A letter? A document?

"I have some things to take care of, but I'll see you tomorrow. I'll call first."

"What about that interview I have with your former teammate this afternoon. Should I cancel?"

"Do the interview. He actually likes me. I'm not all bad."

"Maybe you're blowing whatever this is way out of proportion," Lily says, as much to convince herself as to reassure him.

Brent inhaled deeply. "Here's the thing. I finally realized that I can't be in a relationship with you and be dishonest about my life. And even if you decide you won't have me, I need to do this because you've changed me. You make me want to be a better man."

"Isn't that Jack Nicholson's line?" Lily asks with more than a little sarcasm. "From As Good As It Gets?"

"I knew you'd nail it." Brent laughs weakly. "Just know this. I truly love you, Lily. I'll see you tomorrow." A click, and he's gone.

Lily was still soaking in the sun when the door at the far end of the pool opened with a squawk. Lifting her head from her prone position, she was startled to see a short middle-aged woman dressed in jeans and a T-shirt, standing just inside the doorway. Their eyes met for an instant before the woman raised her hand in a gesture of apology.

"Oh, sorry Kate!" she said. "I didn't mean to disturb you. I can come back and clean here later."

"Okay," Lily squeaked.

The door closed and she quickly pulled on her robe. *Must be Iris, the housekeeper. Thinks I'm Kate. Got an eyeful.* She took a backstairs route to her room.

Before long, there was a tapping sound followed by Clair's voice. "It's just me."

"Come in," Lily called.

"I'm so sorry," Clair said, stepping inside. "I forgot all about Iris coming today." She crossed the room and sat down on the window seat beside Lily.

"It's alright. I was catching some sun beside the pool. She assumed I was Kate. Caught me naked." Noticing Clair's comically arched brow, Lily grinned. "Seems I have a knack for that." Her expression changed. "What if Kate comes home while she's here?"

Clair laughed. "We'll just tell her you're Kate's cousin and you were too embarrassed to introduce yourself."

"Well, part of that is true."

"Meredith called. Iris arrived just as the phone rang, so I couldn't use the intercom to find you. Anyway, she said she'd call back later."

Lily nodded. "She's probably set up the meeting with Dean. I'm petrified."

"There's nothing wrong with feeling fear. Just face it with courage. And think of the wonderful things that are going to happen for Jemma and Dean."

"When I was sent to prison, I couldn't bear the thought of Dean taking her away. It seemed to me that as long as the Mullalys had her, I still had her."

"Oh, my dear," Clair said. "You may need to share Jemma, but you'll never lose her."

"They'll be like this, Clair." Lily said, crossing her fingers. "Looking at the two of us, you'd never guess that I'm her mother, but when you see Dean? She's the proverbial chip off the old block."

"You put too much stock in biology," Clair said. "It may be interesting, all your talk about eye colour and hair and who got what from whom. But let me ask you this. Would you love Jemma any less if she were adopted?"

"No."

"There are all kinds of families, Lily, and some are not blood-related at all. That doesn't make them any less connected. Did you know that Kate's brother, Flynn, is not Ed's biological son? He's Karen's from a previous marriage, but he's just as much a son to Ed as his own flesh and blood would have been. And he's every bit my grandson, too."

"What about your other grandchildren? Are you close?"

Clair sighed. "Well, my daughter, Celeste, has three girls. The jury's still out on the youngest two. They're typical teenagers I guess. Well-mannered, when they stop texting long enough to converse with actual people. The oldest girl, Stephanie, is another story. Apparently, at twenty-three, she knows it all. She's self-centred and often disrespectful. I'm hoping that her better qualities will eventually emerge."

"Your point is that blood ties are not necessarily binding," Lily said.

"My point is, dear, it's the relationships we build, not who resembles who, that is truly important."

"How did you get to be so wise and yet so colourfully different?"

"Equal parts love, common sense and good example with a generous dash of whimsy. And a lot of living." She gave Lily's knee a pat. "And thank you. What a lovely compliment."

The door opened a crack and Kate's amused face appeared. "I hear Iris found me sunbathing in the nude a little while ago," she said.

Lily rolled her eyes. "I'll never live this down."

Disentangling himself from Jemma's hug, Jeff greeted Meredith and Eric warmly as they joined him on the sidewalk in front of their house. The mercury had dropped throughout the day and it was unpleasantly cold.

Eric glanced up and down the street. "What is it that you didn't want to talk about on the phone?"

"I wanted to warn you about listening devices. The search would have been a perfect time to plant something, so take a good look around, Eric. And no more discussions about the situation in the house."

"The bastards," Meredith muttered.

Jemma nudged her in the ribs. "Language!"

"This search was a wake-up call. We mustn't let our guard down."

"Was Mark home when his house was searched?" Eric asked.

"Yes. They seized his computers, but they won't find anything, of course. Actually, our family's *lack* of communication about Lily may raise suspicion."

Meredith frowned. "The effin' assholes took all of ours, too.

Pisses me off." She felt another jab, as Jemma gleefully poked a finger into her side.

"They're doing their job, Meredith," Jeff said. "And Jemma doesn't need to hear that potty mouth of yours."

Eric scowled. "They'd better get those computers back to us tomorrow. My work was on one of them. Any progress in your investigation?"

"Other than the video Mark recovered, it's been slow going, but I've found an interesting little detail that didn't come out in court. Brent's fiancée, Melissa, had hired a private investigator to check up on him while she was away."

"Really?" Meredith gasped. "That was in a police report?"

"Yes, but it doesn't say what was discovered. I haven't been able to track down the investigator yet. This may help us to win an appeal for a new trial. I want to know why the information was suppressed or overlooked."

Jemma shivered and pulled her jacket more tightly around her.

"Get yourselves back into the house," Jeff said. "I'll be heading back to Oakville in the morning and hopefully some more information will surface."

"You would have made a great defense lawyer, Grandpa. I'm glad you're helping Mum."

Jeff smiled. "Mullalys stick together, Jemma."

CHAPTER 19

March 14

Dean was sitting on the stairs outside the audition room, staring numbly into space, his phone still in his hand, when Georgia found him.

"You okay?"

Dean ran a hand through his hair and sighed heavily. "That was Dad. My grandfather passed away this morning."

"Oh, honey, I'm so sorry." Georgia sat down next to him and wrapped her arm around his shoulders. "The one who lived in the Adirondacks?"

Dean nodded. "He was ninety-one and terminally ill, so it was expected, but it still hits hard."

"When is the funeral?"

"On the seventeenth. I'll drive down the day before and probably stay a few days if you can carry on here without me. And Gramma has asked me to sing at the funeral. Don't know if I'll be able to without blubbering."

Georgia gave Dean's arm a squeeze. "You'll do fine and don't worry about things here. Just get there and back safely. How long of a drive is it?"

"Five, maybe six hours." He lowered his voice. "I need to call Meredith. She arranged a meeting with you-know-who two days from now, but I'll have to change it to tomorrow. But I've got the gig at Phil's Room tomorrow. Maybe I can squeeze them both in."

"Okay, let's get you out of here now," Georgia said. "Go pack, make some calls and practise that song."

"But we've got a meeting with the art director this afternoon."

"We can make a decision without you."

"And I wanted to be here when–"

"We'll have video of all the auditions for you to see when you get back."

"Okay, but–"

"No."

Dean rose to his feet and slid his phone into his pocket. "You're a bossy little thing, aren't you?"

Kate waited nervously on the front step of the Newell bungalow. This was to be her first solo interview and Simone had warned her that it might be brief. Momentarily, a petite, pretty woman opened the door and offered her a tense smile. She was blonde, but a quarter inch of dark roots told another story.

"Kate?" the woman said.

"Yes. Stacey? So nice to meet you."

A second face, chest height to Stacey appeared at the doorway and gazed earnestly into Kate's eyes.

"BJ," Stacey sighed. "My son and supervisor."

"Are you writing a book about my dad?" BJ asked, giving Kate a quick head to toe appraisal.

"Ah… yes I am." Kate grinned, giving him a mock appraisal of her own. He had his father's eyes, but his mouth and nose were delicate, like his mother's.

"Well, come in," Stacey said, stepping back. BJ led the way into a living room. A few toys were scattered near the coffee table and

Stacey kicked them aside. "Have a seat," she said, gesturing toward the sofa. A small head popped up from behind one of its arms and Kate found herself looking into the eyes of a mini version of Stacey.

"That's Amanda," Stacey said.

"Hi there," Kate said. "How old are you?"

The tiny girl smiled shyly at Kate and raised her hand, displaying four fingers. "Unlike my other child, this one is mostly non-verbal around strangers," Stacey said.

"Yes, and I have a lot to say if you want to interview me for your book," BJ added.

Kate laughed. The children were proving to be an easy icebreaker. "Tell you what, I'd love to, but first I'd like to talk to your mother."

Stacey reached for Amanda's hand. "BJ, take your sister downstairs and put on a movie for her."

"Come on, Mandy," BJ said.

Kate smiled at Stacey. "Lovely children."

Stacey smiled back. "I don't expect Tom home until dinner time, but I'd appreciate it if we could keep this under an hour. I'd like to set the record straight on a couple of things, but I really don't have a lot to say. And my husband wouldn't..."

Kate waited for her to finish, but it was left hanging. "Whatever you have to share will be greatly appreciated and we'll end this whenever you like."

Stacey settled into a chair next to the sofa. "You know, we get Hamilton radio here in Grimsby and I was a big fan of your show. I couldn't believe it when Simone told me it was you writing this book," she gushed.

"Thank you so much!" Kate said.

"But I guess you've switched careers."

"Time will tell." Kate turned on the voice recorder. "Can we begin with how you met Brent and what it was like to be in a relationship with one of hockey's brightest stars?"

Twenty minutes slipped by as Stacey related her tale of meeting Brent at a party, travelling in high style with him and being lavished with his attention, and of the eventual friction brought about by his suspected infidelities. "And this I want clearly understood," she finished and her eyes left Kate's to focus on the general vicinity of her feet. "BJ was a complete surprise, one I will never, ever regret, but I didn't plan it."

"You moved back to your hometown to have the baby?"

"Yes," Stacey replied. "Then five years ago I got a job in Grimsby and that's where I met Tom."

Kate did the math. If Amanda was four years and some months old, and Stacey had moved to Grimsby approximately five years ago, that left a very narrow window of time for her to meet Tom, marry him, get pregnant and give birth. Was there a pattern here? "BJ was very young when you and Tom married. Can you tell me how Tom and Brent each filled the role of father in his life?"

Stacey found Kate's eyes again. "Tom is a good father. I mean, you know, he'd rather BJ was his own child, but it's complicated. As his biological father, it was Brent's responsibility to provide for BJ, and he did. But then, Brent started wanting to see more of him. And he'd never acknowledged his birthday before, so when he showed up with presents one year, Tom was kind of put off. BJ has never wanted to call Tom 'Dad' so we decided he'd be 'Papa' instead, but after being with Brent for a few hours, it was always, 'Dad this and Dad that' and then BJ wanted to be called Brent and Tom just blew a gasket." Stacey caught herself and almost jumped out of the chair. "Oh, God, don't put that in the book – the part about Tom losing his temper!"

"I won't," Kate said. "BJ, that's short for Brent…"

"Brent James. Anyway, you have to understand how difficult it is for an ordinary guy to compete with a superstar when it comes to a kid's affections. Brent wasn't the one who had to deal with discipline and day-to-day issues. He just swooped in and got to be the fun dad, the big hero. You'll be sympathetic to that, right?"

"I'll make sure your views are represented," Kate assured her. "Now, you may not want to discuss this and that's fine, but I understand Brent's financial affairs were in a mess at the time of his passing. How was BJ's inheritance affected?"

"Well, legally, everything is still tied up in red tape and until the sale of Brent's house closes, there is nothing for us, for BJ that is, to help with child support. Brent supposedly made some really bad investments, but we don't trust his lawyer – that cousin of his – and we're going to court to get full disclosure of what's in the estate, and some kind of settlement. It's not fair that Tom should have to foot the bill for BJ's needs when, really, there must be plenty of money in the estate. I mean, doesn't it seem odd to you that with all of Brent's earnings over the years, there's hardly anything left?"

Kate shook her head. "I–"

"Oh, and furthermore," Stacey said, leaning forward, "That girlfriend of his, Melissa Applebaum? She owes a large sum of money to his estate and that matter is still pending. She's fighting it, claiming it was a gift and they were about to get married. If you ask me, it could have been her that killed him when he tried to ditch her."

"I understand a number of people are beginning to see it that way," Kate said.

"Brent's will did stipulate that the house or the money from the sale of the house, should be held in trust for BJ until he's twenty-five, with some of that available ahead of time at the discretion of Brent's attorney… for post-secondary education expenses. Tom and I expect –hope – that a portion of that money will be directed to child support costs now. I mean, BJ is Brent's kid, after all."

"But Tom considers him his own child, too, right?"

"Well, sure," Stacey said. "But, it's a matter of entitlement. Legally…" Stacey's voice drifted off.

Kate cleared her throat. "Do you have any photos that I might copy for the book?"

"Simone gave me your email address, so I can send you a few if you like."

"Thanks, that would be great," Kate said.

"Is it time for my interview yet?" a voice called from the doorway.

"I'll give you five minutes," Stacey laughed, beckoning her son forward.

BJ darted into the room, sliding on the hardwood floor in his sock feet and landing with a well-executed plop in the empty space on the sofa. "Shoot," he ordered.

"Wow, that was pretty athletic stuff," Kate remarked. "Do you play hockey like your father?"

"Not only do I not play hockey *like my father*, I don't play hockey at all."

"Why not?"

"First of all, I was never really *encouraged* to," BJ began.

"That's not true," Stacey declared. "You were just not *pushed* to do it."

"Okay, whatever, but also I just don't like sports that much. I love watching videos of my dad playing, but I could never be that good. I knew if I didn't try, I wouldn't disappoint him." BJ looked straight into Kate's eyes. "I really miss him a lot. Make sure you say that in your book."

For a moment, Kate couldn't speak. She swallowed and gave him an understanding smile. "What kinds of things are you interested in doing then?"

"I like science stuff and math. I like taking things apart and figuring out how they work, so maybe I'll be an engineer someday. I'm not sure yet. And I love, love, *love* computers." His eyes lit up. "I have my dad's laptop. He gave it to me."

There was a catch in Kate's breath. "Really? When did he give it to you?"

"The same summer he, you know… died."

"BJ, did the police know you had the computer?"

"There was nothing important on it," Stacey said. "Tom checked it."

"It's mine," BJ said. "Tom said I might not get it back if they took it."

Kate noted BJ's casual use of Tom's name and wondered if he ever actually called him Papa… or anything at all, to his face. She gently touched his shoulder. "BJ, I have a good friend who is a computer expert. Among other things, he designs video games and he knows how to retrieve files that have been deleted from computers. Photos and documents and things. If you would let me borrow the laptop for just a few days, I'd take really good care of it and make sure you got it back right away."

BJ hesitated.

"And I'm sure he would be happy to give you a tour of the place where he works and he could show you how video games are made and a lot of other cool stuff, if it's okay with your mother."

BJ's eyes shot to Stacey, then back to Kate. "That would be so cool!"

Stacey looked uncertain, but she nodded. "I guess so, but BJ, don't say anything to anyone about this, okay? We'll visit the video place later, maybe this summer when school's out."

"Alright!" BJ hurried out of the room, returning quickly with the laptop. "You promise, right? Just a few days."

Kate crossed her heart. "I give you my word." She set the computer down on the coffee table and laid her purse on top of it.

BJ was staring at her when she looked back at him. "Are you a celebrity?" he asked.

Kate chuckled. "Are you planning to interview *me* now? No, I'm not a celebrity."

"You kind of are around here," Stacey laughed. "And I'd say…" She was interrupted by the slamming of a heavy door, followed by the scampering sound of little feet. Stacey's eyes flew to her watch and panic registered on her face.

"Daddy!" a voice squealed.

"Hey, punkin," replied a deep male voice.

BJ removed his feet from the sofa and sat back stiffly, his eyes lowered, as heavy footsteps moved toward the living room. Tom. Kate didn't like the man and she hadn't even laid eyes on him yet. She focussed on the doorway as he came into view, holding Amanda in his arms. He was relatively short but not bad looking in spite of a shaggy moustache. A red cap bearing a company logo hid most of his dark hair and the rolled-up sleeves of his work shirt revealed muscular, tattooed forearms. He stopped just inside the room and frowning, set Amanda down.

If Stacey was trying to smile, she wasn't succeeding very well. "It's not even two o'clock. You finished early today?"

"Just driving by on my way to a call. Saw the car in the driveway," Tom said, glancing Kate's way.

"Oh, Tom, this is Kate Young. Remember *Coffee with Kate*? This is her."

Tom didn't look impressed and he made no move to come closer.

"Kate, my husband, Tom," Stacey finished weakly.

Kate stood up. "Pleased to meet you, Tom."

Ignoring her, Tom glared at his wife. "And to what do we owe this visit?"

"Kate is here to see *me*," Stacey said.

"And me," BJ mumbled under his breath as he continued to focus on a spot near his knees.

"She's writing a book about Brent and needed to fill in the parts about his history with… me and… about BJ," Stacey added.

A muscle in Tom's jaw twitched as he took a couple of steps toward his wife. "Without my consent?"

Stacey's face flushed red and she glanced apologetically at Kate. "Tom, I didn't think it was a big deal. Simone set it up yesterday."

"And you forgot to mention this to me? We make all of our decisions about BJ together."

Kate had a pretty good idea who made all the decisions in this family.

"What could it hurt?" Stacey pleaded. "It's a chance for me to make sure nothing about us gets misrepresented in the book."

"Us, you and Brent, or us, you and me?"

"Us, everyone!" Stacey was finally beginning to show some spine and she stood up. "We have a guest, Tom. Show some respect!"

Tom stood stock-still, his jaw twitching furiously and Amanda, who'd been lingering in the doorway, turned and ran from the room. "What's in the past should stay there. It's done. Over."

A less courteous person might have reminded Tom that his efforts to get his hands on BJ's money were far from over, but Kate kept her thoughts to herself. She stuffed the voice recorder into her pocket and tucked the laptop and her large purse under her arm. "I think we're through here, anyway," she said, giving Stacey a sympathetic look. "I'm sorry for any trouble caused by my visit." She turned to BJ. "It was absolutely delightful meeting you," she said with a wink.

"I'll walk you out," Stacey offered and stepped around Tom to lead her out of the room.

At the door, she lowered her voice. "He's not like that all the time. I'm really sorry."

"You'll be alright?" Kate asked.

"It'll be fine."

"Tell BJ I'll talk with him some more another time if he likes," Kate whispered.

Tom brushed past in the hallway behind them. "Anything unflattering comes out in that book of yours, you'll hear from our lawyer."

"Oh, Tom, give it a rest," Stacey said, glancing back over her shoulder.

Kate touched her arm. "Thank you, Stacey. I know this wasn't easy for you." She stepped outside and turned to see Stacey, another strained smile on her face, close the door.

CHAPTER

20

The Tahoe was back. Beryl didn't miss her brother's piece of crap car. She'd been careful this time to avoid parking on Meredith's street, circling the block from time to time to watch for signs of movement. On one of her circuits she'd observed Meredith getting into the driver's side of a car. The girl was with her and Beryl felt certain she was Lily's daughter. She pulled over near the end of the street, waited for the vehicle to pass and then gave chase, catching up a few blocks to the south where she followed them down Yonge Street.

Meredith pulled into the Bay/Dundas parkade. Beryl followed suit and watched as she parked the car and walked toward the Eaton Centre with her niece. There had been no taxis or evasive tactics used in today's outing, so she knew they were not leading her to Lily, but that was okay. Beryl had something else in mind.

For over an hour, she discreetly tailed them from store to store. She was pleased to see that Meredith had that same red suede bag with her. In fact, she was counting on it. Her opportunity would come, perhaps in a lineup or maybe among the crowd clustered around the youth choir that was performing on the ground floor.

As they neared the food court, Beryl watched Meredith rub her back and point to a table. Jemma walked in that direction while Meredith made a beeline for the washroom. Beryl quickly purchased a coffee and sat down three tables away.

When Meredith returned she handed money to her niece and then hung the handles of her tote over the back of her chair. The girl walked over to the Froshberg Gelato counter and stood in line. The place was busy. Lots of bodies moving about between tables. Beryl smiled. She put on her sunglasses, then removed a small grey object from the front pocket of her jeans. The charge on the battery would be good for at least five days, during which time, she hoped, Meredith would connect with Lily. Beryl could follow that plump red bag, anywhere. So long as Meredith didn't find the device first.

Beryl ambled past Meredith's table, her eyes fixed on the tote. She stopped at the tray station and took a last swallow of coffee. As a group of four teens moved noisily toward Meredith from the opposite direction, Beryl made her move. She walked toward the table, timing her arrival to coincide with the approaching traffic. A couple at the adjacent table stood and began to collect their trash, narrowing the space even more. As the bodies converged, Beryl pressed close to Meredith's chair and paused to allow the teens to pass first. The tracker slid neatly out of her hand into the open mouth of the tote.

"Sorry," one of the teens said, simultaneously with her "Excuse me," as the group became momentarily bottlenecked. Humming happily, Beryl departed the scene.

When Jemma returned, she put two drinks and some change on the table.

Meredith scooped the coins into her wallet and stuffed it back into her tote bag. "Remember when I said we'd shop till we drop? Well, I'm about ready to drop. Sorry."

"That's okay," Jemma said. "I'm not that big into shopping anyway. And I'm so excited about seeing Mum tomorrow, I really don't care if I do anything else this whole week."

Meredith smiled. "I'm excited for you."

"Except for one thing I'm dying to do," Jemma said, glancing up coyly from the straw she was twirling around in her smoothie. "I was hoping if I asked very nicely when you're in a good mood, you'd say yes."

"What is it you're *dying* to do?" Meredith asked warily.

"This morning when you told me we'd be meeting Mum at the Chandler Hotel, I went online to read about it and there's this place called Phil's Room that's right next door."

"I've been there," Meredith said. "It's a live music venue."

"Have you heard of Travis Wright and his band, The Wright Stuff?"

Meredith shook her head. "But you have?"

"Oh, Mere, he's incredible! Mark took me to see him at the Waterfront Festival last summer. And he's playing at Phil's Room tomorrow night. So, here's my idea: We're not meeting Mum until around ten, right? We could go to Phil's Room for a couple of hours and slip out in plenty of time to be in our hotel room before she arrives."

"I think seeing your mother will be excitement enough for one day, don't you?"

Jemma looked deflated. "Is it because it would be too much for you in your condition? Or because Eric can't be there? I didn't want to ask you in front of him this morning because he's so protective. It's like he thinks the baby's going to come shooting out if you sneeze or laugh too hard."

"He's not quite *that* bad," Meredith laughed.

"How about if Mark takes me instead?"

Meredith frowned. She was the one who had orchestrated this rendezvous and she wanted to be the one to see it through. Dean had some kind of business at the hotel that evening, but had agreed to meet with Lily when it was over because he was leaving Toronto the following morning. This arrangement made it necessary to have Dean and Jemma meet the same evening. "Are there even any seats still available?"

"Yes! I… um, took the liberty of reserving two seats with my MasterCard."

"*You* have a credit card?"

"It's a prepaid gift card that Grandpa me for this trip. I'd much rather spend it on Travis Wright than on clothes and stuff."

Meredith tapped her nails on the table. What harm could it do? March Break should be fun. Of course, Jemma had no idea that the show would be followed by the shock of her life, but in the meantime, it would be an enjoyable distraction. "Okay, Phil's Room it is."

"Yes!" Jemma jumped from her chair and squeezed Meredith around the neck. "Thank you, Mere. You'll love it." She sat back down, grinning triumphantly. "Oh, and I booked dinner, too. It was the only way to guarantee that we'd get a table close to the stage."

"I see," Meredith said, her amusement dampened by the idea that the evening may be stretching out a little long for comfort. "Well, I'm sure it'll be worth it." She reached for her tote. "I need to get my arse off this chair and home to the couch. You and Eric can get dinner ready while I rest up for this big event tomorrow."

"I can hardly wait," Jemma sighed. "Travis Wright and Mum all in one evening. What more could I wish for?"

"Mark is here," Lily's voice announced over the intercom.

Kate patted her face dry with a towel, changed her shirt and darted over to the cheval mirror, where she fluffed her hair and performed a test smile before heading downstairs.

Lily was busy at the kitchen counter and Mark was leaning on the breakfast bar.

"Hey," Kate said softly as she entered the room.

"Hey yourself," Mark answered, straightening. He read the words on her shirt. Clearly Ambiguous. Grinning, he added, "Since you and I have quite a collection, I thought I should start Lily on one of her own. Show her, sis."

"No," Lily snapped, her back to them as she arranged appetizers on a platter.

"I made her put it on before you came down," Mark said.

With a grumble of resignation, Lily spun around and placed the platter on the breakfast bar.

Kate read the words on the black shirt aloud. "Dinner is ready when the smoke alarm goes off." She covered her mouth to muffle her reaction. "Sorry, but could it be that you've earned your reputation?"

"Absolutely not!"

"Well, you know what they say. Where there's smoke, there's fire."

At this, Mark laughed and high-fived Kate.

Lily poked Mark's shoulder. "Okay, smart-ass, your turn."

Mark slipped off his jacket and puffed out his chest. **World's Okayest Lover** was printed in red across his grey tee.

Lily rolled her eyes and a giggling Kate left the room, returning a moment later with BJ's laptop in her hands.

"Maybe you should have at look at this now, Mark."

"Good job prying it away from the kid."

"Brent would have deleted anything sensitive, but can you retrieve it?"

"Those deleted files may still exist on lower levels, depending on how much space BJ has used. Some of it could be gone for good."

"Let's have a look at what's there before you go to work on it," Lily said.

She and Kate sat down on either side of Mark and watched as he turned on the computer and examined the icons displayed on the desktop. "Hmm… *Thunder King*, *Google Earth*, *Skype*, *Microsoft Office Word*, not much else. Let's check *Documents*." He did some clicking. "Gone. How about *Pictures*?" Another round of clicks produced several files. Mark opened the first one and a series of Brent's fine art photographs appeared on the screen. Another file contained old family photos, all labelled.

"This is probably stuff Brent wanted BJ to have," Kate said.

Other folders contained photos from Brent's career, his travels and his everyday life. Mark scrolled quickly through them. The last photo appeared to be a fairly recent shot of Ben, who had grown progressively heavier in his thirties. He was on a boat, his longish curls blown sideways by the wind, and his large shirtless belly complemented by the Budweiser in his hand. An anchor tattoo was displayed on his right upper arm. Lily lingered on the photo, then asked Mark to open the video files.

There were two. The first one they viewed showed Ben standing at the helm of a sailboat as it crashed through the waves. "Ready about!" he called, followed shortly by, "Helms alee!" He turned the wheel sharply and a rogue wave pounded the boat and drenched the deck. A loud squeal pierced the air and the camera panned to a female figure cowering in the cockpit.

"This is too rough!" the woman exclaimed, wrapping her arms around her knees.

"Got no faith in me, eh?" Ben laughed. "We've been out in much rougher seas than this, haven't we boys?" he yelled to the unseen crew. The boat bounced and a whimper was heard. He threw the woman a look of disgust. "If you're that scared, go below, but it's perfectly safe!"

"Famous last words from one who was soon to die on a sailboat," Lily commented.

The other video began with the camera panning down a long stretch of beach and across a turquoise sea.

"Greetings from paradise, Brent. Beautiful, eh?" A voice they recognized as belonging to Ben was narrating. The view swung slowly around to the patio of a seaside restaurant where a few people sitting around a table smiled and waved at the camera. In the background, the name of the establishment was prominently displayed. *Captain Kipp's Bar and Grill.*

"Too bad you have to be stuck up there in the cold north, but you know, that's the price you have to pay to play for the *Montreal Canadiens.* To be a celebrity," Ben drawled, drawing out the last word. The camera zoomed in on one of the women. "This is Sabrina. Sabrina say hi to my brother, the hockey star."

A busty blonde in a white bikini, looked at the camera. "Hi Brent. I'm a big fan."

"She can't get enough of me," Ben's syrupy commentary continued.

"That is so not true," Sabrina protested.

"That's not what you said last night." The camera panned down to her cleavage.

"In your dreams." Sabrina raised her middle finger.

Ben laughed and the camera moved on to take in more of the

scenery. "This place is incredible. Great beach, great bar, love it."

The picture jiggled as it appeared to change hands and then Ben was in the shot. "I am totally going to retire here someday. Bet you'll miss me, eh? Meanwhile, I'm having a drink for you, buddy. Cheers." He lifted an orangey cocktail to his mouth, downed half of it and grinned inanely as the video ended.

"Slimey, isn't he?" Kate said.

"Where could this have been shot?" Lily wondered aloud.

"Somewhere in the Caribbean, judging by the Carib beer and Mount Gay rum." Mark closed the lid of the laptop. "Okay, I'll see what I can recover from the bowels of this machine."

"Stay for dinner?" Kate asked.

Mark pretended to consider this. "Who's cooking?"

Lily glared at him. "Just for that I *will* cook!"

As the water came to a rolling boil, Dean snapped a fistful of spaghetti in half and dropped it into the pot. "Just spaghetti," he hollered.

Georgia appeared in the doorway and moved toward the stove. "Let me help. How about a Caesar salad on the side?"

"If you like," Dean said, straining to open a jar of sauce.

"Gimme." Georgia took the jar from him, and whacked the edge of the lid with the handle of a knife. She poured the contents over the ground beef that was sizzling in a skillet.

"I can do it," Dean muttered. "Go make your salad."

Moving to the refrigerator, Georgia pulled out a bag of lettuce. "Feeling a little tense, are we?"

"Sorry."

"You know, Travis would understand if you cancelled."

"But he'd be disappointed. Anyway, I'm looking forward to it. And I want to see Lily, too. I'm nervous as hell, though."

Georgia pulled more ingredients from the refrigerator.

"Meredith said I'm to meet Lily in the hotel restaurant. She doesn't know I've told you anything. I don't think she'd understand the complete trust I have in you. But how could I *not* tell you?"

"Yeah, your head would've exploded for sure. And while we're on the subject of complete trust, tell me, how is it again that you failed to mention you were ever married?"

Dean slowly stirred the sauce as Georgia attacked the lettuce. "It was so brief it hardly counted. Not my proudest moment."

"In all this time, you never wondered where she was or what she was doing?"

"I just assumed she'd found someone and married a long time ago. If she got a queer to marry her, imagine all the straight men she'd have chasing her."

Georgia began shuffling through packages on a shelf. "Little did you know she'd made headlines in Canada as a murderer."

"An *accused* murderer."

"No!"

Dean's spatula jerked, sending speckles of sauce across the top of the stove.

"Sorry, I meant, *No, we're out of croutons!* Your secrets are safe with me."

"I don't think we ever had any."

"Secrets?"

"Croutons." Dean turned the heat to low. "One thing I'm sure of – Lily didn't kill anyone."

"Dean, just be careful. Say what you need to say and then get out. I just think it's dangerous, not to mention weird, that the two of you are doing this *now.*" Georgia turned her attention back to the salad. "I can't believe we have no croutons," she grumbled.

Clair Young's bright, modern kitchen with its adjoining solarium was everyone's favourite room in the house. Lily described it as the command centre, the brain. Clair thought of it as the heart of the house. And Kate liked it simply because it was a kitchen, and kitchens were her domain. Lily folded foil around the garlic bread she'd just prepared.

"Dinner in ten," she said, pressing the office button on the intercom.

At that moment Clair walked in, followed closely by Jinx. "What smells so delicious?"

"Just spaghetti," Kate said.

Mark appeared with the laptop under his arm. "All done," he informed them.

Lily closed the oven door and hurried over to the breakfast bar where Mark was opening the laptop. "And?"

"Unfortunately, I didn't find what you were hoping for. If Brent ever used this computer to compose the letter he hid, it's not here now. In fact, there were virtually no text files here at all. He probably used his main computer for that sort of thing."

"Maybe this confession or whatever was handwritten," Kate suggested.

"If it was," Lily said, "that would help to verify its authenticity. And it could still be in that house. Since my statement was never taken seriously, I doubt the place was thoroughly searched." She sighed. "So, what *did* you find?"

Mark tapped a few keys. "These." He angled the computer toward Lily. "Frankly, I expected to find porn, but the raciest photo here is of his fiancée in a swimsuit. There are a dozen or so pictures that I've thumb-nailed here."

Lily paused briefly on the shot of Melissa and then clicked on the next image. The enlarged photo showed an emaciated man in ragged shorts standing on a beach next to a life raft. "What the__" She examined the scene more closely. Part of the image was familiar. It was the photo of Brent on the beach immediately following his rescue. "I have this same photo. Brent gave it to me for the book. But this," she exclaimed, jabbing her finger at the face on the screen, "is not Brent's head!"

Kate leaned in. "Does this mean the picture you have was... Photoshopped?"

Lily's eyes shot to Mark. "How hard would that be?"

"Not hard for someone with Brent's expertise," Mark said and he was already clicking through the other images. "In fact, a photo editing program had been installed on this computer. Could *this* be the head that's on the body in your picture?" he said pointing to another image on the screen. It was Brent sporting a grimy face, a beard and a head of wild, sun-bleached hair.

Lily nodded. "That's it."

"Why would he do such a thing?" Clair asked.

"There was only one other photo of him taken the day after the rescue," Lily said. "He was in a hospital bed in Guadalupe. Maybe he needed to come up with a picture of himself right after the rescue for publicity purposes. But why use someone else's body? Was he trying to exaggerate his weight loss?"

"It's more dramatic. Maybe he was anticipating fame, attention, book deals, and a high profile, big bucks job on TV. That would be quite appealing to someone whose career and finances were in the toilet," Mark said.

As the group fell into momentary silence, Jinx sniffed the air and yipped.

"Ah… is something burning?" Clair asked.

Heads turned to look at the oven and Lily flew into action. "My garlic bread!" she shrieked. She yanked opened the oven door and smoke billowed out. Within seconds the smoke alarm was blaring as Lily grabbed pot holders, pulled the charred remains of the loaf from its crematorium and deposited it in the sink. She turned slowly to face her audience. "Dinner's ready."

CHAPTER 21

March 15

The table for two that Jemma had reserved at Phil's Room was directly in front of centre stage. Meredith nervously checked the time. Dean had promised he'd be waiting at the Chandler Hotel following whatever meeting he had going on there. Meredith intended to be close by to give whatever support was needed to her sister and her niece.

A waiter cleared their plates as the stage lights came on. Meredith gazed at Jemma who was shifting her chair, her face bright with anticipation. She'd changed in recent months, growing nearly as tall as her mother and developing noticeable curves. At Meredith's insistence that they alter their appearances, Jemma had elected to go "boyish". She wore black jeans, a white shirt with rolled up sleeves, a grey vest from Meredith's wardrobe, and one of Eric's funky colourful ties. In the last taxi to Phil's Room she'd gathered her long hair into a ponytail and stuffed it inside a powder blue fedora. Round glasses with pale pink lenses completed her transformation. Meredith had her hair pinned up beneath a slouch tam and had traded her contact lenses for red-framed glasses.

"You look adorable in that hat," Meredith said. "Very hip."

The chatter in the room subsided as the house lights dimmed and The Wright Stuff were introduced. The band began playing a song that was unfamiliar to Meredith. When it ended, the room filled with generous applause. "Thanks so much," Travis said. "That was one of our own from the new CD, but for the rest of our first set we're going to cover some of our favourites from the past."

Jemma leaned into Meredith's ear. "Great, isn't he?"

"I have a special treat for you tonight," Travis continued, grinning. "I recently had the good fortune to jam with someone who has made a name for himself in New York's theatre and nightclub scene and who is here in Toronto working on his first ever major production, *Thin Air*. In the not-too-distant future, you're going to be hearing this beautiful man's tal… I mean this talented man's beautiful music everywhere." Travis laughed and banged his head on the mike. "I'm a little tongue-tied at the moment, but yeah, actually he is a beautiful man."

Meredith, who'd been only half tuned in to what Travis was saying, felt her heart flutter as his words began to sink in.

"I am so honoured that he has agreed to join us on stage tonight. Please welcome Dean James!"

The room filled with applause as a golden-haired, handsome man leapt up onto the low riser that formed the stage.

Meredith held her breath and stared, wide-eyed, as Dean took his place at the keyboard.

"Cool name. Like James Dean, but flipped. Get it? Have you ever heard of this guy?" Jemma asked, turning to look at her aunt. She caught Meredith's deer-in-the-headlights stare. "What's wrong?"

Meredith's eyes flew to Jemma's.

"Nothing. I–"

"You're all red in the face."

"Hot. Hormones. I'll be fine."

Dean's fingers began moving across the keyboard and instantly Jemma recognized the intro.

"That's *Halleluiah!*" she exclaimed. She began rocking side to side in time with the music as Dean's voice took the lead.

Meredith followed Jemma's eyes to the stage. Her mind raced.

Would Jemma recognize herself in the face of this stranger? Would Dean recognize the Meredith of so many years ago? He hadn't seen her since she was thirteen, so probably not. Still… if they were any closer, he'd see the beads of sweat forming on her brow.

While Meredith stared, paralyzed with indecision, Dean was noticing the young woman seated below him at the front of the stage. She oozed joy, her face lit up in a thousand-watt smile. Strangely, the woman beside her looked as though she were watching a horror film. As he began softly singing the chorus, a few voices in the audience quietly joined in.

Travis assumed the lead on the second verse and as they approached the chorus, Dean took one hand off the keyboard and beckoned his audience to sing along. The voices rose up, stronger this time, cushioning the two voices on stage in a blur of melody. Then, above the sound, a single voice rose – clear and strong. Dean's eyes swept the front tables and came to rest on the girl in the blue fedora.

Below the stage, Meredith looked on, quietly stunned, as Jemma finished with a lingering vibrato. She grasped Jemma's arm and fixed her with an open-jawed stare. "I had no idea you could sing like that!"

Jemma simply grinned and turned her attention back to Dean. "Amazing!" she gushed as the song ended. "I love him!" She turned her attention once again to Meredith. "You okay now?"

Meredith opened her mouth to tell her they must leave, but catching the sparkle in those green eyes, she just nodded and smiled. Maybe this was how it was supposed to happen. They could leave before the set ended and deal with the shock later. She became aware of the all-too-familiar pressure on her bladder. Sighing, she squeezed Jemma's shoulder and rose to her feet. "Be right back. Gotta go."

"Again?" Jemma laughed. Meredith waddled off in the direction of the washrooms.

As the applause died down, Travis spoke into the mike. "Told ya he was good." He glanced sideways at Dean who was relinquishing his seat at the keyboard to one of the band members. "Thanks, Dean. That was awesome."

Dean, his cheeks flushing pink, nodded his thank you to Travis and to the audience, then removed a second microphone from its stand.

"This next song is from the nineties and we're going to sing it – *Together Now*," Travis said. The keyboardist began playing the introduction as Dean and Travis waited, poised to sing.

Alone at her table, Jemma blurted out, "Oh, I love this song!"

Overhearing this, Dean smiled at her, then let his attention drift around the room as Travis sang the first verse. He felt somewhat self-conscious, standing next to this man. There seemed to be some sparks of attraction between them. Or not. Travis, for the moment, was singing with his eyes closed and seemed comfortably detached from everyone in the room. There was no girlfriend in sight tonight. But it hardly mattered. Dean knew the last thing he needed right now was to complicate his life with a new relationship. His eyes wandered back to the girl in the blue hat. She looked so cute with her pink shades and her bright tie. Her dimpled grin was strangely familiar.

Travis was halfway through his verse. Dean glanced his way and was startled to see a pair of maple syrupy eyes looking directly at him.

"Heart wide open, wanting, hopin',
You will feel it, too..."

Quickly, he averted his gaze and found himself focussed once again on the girl. Impulsively, he stepped forward and leaned down, reaching out his hand to her. She hesitated briefly, blushed furiously, then stood and placed her own hand in his. With a quick tug, she was on the stage.

Travis had intended to sing the chorus in unison with Dean, but when he saw the pretty young woman pop up from the audience, he made an immediate judgement call, and let Dean take it solo.

Dean turned to Jemma and began singing directly to her.

"When you face the storm, I'll keep you warm
Won't let you down,
Be my guiding star, we'll travel far
Together now."

Meredith, who had been making her way back across the room, noticed the empty table. In the next instant she was astonished by the realization that her niece was standing next to Dean on stage. She grabbed the back of a chair for support and stood, riveted to the spot until a voice from behind commanded her to sit down. Arriving at their table, she collapsed onto her chair and stared at the scene unfolding before her. Until her instincts kicked in. She reached into her tote and fished around. Her fingers brushed various objects – lipstick, a bottle of vitamins, a hard, unfamiliar object and then, finally… the camcorder. Triumphantly, she pulled it from the bag and turned it on.

She remembered Eric's words when he'd given it to her on her last birthday. *What filmmaker worth her own salt doesn't have a camcorder with her at all times?* It was small, but high quality, and tonight it was going to more than pay for itself. People often teased her about the size of her purse. "Who's laughing now?" she chortled softly. Concentrating to steady her hands and calm her breathing, Meredith flipped open the monitor and began recording.

During the instrumental break between verses, Dean whispered something in Jemma's ear. She nodded gamely as he raised the mike just in time to lead off the second verse. He looked into Jemma's eyes as he sang and a few feet away, a sob caught in Meredith's throat.

"Got this feeling, shaking, reeling,
Knowing this is true,"

Dean held the microphone to Jemma's lips and her magnificent voice sprang to life, gently at first, then with more intensity.

"Hardly breathing, words are leaving,
Softly finding you,"

Dean was astonished. He'd heard a dampened version of the girl's voice singing *Halleluiah,* but it hadn't prepared him for this rich, pitch-perfect flow of lyrics. He exchanged exuberant glances with Travis. In his shock he failed to take the mike back at the end of the lines he'd previously whispered to her, and she slid right into the bridge.

"You smile and tell me how long you've waited
And this is where you belong."

She knew the words! Dean recovered his composure in time to bring his mouth to the microphone for the chorus, but he moved in close and held it between them, inviting her to follow along. Dean heard himself sing the first note and then Jemma's voice was there. But not just *there*. She came in higher and strong, singing harmony. A spine-tingling bubble of pure joy shot up from deep inside and burst across Dean's face in a huge grin.

At the table down front, Meredith was trying to contain the volcano of emotion that threatened to erupt. Dean and Jemma held the final note, their voices vibrating as one, and the crowd went wild, jumping to their feet. The band applauded as Dean pointed both arms toward Jemma like a human spotlight. Amid the hoots and cheering, Jemma executed a quick bow, then pointed her own arms in Dean's direction, sharing the adulation.

As the noise died down, Dean spoke into the microphone. "Who are you and where have you been all my life?"

Just below them, Meredith uttered an involuntary squeaking sound.

Travis had moved forward to stand on the other side of Jemma. "I'm in shock," he said. "What's your name?"

Jemma's eyes darted to Meredith and for the first time she noticed the camera. She gave her a little wave and looked back at Travis. "Ella," she said.

Dean ran his fingers through his hair as he brought the mike to his mouth. "Well, Ella, obviously you're a performer. Tell us about yourself."

"I've never performed anywhere," Jemma replied.

"Seriously?" Dean asked. "Where did you get that beautiful voice and how did you know that song?"

"I've taken lessons. And the song? I listen to my grandparents' music. They like all that old stuff."

At this, the audience laughed and the drummer played a bada-boom.

"Hey, I'm not criticizing, 'cause I like it, too," she quickly added. She shrugged. "Guess I'm not a typical fourteen-year-old."

"You're only *fourteen*?" Dean gasped. He looked more closely at her face. "Kind of hard to tell behind those pink shades."

"And what brought you here tonight?" Travis asked.

Jemma looked at Travis. "Well, I heard you once last year, live, and I'm a big fan, but I'd never heard of him before," she said, motioning in Dean's direction.

Again, laughter rolled through the audience, punctuated by another short burst from the drums. Jemma's face turned red and she lowered her head, smiling sheepishly.

"Gee, you blush almost as brightly as Mr. James here," Travis said.

Dean immediately felt his cheeks grow hot.

"Just look at the two of you! Well, let me tell you something. This guy is a lot more famous than I'll ever be."

"And better-looking!" the bass player shouted from the background.

"Better smelling, too!" the drummer added, hitting the cymbals.

"Enough!" Dean said, raising his free hand. "So… is this your mother down here with the camera?" He was pointing at Meredith.

"No," Jemma giggled. "That's my aunt. She's only twenty-nine."

"I see. And does she sing, too?"

"Like a donkey," Jemma bantered. "Just kidding, Mere… Aunt Mary." She looked at her feet. "I'm nervous."

Meredith squirmed. Her anxiety was off the chart and her bladder was full again.

"Well, you don't seem nervous when you're singing," Travis said. "How about one more duet with Dean while you're up here?"

The audience shouted encouragement and Jemma nodded. "Sure."

"What would you like to sing? Maybe we can fake our way through it. Keep it *old*, though."

"Um…" Jemma thought for a moment. "I heard you do *Feeling Good* last summer and I know that one."

"I think we can handle that, right boys?

"Can you boys handle it in the key of G minor?" Jemma asked, smiling slyly.

Dean laughed, delighted at the girl's moxie. "Just a minute," he said, grabbing the waistband of his jeans. "I'll have to hitch up my pants if I'm going to hit *those* notes!"

The audience hooted, and Jemma now seemed totally at ease with the men on stage. "Actually, your key is fine," she said. "I have a fairly strong lower register. Do you know the words?" She looked calmly at Dean.

"Ah… yeah," he replied, confounded by her sudden show of confidence. "I'm… up to speed."

"Great," Jemma said. "How about you start and we alternate lines on the first two verses and then wing it from there?"

Dean nodded, slipping further under her spell. "You're not really fourteen, are you?" he said as the band began to play.

Jemma grinned as he turned to face the audience. Meredith zoomed in on their faces, two faces slashed with identical sets of long dimples. Dean wiped his hand over his mouth, smoothing it into a serious expression, waited for his cue and then sang the opening lines. The camcorder wobbled as Meredith dabbed at the tears trailing down her cheeks. She snuffled audibly when Dean finished his next line and Jemma's voice cut in again, eliciting a burst of applause.

As Dean began the second verse, Jemma turned toward the man she did not yet know as her father and looked into the mirror that was his face. They continued alternating lines, eyes connected. She was focussed on the song, remembering the lyrics, listening to the instruments, aware of every nuance of emotion she was projecting – but there was something in those eyes that was unsettling and as her mind reached for the next line, she returned her gaze to the packed room, her voice rising and swelling to fill the house.

Whistling and more applause erupted and then tapered off as the voices of Dean and Jemma fused into one melody. Their faces glowed as the intensity of the song peaked. The image in the monitor was shaking now and Meredith had to put both elbows on the table and support her wrist with her left hand. She wiped her nose on her shoulder and let her tears drip freely off her chin. This moment would be captured for posterity at all costs. She squeezed her legs together.

On the final verse, as Dean came to the end of the first line, Jemma's voice joined in, overlapping his last note and repeating his words with a higher, jazzy counterpart. Dean instinctively held the melody, and Jemma echoed, their voices climbing. The band slowed the tempo and they sang the last line in unison.

Thunderous applause followed. Jemma whipped off her fedora, pulled the band from her ponytail and shook her head, allowing her long gold hair to cascade over her shoulders. Meredith's heart pounded. *That girl is going to be the death of me.* But she kept recording. She swung the camcorder over the room, then turned it back to the stage, where Dean and Jemma were bowing, hands clasped.

On the stage, Dean turned to stare at the girl beside him. Fresh-faced, joyous and gorgeous, she ran a hand through hair that now flowed freely. Something tugged at his heart, but he couldn't interpret the feeling. He looked back at Travis. This was his gig, and Dean had promised him the set they'd been rehearsing. The crowd waited expectantly as quiet descended.

"Ella," Dean said at last. "Thank you so very much for joining us here on stage and for sharing your outrageous talent with us. I know your name will be in lights someday." He gave her a quick hug, handed off his microphone, and escorted her off the stage.

As Jemma took her seat, Dean leaned over the table. "I have to rush off at the end of this set, but I'd really like to talk to you and your parents about some opportunities for you. I'm going to be out of town for the next week or so, but…" He looked at Meredith. "Would it be alright if I contacted your family when I return?"

Jemma didn't wait for her aunt to respond. "Really? Oh, Wow! I'm actually living with my–"

Meredith cut her off. "That would be amazing. Here." She rummaged through a side pocket in her bag and came out with a pen and a pad of Post-it notes. She wrote her husband's name and cellphone number on the paper.

"Thanks," Dean said, smiling. "I'll see you when I finish the set. We'll have a proper introduction later."

Meredith nodded politely. *You have no idea.*

At the very back of Phil's Room, Beryl watched the proceedings. The GPS device had been her best idea yet. She'd arrived shortly after Meredith and Jemma and had purchased one of the few tickets left for *Dinner and Show*. She'd scanned the crowd and kept her eyes on the door when the *Show Only* group filed in. She hadn't seen anyone resembling Lily, but the fact that Meredith and Jemma had used a convoluted route to get there told her something was up.

Beryl wasn't sure if the hats and glasses were intended to throw anyone off or if they were simply fashion statements, but she'd spotted them with little difficulty. As for her own appearance, she'd made just one change, donning a dark brown wig. It was shoulder length and wavy, and with her aviator sunglasses and leather jacket, she resembled a chubby Howard Stern.

She'd never heard of the cover band or the special guest, this Dean James person, but they were actually very good, and when Jemma had been invited to join them on stage, Beryl could hardly believe her ears. Lily Mullaly's daughter was some kind of musical prodigy. She gritted her teeth. Of course she was. Lily was beautiful, successful and privileged. Why not have a super-talented, extra-precious daughter as well? That's just how life worked for some people.

Disappointment and doubt nagged at Beryl. Maybe they were simply here for a fun night out. This could be a dead end, but she intended to stick around and find out.

The evening was slipping by. Meredith knew she needed to get Jemma out of there before the set ended. Dean and Travis were circulating through the audience with their portable microphones singing *Dream Come True*, a power ballad from the seventies.

"We need to go," she said, leaning into Jemma's ear.

"But Mere, Dean wants to see us before he leaves," Jemma said. "Can't we just hang in a little longer?"

"Not this time."

Jemma started to object and Meredith cut her off. "Listen. Do you trust me?"

"Well, yeah, of course."

Dean was nearing their table. He stopped in front of Jemma and looked into her eyes as he sang. Meredith sat rigidly, thighs trembling, lips pressed into what she hoped would pass for a smile, as she endured the lyrics – about how the "you" in the song had turned his stale life into a fairy tale and how he'd always be there for her. Jemma turned to watch as Dean moved on, making his way toward the back of the room. Meredith placed her hand on Jemma's cheek and recaptured her attention. "Then just do what I ask. I promise you'll see him again."

Jemma's eyes were pleading. "But–"

"I promise."

Meredith hooked her tote bag over her shoulder and waited until Dean's back was turned, then nudging Jemma, quietly stood and led her across the room. They slipped into the corridor that connected with the Chandler Hotel, the music fading behind them.

"You're late," Mark scolded as his father slid into the booth.

"And starving."

"That's what happens when you skip dinner." Mark caught the waitress's eye and she took their orders, her smile lingering on his face a little longer than necessary before she sashayed away.

Jeff cocked an eyebrow. "What, no flirting with the cute employees?"

"That all happened before you got here," Mark said, checking his watch. "Twenty minutes ago."

"Sorry, I lost track of time. Wait, isn't that your line?"

"I may have uttered it a time or two," Mark said. "Actually, I'm not really putting the moves on waitresses or anyone else these days, except–"

"What? Are you off the market again?"

"Not exactly," Mark hedged. "There is *someone.* I'm not even sure she's interested in me, but I'd like to find out."

Jeff chuckled. "Who is she?"

"Kate, Clair's granddaughter. She's three years older than I am, but–"

"Cradle robber!" Jeff exclaimed, suppressing a smile.

Mark leaned forward. "It's strange, Dad. I haven't spent much time with her, but ..."

"Then go for it. That's great news. You've made my day."

Mark grinned. "Okay, your turn. Go ahead, make my day."

"How about this? I found the woman who saw Lily parked several streets away from Brent's house the day of the murder."

"The woman Lily gave the finger to?"

Jeff nodded. "It doesn't exactly clear her, but it messes up the prosecution's timeline."

"Wow. How did you track her down?" Mark asked.

"I highlighted the streets Lily thought she could have been on and went door to door. Turns out she was seven blocks from Brent's place."

"I thought Lily's defense team combed that whole area."

"Combed? Hardly. They missed Anita Burns, the eighty-two year-old woman who lives in the basement granny suite at her daughter's house. She didn't get a good look at Lily, just her finger, but she identified the vehicle as a blue Nissan SUV and said there was a green leaf sticker on the right side of the rear bumper."

"Lily's Nature Conservancy of Canada decal."

"*And* she knows what time that was because Lily's vehicle pulled away just as the in-ground sprinklers came on. They were on a timer set for five-thirty. That only leaves Lily about five minutes to drive the seven blocks to Brent's house, argue with him and kill him."

"Wow! Good work."

"And that's not all," Jeff said. "I canvassed Brent's neighbourhood and found someone who remembers seeing a silver car parked near the Baines home late in the afternoon on the day of the murder. He said he reported it to an officer who was at the scene that day, but no one ever called him back to follow up. Unfortunately, he doesn't recall the exact time, the make of the car or if anyone was in it."

"More good evidence for an appeal."

"We'll talk to Lily in the morning. She has enough to deal with tonight."

"I'm glad Meredith's with her." Mark was tearing away at the corner of his paper napkin.

"She's got the support of Kate and Clair, too," Jeff said. "They've been a godsend to Lily."

"And to all of us," Mark breathed, tearing a piece of the napkin free.

Jeff snatched it from Mark's fingers and found himself looking at a paper heart. "Yup. Cupid has hit his target."

When Meredith and Jemma entered the lobby, they found Eric waiting for them. "Honey, what are you doing here?" Meredith exclaimed.

"I put in an appearance, did some fast networking and then ducked out early so I could be here for my girls."

"I definitely married the right man!" Meredith said.

Jemma grabbed Eric's arm as they headed for the elevators. "Eric, wait till you hear what happened!"

"Yeah, just wait till you hear," Meredith mumbled.

Several paces behind them, Beryl watched as Eric pushed the elevator button. The idea that Lily could be hiding in a room in this very hotel had set her pulse racing. But in what room and on what floor? The GPS device wasn't capable of tracking in a 3D environment. She made a dash across the lobby.

Inside the elevator, Meredith pushed another button and the doors began to close. Only a sliver of space remained when a hand suddenly gripped the edge, forcing them to reopen. A person of indeterminate gender stepped inside and leaned against the rear wall. Meredith raised her arm to press the button for the twelfth floor and felt a shiver crawl up her spine. She pressed five instead and gave the stranger a questioning look.

"Five please," the stranger said in a voice identifying her as a probable female.

They rode in silence for a few seconds until the elevator slowed to a stop and the doors slid open.

"Go ahead," Meredith said as she stepped aside.

Their fellow passenger hesitated and glanced at the panel. "Not your floor?"

Meredith shook her head and the woman stepped out into the hallway. The doors closed and she pressed numbers eleven through sixteen.

"What was that?" Jemma asked.

"I don't know, but we're not taking any chances." Meredith sighed as she retrieved the key card from her bag.

At the twelfth floor, the trio disembarked. Eric opened the door to a large, attractive suite.

"This is beautiful," Jemma said, tossing the knapsack she was carrying onto one of the beds. "I'm going to check out the bathroom."

Jemma disappeared and Eric turned to his wife. "You two had a good girls' night out?"

"I was close to peeing myself the whole time!" Meredith rasped. "Dean was there with the band. He didn't tell me on the phone what kind of meeting he had or that he'd be next door at Phil's Room. On. The. Stage. And Eric, OMG! I went to the washroom and when I came back, Jemma was up there singing with him. And she's good. No, phenomenal! You won't believe it till you hear it. And oh! You'll be so proud of me. I got it on video! Meanwhile, it was all I could do to…"

"Calm down, sweetheart," Eric interrupted. "Deep breaths, relax."

"I'm fine. *You* relax."

"She sang with him, but she doesn't know who he is?"

"No clue."

Eric rubbed his hands over his face and chuckled. "What a night! If this wasn't such a serious thing, I'd have to laugh."

"You *are* laughing."

"That was my ironic chuckle, not actual laughing," Eric said. "Look, I was going to go wait in the bar and let you handle the sensitive chat thing when Lily gets here, but if you want I can stay and you know, support you."

"Thank you, honey, but it would be better if it's just me." Meredith patted her belly. "Baby's doing Karate tonight."

Eric bent to kiss the baby bump as Jemma emerged from the bathroom.

"Ew, get a room!" She opened the bar fridge and removed a bottle.

"We've got a room and Eric was just saying goodbye to Miss Petunia," Meredith informed her. She was rewarded with an expression of wide-eyed delight from her niece.

"It's a girl?"

"You're the only one we've told. It'll be our secret."

"Really?" Jemma made a face. "You're not actually going to call her Petunia, are you?"

Eric laughed. "We can't agree on a name so it's temporary. Kinda cute, though."

"Yeah, for a piglet," Jemma snorted. "I just hope she loves me someday as much as I love you guys."

"Oh, sweetie, that's so beautiful!" Meredith's chin quivered.

Eric and Jemma stared as a tear streaked down her cheek, then looked at each other. "Hormones," Jemma said. "Here, have some cranberry juice. Good for the bladder."

"Speaking of bladder, Petunia is pressing on it," Meredith said, "so my next stop is the bathroom, but come give me a kiss before you leave, honey."

"Ah, once again, I'm standing *right here*, you guys," Jemma complained.

When Eric leaned in to kiss her, Meredith whispered, "Keep an eye on the restaurant, but give them their space." Then she handed him her tote bag. "Why don't you take my Kobo with you and read. And while you're at it, get yourself something for that coffee breath. I've got Tic-Tacs and peppermint gum in there somewhere."

Eric rifled through her bag. After removing the Kobo he felt around for the Tic-Tacs. He pulled out a small, hard object and set it on the table. "Really, Meredith? A lighter? No one we know smokes."

Meredith was halfway across the bedroom. "Hey, you never know when we might need to light a fire. It's part of my survival strategy and you'd be really glad I had it if we ever…"

"Got lost in the woods of downtown Toronto, yeah." Eric

continued searching until he came upon another candidate. He stared at the little boxy gadget that appeared in the palm of his hand. Eric was a techie, a gadget aficionado, and he knew exactly what this was. He'd read about them, handled them and might have purchased one if he'd had a use for it. There was no reason for Meredith to have one. He briefly considered bringing it to her attention, but the last thing his pregnant wife needed was more stress.

"Did you find anything?" Meredith called from the bathroom doorway.

"Yeah, thanks," Eric said, slipping the Kobo back into her purse. "See you later, ladies." When the door closed behind him, he headed for the elevator, clutching the tracker in his hand. *Let's see who you can flush out of the shadows for me, my little charm.*

CHAPTER

22

Lily rose from her seat in the corner of the restaurant, raised a trembling hand and met the eyes of the man she'd once promised to love forever. Dean crossed the room and looked at her uncertainly. Lily smiled. "Yes, it's me."

He opened his arms and they embraced. "Lily, I–"

"Shhh. No names," she said, nodding at a couple seated a few tables away.

"Sorry," Dean said.

They sat down across from each other and Dean took her hands in his. "It's so good to see you." He glanced toward the door as another couple wandered into the restaurant. "I could get us a room if you like." He blushed as he heard his own words. "I mean, so we can talk in private."

Lily smiled and squeezed his hands. "No, this is fine." She spotted the approaching waiter. "I ordered two glasses of wine and asked the waiter to give us some privacy."

They fell into momentary silence as the wine was delivered.

"Enjoy," said the waiter before he retreated.

Memories were rushing over Dean. He wished he could see those brilliant blue eyes, now masked in brown.

"I'm sorry about your Grandpa James," Lily said.

"Thanks," Dean replied softly.

Lily set her glass aside and folded her arms on the table. "We have a lot to talk about."

Eric scanned the lobby, then walked over to the front desk. "I don't suppose you have an envelope I could use," he asked the woman on duty.

"Certainly, sir."

Eric thanked her, accepted the envelope and wrote a name on it. Then he sealed the GPS tracker inside and handed it back. "Would you hold this here for one of your guests, Meredith Larson?"

"Of course."

Eric walked into the lounge, picked up a newspaper and sat down.

He'd hardly had time to open the paper when an elevator dinged and a moment later the same woman who'd shared theirs earlier entered the lounge. Eric watched with interest as she examined her phone and glanced around. He felt her eyes pass over him and pause for a moment as he pretended to read. She walked in the direction of the front desk and stopped a few paces short of it, staring again at her phone.

Eric studied her movements. Could she be the stalker? If so, the police were getting pretty sloppy. After a moment, the woman looked at the ceiling, shoved the phone into her pocket with obvious frustration and walked in the direction of the restaurant.

Beryl had searched in vain for signs of her subjects. When she'd noticed that the signal was moving again, she'd hurried to the lobby. She'd found Eric there, and that implied that he was waiting. The dot on her phone had led her to the area of the front desk and she'd realized the target had probably come to rest on one of the many floors above it. She'd decided to wait. Eventually Meredith and, hopefully, Lily would come down that elevator. Lily was likely to be wearing a disguise.

A malicious grin came to her face as she pictured the scene – tackling Lily as she emerged from the elevator, yelling for the desk clerk to call the police, snapping handcuffs on Lily's slender wrists. What a great time she would have describing the whole affair to the media. There would be interviews, talk shows…

In the midst of this fantasy Beryl collided with a young waitress who'd just materialized in her path. "Slow down!" she snarled, abruptly stepping around the girl who had been innocently wiping a table.

"Can I help you… madam?" asked the bartender.

Beryl shook her head and continued on through the bar area into the restaurant. She strolled into the middle of the room and looked around. Only three tables were occupied. Briefly, she considered ordering a burger. She'd only picked at the fishy-tasting salmon she'd been served in Phil's Room.

Her gaze travelled to the couple seated in the corner of the room and she recognized the man as the singer who'd appeared in Phil's Room. He was engaged in conversation with some blonde chick, one of those classy types she detested. Like Lily Mullaly. *Yep, just the type he'd go for.* Dean's eyes shifted her way and Beryl resumed her walkthrough, heading slowly back to the lobby.

Eric, who'd been watching apprehensively, followed a discreet distance behind her. When she plopped down on a chair in the lounge, he turned on his heel and went back into the bar where he sat on a stool that afforded him an unobstructed view of the restaurant.

At their corner table, Lily and Dean were still engrossed in conversation. They'd updated each other on their careers and Lily had just given Dean an abbreviated version of the events that had led to her incarceration and escape.

Dean looked earnestly into her eyes. "I rather purposely lost track of you. It was too painful to face the truth. And the truth is I did love you, just not in the way you needed and deserved to be loved. I wasn't much more than a stupid kid then. I'm so sorry."

Lily focussed on the white tablecloth between them. "I'm to blame, too."

"None of it was your fault," Dean said.

Lily swallowed. "I could've given you a chance to explain. I didn't want to hear what your mother had to say, either."

"My mother," Dean shook his head. "It was so hard to face everyone, but especially her."

"Why is that?"

"You remember my parents were very religious, my mother in particular. Just like her parents and her grandparents and the whole extended family. Their beliefs were dictated by the doctrines of their church. And their entire social life was built around it. When you're in that deep, it's hard to change your thinking."

"Her religion regarded homosexuality as a sin?" Lily asked.

"An abomination, although these days, that religious organization is trying to back-peddle from their use of such strong words. Still opposing it, though."

"Did she ever question your sexual orientation?"

"Not directly. In high school, she was forever urging me to ask out nice girls from church. I lived with the hope that when the right woman came along, the feelings would magically blossom. As an only child, I was anxious to please my parents. They'd always wanted more children, but after two miscarriages, a hysterectomy ended that hope." Dean sighed. "They would have been overjoyed to have a grandchild. And for me, that would have been a miracle."

Lily bit her lower lip to stop her jaw from trembling.

"But it wasn't meant to be. I'd gone all the way through university without ever getting seriously involved with anyone. I dated a few girls, but it was never…"

"You mean I was your first?" Lily asked.

Dean nodded. "I may have led you to believe otherwise. We never really talked about it, did we?"

"In hindsight, there was a staggering lack of intimate communication."

"There are those who say it's not about gender, it's who you happen to fall in love with. I guess they're somewhere in the middle of the gay-straight spectrum. But others, like me, are closer to one end or the other. Years ago, I couldn't accept that, because I'd been taught to think of it as evil and shameful. It sounds naive now."

Lily lowered her eyes. "I'm sorry I reacted the way I did."

"You were angry. Not because I was gay, but because I'd deceived you. And married you! I knew you'd had at least one serious relationship that ended before we met. This may surprise you, but I was jealous of him."

"You felt threatened by someone who wasn't even on the scene anymore?"

Dean nodded. "I was afraid he'd show up again and steal your heart."

"But why did you even want me?"

"I thought you might be my 'cure'. That first time we were together it was..." Dean's cheeks reddened, "quite... nice. I felt like I'd walked on water. I wanted to show you off. 'Look at me, I finally have a girlfriend!' I was in love with an idea. I wanted to hurry up and marry you so it wouldn't go away, like... maybe I could fan that ember of attraction and it would grow into a real fire. Once we decided to get married, my mother was thrilled and everyone was so encouraging, I ignored my instincts and got swept straight to the altar."

"And then reality set in," Lily stated solemnly. She felt the last small vestige of resentment she'd held on to all those years evaporate. "If I'd been a little older and wiser, I'd have known you weren't all in from the beginning."

"The honeymoon was when it really hit me. I tried to block my doubts, but I felt like such a failure."

"Then you met that handsome tourist. Vince. Did you two..."

"No. We just talked. He helped me take an honest look at my life. Meeting Vince served to reignite all those suppressed feelings, but nothing more happened, not then or after you left. I had enough to feel guilty about."

"Did you ever find a special someone?"

"I was in a relationship for five years. Long story for another time. Truth is, I'm too busy to get involved with anyone at the moment. How about you? Or did I scar you forever?"

"Short term dating. Nothing serious. I get wrapped up in my work, too." She made a conscious effort to breathe. "And family."

"You Mullalys always were a tight bunch," Dean said. "I thought you'd have kids of your own by now."

Lily took a deep breath. "How are your parents with the whole gay thing now?" she asked.

"They understand that this is how I'm wired and it doesn't make me any less decent or deserving of the same happiness and rights as anyone else. And they've broken from that church. It was a painful but enlightening process, and they're much happier now. But there are others on both sides of the family whose minds are still slammed shut. They pat themselves on the back for being so *tolerant*."

Lily nodded and searched for her next words. And her courage.

Eric noticed a sudden influx of patrons. He checked his watch. The show was over and some of the hotel guests were stopping in for a nightcap. Other audience members were probably on their way to the parking garage. *The parking garage*! Eric abruptly left the bar and hurried into the lobby. He ventured a quick peek at the lounge and spotted Beryl, still slouched in the chair, her gaze trained on the elevator corridor. Neither the front desk nor the smaller elevator to the parking garage were visible from her vantage point.

Eric retrieved the envelope containing the GPS tracker and ripped it open as he descended in the elevator to the parking garage. One level down, he stopped and looked around. He needed a pickup or, better yet, an unlocked car. As he watched, a white Honda Accord rounded the corner, heading for the exit. The driver's window was down, a grey-haired gentleman at the wheel with a woman in the passenger seat. As Eric hailed the driver, he was recalling the sleight of hand tricks he used to practise as a kid. Most of them involved an element of misdirection. Maybe he could perform one more feat of magic.

The car slowed and the man eyed him warily.

"I'm looking for my son," Eric said, bending so that his face was level with the window. "He's seven years old, wearing a Toronto Blue Jays cap and a red jacket. Have you seen him?"

"No, sorry," replied the man, whose expression turned to one of concern.

The woman beside him leaned in to squint at Eric's face. "Oh, you must be frantic. When did you last see him?"

"Just five minutes ago," Eric said. "See that sign right there by the elevators?" They both followed his finger to look forward and to the right at the large sign on the wall ahead of them. At the same, Eric slipped his other hand through the window and dropped the GPS tracker behind the seat. "He was waiting there for my wife to come down the elevator."

"Maybe he went back up to the lobby," the man suggested.

"You know, you're probably right," Eric said. "I just panicked. Sorry to bother you."

"Children should never be left unattended," the woman lectured.

"You're right. Poor judgement on my part," Eric said, his voice hurried, but sufficiently humble. "Safe trip, folks." He jogged to the elevator, pressed the up button and waved to the couple as they drove slowly past.

Back in the lounge, Beryl was studying her phone, irritated and perplexed. The signal had disappeared completely. She wondered if the battery had died or been removed or destroyed. Or perhaps it was now in an area that was blocking the signal. Her eyes darted around the lobby, then back to her phone. Suddenly, she was on her feet. The signal was back and the target was moving away from the hotel. Eric watched from behind a tall planter of greenery as Beryl flew to the garage elevator and pounded the down button repeatedly.

"Almost too easy," he said to himself as the elevator doors closed and she vanished from sight.

She couldn't stall any longer. Lily's toes were at the edge of the precipice and she was staring down at the void. "There's something I need to tell you," she heard herself say. She looked through the restaurant window to the barren patio beyond. "I know it's a bit chilly, but could we go out there?"

"Sure." Dean rose from his chair and together, they navigated around tables to the patio doors, leaving their untouched wine behind.

The air outside was crisp and a light breeze ruffled their hair. Lily led him to a corner away from the windows. She inhaled deeply, then let out her breath, watching it fog between them.

Dean stuffed his hands in the pockets of his jeans. "You're starting to scare me a little."

Lily leaned her back against the wall. "You may want to sit down," she said pointing at the low stone wall beside them.

"I'll be fine. Tell me."

"You and I..." Lily looked him in the eye, "we have a daughter together."

Several seconds of silence followed as Dean slowly brought his hands to his head. "What?"

"I got pregnant in St. Kitts. Beginner's luck. I had the baby the following July."

Dean's legs crumpled and he sank to his knees in front of Lily, hands still pressed to the sides of his head, his mouth ajar.

"Should've sat down," Lily said softly. She helped him to his feet and they seated themselves on the wall. "I don't deserve your understanding, but I hope you'll listen anyway."

Dean stared straight ahead, his face suspended in shock.

"I'd cut myself off from you and I figured what you didn't know wouldn't hurt you. Actually, I didn't think I'd get away with it for long, but as time went on and nothing happened, I simply avoided dealing with it. When people outside the family became aware of the baby, I was evasive. My daughter… I mean our daughter… thinks I used a sperm donor. And that's how I tried to think of you."

Dean slowly turned his head to look at Lily. "I'm a father?"

Lily nodded. "My family was ambivalent about going along with the whole thing, but I used my pain and neediness to convince them to keep my secret. Each day turned into another and we let time pass. Then came the murder and the conviction and I felt like I'd lose her for good. Sorry doesn't cut it, but I *am* sorry."

"I'm a father!" Dean lowered his head and rubbed his temples.

"What's her name?"

"Jemma."

"Jemma. Is that for your parents, Jeff and Emma?'

"Yes. I moved back in with them and during my pregnancy I did some serious writing. Somehow, within the first two years of Jemma's life I managed to publish my first book and get the job with *Canadian Voice*. Are you alright?"

Dean was leaning forward, his head close to his knees. "A little light-headed." He sat up again. "I know you were hurting, but I had a right to know."

"It was unforgivable."

"This news, it's the most incredible thing I could ever imagine, but I can't believe how selfish and… and cruel you were to keep her from me all these years."

"I'm trying to do the right thing now," Lily said, her voice trembling.

Dean gave his head a shake. "I have so many questions, I …does she know about me?"

"Not yet."

"Where is she?"

"Here."

"What do you mean, *here*? Here in Toronto?"

"She's in a room at this hotel. I need to have a few minutes with her and then I was hoping you'd meet her tonight – since you're leaving tomorrow."

If Dean hadn't been sitting down, he might have crumpled a second time.

"I don't know what's going to be happening here in a week's time. Worst case scenario is that I could be back in prison by then, so I want to do this now while I have the chance." When Lily spoke again her voice was strained and tearful. "If she hates me over this, it'll kill me. I can't lose her."

Dean wrapped his arm around her. "Whatever mistakes have been made, I would never let that happen."

"Some people say *Halleluiah* is about a destructive relationship and some say it's about sex, but I think Leonard Cohen was deliberately vague about the meaning. He used phrases that sound really deep, but don't tell you what's he's thinking, because maybe he's not even sure – you know, like, what would rhyme with this and sound like poetry? Kind of like abstract art. A bunch of shapes and colours that look cool together, but you only get muddled ideas about what it could mean and everyone stares at it and says how great it is."

"You're saying his songs are pretentious?" Meredith asked, pressing the cool washcloth to her forehead. Forty-five minutes of listening to Jemma's over-stimulated rambling was proving to be exhausting.

"No, I just think…"

Meredith's phone jangled, finally signalling the end of their wait. She listened, responding, "Yes… fine… okay," and shoved it back in her pocket. "Your mother's on her way up," she informed Jemma.

Two minutes later there was a light tapping at the door and Jemma, who had been standing at the peep hole, jerked it open and threw herself into her mother's arms. They clung wordlessly to each other just inside the doorway while Meredith withdrew quietly into the bedroom. At last, Lily took Jemma's face between her hands, kissed her cheeks and then stood back to look her up and down. "I swear you've grown since I saw you. I've missed you so much."

"I love you, Mum."

"I hope you never stop feeling that way."

"Of course I won't! Why would you even say that?"

Lily took Jemma's hand and led her to the sofa. "There's something I have to tell you and it can't wait any longer." They sat facing each other. "First, I just want you to know that I love you with all my heart and I always will."

Jemma looked panicked. "What's wrong? Are you sick or something?"

"No, honey." Lily took a deep breath and felt her chin begin to quiver. "A long time ago I told you a big lie. I always meant to tell you the truth someday, but I didn't. I waited too long and couldn't bring myself to do it."

Jemma said nothing, but stared so intently at her mother, it made Lily wince.

"I was married very briefly when I was twenty-two. You are the product of that union. Your father broke down on our honeymoon and told me that he couldn't go on with the marriage because he was gay. I left and we never saw each other again. He didn't know about you."

Jemma continued to stare, her lips pressed hard together, but her countenance had changed. Her cheeks were flushed, her eyes were shining wet and her entire body seemed to vibrate.

"Aren't you going to say anything?" Lily asked softly. "Tell me that you despise me?" She waited and reached for Jemma's hand. "Or that you don't understand, but you still love me anyway?"

Jemma withdrew her hand. "How could you do that to me? All these years, when other kids talked about their fathers, I felt this huge emptiness. I felt second-rate."

"You never told me that."

"I didn't want you to feel bad. You'd given me life. A great life. How could I complain?"

"I'm so, so sorry, Jemma. It was a terrible thing to do, and I can never make it up to you, but starting tonight, I'm going to do whatever I can to make it better."

Jemma folded her arms, hands tightly gripping her elbows. "Who is this guy, this father of mine? And where does he live?"

"I'm going to let him tell you all those things in about five minutes."

Jemma shot to her feet. "He's *here*?" She took a few rapid steps across the room, then turned, hyperventilating and stared back at her mother. She caught sight of Meredith through the French doors and yanked them open. "And *you*! Have you known about this all along?"

Meredith lowered her eyes.

"I can't believe this! I should have known. Who goes looking for a sperm donor fresh out of university?"

"Tell me if you want to go ahead with this tonight. There won't be another chance for a while and I'd like to be here when it happens," Lily said. "But if you're not ready…"

Jemma, still seething, leaned against the wall and closed her eyes. "I'm ready."

Lily nodded at Meredith, who pulled out her phone and tapped in a number. She turned her back, spoke in a hushed tone and then began slipping on her shoes. "Eric and I will wait for you in the lobby, Lil," she said.

"No. I mean, would you stay here with us… please?"

"Sure, whatever you want."

Lily inhaled deeply and released a shaky breath. "Thank you. That doesn't say enough, but you know how much it means to me, right?"

Barrelling down the 401, travelling steadily away from Toronto, the black Tahoe kept pace with the white Honda Accord ahead of it. It was zipping in and out of traffic that was heavy with transport trucks, making it difficult for Beryl to keep it in view. But the GPS tracking device was doing its job and she felt confident Lily was in her sights.

They were heading east. Most likely, Beryl reasoned, on their way to Mullaly turf. Beryl's stomach growled, reminding her that she should have stashed some snacks in the vehicle. Suddenly she thought of the Milk Duds, the ones Lily had waved at her the last time they'd locked eyes. *Bitch.* Beryl drove on, tired and hungry, and starving for revenge.

Dean's pulse pounded as the door opened in front of him. There stood the blonde, brown-eyed version of Lily.

"Come in," she said quietly.

Somehow, Dean's feet moved, taking him over the threshold. His throat felt dry and a slow paralysis seemed to be invading his muscles.

Behind Lily, at the far end of the room, two figures stood, and as Lily drew him into their view, she stepped aside and spoke. “Dean, this is Jemma.”

Two sets of identical green eyes met and the space between them was instantly charged, sending a powerful wave of shock through Dean that left him light headed as it receded.

“It’s you!” His voice came out in a hoarse gasp and his hand found the wall as the weakness in his legs pitched him sideways.

Jemma stood, motionless, her eyes wide. Then her mouth gaped open. “Dean James?”

Lily, appropriately confused, stammered, “What... how...”

Meredith squeezed Lily’s arm, cutting her off. They watched as Dean straightened and took a shaky step toward his daughter. Jemma closed the space between them and he drew her into his arms.

Lily’s composure dissolved and she turned to Meredith, her eyes imploring.

“Let me explain,” Meredith said, tugging Lily into the bedroom.

When Dean finally released Jemma, he stood gazing at her, an arm’s length away. “I can’t believe it’s you,” he said, his voice quivering.

Jemma stared back and blinked. “I look like you. I’ve got a million questions. I don’t know where to begin.”

“Me, too,” Dean said. “I’m too shocked for words. In a wonderful, impossibly magical way.”

“Are you a well-educated man of English-Irish descent? That’s all I knew about my so-called sperm donor father.”

“I am.”

“At least she got that right,” Jemma muttered.

“Let’s not go there. It’s all too fresh.”

“I guess you’re kind of famous.”

“Only in a very small realm. And *you* – where did you learn to sing like that... *Ella*?”

Jemma grinned. “That was just my stage name for tonight.” Suddenly her face lit up. “My name! As your daughter, I would be Jemma James! What a great stage name!”

Dean took a deep breath. “Wow, this is actually starting to feel real." With a trembling hand, he smoothed an errant strand of hair into place along the side of Jemma's head. "I'm pretty sure your mother must have tried Jemma and James together when she chose your name."

"Then why didn't she put it on the birth certificate and, I don't know, maybe *tell* me about it?"

"You didn't answer my question. How is it you can sing like a pro?"

"Obviously, I got my natural talent from you."

"You've had training, too."

"For the past couple of years, I've been practising on my own and for four months now, I've had a voice coach. But tonight was my first time on stage."

"Have you always been interested in music?"

"Oh, yes! Mum taught me some piano. Then I got interested in the guitar and she bought me a Gibson J-45 acoustic."

"Serious guitar."

"I love it. The top is Sitka spruce and the sides and back are mahogany. It sounds incredible."

"They're beautiful instruments," Dean said. "I have a vintage SJ myself."

"Southern Jumbo? What year?"

"Fifty-two." Dean studied his daughter's face. "You're brilliant, just like your mother."

"I want you to teach me everything you know," Jemma said, ignoring the reference to Lily.

Meredith and Lily emerged from the bedroom and stood slightly apart from father and daughter.

Dean turned to Meredith while Jemma studiously avoided her mother's eyes. "Meredith, you've changed from Lily's kid sister to a beautiful woman. Thank you for arranging all of this."

"Glad I could help," Meredith said.

His attention shifted to Lily. "We need to talk about a custody arrangement. With Jemma's consent, of course."

"Yes," Lily said. "Jemma needs you. Just promise me she'll continue to be a regular part of the Mullaly family, too. None of us could bear a long separation."

"I promise." Dean looked at Jemma who had fallen quiet. "Tomorrow I'm leaving for a few days to attend my grandfather's funeral, but…"

"Take me with you!" Jemma interrupted. "They're my family, too, right?"

Dean cast a questioning look at Lily, who nodded, then turned away. "Alright then! How about if I pick you up at ten tomorrow? Could you be ready by then?"

"Yes!" Jemma exclaimed. Then quieter, "Dad."

Dean's face flushed pink. "You'll have to bring enough clothes for a week," he said, his words tumbling out quickly. "And school. What about school?"

"They already know I'm taking an extended break."

"We'll talk on the way to Saranac Lake," Dean said, still beaming. "We all have things to do before I pick you up." He rested his hands on Jemma's shoulders. "Please don't close your heart to her and your aunt. This has all happened suddenly, and you need to keep an open mind. I know you love them."

Jemma slid into his arms. "Are you sure you haven't done this father thing before?"

"Not in my wildest dreams," Dean said, and he kissed the top of her head.

Meredith was writing on a small card she'd taken from her bag. "My address," she said, handing it to Dean. "You'll have to stop just before the border to pick up Jemma's passport at her grandparents' house. I'll tell them you're coming."

Dean accepted the card, said his goodbyes and stepped out of the room. The hallway looked the same – the same floral carpet and taupe walls he'd navigated minutes ago, but his entire world had changed. He floated to the elevator, grinned excessively at the family of four grouped inside, and descended in a fog.

Beryl followed the white Honda Accord for an hour and twenty minutes all the way to Port Hope. When the car pulled into a driveway in a quiet neighbourhood, she slowed to a crawl. She was almost in front of the house when the passengers, who appeared to be about the same age as Lily's parents, made their way to the front door. But they weren't Lily's parents. They weren't anyone Beryl recognized at all.

The man turned to look at Beryl's vehicle as it slowly passed and then accelerated under his suspicious glare. In that instant, she understood. She'd been duped. Slamming the gas pedal, she squealed away, cursing at the unknown architect of her wild goose chase.

Passing through the downtown core, she spotted a bank and decided to pick up some cash at the ATM. She was light-headed from hunger and boiling with frustration. In this distracted state, she collected her money and walked away without her debit card. Realizing her mistake, she dashed back to the machine just in time to see it swallow the card. Beryl snapped. Her fury ignited an explosion of kicks and punches directed at the ATM. In weeks to come, the surveillance video would go viral on YouTube. But in that moment there'd been no thought of the future, only hunger and unmitigated rage.

CHAPTER

23

March 16

Brent is focussed on the image on his laptop as he makes some final touches. He zooms out to full screen. "There. What do you think? I made him Caucasian with a tan and put salt water sores on his arms and legs. That sick, skinny guy will never see this and it was well worth the hundred bucks I gave him."

"Yup. You look truly starved. You'll have to hide under baggy clothes, eh? Until it seems reasonable that you could've regained some weight."

"Meanwhile, I'll try to lose a little more. This picture will be seen far and wide after I'm rescued. It has to be convincing and so do I."

Lily's eyes opened slowly to weak morning light as her dream dissolved into consciousness.

It was beginning to slip away, as dreams will, and she held it while the details lingered. Brent... Photoshopping the image... paid some guy, someone who was thin, ill... talking to... who? Lily stared at the ceiling, replaying the voice, recalling the face. Ben. Ben, who died in the sinking, talking about... the faked rescue photo. What was her subconscious mind saying? Dreams are often weird, reviving the dead, ignoring sequence, altering facts. But… Ben and Brent discussing his rescue… before it happened?

Lily gasped, threw off her covers and ran to Kate's room. When her knock drew no response, she slipped inside, shook Kate's shoulder and plunked herself on the edge of the bed.

Startled from her sleep, Kate jerked to a sitting position. "Lily! You scared me half to death! What's wrong?"

"I just had an epiphany. Well, a dream."

"And you had to tell me at this hour?"

"Yes." Lily, fully awake now, spoke in a rush. "Sorry, but it just hit me. I've been so preoccupied with the Jemma and Dean issue that it didn't occur to me until now. Because of my dream."

"What?"

"That photo of Brent, the one he apparently Photoshopped? I think he faked more than that. He faked the entire tragedy!"

"You mean he staged the sinking?" Kate's eyes grew wide as another thought sank in. "Because he killed Ben!"

"I think they both staged it. Ben could be alive. Brent had his problems, but I can't imagine him as a killer."

"This is incredible!" Kate exclaimed. "Brent had a lot to gain from the publicity, but what was in it for Ben?"

"His biological brother and the wife, Nicole, are serving time for the Ponzi scheme. Maybe Ben was involved in that and was anticipating being linked to the crime. Or he had access to the money and wanted to get his hands on it while Richard and Nicole were locked up."

"But later, after convincing the world that Ben is dead, Brent falls for you, realizes he can't pull off the deception and decides to confess."

"Right," Lily said. "He contacts his brother first to give him fair warning and then arranges to meet with me to tell me everything. And then…"

Kate made the connection. "Ben murders him to shut him up! Can we go to the police with this?"

"No, not yet. We need proof and I'm not going to sit around in prison waiting for it." Lily stood up and began to pace. "This is wild. It never occurred to me that the whole sailing-the-Atlantic story was a lie!"

Sue had been quite certain she wouldn't be followed in her borrowed car, but she'd taken the precaution of making several stops along the route to monitor the traffic around her. The street was empty when she picked Lily up at Clair's front gate. After an exuberant greeting, they headed west out of Rosedale.

"Meredith told me all about last night," Sue said. "How are you doing?"

"Oh, Sue, it all had to happen the same night. It was like ripping off a bandage really fast."

"It must have been hard."

"Dean and Jemma are thrilled with each other, but Jemma is none too happy with me. Apparently, she can sing quite well," Lily said. "Meredith she says she got all of it on her camcorder."

"Maybe you'll be the mother of a rock star someday."

Lily laughed. "Let her dream. She'll be grown up all too soon."

Sue glanced sideways at her. "I can't believe how different you look."

"I hope I don't have to fool too many people with this disguise."

"The only people we should see at Brent's house are the lawyer and the caretaker, but are you sure this is a good idea?"

"I need to get inside the house to look for that letter. In my reading with Abby, she said there was something important about the house."

"Lily, do you seriously believe in that psychic baloney?"

"I don't know what to think anymore. I know it sounds crazy, Sue, but she knew so much about my life."

"Clair might have filled her in."

"She didn't tell her anything. And get this – she made a pain in my neck disappear."

"Power of suggestion."

"Perhaps. I was as skeptical as you are, but I can't explain what she did."

Sue shook her head. "A few years ago, one of our authors wrote a book about unmasking the psychic business – mediums, televangelists and faith healers – anyone who profits from the suffering and gullibility of others. It covered everything from the obvious scams of spiritualism in the nineteenth century to the more sophisticated operations today. There are all kinds of tricks."

"I know," Lily said. "But Abby isn't using any technical tricks or researching me or having an assistant go through my coat pockets."

"Mediums use 'cold readings' – highly probable guesses by analyzing your appearance, speech and mannerisms. They ask a lot of questions and throw out vague information and watch your reaction. When they get a hit, they pursue it, and they move on quickly from the misses. It's all about deductive reasoning, quick thinking and a sense of psychology."

"Either Abby has some psychic ability or she's a very lucky guesser. She may not be a medium, but I don't believe she's a fraud."

"Some so-called mediums aren't aware that they're actually using cold reading."

"Anyway, Abby said that I should 'take hold of the reins and step into the arena myself,' and that's what I'm doing today."

"That's a mixed metaphor," Sue commented dryly.

"Hey, she's *ninety-nine.* I think she expresses herself remarkably well. Meredith is all excited about making her the subject of their next documentary film."

They drove in silence for a few minutes and then Sue said, "Lily, if you never want to write this book, I can accept that." She waited a beat. "But it would make one hell of a story."

Mark watched the surveillance video, noting any potential matches for the vehicle Lily had seen within a one-hour time frame before and after the murder. Suddenly he leaned toward the screen and focussed on the image. "Oh, man!" he mumbled. He was looking at the side view of a light-coloured sedan with a triangular piece of fabric protruding from the bottom of the rear door. He clicked on the back arrow until the vehicle entered the frame and watched as it moved across the deserted school parking lot and came to a stop. It was a Ford Focus, not Kristie's car, as he had anticipated. He couldn't quite make out the entire plate number, but some good image processing equipment might do the trick.

The parking lot was several blocks from the Baines house and the time indicated on the recording placed it there twelve minutes after Lily's estimated arrival. Mark continued watching the video, but no one got out of the car. The lone occupant was indistinct and the visor was down. After several seconds, the vehicle pulled away and entered the street.

A stocky, clean shaven man was leaning against a black sports car in front of the Baines home.

"That must be Ryan Cross," Sue said as she pulled up behind him. "And check it out. He drives a Crossfire." She snickered.

Next to him stood a much larger man, biceps and pecs bulging beneath a tight shirt.

"Crap! That's Drew Fowler, the neighbour who tackled me right here in the driveway!" Lily hissed.

"You don't look like the Lily he saw, but stay here for now. I'll run interference."

Ryan moved toward Sue as she opened her door. Lily shuffled things around and reached into the back seat, pretending to search for something.

"Would you be Ryan Cross?" Sue asked, extending her hand.

"I am," he said, giving her a firm handshake.

"Sue Emerson."

Drew shuffled closer and introduced himself as the neighbour who'd captured Lily. "I'd be happy to answer any questions about what happened here," he said.

"Thank you. Perhaps another day? Our time is short today." Sue dismissed him with a polite smile.

Lily emerged from the car, dark glasses firmly in place. Drew glanced at her as she opened the trunk and began rummaging around inside, then he said goodbye and strolled away.

"This is Kate Young," Sue said, introducing Lily to Ryan when she finally arrived at their side, camera in hand.

Ryan smiled and shook her hand.

"We appreciate this opportunity to see the house," Sue said. "In addition to taking a few photos, we'd like to look around."

"Fine with me," Ryan said, smiling. "My mother told me you're curious about the rumoured letter that was left by Brent, but the police checked and nothing was ever found. But have a look. I can give you forty-five minutes, then I have to be on my way."

Lily felt her hope deflate. She'd thought they'd have more time.

"The caretaker's been packing up the contents of the house for an auction sale next month. The place finally sold, but it doesn't close until May. I'll be glad when it's done. Brent's ex and her hubby are breathing down my neck."

"Anxious to get their hands on the money?" Sue asked.

"Oh, yeah. And accusing me of siphoning cash from some imagined fortune Brent had stashed away. But actually, aside from the house, there was very little. Anyway, the Newells are dying to get in here and grab anything of value. Brent saw that coming and his will is very specific about how and when BJ will get his inheritance."

"How long has the caretaker been here?"

"About five weeks. First thing I did when the police were finished with the house was make an inventory of the contents. Then I hired a security company to do regular checks on the place, but when it finally sold, I arranged for a caretaker to live here until the closing. I neglected to tell him we were coming and his truck is gone, but if he shows up, I'll explain what's going on." Ryan took a key from his pocket. "Follow me." He unlocked the door and led them inside. "I suppose you'll want to see *the* spot. We'll start there."

When they arrived at the kitchen, Ryan pointed to an area on the floor. "Different tile now, otherwise it's unchanged. The body was right here," he said, pointing. "Partly on his side, feet angled in this direction."

Lily shuddered, remembering all too well.

"I want to check on a few things while I'm here, so go ahead and look around. I'll be out back if you have any questions."

When Ryan left, Lily removed her sunglasses and slipped them into her jacket pocket. "Let's be quick. You take photos and search down here while I look around upstairs. I've never been up there."

"Okay."

The handsome staircase that led to the second floor was bordered by a railing on one side and an elegantly panelled wall on the other. As Lily ascended, she examined the panels, looking for indications that one of them might be hinged. At the top, she noticed that several boxes and some furniture lined the hallway. She entered the master bedroom. It had been stripped bare. The closet was empty and the bed had been dismantled and left in the middle of the room. A cursory check revealed nothing.

As she exited the room, she noticed a broad, retractable wooden ladder that led to an opening in the ceiling at the end of the hall. Several boxes sat on the floor beneath it. She walked down the hall, climbed the first four steps and poked her head through the opening. Lily gasped. A woman was kneeling over a trunk, inches from Lily's face.

"Aaaa!" the woman shrieked as she spun around.

"Sorry, I didn't mean to frighten you," Lily apologized.

"Who are you?" the woman demanded.

"I'm a writer. I'm working on a book about Brent Baines and I've been given access to the house. Mr. Cross is outside if you want to check." Lily realized that her sunglasses were not in place, but at least she was wearing the brown contact lenses.

The woman stared at her. "Oh," she said finally. "Let me come down and introduce myself."

Lily backed down the attic steps and the woman followed.

"Way up there, I didn't hear anyone come in. I'm Hannah, the caretaker's fiancée. I'm helping him pack things up." Hannah wiped a hand on her jeans and offered it to Lily.

"Kate Young. Nice to meet you," Lily said, shaking her hand, "and congratulations on your engagement. Is it recent?"

"Just a few days ago. I told Leo he has one week to put a ring on it or I go on strike!" Hannah laughed, wiggling the fingers of her left hand.

Lily detected a faint German accent and noticed that she bore an uncanny resemblance to Vanna White, the Wheel of Fortune celebrity.

"It looks like you've made a dent in it."

"We have about four weeks left to clean and organize everything," Hannah said, smoothing her long hair into place.

Lily looked away from the penetrating brown eyes. She fished in one of her pockets for the glasses with the fake lenses, then focussed on the box near her feet. A paperback at the top caught her attention and she picked it up. "*Adrift.* Seventy-six days lost at sea." It was the book she'd told Brent about, the one she'd said reminded her of his experience. And now, she realized, the one from which he'd borrowed to fabricate his own story.

Hannah studied her expression. "What is it?"

"Just a book I read a long time ago." Lily put it back in the box. "Well, I've only got a few minutes to look around. I was told the office is up here somewhere."

"Yes, yes," Hannah said. "Let me show you. We haven't done much with that room yet."

Hannah led Lily down the hall to the large room at the back of the house. "This used to be the senior Mr. Baines' bedroom, but after he died, his son turned it into the office."

"I see," Lily said. "Look, I don't want to keep you from your work, so..."

"Oh, believe me, I can use the break."

Lily walked slowly around the room perusing the furnishings and walls. Like Clair's house, this one had an intercom system and Brent's desk was positioned close to the wall-mounted speaker.

"Just being among his possessions gives us a strong sense of his presence," Hannah said.

"I'm sure it does." Lily bent to inspect what looked like a computer screen.

"That's a portable home monitor. Apparently, in the last year or so that the father was alive, he started wandering off and falling down, so Brent had a system installed." Hannah pushed a button and Lily watched as a series of squares appeared, each displaying a different view. She tapped on the bottom right square and a live image of Ryan Cross walking alongside the empty pool filled the screen. "That way, he could keep tabs on him. Personally, I'm guessing he got more use out of it recording his sexual encounters and spying on his girlfriend's kid.

"Did you know Brent?" Lily asked, moving away.

"No, but stories get around. The neighbours have told Leo some interesting things."

Lily was staring at one of Brent's framed photographs. This particular photograph, taken from behind, showed a man sitting in a beach chair under a palm tree, gazing out at a tropical sunset. She moved closer and read the title that had been penciled in on the mat board. *Escape to Paradise.* A subtitle written smaller below it read, *gazing west.*

A companion piece hung a short distance away on the same wall. It too, depicted a tropical scene, this one of a sailboat moored peacefully in a blue lagoon. On the deck stood a solitary man, his back to the camera and one hand resting on the boom. It was titled simply, *Getaway.* It, too, had a subtitle, *gazing north.*

Lily felt a tingle of excitement. Brent's framed photos. Could these be the works of art, the "pretty paintings" Abby had glimpsed? She studied the photographs closely, but there were no distinctive landmarks or signs that might give away the locations. It could be any place where palm trees grew and the sea was vivid blue. She tipped first one frame, then the other, away from the wall and looked behind them. Nothing was fastened to the back of the pictures, but it was apparent that the paper backing had been cut, then reattached with masking tape.

"If you're looking for the mysterious note that Brent Baines left, the police have already looked there," Hannah said. "We found that every photograph and painting has had its backing cut."

"Guess they took Lily Mullaly's story seriously after all," Lily said.

"Is your book going to support the idea that she was the killer?"

Lily carefully released the frame she was holding and went back to studying the scenes in the photos. "We're not planning to draw any conclusions, just present the facts," she said.

The next time Hannah spoke she was standing next to Lily. "If you ask me, I think it's possible that Brent's fiancée got away with murder."

"Really? And do you think there could still be a letter somewhere in this house?"

"Oh, sure. We'll be going through every inch of this place. If we find something, Mr. Cross wants us to hand it over to him in exchange for a big reward." In a hushed voice she added, "*Five grand!* But we would turn it over to the police instead."

Lily looked her directly in the eyes. "Oh, really!"

Hannah was suddenly flustered. "I shouldn't have said anything. Please don't mention this to him. He'd fire Leo. I… I think he's just concerned about Brent's reputation. I'm sure he wouldn't hold back any important information."

"You should make a photocopy before you turn it in." Lily hesitated. "I don't suppose… um, if you did find something, you could let me know? My book would likely be published before police ever got around to releasing new information. And I'm sure my publisher would match the reward."

"Certainly. Give me your phone number and I'll get in touch if we find anything."

"Thanks, I'll do that." Lily printed both Kate's cellphone and Clair's landline numbers on note paper she found on the desk and handed it to Hannah. Then she returned to her examination of the photograph.

"You know these places?"

"No. They're beautiful, though." Lily looked again at the titles on the mats, then to the signatures. Both were signed B. Baines. His other framed photographs had been signed Brent Baines. A simple variation?

Her eyes travelled to the left side of the mat where the photo was neatly numbered and immediately she recognized the anomaly. Most of Brent's gallery photos had been printed in round-numbered quantities – usually twenty or, at most, fifty. Oddly, this print was numbered, *17/1167*. It wasn't the kind of thing a casual viewer was likely to notice.

Moving to the photograph on the right, she checked the small pencilled numbers. This one was labelled *61/8500*. She stepped back and looked at the overall presentation of the photos – the tropical locations, the titles, the signatures, the strange numbers. And that's when it hit her. Those numbers weren't referencing a quantity of prints, they were map coordinates! And B. Baines wasn't Brent, it was Ben. Brent was telling the alert viewer that his brother had escaped to paradise, made his getaway. Ben's words played back to her. *Greetings from paradise, Brent. Beautiful, eh?* The photo of the sailboat that was subtitled gazing north was on the left. This would represent the latitude, since latitude was always noted to the left of longitude. Lily memorized the coordinates: *17.1167 degrees north, 61.8500 degrees west.*

This revelation had transpired in less than a minute, but it was long enough to prompt another comment from Hannah. "You are intrigued by those pictures."

Lily realized she was smiling. "I am. I was just wondering if I might be able to pick them up for a reasonable sum at the auction sale."

"Perhaps you could make a deal with Mr. Cross before the sale," Hannah suggested.

"Good idea," Lily said. "I should probably go. My publisher is waiting downstairs." She turned to Hannah. "If you find anything you'll let me know, right?"

"I promise. Good luck with the book, Kate. I can't wait to read it."

"Thanks," Lily said as she left the office. "Sorry again about the scare."

They parted in the hallway and Lily descended the stairs. On her way through the living room, she glimpsed Ryan through the window. He was standing in the driveway, engaged in conversation with a man wearing wraparound sunglasses and a blue cap. Leo, she guessed. She found Sue in the den, sliding books around on a built-in shelf. "This is pretty hopeless," Sue said, stepping down from the chair she'd been standing on. "How did you do?"

"Oh, alright," Lily replied. Then she cracked a big smile. "I know where Ben is."

"What? You're kidding! Lily, how?"

"I found map coordinates on Brent's photographs. I'll tell you all about it on the way home."

They reached the front door at almost the same time as Ryan. "Sorry I have to rush you out of here," he said. "Did you get your pictures?"

"Yes, thank you," Sue said graciously.

The sunny weather had worked to Lily's advantage – her dark sunglasses were back in place as they parted ways with Ryan. Leo was gone, but his truck was parked behind Sue's car. Ryan pulled out of the driveway first and Sue followed, driving slowly out of the neighbourhood, as she listened, spellbound, to Lily's account of her discovery.

At the third stop sign, she turned to stare at her friend. "I take back what I said about being okay with you not writing the book."

Every time Jemma called him Dad, Dean felt his stomach do a little somersault. They were travelling east on the 401, just twenty minutes from the Thousand Islands Parkway and the US border.

"Did you know my grandparents very well? The Mullalys I mean, not *your* parents," Jemma laughed.

"Not really. I met them only once before the wedding. They're very nice."

"They're amazing. I just don't get how they could keep me from you."

"Maybe they loved you too much to imagine you spending half your life far away with some guy who'd ripped your mother's heart out," Dean said. "When we get to your grandparents' place we're not going to have that discussion. For now, just get your passport and let them know you love them."

"Okay, Dad. You're right."

"Memorize those words," Dean said.

"You're off to a good start, but don't let it go to your head." Jemma's playful smirk melted into a smile. "You know it's so weird. In a way, I feel like I've known you forever."

"I feel the same. It's like you're a piece of me that I didn't know I was missing."

Dean glanced at Jemma. Had he not been driving, he would have stared. He could scarcely believe that she – his progeny, his daughter – was sitting right there beside him! Mere hours ago, she'd materialized in his life almost fully grown. He thought of those magic grow-a-dinosaur toys, the tiny capsules you drop into a container of water and leave until they've expanded about six times in size to resemble the surprise creature promised on the package. Dean had unwittingly walked away from the tiny cluster of cells that was to become Jemma and had missed the miracle of her expansion. Not just her birth or the first smile, steps and words, but all the ordinary moments that reveal themselves in scraped knees and slumber parties and school field trips and birthday cakes. The simple act of holding your child's hand in the grocery store or seeing the wonder in her eyes when she discovers some exciting new thing in her world. He'd missed it all.

As though on cue, Jemma said, "We have loads of pictures of me growing up. And Mum took a bazillion home movies. I'm going to make you watch every one of them. I want to see all your pictures and stuff, too."

Dean grinned. "I'm sure my mother will be more than thrilled to show you the minutia of my childhood and career that she's collected."

"Your parents are going to be blown away when they meet me."

Dean felt his stomach flutter and he grinned at Jemma. "They'll be over the moon! And Gramma too, Jem. You'll lift her spirits."

"I'm nervous."

"That's normal. *I'm* nervous about the song I have to perform at the funeral. It might be too emotional for me."

"What song?" Jemma asked, ears perked.

"*I'll Be Seeing You.* It's from the thirties. One of Grandpa's favourites." He sang a bar.

"I've heard it before, but I don't know it well." There was a gleam in Jemma's eyes. "I'm a quick study, though. What if the two of us were to sing it together?"

Dean stared at her. "Seriously?

"Yeah, let's go for it! We've got four hours to make it perfect. We'll rock that place! Oh," Jemma said, instantly sober. "Almost forgot. It's a funeral, and it's not about us. Sorry, I don't know your family, so it doesn't feel real to me yet."

"You *will* know them. I've written an extra verse that I hope will be a touching tribute. And a duet would be beautiful."

Jemma nodded. "Teach me."

"Okay, one line at a time. First listen, then sing it back and then we'll work on harmonies and nuances. Hmm. I could lower the key so that you can take the lead an octave higher on the second verse or I could modulate the melody between verses so it'll transition to a key in your best vocal range. *Or* we could–"

"Dad," Jemma interrupted.

"What?"

"To quote the Dixie Chicks, shut up and sing."

Dean laughed and the familiar crimson flush tinted his cheeks. "Okay." He launched into the melody.

CHAPTER

24

Beryl was discouraged. She'd driven back to her brother's apartment in the wee hours of morning and slept in late. A sense of trepidation had crept in at the memory of the damage she may have inflicted to the keypad of the ATM the previous night. The way the screen had flickered and then gone black – that couldn't be good. The hunt for Lily had hit a dead end.

Now she was contemplating her next move. Lily was here in Toronto. She was sure of it. She could go back to the Chandler Hotel, but someone had discovered the GPS tracker and that meant Lily would have cleared out of there by now.

Beryl picked up her brother's car keys from the hall table. Time to switch it up again. She'd go back to the stakeouts until she came up with a better plan.

The anticipation among the four women gathered around Clair's computer was palpable.

"How did you know these were map coordinates, Lily?" Kate asked.

"You've probably seen geographical coordinates written as DMS – degrees, minutes and seconds. Since the earth is almost twenty-five thousand miles around, each degree is many miles apart. Adding minutes and seconds makes it more precise. But degrees are often written simply as whole numbers with decimals. The more decimals, the more exact the location."

"How precise are the coordinates you have here?" Clair asked.

"Very. Four decimal points might even narrow it down to a single building. Based on the bearings – north of the equator and west of the prime meridian – and based on the tropical scenes in the photographs, we should be looking somewhere in the Caribbean."

Lily pulled up a Google Map and within a minute she'd zeroed in on the back yard of a property in the town of St. John's, Antigua.

Sue uttered a little gasp. "You nailed it!"

"Maybe," Lily said. She minimized the page and typed "coordinates of St. John's, Antigua" in a new search bar. "I want to see what result someone would get if they were to look up the location of St. John's." A moment later she had her answer: 17.1167N, 61.8500W. "Same. That's what I was afraid of," she said. "Brent got these bearings online. He was telling us that Ben is in the St. John's area, but not exactly where."

"Why is that?" Kate wondered aloud.

"Maybe he didn't know."

"Why do you suppose Brent left this cryptic message to begin with?" Clair asked.

Lily leaned back in her chair. "I suppose Ben came up with a scheme to abscond with the millions from the Chicago scam and Brent went along with it for whatever reason. Maybe it helped to assuage his guilt over Ben always getting the short end of the stick. Brent was the biological son, and he was gifted, successful and handsome. Ben was… not."

"And it would've removed Ben from his life once and for all," Kate added.

"Exactly," nodded Lily. "Also, this would have been a financial gain for Brent. He could have lost a half share in the house, which

I'm guessing is worth three to four million, if Ben decided to proceed with the challenge to their father's will. And I'm sure Brent anticipated the media attention and subsequent opportunities that would follow his dramatic escape from death.

"But I think when it was all done, Brent may have regretted his involvement or felt some remorse. And he may have feared his brother and anticipated trouble. I think he wanted the truth about Ben to come out if something bad were to happen."

"By 'bad' you mean murder," Sue said. "And then you came along."

Lily sighed. "Once Brent and I got involved, his lies started crashing down on him. I believe he communicated with Ben, then…"

"Because?" Kate interrupted.

"Perhaps he felt that he at least owed Ben a warning, a chance to either turn himself in or disappear."

"And then Brent wrote something explaining what happened and hid it."

"We don't know when he wrote it. Could have been recently or a long time ago. Perhaps he wanted it to be found, but not by the wrong person. He wouldn't want it lying around in plain sight."

Sue sank onto a nearby chair. "Wow. Now what? Is it time to go to the police?"

"No," Lily said. "We're not even certain Ben is in Antigua. He may have moved on by now. And the evidence we have doesn't really prove much. I'd end up back in prison and this whole mess could drag on."

"Well, at least you're on the right track," Clair said.

Lily swivelled around in her chair. "To quote my mother, who is fond of quoting Will Rogers, 'Even if you're on the right track, you'll get run over if you just sit there'." She paused. "I'm going to Antigua."

"That's crazy!" Sue exclaimed.

"Let's just call your father and get some legal advice," Kate said.

"Hear me out. This is my problem and I'm the one who needs to fix it. I'm motivated to find Ben more than anyone in law enforcement and I trust my instincts. I could pass myself off as Kate."

Sue shook her head. "You'd have a stopover in the US which means you'd have to go through preclearance in Toronto."

"I use a Nexus card when I cross into the States," Kate said. "A retinal recognition scan is used for ID."

"I can do it the regular way. Is your hair styled the same in your passport photo?"

"Yes, but…"

Lily held up her hand to silence them. She turned to Clair. "I could do this through my parents, but I don't want to alert them or the police to the fact that I'm accessing my account. I have some money left from the sale of my house, so I would pay you back."

"Of course, my dear, anything you need,"

Eventually a consensus was reached. Lily would book a flight for the next day. She extracted promises from the others to keep her mission a secret, at least until she was out of the country and promised to make contact with them at predetermined times. Now, having seized the reins, Lily felt that she had some control of her destiny. It would be an interesting ride.

At a loss for any new ideas, Beryl had been cruising the neighbourhoods where Mark and Meredith lived. She was rounding Mark's block when she spotted him walking east. At the end of the street, Mark turned left and Beryl moved forward in pursuit. She slowed near the corner in time to see him lope to the other side. He continued walking north, then looked back and raised his arm. A taxi slowed to a stop and Mark boarded it. Quickly, Beryl darted out into the traffic and took her place a few cars behind him. She was driving her brother's crappy car again and for once she was glad. Beryl was able to keep the taxi in sight all the way to the corner at Eglinton Avenue until a red light brought them to a halt.

She cussed as Mark disembarked and walked down Eglinton. Most likely, he was changing taxis which meant he was almost certainly on his way to see Lily. The light changed and Beryl turned right onto Eglinton. As she rounded the corner, she spotted Mark heading east ahead of her. She passed him and turned into a laneway then zipped ahead until she found a place where she could turn around. By the time she arrived back at the lane entrance, he was on her right, not too far ahead, flagging down another taxi. She waited. The taxi stopped. Mark got in.

Beryl forced her way into traffic, eliciting a honk and a nasty gesture. She stayed close as the taxi turned south onto Mt. Pleasant Road, then backed off when the street stretched away from the business area and opened to parkland and residential settings. They had travelled about three kilometres when the taxi turned into the Rosedale neighbourhood. Beryl's senses were suddenly on high alert.

Hanging back just enough, she tailed Mark down twisting streets, deeper into Rosedale until the taxi slowed and turned into the driveway of a beautiful stone mansion. She drove by as Mark was paying the driver, then turned around and parked a short distance from the property. By the time she'd made her way back to the house, the taxi had departed and Mark was standing at a side entrance. The yard was enclosed by high iron picket fencing erected between a series of stone pillars. She stopped at one of the pillars and peeked through the bare vines that had woven themselves through the fence.

As Beryl watched, the side door opened and a blonde woman appeared. Mark began to step inside, but before the door could close, a small, ginger-haired dog darted out and began barking and bouncing about the front yard. Mark walked toward it, calling, "Jinx! Come here, boy!"

The dog spun around in a circle and then raced toward the street as Mark moved in its direction. The woman followed and soon both of them were giving chase. Finally, the woman said, "Mark, stay there. You're the one he's teasing." She moved slowly toward the front gate where Jinx was looking back, panting. As she drew closer, Beryl experienced a flash of recognition that jarred her memory of the previous night. Could this be the woman from the restaurant at the Chandler Hotel? She'd seen her only in profile, but the short, highlighted hair was quite distinctive and the facial features were so… familiar.

"Jinx, want a treat?" The woman moved closer and Jinx backed away. "Come here, you little turd brain."

Beryl moved slightly to get a better look. The woman was

crouched down about twenty paces away and suddenly she knew. She was looking at Lily Mullaly.

A twig snapped underfoot as she drew in her breath and stepped back behind the pillar. Jinx heard the sound and tore away from Lily. Beryl quickly turned her back to the fence and began walking toward her vehicle as he charged down the sidewalk behind her.

"I'll get him!" Mark shouted and Beryl heard his footsteps as he came pounding along the pavement. She was doing her best to ignore the dog who trailed her, barking furiously. Mark scooped Jinx up in his arms and called after her. "Sorry about that."

Beryl kept moving, but turned her head slightly and said, "No problem."

When she was sure Mark was out of sight, Beryl returned to her car and, with a cackle of elation, pulled out her phone.

Back at the house, Lily scolded Jinx who looked at her with remorseful eyes. She sighed and gave him a biscuit. She glanced at Mark who'd gone very quiet. "What?"

"When you were near the front gate, did you see the woman Jinx was chasing pass by the driveway?" Mark asked.

"I didn't see anyone."

"I could be wrong, but she looked an awful lot like the cop who was following me a week or so ago."

Kate entered the room just as Lily's face took on a panicked expression. "What's wrong?"

"Hi Kate," Mark said, then tore his eyes away from her and looked back at his sister. "The police may have tracked me here."

"Mark, did you take the usual precautions?"

"Absolutely. I didn't get a good look at her face, but it's pretty hard to miss an Amazon like that."

"Amazon? Could this be the person Eric saw in the lobby last night? What exactly did she look like?"

"Tall, big-boned, hefty. Um... short, light brown hair, aviator style sunglasses, black leather jacket."

Images of Beryl formed in Lily's head. "No, it can't be," she murmured.

"Let's see if she's still out there," Kate said and she was already moving. "We have a good view of the street from a window upstairs."

Crammed into the driver's seat of her brother's small car, Beryl was on the phone with a Toronto Police Service dispatcher. "Tell them not to come blaring up to the house with their sirens on. She doesn't know… what? I don't know the number, but… no, I didn't notice the street name. I was busy watching the damn vehicle." Beryl opened the car door and jogged to the corner where the street sign was posted. Huffing into her phone, she walked slowly back to the car.

From the upstairs window Lily peered through the binoculars Kate had fetched at the figure approaching the car parked in front of the neighbour's house. "It's her! Beryl Sweeney. How the hell did she find me? And why is she even looking for me?" She adjusted the focus. "Looks like she's on the phone. She probably recognized me so I expect the police will be arriving soon.

"What are we going to do?" Kate fretted. "We could both leave right now. You could cut through the backyard and I could pick you up, but you'd have to get yourself over a high wall and through a neighbour's property."

"Beryl would see your car coming and block the driveway," Mark said, "and Lily wouldn't get far on foot in broad daylight. Any good hiding places here?"

"I have an idea," Kate said. "Trade tops with me, Lily. Hurry!"

Lily took off her long-sleeved blue and white striped top and Kate pulled her T-shirt over her head.

"Mark, go and find Gram. Tell her what's happening. I'm going to hide Lily."

Mark stood, transfixed and mouth slightly ajar, seemingly spellbound by Kate's lavender satin bra.

"Mark, go!" Lily shouted.

He ran from the room.

"We're both wearing similar jeans, so this could work," Kate said. "I'll go to the front door when the police arrive and tell them it was me out there chasing the dog. They need a warrant to come in here and look around, but if we don't let them in voluntarily, they'll put the house under surveillance until they get one."

Downstairs they ran into Mark, still talking to Clair.

"I'm going to delete some stuff on your computer and hide Lily's research material," Mark informed them as he left the room.

"And I'm hiding Lily," Kate said, tugging her in the opposite direction.

Clair remained at the bottom of the stairs, wringing her hands. Jinx trotted over to her.

"What have you done now?" she asked, eyeing the cotton batting that trailed from the object clamped between his teeth. It was a partially disembowelled toy cat, its stuffing protruding from a hole ripped in the belly seam. He lowered his head and rolled his eyes up at Clair, playfully daring her to scold him.

"This is all your fault!" she chided. "And look what you've done to poor Mittens!"

Jinx flipped the limp blob that used to be Mittens into the air and pounced on it, oblivious to the unfolding drama.

Kate led the way into the wing that housed the pool. The chlorine-scented air, warm and humid as it hit her lungs, transported Lily back in time to her childhood swimming lessons and she saw her five-year-old self, filled with excitement and trepidation, padding barefoot toward the pool. It was that exotic mix of anticipated fun and fear that triggered her memory whenever she entered the climate of an indoor pool. It kicked in again as she raced after Kate, but it was purely fear that flooded her senses this time.

"Over here," Kate said. She pointed to a narrow door that was recessed into the tile wall. Beside the door stood a tall, open cabinet that was filled, top to bottom, with neatly folded, fluffy white robes and towels. "This is a utility closet," Kate said. "If I push the cabinet in front of it, the door will be completely hidden behind the stacks of towels."

She opened the door and Lily stepped inside the cramped space between the sink and the cleaning supplies.

"I'll get rid of them as soon as I can," Kate assured her.

"Before I suffocate would be great."

"The door doesn't lock. You'll be fine." Kate closed the door and then pushed on the cabinet, putting all her weight behind it until it obscured the door. Stepping back, she assessed the wall. "Brilliant."

Kate found Mark and Clair standing at the living room window gazing at the street.

"That didn't take long," Mark said as, minutes later, a police cruiser turned into the driveway. "The curtain is rising. Ready Jinx? You're on."

Beryl flagged down the car at the gate. "I'm Beryl Sweeney, the one who called," she said.

Detective Krueger was in the passenger seat, with Alvarez at the wheel. "We have officers patrolling the neighbourhood and watching the rear of the property," Krueger told her. "How do you know it's Lily Mullaly?"

"I recognized her!" Beryl squawked, as though that's something he should have known. "She was in the front yard. I was the one transporting her when she escaped.

The detective frowned, started to speak, then thought better of it and signalled his partner to pull forward. Suddenly Jinx came charging out of the house with Mark on his heels. Kate stepped out after him onto the front lawn.

"That's her! In the striped top!" Beryl shouted and both officers got out of the patrol car and walked quickly toward Kate, who made no effort to run, but instead, shoved her hands casually into the pockets of her jeans.

Jinx charged the officers and yipped excitedly until Mark picked him up and carried him back into the house. The male officer held up his badge. "Detectives Krueger and Alvarez," he said and he looked closely at Kate's face, then at his partner who shook her head. "What is your name?"

"Kate Young. Is there a problem?"

Krueger turned and motioned to Beryl, who was still some distance away. As she came forward, he asked, "Is this the woman you saw?"

"Yes!" Beryl said with a self-satisfied smirk. "It's Lily Mullaly.

She's changed her appearance, but it's her and that," she said pointing at Mark, "is her brother."

Alvarez turned to Mark. "And your name is?"

"Mark Mullaly," he said. "And yes, I'm Lily's brother. But *she's* not here."

"We're responding to a call that your sister is on the premises. What is your relationship to this woman?" he asked, nodding to Kate.

"She's my girlfriend," Mark said, putting his arm protectively around Kate's waist.

Beryl started sputtering and all eyes turned in her direction. "B-but I… I could have sworn it was her. I followed him," she said pointing at Mark, "and he did this thing where he… he went north to Eglinton, then switched taxis and circled back here… to throw me off!"

Krueger gave Mark a questioning look.

"I've no idea who she is. And not that it's any of her business," Mark said calmly, "but I was on my way to a friend's place when Kate called to tell me her evening plans had been cancelled, so we decided to go out for dinner. I got out on Eglinton because I needed to stop at the drug store for, um… okay, this is embarrassing… for condoms, but…"

Kate blushed. "They don't need to know every detail," she muttered.

Detective Alvarez shot a quick look at her partner and was rewarded with the wry smile she'd expected.

"Anyway, I didn't go in because I suddenly realized I'd left my debit card at home and I needed whatever cash I had left for the second taxi." He glanced at Kate. "FYI, you're buying dinner."

Alvarez turned her attention back to Beryl. "This person does not appear to be Lillian Mullaly. Would you agree?"

"Well, I… I guess," Beryl stammered. "I thought it was at the time, but… I don't understand how…"

"Sometimes we see things the way our mind wants to see them," Alvarez said.

The front door of the house opened and Clair stepped outside. "What's going on out there?" she called.

"That's my grandmother, Clair Young." Kate said. "This is her house. I'm here visiting her today."

"Give us one moment," Alvarez said and she took Krueger aside. "Recognize the name? Clair Young is the widow of Bill Young."

"The media mogul?"

"That's the one. She's very high profile, still politically connected. We don't need any trouble, so let's handle this gently."

"Okay, you deal with her," Krueger said. "I have some questions for Ms. Sweeney."

"I'm on it."

Kate and Mark followed the detective to the front door where Clair awaited them.

"I'm sorry to bother you, ma'am," Alvarez said, flashing her badge. "We had a report that Lillian Mullaly was on the property."

"Nonsense!" Clair exclaimed.

"This is likely a case of mistaken identity," Alvarez explained. "It seems the woman in the black jacket had some connection to her. She followed Mark to this house and believed she saw her in the front yard. She now realizes she was mistaken. We're sorry for the intrusion, but I'm sure you understand that we were obligated to respond."

"What must the neighbours think? I'm mortified. And poor Mark. Just because of his sister, *he* comes under attack," Clair said, casting him a sympathetic look.

"I'd like to have a restraining order issued against that strange woman so she won't be allowed to come near me or my residence," Mark said.

"Or this house," Kate added. "She's creepy."

"If you proceed with that, we can certainly verify the events of today for you," Alvarez said. "Mrs. Young, would you mind if we had a look inside?"

"That depends," Clair said. "I could insist that you get a warrant to do so, but I have nothing to hide. However, I don't want anyone touching my possessions or being too nosey. What exactly would you be doing?"

"Just walking through the rooms, opening a few doors, nothing very invasive. You could ask us to stop at any time."

"Okay then, but please be brief," Clair said with a sigh. "And we will accompany you."

"I'll unlock the carriage house if you need to look in there," Kate volunteered.

"Thanks, we will." Detective Alvarez stood and spoke into her handset.

Two more police cars had appeared in the driveway and three officers came forward to join Alvarez at the front door. She sent one of them to the carriage house with Kate and pulled the other two aside to speak privately with them.

"Since Mark Mullaly is here, it merits a check. You take the upstairs, Fletcher," she said. "Look anywhere a body could hide, but don't touch anything else or Clair Young will call it off."

Alvarez led them into the house and Fletcher followed Mark upstairs. The other officer was assigned to check the basement. She began a search of the main floor with Clair at her heels. She was quick, but systematic, starting at one end and working her way to the other. The officer who had inspected the carriage house returned and shadowed her, watching the hallways.

Clair followed nervously as the detective entered the doors to the pool wing. To the right was an enclosed area that housed a treadmill and a few other pieces of equipment. Alvarez poked her head inside, looked around, and moved on to the sauna, checking to see if the wooden bench seats lifted up. The shower was empty as well. Next was the sunken hot tub, positioned in the corner near the edge of the pool. She knelt down to grasp the cover.

"It folds back," Clair said. Her eyes wandered to the floor near the towel cabinet where faint scratches in the tiles hinted at its recent movement.

Alvarez pulled the first section of the cover back and leaned down to look inside, then reclosed it and rose to her feet, tugging her now wet pant legs away from her knees. "Looks like someone was splashing around in here recently," she said.

"That would be me," Clair laughed. "I try to swim every day."

"Good for you. I would, too, if I lived in a place like this." Alvarez moved toward the towel cabinet. "Do you mind?" she asked pointing at the towels.

"Help yourself." Clair's heart hammered as the detective pulled a folded towel from a centre stack resting at eye level.

Alvarez froze, the towel hovering just below her chin. She turned slowly to Clair. "This smells so nice," she said, lowering her face to the fabric.

"Lilac-scented," Clair said. She watched as Alvarez rubbed the towel vigorously over her pant legs.

"We're done here." The detective held the towel up and pointed to a laundry receptacle next to the shelves. "In there?"

"Yes, thank you," Clair said, her tension easing as the detective moved toward the door.

In the backseat of the patrol car Beryl waited in glum silence. Detective Krueger, who had been talking with dispatch on his police radio, walked wearily toward the car and nodded to the female constable who was standing nearby. She opened the door. "Please step out of the vehicle, Ms. Sweeney."

Beryl grasped the edge of the door frame and hauled herself up to her full height, glaring down at the much shorter constable.

Krueger spoke slowly and evenly, "Beryl Sweeney, where were you between twelve fifteen and twelve twenty this morning?"

Beryl closed her eyes and blew out a lungful of air intermingled with a long, breathy "Fu............"

"Answer the question, please."

"...ck." Beryl turned her head away and opened her eyes. "Obviously, you *know* where I was."

"You'll need to come with us to the station," Kruger said. "This is Constable Richie. She'll drive you there."

"Turn around, spread your legs and place both hands on top of the vehicle," Constable Richie instructed.

"Oh, come on!" Beryl shouted. She backed away from the police car. "You don't understand. I was in Port Hope because I was following... listen, I was only trying to..."

"Ms. Sweeney, if you don't cooperate, I'll have to use force and place you under arrest," Ritchie said.

All reason abandoned the part of Beryl's brain that dispensed common sense and she stepped angrily forward, her arms whipping about in a manner that could only be perceived as threatening. "Yeah, right. As if a scrawny bitch like you…"

In the next instant, Beryl was face down on the driveway with her arms pinned behind her back.

"Need some help?" Krueger asked Ritchie.

"I've got it," she said, snapping a set of handcuffs on the wrists beneath her.

Detective Alvarez and her crew arrived just in time to see Constable Ritchie pull her upright, pat her down and load her into the back seat.

"Did things deteriorate just a bit while I was gone?" she asked.

"Just a bit," Krueger answered, holding up the car keys they'd confiscated from Beryl. "Fletcher, you get to drive her car to the station," he said. "It's the grey beater down the street. Can't miss it."

"Goodie," Fletcher said dryly and snatched the keys out of the air as Krueger tossed them his way.

"Seems our delicate little friend here practised some Karate on an ATM in Port Hope last night."

"I knew that call was too good to be true," Alvarez said.

"How did your search of the house go?"

"Dead end."

Kate and Mark watched as the police vehicles disappeared down the street, then joined Clair in the pool area. Together, they pushed the cabinet out of the way and opened the door.

"Did I mention that I'm claustrophobic?" Lily asked, drawing in a deep breath.

"Sorry," Kate said. "Are you okay?"

Lily looked down at the T-shirt she was wearing, the one she'd acquired in the hasty exchange of tops with Kate. The front featured a realistic rendering of four bloodstained bullet holes with **I'm fine** printed at the bottom. "I'm fine," she said.

Clair laughed and clapped a hand to her forehead. "I thought I'd have a stroke when the detective grabbed that towel off the shelf. Her eyes were lined right up with the door."

"We're going to have to be more careful from now on," Lily said. "I'll need to find a different hideout."

"I'm sorry," Mark said as they walked in the direction of the kitchen. "I can't believe she tracked me here."

"Why *are* you here, by the way?" Lily asked.

"I, ah… I have more good news. I found surveillance video of a Ford Focus with a piece of fabric caught in the back door."

"No way! Was it silver?"

"Probably. The video is black and white and a bit blurry. I've been promised access to some good image processing equipment, the kind forensic investigators use, so tomorrow, if we can enhance the image, I'll be able to look for licence plate matches. The police had collected plenty of surveillance video."

"I'm sure they were hoping to spot *my* vehicle at a time that fit their theory. And what else brings you here… Marcus?"

Whenever Lily used his formal name, Mark knew she was either making a point or teasing him. He cleared his throat as they arrived at the kitchen. "I, um, just wanted to see you." He was staring at Kate, who was opening the refrigerator.

"Of course." Lily snapped her fingers in front of his face. "I'm over here." When he turned, she gave him an evil grin.

Kate was studying the contents of the refrigerator, her back still to them. "I'm starving. How about you guys?"

"I'm not that hungry," Clair said. "but you kids do whatever you like."

"How about we order takeout?" Mark said.

Lily glanced at the clock. She'd booked a flight to Antigua with a stop in Miami for the next morning and had only that evening to prepare for it. She couldn't tell Mark what was going on, but she knew how to get rid of him.

"I'm not hungry either, just tired." she said. "But Mark, why don't you take Kate out for dinner?" She yawned.

Kate whirled around and looked wide-eyed at Lily.

Mark brightened. "What do you think, Kate?"

Lily flicked her eyes in the direction of the front door and Kate quickly caught her meaning. "I, ah… sure, we could do that."

"Great!" Mark said. "You don't even need to change. We'll go somewhere casual."

"Come to think of it, you did tell the police we were going out for dinner – we must keep up the charade, right?"

"Right. I just have to stop at the drug store on the way." He grinned and Kate blushed.

She threw Clair and Lily a conspiratorial wink as she left the room. "I won't be late."

"Now we really must play our parts convincingly," Mark said as he followed her into the hall. "In case the police are watching." Their voices faded as they moved farther away and the door closed on notes of laughter.

"They'd make a wonderful couple, don't you think?" Clair said, smiling.

"I'd love to see them together," Lily said, "but Kate doesn't feel ready for another relationship."

"I think she just needs to have a little more faith in herself and open up to some new experiences, test her wings."

"Mmm… wings. I lied. I'm starving, too." Lily crossed the room and opened the refrigerator. "Shall I warm up some of those leftover chicken wings?"

"Didn't we take away your licence for that oven?" Clair teased.

The unveiling of Jemma to his parents and his grandmother had been a more thrilling and dramatic performance than anything Dean had ever given on stage. There had been gasps, squeals, tears of joy and, from his father, Doug, a near fainting. "Like father, like son," Jemma had joked.

The trio were standing in Gramma James' living room in a tight knot around Jemma, fawning over her, hugging her, shaking their heads in disbelief.

Dean's mother, Janet, her eyes still wet with emotion, took Jemma's hands in hers. "I can't wait for you to meet your other great grandparents. They'll be ecstatic." She giggled like a teenager. "Oh, wait till my sister hears! And the rest of the family." She pulled Jemma into another crushing hug.

Doug turned to Dean. "Tell us the rest of this amazing story."

CHAPTER 25

March 17

In her purse, Lily had Kate's credit card, passport, phone, and some US cash that Clair had taken from her safe. Everything else she needed was in her carry-on. The sky was soft pink with the awakening of morning and the streets were wet from rain that had fallen during the night. Rosedale lay in peaceful slumber, but as the blue Toyota Prius left the neighbourhood and headed north, the spell was broken. Early commuters rushed to their destinations and many more were collected as they entered the Allen Expressway.

"We should be at Pearson in about twenty minutes," Kate said. She eyed her passenger. "You look worried."

"I'm thinking about getting through Customs."

"You'll easily pass for me," Kate said with more conviction than she felt.

"It doesn't help that I'm five years older than you and your passport's two years old."

It wasn't lost on Kate that their roles had momentarily flipped and Lily was the one now expressing doubts. "You don't have to go through with this," she said.

"It's just nerves."

Kate changed the subject. "Did you have any luck last night tracking down that bar in the photo?"

"Captain Kipp's? No. Nothing showed up on the web for Antigua or anywhere else."

They drove in silence for a while, then Lily glanced at Kate. She'd seemed happy these past few days and it had been easy to forget that she was in a recuperative phase of her illness. She looked tired. She'd been out late the night before – Lily had heard her returning from her dinner date sometime after midnight.

"Yeess?" Kate said, looking straight ahead at the road, and Lily realized her glance had turned into a steady gaze.

She laughed. "Just wondering how your date with Mark went."

The corners of Kate's mouth twitched. "We had a nice dinner and then we drank decaf and talked – for hours."

"And?"

"Just talked." She let a smile bleed through. "He's an amazing guy, great sense of humour, genuine and caring. I could ruin him in no time."

"Why are you so hard on yourself? You're amazing, too!"

"Just being realistic. We'll talk about it some other time."

Lily glimpsed the sign for Pearson International Airport as they exited to the 409 and her anxiety spiked.

By the time they arrived, parked and entered the terminal she'd passed anxiety and was heading straight for nausea. She checked in at a kiosk and they moved on to the processing area for US Customs and Border Patrol.

"This is as far as I can go," Kate said. "I'll hang around until you clear Customs."

"*If* I clear Customs." Lily shouldered her carry-on bag and looked into the eyes of her near-twin. "I couldn't ask for better friends than you and Clair. I love you both."

"We love you, too," Kate said. She gave Lily a hug. "Be safe. Make sure we get those calls, not just texts."

"I will. See you soon." Lily took a couple of backward steps and felt the lifeline between them dissolve.

Kate nodded. "You'd better."

The CBP officer to whom Lily was directed wanted to know, among other things, why she was travelling alone, but he gave her passport photo only a cursory look and before long, she was cleared to move on to the security screening area. With a sigh of relief, she fell in step behind her fellow passengers, texted Kate, and turned her thoughts toward her destination.

With a self-satisfied smile, Mark tapped a number into his phone. "Hey, Dad," he said when Jeff picked up. "Is your conjugal visit over yet?"

"I just got here last night," Jeff groaned. "I don't think your mother is ready to let me go just yet. Why, what's up?"

"I got the number from the plate of that Ford Focus."

"Really? That's terrific!"

"I don't think the folks here at 2 District would be too keen on running the number for us, but I thought your OPP commander friend might bend some rules for you. Got a pen handy?"

"Fire away." Jeff wrote as Mark dictated. "Thanks, Mark. See you soon."

Getting through the V.C. Bird Airport in Antigua was a slow process, but no one questioned her passport or her identity. For the next few days, Lily would be Kate from New Zealand. She planned to begin her search with bars, resorts and taxi drivers. Hopefully someone would recognize Ben's photo or know of Captain Kipp's Bar and Grill. She suspected that Ben's choice to live in Antigua had been influenced by a previous visit, during which he'd shot the video and posed in front of the bar.

The Heritage Hotel was close to the Heritage Quay on St. John's Harbour. It was far from luxurious, but the room was spacious and clean. Dropping her bag and purse on the bed, Lily walked onto the balcony and gazed out at the waterfront. She was steps from the duty-free shops, restaurants and boutiques of the Heritage and Redcliffe Quays.

After calling Kate and Clair to let them know she'd arrived safely, she changed into lighter clothes and went downstairs. The receptionist in the lobby couldn't recall a bar and grill called Captain Kipp's and when she checked a phone directory, it was not listed there.

Lily left the hotel and proceeded toward the waterfront, drawn by the sound of steel pan music. She walked along Heritage Quay, past palm trees and colourful shops. Four huge cruise ships lined the finger piers, dwarfing the surrounding architecture. Finally, Lily stopped at a bar and ordered some food. The waiter there knew nothing about Captain Kipp's. She paid her bill and strolled the darkening streets back to the hotel, enjoying the light breeze that caressed her skin. When at last she fell into bed, sleep overtook her quickly. But her dreams would not let her rest. In the black of night, she wandered through Heritage Quay.

Lily is running, but the street is clogged with people. At last she breaks through and she finds herself in an alley with only a dim light marking its end far ahead. Suddenly she is thrown against the wall.

"You thought I wouldn't recognize you?" he growls. Ben is panting, his breath boozy and hot against her face. One hand is pressed to her throat, the other gripping the wrist that is trapped between them by his large belly. Her free hand smacks him on the side of the head and he just laughs. The hand on her throat begins to squeeze and her tongue writhes as she struggles to draw in air.

Gasping, Lily sat bolt upright. She took a long drink from the bottle of water on the night stand, then threw off her covers and walked out onto her third-floor balcony. She looked down. There was no way for anyone, short of Spiderman, to scale the side of the building. For several minutes she stood still, as the pounding in her chest subsided and the sweat on her skin evaporated.

When, at last, her nightmare was fully extinguished, thoughts of another Caribbean night descended on her. Her first night in St. Kitts with Dean. She remembered every detail – the clothes they'd worn, the name of the perfume she'd dabbed behind her ears, the meal they'd ordered from room service, the name of the maid who'd delivered it and the song that had played from the patio below their balcony as they'd dined. Lily knew she had an exceptionally good memory. She'd never imagined that she might be able to discern things not seen, not experienced. But tonight she could sense him. Ben was close, here in Antigua, and she would find him soon.

The grandfather clock in the hall chimed eleven times as Jemma, clad in flannelette pajamas, sipped the last of her hot chocolate. She was seated at one end of the sofa and Dean at the other, his legs propped up on the coffee table.

"I should probably go to bed, but I'm not the slightest bit tired," she said, as she stretched out and rested her feet on her father's leg.

Dean and Jemma were riding high on the wave of excitement that had followed her introduction to the rest of the family. The service for Grandpa James had been beautiful, a touching tribute to a life well-lived. When Dean and Jemma had performed *I'll Be Seeing You,* there was not a dry eye in the room. At the reception that followed, they'd been inundated with praise, flooded with questions, and generally swarmed. They'd kept their responses vague, obscuring details about Lily.

Relatives had whispered about Dean's brief marriage for years, but most of the family's friends had no idea. The fact that he was gay was old news, but the unveiling of his daughter was an astonishing revelation, a titillating morsel of information that would fuel their speculations for weeks to come. Jemma projected poise, oozed intelligence and screamed talent. Dean had spent the afternoon basking and often blushing in the glow of compliments that were heaped upon her, as though he, himself, had raised her and nurtured those gifts. He'd contented himself with the knowledge that he had, in fact, created this magnificent being through the very gift of his genes.

"So..." Dean said, squeezing one of her bare feet. He momentarily let his mind wander to her toes and he imagined himself playing

This Little Piggy with a three-year-old Jemma. One more thing he'd missed.

"Dad." Jemma wiggled her toes. "You were saying?"

"Did your mom ever play *This Little Piggy* with your toes?"

"Don't even think about it," Jemma warned him, narrowing her eyes.

"Actually," Dean said, "I was going to ask how you'd feel about taking on the role of young Valerie in *Thin Air*?

"What?" Jemma exclaimed, snapping to a sitting position. She sat cross-legged and leaned toward him. "Me?"

"I wanted to talk to you about it sooner, but you already had an avalanche of new things coming at you."

"What will the producers think? Maybe they won't like me."

"How can they not like you? Anyway, I plan to have you audition anonymously. I want their unbiased opinions. No one, not even Georgia, even knows that you exist."

Jemma giggled, bouncing lightly on the sofa cushion. "I… wow… what about school?"

"We'll get you a tutor. If your mother agrees, that is."

"She'll be guilted into it. As she should be."

"You need to know that we use more than one actor in each role, so it won't always be you on stage. And if the show has a long run, you may outgrow the part."

"I'm so lucky!" Jemma beamed. "I didn't just get a father, I got you, the super-talented, incredibly wonderful, semi-famous Dean James!"

Dean laughed. "Someday, my claim to fame will be that I'm your father."

Jemma plopped back down on her cushion, stretching out once again. "Jemma James. It has a nice ring to it." She closed her eyes and yawned.

Dean scratched his chin thoughtfully. "In the story, the young Valerie is supposed to be fifteen. You'd be playing her as she ages to eighteen. Then the story jumps ahead to the eve of her fortieth birthday and the role is played by the principal actor. Also, we need to talk about your future beyond all this. Like, do we launch right into your career or do you go to university? I think your mother would want you to continue your education. I mean… Jemma?"

He stopped and looked at his daughter. Her eyes were closed and her breathing was slow and nasal. "Honey?" he whispered. There was no response, only a shift in her breathing as it morphed into a light snore. Dean let his eyes linger on her face, serene in deepening sleep. With feather-light pressure he pinched her big toe. "This little piggy went to market…"

CHAPTER 26

March 18

The sky above Toronto was cloudless and bright as Kate and Mark set out for Grimsby. They had arranged with Stacey to return BJ's laptop and were taking both children gifts. The morning was warm and Kate, who was driving, lowered her window.

"I adore spring," she said, inhaling deeply.

"It's not officially spring for three more days," Mark said.

"Two more days," Kate countered.

"Wanna bet?"

"You're on. Loser buys lunch." Kate chuckled. "BJ is going to be so thrilled to meet you. He thinks of you as some kind of nerdy superhero."

"Like Superman or Iron Man?"

"I said nerdy. More like Computerman."

"Well, I'm not saying that I'm Computerman. I'm just saying nobody has ever seen me and Computerman in a room together," Mark said as he pulled his phone from his jacket pocket.

As the car picked up speed, Kate closed her window and glanced over at him. "What are you doing?"

"Calling Lily."

"Why?"

Mark began to punch in the number. "Meredith wants to show her the video of Jemma singing with Dean and I told her I'd set it up for tonight. Do you have any plans?"

"Wait!" Kate pulled over to the curb and Mark aborted his call. She put the car in park and turned to face him. "You're not going to like this, but..."

Mark's jaw twitched and he looked away. "It's alright. I think I know where this is going. I have no right to expect that you wouldn't go out with other guys. I mean if you're seeing someone tonight..."

Kate's head whipped up. "You think I'm seeing someone else?"

"You're not?"

"No. I was going to tell you that Lily's not here... exactly... in Toronto."

Mark's expression changed to relief, then concern. "What do you mean?"

Kate sighed. "I expected this might come up, but not before we reached the end of your block. Look, Lily asked us to keep it from you as long as possible. She thinks she's figured out where Ben is hiding – and she's gone there to look for him. She knew you and your parents wouldn't approve."

"Damn right we wouldn't." Mark's eyes bulged. "Where exactly did she go?"

"Antigua."

"Are you freaking kidding me?" Mark stared at Kate, his mouth opening and closing like a fish as he floundered for his next words.

Kate updated him on the latest development. "She doesn't expect to be gone long," she finished. "If she finds him, she'll let us know and come right home."

Mark shook his head and fixed his gaze on a robin hopping across a patch of lawn.

"Are you angry with me?" Kate asked.

"At Lily, mainly. For being stubborn and foolish," Mark muttered. There was a long pause as his finger tapped against the phone that was resting on his thigh. "You said you weren't seeing someone *else.*

Does that mean you're seeing *me*?" He turned his head and found her eyes.

Kate smiled and put the car in gear. "First, let's go see BJ. We can talk about it over lunch. Which you will be buying."

Lily looked with distaste at the orange bikini she'd just purchased at a shop in the Quay. Should she find Ben, a little wardrobe assistance could be helpful in keeping his attention. Although Lily never flaunted her attractiveness, she was well aware of the effect she still had on men. Straight ones, anyway.

After making inquiries at a couple of local bars and flashing Ben's picture around with no luck, she decided to try some of the more expensive waterfront establishments. She hailed a taxi and spoke to the driver through the open passenger window. "Sandals Resort?"

The driver nodded. "Five kilometres."

"Thanks." Lily settled herself into the back seat.

"You here on vacation?" The driver, a middle aged, dark-skinned man with silver-flecked hair eyed her in the rearview mirror.

"Yes," Lily said. "Meeting up with friends." She leaned forward. "Ever heard of a bar called Captain Kipp's?"

"Sure. It's gone now, maybe eight, ten years ago, but I remember it, yes."

"Oh, really?" Lily practically climbed into the front seat.

"Yes. It's still there, but it has a different name now. It's at a beach not far from Jolly Harbour."

"Could you take me there now?"

"Of course, yes."

"What is this place called now?" Lily asked.

"Skipper's Bar and Grill. Nice, good food."

"I'm trying to find someone who may still go there sometimes."

The driver whipped around a corner and sped off. Lily lurched sideways in her seat and her mind flashed back to those terrifying moments in the corrections van as it slid across the icy intersection, the dark shape of the dump truck bearing down on them. The scene outside these windows was as different from that snowy day as anyone could imagine. Palm trees, colourful buildings, walls covered with bougainvillea in bright yellows and magentas, the turquoise sea. Is this what Ben, with his hatred of winter, imagined when he planned his "escape to paradise"?

"Paradise," the driver said suddenly, snatching the word from Lily's brain. "That's what the place was called after Captain Kipp's and before Skipper's. Paradise Bar and Grill."

"Interesting," Lily said. "When did it become Skipper's?"

"Maybe two years ago?"

When the driver pulled up in front of Skipper's, Lily showed him the photo of Ben on the phone. "Have you seen this man before?"

"No, sorry," the driver said.

The door to Skipper's Bar and Grill was set into a protruding, barrel-shaped entrance designed to resemble a cask of rum. A large bar sat like a cube in the centre of the spacious dining area. Wooden stools with black leather seats were scattered around it. The theme of the bar was sailing, with mismatched references to pirates here and there. In spite of the incongruous decor, the overall tone of the place was one of tropical charm.

Three men and a woman sat at the bar, joking and laughing loudly. One of the men turned to look at Lily as she approached. She avoided his eyes, but could feel them travelling up and down her body as she passed.

Two large sliding doors opened onto a large deck overlooking the beach. Palm trees with strings of lights wrapped around their trunks lined two sides. Outdoor dining furniture was arranged beneath canvas sails stretched between the trees. Most of the tables were occupied. Lily stood at the opening, admiring the view of the bay, then turned and walked up to the bar.

"What can I get for you, beautiful woman?" The bartender's Antiguan accent was thick.

"I'd love a rum punch," Lily replied, smiling.

"Oh, you came to the right place, my friend." Large white teeth flashed against copper skin as the man reached for a glass.

Lily glanced outside. "I'll take a table on the deck."

"Go ahead," he said. "Enjoy the sunshine."

As Lily seated herself, she reached into her purse and brought out the phone. Scrolling through the photos, she found the headshot of Ben. By now, she knew every crease, freckle and defining feature.

A younger waiter bustled by with plates of appetizers. She waved him over on his way back to the kitchen. "Could I order a serving of whatever that was. It smells delicious."

"Yes, miss. It is delicious, very popular here."

"Have you ever seen this man in here?" Lily turned the screen of her phone toward him.

"I don't think so," the young man replied, "but we see many people here every day."

"Thanks, anyway."

As the waiter hurried away, the grinning bartender appeared in his place. "Here you go, my lady. One rum punch, Antigua style."

Lily thanked him and showed him the same photo. "Have you seen this man in here before?"

He shook his head. "My boss might recognize him, though. He's at the bar now." He leaned in closer and studied the photo. "But you know, it is familiar." He strode back toward the bar. "Hey, Skipper, this lady is looking for a man."

Lily felt eyes turn her way.

"She has a picture. She wants to know, have you seen him?"

Lily watched as a man with a blonde buzz cut rose from a bar stool and began moving her way. It was the same man who'd given her the once over when she'd entered the place. She sighed. This might be her last stab at tracking down Ben through what she'd hoped would be his continuing patronage of the bar and grill once known as Captain Kipp's.

Skipper, though she doubted that was his real name, threw some remark back over his shoulder and laughed, rounding the corner of the bar. He was squarely built, tanned and toned. A diamond stud winked from his ear. Lily noted the casual chic appearance – neat, navy shorts and white linen shirt, opened at the top to expose a waxed chest. If he hadn't leered at her earlier, she might have found him mildly attractive.

Someone from the far side of the bar spoke and Skipper chuckled and pivoted back in their direction. "Chickening out now, eh? Well, I'm not about to let you forget." He laughed again and turned to face Lily.

As their eyes connected, pure terror rose from her core, leaving a tingling sensation on her scalp. Her gift for registering intonation, pitch, and subtle inflections in speech had just unmasked this man. The voice she'd heard in the video of Ben on his sailboat played back in her head. *Got no faith in me, eh?* That little Canadian *eh* at the end left no doubt.

The bartender wasn't finished torturing Lily. "She's got a picture that looks like you, boss. Dark hair, but eyes like your eyes. And uuuugly," he sang. He leaned on the counter and grinned.

The amusement drained from his boss's face as Lily quickly looked down and flicked away the image on her smartphone.

"You got something there you want to show me?" he asked, moving closer.

"Oh, ah…" Lily's eyes darted from her phone to him and back again. She scrolled quickly through the file of photos, as her mind tangled with this sudden turn of events. Somewhere on Kate's phone, there was a photo that might work. Kate had shown it to her days earlier. "Sorry, I didn't mean to take you away from your friends."

Then she had it, a head and shoulders shot of Kate's ex-husband, Steve. Dark wavy hair, brown eyes. It would do. Ben/Skipper sat down across from her, his expression hard.

Lily turned the phone around and showed him the picture of Steve. "Have you seen this guy around here recently?"

Ben's face relaxed. Close up now, she could see that it was definitely him. He'd changed almost beyond recognition, but his eyes and his mouth gave him away. He'd had a nose job and his curly hair had been shaved to a stub and dyed blonde. Incredibly, he appeared to have lost at least fifty pounds.

Ben's fingers gripped the edge of the phone, but Lily held on tightly. "Not even close, Jenson." He spoke loudly, turning to the bar. "Smart ass."

Jenson shrugged and turned his attention to one of his customers.

As Lily returned the phone to her purse, Ben leaned on the table, hand in chin. "What's the story on this guy?" His eyes roved over her breasts before settling back on her face.

"He's my fiancé, but maybe not for long. We're here on vacation.

Yesterday we had a fight and he took off. He likes upscale bars and beaches, so I'm checking places near the water."

"And you're worried about him?"

"Not really. I just want to resolve the problems or call it off and go home."

"He's a jerk. Call it off, but don't go home. Enjoy your vacation."

Lily laughed. "Maybe I'm the jerk."

"You don't have a jerk vibe. My name is Oliver Tate, by the way. Skipper's just a nickname."

"Nice to meet you," Lily said, offering her hand. "Kate Young."

Ben reciprocated, but instead of shaking her hand, he brazenly kissed it. "What did you fight about?"

"It's not something I want to talk about right now," she said. She took a sip of her drink, then pushed it aside.

"Rum punch not to your liking?"

"It's okay. I guess I'm not that fond of dark rum."

"Let me get you something you *will* like. My treat. I own this place, you know," Ben boasted with a sweep of his hand.

Lily noticed that the hair on his arms and legs had been bleached blonde, too. "It's wonderful, very charming… like you."

"Why, thank you. Now about that drink." He leaned forward and wiggled eyebrows that had been thinned and bleached. "Wanna try Sex on the Beach?" He laughed at his lame joke. "The drink, I mean," he clarified, noticing Lily's failure to react.

"I'm not much of a drinker," she said, forcing a small smile.

"Tell you what. I have a personal favourite that I invented. I call it a Faceoff. That way I can say to people, 'Drink your Faceoff!'"

"I see. Any connection with hockey?"

"Yes, actually. See, the drink is blue with red cherries and an icy white layer on top – the colours of a hockey rink."

"Clever." Lily made eye contact, daring to flirt. "You're a hockey fan?"

"Nah," Ben said. "But a lot of our customers are." He called out to the bartender. "Two Faceoffs, Jenson."

The waiter arrived with Lily's platter of stuffed mushrooms, deep fried veggies and toasted wedges with dips. She thanked him and picked up a mushroom. "This is a huge serving. Will you stay and join me? Or am I being presumptuous?" She smiled coyly.

Ben lifted a breaded zucchini stick from the plate and dunked it in the white cheese sauce. "Do you allow double dipping?" He licked the sauce with his tongue.

Lily ignored the double entendre. She popped the deep-fried mushroom in her mouth. "Oh... heaven," she said, licking her fingers as she chewed.

"Mmm, glad you like it," Ben purred. "This is my treat. The drinks, too."

"Wow, thanks. That's so kind."

"Watching you lick those beautiful fingers is all the thanks I need."

Lily caught his sappy expression and turned the conversation to her impressions of Antigua. Before long, Jenson arrived with two creamy blue drinks. As Lily looked up, she noticed the woman who had been seated near Ben earlier, standing just inside the bar, hands on hips, glaring her way. She was slender with red, shoulder length hair and pale, freckled skin. Lily guessed she was in her mid-thirties and was probably good looking when she wasn't glowering.

"Is that your girlfriend?" she asked, nodding in the woman's direction.

Ben looked over his shoulder. "She's a friend who comes by sometimes."

Jenson grinned. "Anything else, Skipper?"

"Just the bill." Both men laughed and Jenson ambled back to the bar, hands in his pockets.

The redhead crossed the deck in a huff, thumped down the stairs and took a few steps toward the beach. She leaned against a palm tree and lit a cigarette. Lily popped another veggie in her mouth and glanced back at Ben. Whoever had done the work on his nose was good. The new one was straight and GQ perfect, leaving no trace of the wide, bulbous shape that had once dominated his face.

"I love your accent," Ben said. "Where in Australia are you from, Kate?"

"New Zealand, actually. Auckland. And you?"

"All over. Maine, originally. Let's see if you can guess what's in this drink."

Lily took a sip. It was delicious. "Um… pineapple juice…"

"Check."

She sipped again. "Coconut rum…"

"Check."

The rim of the glass had been dipped in maraschino cherry juice and rolled in sugar, resembling a face-off circle. "Curacao for the blue and cherry for the red."

Ben licked his lower lip. "You're good."

"Crushed ice."

"Obviously."

"Ah… lime?"

"Nope. There's two more. I'll just have to keep buying you drinks until you get it right."

"Well, hopefully not all in one day." Lily forced a giggle.

Ben leaned forward. "So, you'll see me again… even if your jerk boyfriend comes back?"

"What boyfriend?" Lily held his gaze, blinking in slow motion, then backed off a little. "Oh, Sam."

"How about going out with me for a morning sail tomorrow? I have a big catamaran and I could show you the sites of Antigua from its beautiful waters."

Lily fought the urge to flee. She'd come all this way to find Ben and now, here he was. She could leave now or she could take one more day to gather valuable evidence. If the authorities were to arrest him before he could vanish, knowing where he lived, where he had bank accounts and what he owned here in Antigua and elsewhere would be useful. She hoped to get photographs, DNA and fingerprints, as well. But she wasn't comfortable with the idea of being alone with him on a boat. "Listen, I like you a lot" she said, "but I *am* engaged, at least for now. Even if I weren't, I'd want to take things slow."

"I expect no more than a beautiful day on the water with a beautiful woman. No strings attached. In fact, I'll bring some friends along. You'll love it."

"Will she be one of the friends?" Lily tilted her head in the direction of the redhead.

"Mona? No." Ben ran a hand over his bristly head. "Okay, to be honest, we've gone out once or twice, but she knows I'm not interested in being in a relationship with her. Now, how about that boat ride?'

"As long as I'm not coming between anything."

"Absolutely not. I'll pick you up at eight o'clock. Where are you staying, Kate?"

"The Heritage Hotel." Lily gritted her teeth behind closed lips and smiled, reaching across the table to touch Ben's hand. "This is really nice of you. I thought my vacation had been ruined. If Sam comes back in the meantime, I'm just going to tell him I have other plans."

"Nah, bring him along and we'll feed him to the sharks." Ben laughed and turned his hand over, so that Lily's fingertips rested in his palm.

An involuntary shudder rippled through her and Ben, noticing, attributed this to the thrill of his touch. He closed his fingers around hers just as a third hand slammed down on the tabletop.

Lily jumped, quickly pulling away from Ben as the freckled hand with Zebra-painted fingernails lifted to reveal a pack of cigarettes.

"These are yours." Mona directed this to Ben, but her eyes were boring into Lily's. "I'm not waiting around any longer." With that, she stormed away.

"Ouch," Lily mumbled when Mona was out of earshot.

"I know, eh?" Ben shook his head.

Lily hadn't noticed she'd drained her glass until her straw started sucking air beneath the frothy foam. "Cream," she announced.

Ben watched her lick her lips. "Right. There's one more ingredient, but save your guesses for tomorrow. I'd offer you a tour of the island today, but I have some business to take care of this afternoon."

"I should be on my way," Lily said.

"I can give you a lift. Unlike you, I've hardly touched my drink."

"Okay then, if you don't mind. Thanks, Oliver."

Ben led her through the restaurant and ushered her out a side door to a private parking area. "Here, put this on," he said, and Lily turned to see a silver helmet in his extended hand. Above the visor there was an image of a skull wearing an eye patch and a pirate hat with a pair of cutlasses forming an X behind it. A fitting emblem for a killer-thief.

"That's yours?" she asked, pointing to the silver and black Harley Davidson Electra Glide near the staff entrance.

"Yup, that's my baby." Smiling, Ben swung his leg over the bike. "Hop on."

Lily straddled the motorcycle and as Ben eased the machine forward onto the street, she reluctantly placed her arms around his waist.

A steady stream of relatives had come and gone from the house on their way out of town. When the last of them finally backed out of the driveway with a honk and a wave, Dean put his arm around Jemma's shoulders. "Feeling overwhelmed yet?"

"A little."

Grandma James headed to her room for a "little lie down" and Dean's parents went into the kitchen to start preparing their legendary stew.

Jemma sat beside Dean on the living room sofa and picked through the bowl of party mix on the coffee table, looking for the cheesy bites. "You know, they all seemed nice, except the whiney twins, your cousin's kids."

"They're your cousins, too, you know," Dean said. "Let's see, as my first cousin's children, that makes them my first cousins once removed, so they'd be your…"

"Can we remove them altogether?" Jemma tipped her head back and knocked a handful of party mix into her mouth.

"Be nice," Dean laughed. "And lay off the Cheezies. You'll spoil your appetite."

Jemma wiped her hands on her shirt as she chewed. "Seriously? You sound like my mother. Did you speed read a copy of *Parenthood for Dummies*?"

A flush of pink crawled up Dean's neck and, crossing his arms, he leaned toward Jemma and gave her a withering look. "No, and I don't know enough about raising a daughter to fill page one. But if you like, I can lend you a copy of *Respect for Dummies*."

A blast of air shot orange bits from Jemma's mouth. She grasped her stomach and bent forward in a spasm of laughter. "But I do respect you, Dum… I mean Dad," she managed to gasp between fits. She took a breath, coughed and started up again, flopping onto her side on the couch.

Dean, his face bright red, raised his voice. "What I meant was, *Respect Your Elders for Dummies.*" He brushed a moist particle of something orange from his forehead.

This set Jemma off again and she rolled onto the floor in hysterics. "That's so bad!" Soon Dean was laughing at the absurdity of his own words.

He pounced on Jemma and playfully shoved a cushion into her face. "Thou shalt not laugh at thy father, young lady!"

Janet came into the room, wiping her hands on a towel. "What in the world is so funny?"

Grinning, Dean stood up and pulled a still-giggling Jemma by the arm to her feet. "Just teaching my daughter a little respect."

"Mm hmm. Well, that noise could raise the dead," Janet said, affecting a look of consternation that failed to conceal her pleasure. "Remember your grandmother is trying to have a nap." She eyed the bowl of party mix. "And don't you two fill up on junk. You'll spoil your appetite."

This elicited another fit of giggles from Jemma and Dean clasped a hand over her mouth.

Jemma ducked away. "Sorry, Dad. Sometimes I just blurt things out and it's okay if you tell me off."

"I'll get better at it, I promise." Dean turned to the window and stared out at the road in front of the house. "How would you feel about going back to Toronto in a day or two, Jem?

"I'd be living with you, right?"

"Yes, but we'll have to notify your school and talk to your mother about an alternative. Meanwhile, you could still audition."

"Yes!" Jemma pumped her fist in the air. She gazed out at the road, one that would lead them back to Toronto and into her future. The tingle of anticipation she felt was real, but just below the surface, she felt a deep longing. She pictured the road stretching west, connecting to Interstate 80, snaking its way north to cross the St. Lawrence and leading her on to a solitary destination – her mother. There was no denying it. She was homesick and Lily was her home.

CHAPTER

27

March 19

At eight on the dot Ben pulled up in front of the Heritage Hotel in a black open Jeep. Lily was waiting near the doors with a beach tote in hand.

"Morning, Kate! Hope you've got a swimsuit in there," he said, raking his eyes up her long legs, over the black shorts and pink T-shirt to her face. "Of course, skinny dipping is not out of the question."

Lily wanted to punch him. Ben had greatly improved his appearance, but his manner was still crude. *Like pond scum,* she thought. *No matter how pretty the pond is, the scum floating on the surface ruins it.* "I'm wearing a swimsuit," she informed him, smiling sweetly.

"You need to get some sun on those legs, girl," Ben said, racing around to open the door for her. He put his hand on her back and let it slide over her butt as she stepped up into the Jeep. "But be careful. If you get a bad burn, you'd be untouchable and we wouldn't want that."

"Ah, remember our conversation yesterday about this date not involving anything physical?"

"Just kidding around, Kate." Ben smiled at her, but his eyes showed displeasure.

As they pulled into traffic, several large motorcycles passed noisily by, moving in the opposite direction.

"I didn't realize motorcycles would be so commonplace here," Lily commented.

Ben pointed toward the Quay. "See that Royal Caribbean Cruise ship straight ahead?"

"What about it?"

"They're disembarking from there. Motorcycle cruises come through here from time to time. The ship stops at several ports in the Caribbean where passengers unload their bikes and tour the islands."

"Sounds like fun. Loud, though."

The drive to Jolly Harbour didn't take long. Ben parked the Jeep and they walked down the pier. The view before them was expansive and expensive. Gleaming white boats studded the blue water. Lily's eyes swept over the splendid buildings and tiled red roofs, the swaying green palm trees and colourful blooms, all set against the backdrop of verdant hillsides.

Ben pointed to the largest of the yachts. "I'm not allowed to tell who that one belongs to. Let's just say she's a huge celebrity. I had drinks with her two nights ago."

Lily found herself straining for a closer look when two indistinct figures emerged on the aft deck. She followed Ben along the harbour's edge and down a pier until he came to a stop beside a gorgeous white catamaran. *The Swan* was emblazoned along the side in blue.

"Here she is," Ben announced. "She's a sixty-two-foot multi-hull." He offered Lily his hand and helped her step onto the aft cockpit which was furnished with a dining table and covered bench seats. The engines were already running.

"Wow!" Lily said and she meant it.

Jenson emerged from the saloon and joined them. "Hey, Skipper."

A deeply tanned, middle-aged couple appeared behind him. The woman wore a bright yellow bikini with a matching sarong fastened about her waist. She had French-manicured nails, several shiny gold rings, dyed blonde hair, and firm, round, silicone-enhanced breasts.

Ben slid his arm around Lily and made introductions. "Kate, you've met Jenson and these are my friends, Dennis and Cece Windle.

They exchanged greetings. Ben and Jenson set about preparing the boat for departure as the others stood under the canopy gazing out at the harbour.

There was a prolonged silence, prompting Dennis to speak. "Lovely day for a sail." He pointed to a large sloop. "*Brooklyn Jewel* is ours."

"Nice name. Are you from Brooklyn?"

"No," Cece laughed. "We named it after our daughters, Brooklyn and Jewel."

Lily wondered about Ben's choice of name. Her mind had gone immediately to the Hans Christian Anderson story of the ugly duckling who was tormented by his siblings until he matured into the beautiful swan. Could this be how Ben viewed his own transformation?

"You're from New Zealand?" Cece was saying. She spoke with a southern inflection that was tempting to mimic.

"Yes, I..."

A ragged scream broke the morning calm. Lily spun around to see Mona, Ben's non-girlfriend, weaving unsteadily on the pier, her eyes on the fly bridge where Ben was at the controls. Jenson, who was casting off the last rope, jumped on board as the catamaran went into reverse and began to ease out of its berth.

"Ollie, you son-of-a-bitch!" Mona had a nearly empty wine bottle in one hand and she pitched it hard at the fly bridge. "You lying bastard! Get back here!"

The boat turned so that the stern was facing Mona. She wrenched off one of her sandals and threw it at Lily, who batted it to the floor. "Slut!" the redhead spewed.

As they began to move forward, Dennis picked up the sandal and tossed it back onto the dock. "You might need this to walk back to whatever hole you crawled out of this morning," he hollered.

Mona's stream of curses was drowned out as the engine propelled The Swan toward the mouth of the harbour.

"That's disgusting!" Cece grumbled. "I don't know what Oliver ever saw in her."

"Were they actually a couple?" Lily asked.

"Well, yes..." Dennis started to say. He caught a look from his wife.

"They were never exclusive," she said emphatically.

"I'm just here for a boat ride today." Lily explained. "I have no... designs... on Oliver."

Cece huffed. "You know, she puts on airs when she's sober, but she's a rough sort. She's a real estate agent. Sold Oliver a house a few months ago and she's been like gum on the sole of his shoe ever since."

"Oliver is quite taken with you," Dennis said.

Lily suppressed a frown. "We hardly know each other."

"Well, just don't let Mona ruin what could be the romantic beginning of something good."

A few more minutes of painful conversation ensued while they cleared the harbour. Dennis helped Ben and Jenson hoist the sails and soon they were cutting swiftly through the water with Jenson at the helm.

"Come." Ben took Lily's hand. "Let me show you around *The Swan.*"

As if on a pre-arranged signal, Dennis announced, "Well, if you'll kindly excuse us, Cece and I are going to go up to the bridge for a bit, Skipper."

Ben gave him a mock salute, then propped his expensive sunglasses on his forehead and led Lily through the open aft doors into the saloon, where he prudently dropped her hand and began his spiel. "She's a Lagoon 620 that I had custom outfitted," he said. "I opted to put the galley below. That meant sacrificing some cabin space, but there's plenty left."

The floors and wood surfaces of the salon were finished in a teak tone that complemented the cream cushions, ottomans and area rug, giving the space a feeling a soft luxury. A bank of windows wrapped the entire room in a U shape, flooding it with light. Ben pointed out the height adjustable table, the electronic blinds, the navigation station and the stowaway flat screen TV.

"It's beautiful," Lily said.

"Nice, eh? Wait till you see below. A master suite and three guest cabins with their own heads." He swept his arm toward a stairway. "After you."

Lily made all the right sounds as Ben continued the tour. Finally, he took her up to the fly bridge and pointed out the dual helm controls and spacious seating area.

"Quite the vessel, isn't it?" Cece remarked.

"Impressive," Lily nodded, but as he continued to spew details about the monocrystalline solar panels and the carbon canoe boom, she imagined herself stuffing a sock in his mouth and wrapping duct tape around his head.

Ben took her smile as an encouraging sign.

"I hope you're calling with good news," Mark said when he heard his father's voice on the other end of the line.

"Good news and bad news," Jeff said. "My buddy, Bob Gaynor ran the plate number you gave me and was able to trace it to the owner."

"Better give me the bad news before you get my hopes up."

"Okay. It doesn't tell us who was driving the car."

"And the good news?"

"It was stolen."

"The car?"

"No, the plate. Taken off a car in a south Toronto neighbourhood. The owner is a sixty-seven-year-old woman who had left her car parked on the street. She doesn't drive it that often and didn't notice the plates were missing until three days after the date your mystery car appeared on the video," Jeff said.

"Interesting. Now we know there was criminal activity associated with the car that was parked near the murder scene."

"Yes, the plot thickens."

From her seat in the aft cockpit, Lily admired the scenery of the coastline. "It's so beautiful here. How long have you lived in Antigua, Oliver?"

"A couple of years. I rented for a while, then finally bought a house five months ago."

"So… Skipper's must be doing well to afford you this lifestyle," Lily said.

"It pays the bills. Originally, I bought and sold properties. Then I branched out, scooped up some small companies."

"Like what?"

As expected, Ben was evasive. "They're sold off now, but I have other investments. I bought Skipper's because I've always wanted to own a bar. I oversee the business, but I've got people to run it for me."

"Like Jenson."

"Yeah, Jenson. He's many things all rolled into one. I have a small guest house, so in exchange for free rent he takes care of the gardens and pool and does repairs. And he looks after the place when I'm away, which is often." He edged closer on the bench until their legs touched.

"I could use some sun," Lily said. "Could we move to the open deck?"

"Sure." Ben slid out from behind the table. "I'm going to take over for Jenson while he prepares lunch. Why don't you go out front and work on that tan? I'll drop anchor in a few minutes, so we can have a swim."

Lily stripped down to her orange bikini and stretched out on one of the trampolines for some Ben-free time. Twenty minutes later the sails were lowered and they anchored in a pretty cove. Lily made her way along the side deck to the stern. Dennis and Cece were descending the steps of the cockpit skirt to the water.

"Are you a good swimmer, Kate?" Ben asked, stripping off his shirt.

"Good enough, but I'd prefer not to get my hair wet." Lily checked out his waxed chest and firm, tanned abs. He wasn't as tall as Brent, but he'd done a good job sculpting his body. A colourful mermaid tattoo had been inked over the anchor that had once decorated his right arm. Ben noticed her looking and playfully flexed his pecs before pulling off his trunks to reveal a Speedo.

With a squeal, Cece took the plunge, followed closely by her husband. Ben dove headfirst over the side. Lily sat on the lowest step and eased herself into the water, careful to keep her brown contact lenses in place. Much to her relief, Ben didn't engage in any splashing nonsense and a short time later, they all climbed back on board.

For lunch, Jenson served them a fish stew with ducanna, a savory side dish. When they finished eating, Lily slipped down to the galley where he was cleaning up, and complimented him on the meal.

"You must try more of our Antiguan foods while you are here. Fungi and pepperpot is our national dish and I think you would like goat water, too," he said, genuinely pleased.

Lily wrinkled her nose and he laughed.

Ben poked his head through the galley doorway. He seemed a little annoyed that she was talking to Jenson. "Let's go up top," he said.

Lily could feel his eyes on her body as she went ahead of him up the stairs to the fly bridge. Ben ushered her into the control station cockpit. He knocked a cigarette out of a pack and held it out to her.

Lily shook her head.

"Didn't think so. Nasty habit, eh? My last vice. I'm going to give it up, though." He lay back on the long-cushioned seat, one arm behind his neck, and Lily noted with some amusement that he'd trimmed and dyed his armpit hair to match the rest of his new body.

"Has Romeo turned up yet?" Ben asked.

"In fact, he did finally call early this morning. Said he was sorry and that we needed to talk."

Ben exhaled a cloud of smoke.

"I told him I'd think about it, but meanwhile I'd be spending today in the company of a rich, handsome guy on his yacht."

Ben snickered and looked very pleased.

"I don't think he believed me, but he'll find out soon enough."

"Good for you."

Lily turned her head as some smoke drifted her way. "And what about Mona? Somehow I don't think you've seen the last of her."

Ben took a last drag and tossed his cigarette over the side, sending the DNA sample Lily had been contemplating with it.

"Mona is unstable. And she's a raging lunatic when she's using."

"Using what? More than alcohol?"

Ben nodded, but didn't explain.

"I feel somewhat responsible for that last unpleasant scene," Lily said.

"Don't. It's not about you. It's about her own problems."

And about the way you flicked her away like that cigarette butt, Lily thought. "I'd be watching my back if I were you."

"Let's forget about Mona and talk about you. Who are you, Kate?"

It took a frightful moment for Lily to realize that Ben was simply asking her to tell him more about herself. She proceeded to share fabricated details about her life in Auckland.

When she finished, he sat up and reached for her hands. He leaned close and looked deeply into her eyes. "Do you wear contacts?" he asked suddenly.

Flustered, Lily dropped her gaze. "I… yes, I do."

Ben lifted her chin. "I didn't mean to embarrass you. Your eyes are beautiful." He grinned. "You thought I was going to kiss you, didn't you?"

"Well, I…"

Before she could react, Ben's mouth was on hers, wet and insistent. Lily put her hands on his shoulders and pushed him away.

"Listen B… buddy, we had a deal. I was clear when I said I needed to resolve things with my fiancé before I got involved with anyone else. I thought you would respect that." Lily squirmed. She had nearly called him Ben.

"Sorry." Ben stood and moved a couple of steps away. "I was out of line. It's just that I really like you and I know you won't be here long. I'm afraid you might patch things up with your boyfriend and I'll never see you again."

"Fiancé. And if you want to win my affections, that's not the way to go about it."

"Yeah, I know. I just thought we were having a moment there. I thought you were attracted to me."

Lily sighed, "I *am* attracted to you."

"Okay, look, I give you my word. If there's a next time, it will be totally up to you to make the first move."

Lily smiled at him. "Alright, then what does a girl have to do to get a drink around here?"

Ben brightened. "What would you like?"

"How about one of those Faceoffs you invented?"

"Do you honestly like those?"

"They're delicious."

"Well then, I'll make it myself. Let's spend some time with the Windles before we head back."

They descended to the aft deck and Lily pulled her shorts and top on while Ben disappeared into the galley. When he returned, he handed her the drink in a tall glass. The Windles came out of the saloon, their own drinks in hand.

"Kate's having a hard time nailing down the last ingredient in my Faceoff drink," he told the others.

Lily took a sip. "Triple sec?"

"Nope."

"How about some photos?" Lily suggested, pulling her smartphone from her bag. She snapped a close-up of the Windles then handed the phone to Cece. "Now one of us."

Ben reluctantly allowed Lily to remove his sunglasses. He seemed mollified when she put her arm around him for the photo.

"Okay," Ben announced, "time to pull up anchor. We're going to motor back."

Once again, the Windles went up to the fly bridge and Lily found herself alone with Ben. "I'm curious about what Americans living in places like this do to make a living," she said. "The Windles, for example."

"The Windles are major shareholders in a US restaurant chain. They also own stock in a medical equipment company and the oil industry. At one time, Dennis had a marketing company that made millions off a non-profit charity run by – guess who – Cece," Ben laughed. "They have loads of money socked away in foreign accounts."

"I've heard about people doing that to hide their money from the IRS," Lily said. It occurred to her that *Windle* preceded by *Dennis* sounded a lot like *swindle.*

"It's more common than you might think," Ben said. "There are places where it's next to impossible for the government to track it down."

"Well, I'll never be rich enough to worry about it," Lily laughed. "Did you sock away your millions in foreign banks, too?"

Ben gave her a sly grin. "Let's just say I'm not careless with my money."

The engines began to throb and Lily glanced at her watch. It was not quite one o'clock.

"My house is nice, but comparatively small. I don't want to have a lot of money tied up in real estate. Too hard to sell if I decide to move on."

"Why? You're not sure you'll stay here long term?"

"I like to keep my options open. Anyway, the grander the home, the more attention and danger you attract."

"There are thieves everywhere, I suppose."

"Tell you what. How about when we get back to Jolly Harbour, I'll show you my place. And don't worry – hands off. We could have a nice dinner then I'd deliver you back to your hotel."

It was what Lily had been hoping for. A quick look at Ben's house, perhaps enough time to snoop around and get more information out of him.

"That would be nice. I'll need to be back fairly early though. I still need to have that talk with Sam," she said.

Ben nodded and lit another cigarette. They were moving now, slicing through the sea at a good clip. Lily moved out from beneath the canopy into the strong light. The novelty of it all was still fresh – the balmy air, the pale sea, the lush tropical foliage. Toronto would still be mostly dull and brown this time of year, with temperatures fluctuating unpredictably, but she was eager to go back. Hopefully tomorrow. It would be the first day of spring.

Jeff wanted to learn more about the news Simone had shared with Kate concerning Ben's biological brother and the Ponzi scheme in Chicago. He scrolled through the pages of an archived news story on the arrest and conviction of Richard Hogan and his wife, Nicole. There had been a third person, a fifty-seven year old Jarvis David Guzman, who'd been involved in the investment scam and who, as it turned out, had initiated everything. He'd been previously convicted on six counts of securities fraud, wire fraud and conspiracy to commit fraud in Texas, and had been released after serving four years in a federal penitentiary, only to vanish and re-emerge as Dave Powers in Chicago. He'd started a new business, Lakeshore Investors, with Richard and Nicole as partners and they'd been phenomenally successful at their scheme, bilking clients out of nearly twenty-seven million dollars.

Everything had been going as planned until Dave Powers had a heart attack and died. He'd been found slumped at the wheel of his Jaguar which had rolled to a stop against a *Bump Ahead* sign outside the Royal Melbourne Country Club. The discovery of suspicious documents in his possession had led to a search of his home office, where investigators found evidence of his criminal activities.

Before Richard and Nicole could disappear, authorities had arrived. The Hogans had claimed to know nothing about Guzman's past or his misappropriation of client funds, but it was clear that at least some of the money had found its way into their pockets. A woman named Lisa Chan, who was Guzman's live-in girlfriend and personal assistant, had testified for the prosecution in exchange for immunity. In the end, only thirteen million dollars in assets and funds had been accounted for. It had been alleged by the Hogans' defense that Guzman, as the head of the firm, had hidden the rest and taken the information to his grave. Richard had been convicted and sentenced to nine years in prison and Nicole, to five.

Jeff typed *Ben Baines* along with *Lakeshore Investors scam* in the search bar and found a longer article that mentioned him. A few unhappy clients from the yacht club had identified him as the person who'd introduced them to Lakeshore Investors, but no proof of collusion between Ben and the company was ever found.

Jeff suspected that Ben had been involved in the scam. It seemed likely that something more than brotherly love had made him pull up roots and move to Chicago. Richard and Nicole would have tried to cover any connection to the stolen funds after Guzman died. Knowing they were headed for prison, they may have entrusted Ben to move the money or, at the very least, safeguard it for them.

Jeff tried to imagine what must have been going through Ben's mind. He may have feared that it was only a matter of time before his involvement came to light. He might have seen the convictions of Richard and Nicole as an opportunity to take the money and run, break from his past and live a life of luxury. But he needed them to believe he was dead and for that, he needed Brent. The plan had worked for a while. Had Ben known that Brent was about to talk? Or had he planned to kill him – or have him killed – all along?

Jeff rubbed his temples. What had Lily been thinking, going after Ben like that? If she got out of this unscathed, he was going to wring her neck.

The yellow house was on a mountainside and although it didn't resemble the palatial, fortressed homes they'd passed on the ride there, it was impressive. The guest cottage matched the main house and an infinity pool bordering a hillside garden stretched between the two buildings. Ben unlocked a side door and held it open for Lily.

This entrance opened to a hallway with a small laundry room on the left.

"The tour starts here," Ben said.

Leading her down the hallway to the right, he showed her a guest room and a bathroom.

"And what's in there?" Lily asked, pointing to a third, solid-looking door.

Ben took his key ring from his pocket and unlocked it. "My office," he said. The room was tastefully decorated and afforded a view of the patio and pool. Lily noted the bars on the window. She glanced at the door. It had a double cylinder lock. Ben led her back into the hall, leaving the door ajar.

The bright, airy central space with its vaulted ceiling incorporated kitchen, dining and living areas. From there, Lily followed Ben into a second hallway that connected to the front entrance on the opposite side of the house. The foyer blended into a cozy sitting area lined with bookshelves. He showed her the spacious master bedroom and en suite and led her through French doors that opened to a large veranda at the back. Lily admired the lovely rattan furniture and bright patterned cushions, the overhead fans and the white-painted wood of the columns, railings and high ceiling. But the best thing about the space was the magnificent view down the hillside to the curving coastline and sea beyond.

"Great view, eh?"

"Breathtaking!" Lily imagined Ben sitting in his prison cell, remembering all of this. His home, his bar, his boat.

"Where shall we sit? Here or by the patio? Same view."

"The patio."

They picked up drinks in the kitchen and sat at a table near the pool. Several minutes passed as Lily peppered Ben with questions about his interests and his travels.

Finally, Ben leaned toward her. "You feel so familiar, Kate."

"People feel that way when they really click with someone," Lily said. "Maybe that's what I'm lacking with Sam." She put her nearly empty glass down. "Too much iced tea. May I use your bathroom?"

"Of course," Ben said. "Take your time. I have a call to make."

Lily slipped in through the open office door and surveyed the room. Quickly, she searched the drawers in Ben's desk. There were office supplies and printer paper, but no folders or records of any kind. The right bottom drawer was empty except for one item – a semi-automatic Smith and Wesson SD40. She grimaced and turned her attention to the computer. A tap of the mouse brought it out of sleep mode and Lily navigated to Ben's bookmarks. Only one bank, First Caribbean International, appeared on the list. Lily clicked and waited anxiously for the page to load. When it did, two windows appeared, requiring an account number and password. She went to email, but found that it, too, was password protected.

Lily glanced out the window toward the pool. Ben was still sitting there, tapping on his phone. She went back to the computer and clicked on Documents. A list of files appeared and she scanned them quickly. There were items pertaining to *The Swan* and Skipper's Bar and Grill, but not much else.

She opened the top drawer of the filing cabinet next to the desk. There were a few hanging folders, but a quick search revealed only a handful of bills and receipts associated with household expenses. The next drawer contained a small briefcase. She was about to unzip it when the creak of a floorboard at the doorway made her jump.

"Find what you were looking for?" Ben asked, his voice tight.

"Oh, I was looking for a phone directory so I could..."

"Save it." Ben stepped into the room, closed the door and leaned against it. He held up a phone. With shock, Lily recognized it as her own. She'd left it in her tote bag on the patio.

"What's this doing on your phone?" He turned the screen toward her and she saw the photo of Ben – the old Ben.

"You went through my bag?"

"I wanted to delete that picture you took of me today, *Kate from Toronto*. Or is it Lily?"

Lily made a wild dash for the desk drawer and Ben was on her in an instant. He grabbed her wrist and twisted her around, pressing her against the wall while he reached into the drawer and withdrew the gun. Lily kicked his leg, but didn't have the angle or the force to do any damage.

Ben clamped his arm around her neck and forced her into a corner chair. "Sit!" He backed away toward the door, levelling the gun at her.

"How did you know it was me?" Lily had dropped her Kiwi accent.

Ben glared at her. "You don't think I follow the news up there in Ontario? I know all about your great escape. But I didn't recognize you until I found those pictures on your phone. I especially liked the before and after shots when you changed your appearance."

"You changed your appearance, too. You look so good now."

"It wasn't easy." Ben leaned his back against the door and lowered the gun. "But it was worth it. My life is finally great. I live in paradise and have everything I want, a beautiful house, beautiful women. And respect."

Lily wanted to say, *Yes, with money stolen from people whose lives were ruined.* But she had to play to his ego. "You worked hard for it."

"How did you find me? How the hell did you even know I was alive?"

"I was able to retrieve some deleted files from one of Brent's old computers. I found a faked photo of him looking extremely thin, supposedly taken when he was rescued. That tipped us off and –"

"Us?"

"I've got help. People who are hiding me."

Ben sighed wearily. "Go on."

"Then I managed to get a look inside Brent's house and I found some clues. Map coordinates. So, I… we came here."

"Who's 'we'?"

"My… brother is with me," Lily said.

"I don't believe you." Ben studied her face. "And this fiancé of yours, this 'Sam' guy doesn't exist?"

"No."

"Humph. Well, that is sad consolation."

"You know, Ben, under different circumstances, it could've worked for us."

"Yeah, right."

"There was a strong connection between us. Didn't you feel it, too? I could've left as soon as I found you, but you intrigued me and I wanted to spend more time with you."

"Right. You didn't come all the way down here to get some money back for a bunch of people you've never met. And don't lie to me. I'm not stupid."

"That's for sure. No one I know could have pulled this off. You completely reinvented yourself and orchestrated every brilliant move."

Ben stared at Lily in silence for several heartbeats, then he gestured at her face with the Smith and Wesson. "Take those brown contacts out."

"What?"

"I want to see those blue eyes everyone raves about."

"Are you serious?"

"Take them out."

Lily extracted the lenses.

Ben came closer, leaned forward and stared into her eyes. "They're Caribbean blue. You're even more beautiful than you were as Kate." He stepped back. "Why did you have to ruin everything?"

"I had a chance to escape and I took it. But I knew I couldn't stay out of prison unless I…"

"Tracked me down and turned me in as my brother's killer," Ben finished for her. He stared at the gun.

Lily sidestepped the subject of Brent's murder. "You don't have to kill me," she said quietly. "You must still have money stashed somewhere. You can disappear again."

"Not before you run to the police."

"There's no way I'd do that," Lily said. "We're both outlaws. I don't want to be recaptured, especially in a foreign country. And believe it or not, I like you."

Seconds ticked by before Ben spoke. "Do you or do you not have someone here in Antigua with you?"

"No. I'm in contact with my friend, the real Kate, every day, though."

"Who else knows you're here?"

"By now, the rest of my family. They'll stop at nothing to bring you down if I disappear."

"Why didn't you just tell the police where I was?"

"I wasn't sure you were here. And frankly, I thought I'd be better at tracking you down."

Ben stared at the gun. "I don't want to kill you, but I don't see how letting you go could work."

"Look at me," Lily said.

Ben met her eyes.

"They would all know you did it. My friends know where I found you and what name you're using." She watched his eyes as he mulled this over. "You have money left, don't you? In accounts in other places. Belize, Cayman Islands, Switzerland?"

"About six and a half million," Ben said. "Half what I started with. This was supposed to last me a lifetime."

"You can still live in style for the rest of your life. Grab a suitcase and catch a flight out of here right now. You can get a new identity and start over somewhere."

"I have multiple identities already," Ben said.

"Then you're prepared."

Silence.

"Why did Brent go along with this scheme? What did he get out of it?" Lily asked.

"The house. I agreed not to sue him. And he figured a good survival story would put him back in the spotlight."

"And did you and Brent actually buy a ketch and sail it across the Atlantic?"

"Yeah, an old one. We figured someone would probably check our story. We scuttled it off the coast, then used false IDs to fly to Costa Rica where we went through a gruelling routine to drop weight. Brent spent hours in the sun and roughed up his skin." Ben waved the gun at her. "And you and my idiot brother screwed it up!"

Lily sucked in her breath. "Tell me one more thing."

"What?" Ben glared at her.

She gave him a meek, half smile. "What's the last ingredient in your Faceoff drink?"

With a small snort, Ben sank onto the edge of the desk. "Creme de Cacao."

"I want to live to taste more of those."

"I'm not going to prison," Ben said.

"You won't if you leave now. But if I don't talk to Kate at the appointed time today, in less than four hours, the cops will be all over this place. You won't get out of Antigua."

There was silence as doubt wavered in Ben's eyes.

"I'm sorry I messed things up for you. Nothing I do to keep myself out of prison will be at the expense of your freedom, I promise."

Ben made a sudden decision. "Lie face down on the floor under your chair."

Lily did as she was told, wriggling her body into position between the wide legs of the antique oak chair.

She watched as Ben tucked the gun in his pants pocket and retrieved the briefcase from the filing cabinet. He removed a painting from the wall, exposing a safe. From inside, he withdrew a small laptop computer, a file folder and some fat stacks of American bills, all of which he stuffed into the briefcase.

"I'm going to pack a bag," Ben said. "Then we're out of here. I have a friend who's away in Barbados for a few days. I'll take you to his house and lock you in his wine cellar."

"No, please listen, just–"

"There's an air duct. I'll leave you food and water and whatever you need and when I'm safely out of the country, I'll let someone know where you are." At the doorway, he gave Lily a long look. She wasn't sure if it was anger or anguish that she saw in his eyes. "Too bad. We could've had a good thing."

Lily heard the key turn in the lock and listened to the sound of his retreating footsteps as he moved down the hall. She crawled out from beneath the chair and examined the door hinges. In the desk drawer, she found a wooden ruler, a heavy stapler and an expensive looking silver pen. She turned her attention to the top hinge, positioning the tip of the pen on the bottom of the pin. She pounded upward with the stapler. It budged a little, moving as far as the tapered end of the pen would allow. Switching to the ruler, she angled the end of it under the cap of the pin and tapped. With a little coaxing, the pin lifted out of the cylinder and dropped to the carpet.

Next, Lily unscrewed the pen and used the top half so she'd have more room to swing the stapler at the bottom pin. She went to work, grumbling as the awkward angle slowed her progress. "Come on, you son-of-a–"

"Skipper?" Jenson's voice was coming from down the hall, near the patio door. He'd stayed behind to "put *The Swan* to bed" when they'd parted on the dock and hadn't been expected back before dinner.

Lily lowered her mouth to the crack beneath the door. "Jenson!" she called. "Help!" She heard footsteps approach and stop just outside the door. The knob wiggled.

"Kate? Is it you?"

"Jenson, listen! I can't explain it all now, but you need to get out of here and call the police. Oliver is not who you think he is. He said he's going to lock me in a friend's wine cellar, and then he's going to flee the country."

"What? This does not–"

"Jenson, just do it! Hurry!"

Lily heard the sound of Jenson's feet running back down the hall. She resumed her attack on the hinge. Slowly a small gap appeared between the cylinder and the pin. She snapped the ruler in half so she had room to swing at it. Precious seconds elapsed before her short taps budged the pin, then a few more good knocks released it. She slid the ruler beneath the door and levered it toward her, creating a space for her fingers on the hinged side. At last, she pulled the door free, leaned it against the wall and bolted down the hall.

As she burst outside onto the patio, she spotted Ben's phone sitting on the table next to her tote bag. She snatched them both and was running along the driveway when she saw Jenson, sprawled near his truck, blood saturating the ground around his head. His chest was not moving and the aura of death shrouded his body just as it had Brent's on that terrible day when she'd knelt in his blood.

Lily sprinted, anticipating at every step, the crack of a gun. But she made it to the road and kept going as the alarm blaring in her head drove her down the hill. The sound of an engine brought her to a halt. She looked back up the hill and, with great relief, saw that it was a taxi van. She stood in the middle of the road and waved her arms frantically. As the van slowed to a stop, she tried to affect a casual air.

"Got room for one more?" she asked, smiling at the driver and his two passengers.

"Are you alright, Miss?" the driver asked, as a group of motorcycles roared by.

"My husband and I had an argument and he left without me," Lily said. "He'll be back, but I don't want to wait for him." The fictitious Sam was turning out to be a real bastard.

The woman behind the driver said, "Let her in. We don't mind."

With that, the door was opened and Lily climbed into the front beside the driver. "Thank you," she said, still catching her breath.

"You look shaken," said the male passenger. "Are you hurt?"

"No, just out of shape," Lily replied with a laugh.

"That's terrible, him leaving you like that!" said the woman.

"Where are you staying?" asked the driver.

"The Heritage Hotel at the Quay." Lily glanced out the back window. Another half dozen motorcycles were strung out behind them.

"We're going in that direction, anyway," said the man.

The taxi made its way down the curving mountain road and into St. John's. Motorcycles were everywhere, all moving in the general direction of the harbour.

"Must be time for that motorcycle cruise to load up," the woman said, glancing at her watch. "What a racket."

They came to at a standstill in traffic on Thames Street, two blocks from Lily's hotel. "You can let me out here," she said. "What do I owe you?"

"It's on us," the woman replied. "Our pleasure."

"That's very kind of you," Lily said. "At least let me get the tip." When she pressed a twenty-dollar bill into the driver's hand, he rewarded her with a wide, grateful smile.

Lily decided to make a quick stop at the hotel, grab her things and find different accommodations for the night. At the corner of Thames and High, she began jogging toward the hotel. She didn't notice the silver Harley Electra Glide among the other motorcycles at first, but as it drew closer, the recognition hit her like a thunderbolt. The silver helmet with the pirate skull emblem, the dark visor – it had to be him.

Without breaking stride, Lily veered away and cut through the parking area of the Heritage Quay complex. She exited on the other side and made her way to Redcliffe Street where she looked frantically in both directions. More motorcycles, moving slowly, approached from the east. Lily spotted a taxi to the west and streaked toward it, but it turned south. She followed in its wake and found herself at the corner of Redcliffe and Nevis Streets with the harbour on her right. She had just rounded the corner, when the sight of the silver Harley coming swiftly her way stopped her in her tracks. With no time to think, she turned on her heel and ran out onto the pier where the *Grand Princess* was docked.

All around Lily, a steady flow of passengers drifted toward their checkpoints, still a good distance away. As she jogged forward, weaving in and out of the crowd, she heard the low growl of the Harley's engine. She melted into the group ahead of her, emerging in front. She now had two options. Stand there in her neon pink bull's-eye of a shirt waiting for Ben to do something or ask the crew to summon the police. She glanced back at the Harley. It was idling at the corner of the street. She doubted Ben would come down the pier with so many passengers and crew members around.

She was almost at the first checkpoint. People were showing their ID cards before proceeding around the corner and up the gangway. Two lines were forming at machines set up just inside the door of the ship where passengers were having their faces and cards scanned. As she stepped aside to let some of the people behind her move past, a shot rang out. There was a split second of confusion. Heads turned. A woman screamed, "It's a gun! Someone's shooting!" In the next instant, there was a stampede toward the cruise ship. A second shot sounded and Lily felt the ripping air close to her head. She charged past the checkpoint, up the gangway and burst through the entrance to the ship along with the others.

Panic ensued. Bodies charged and pushed. Bags were dropped, people stumbled and fell. Those still upright didn't stop in the reception area. Up the steps they fled and Lily fled with them. "What's happening?" she heard, as some of the passengers already on board were swept up in the chaos.

The trampling of feet slowed as the hysteria began to subside, but Lily kept running, up and away, until she spotted some elevators. One of the doors was opening and when a gentleman exited, she slipped inside. She pushed the button for the Promenade Deck, and tried to slow her breathing as the elevator rose. Its sedate music was an unlikely accompaniment for the fear still coursing through her. When she got off on the seventh level she was greeted with a view of elegant, curving staircases that descended two levels to the Piazza below her. Cutting through a lounge, she made her way outside to the nearly empty deck and looked cautiously over the side. The Harley was gone and a lone figure was directing returning passengers off the street at the entryway to the pier. Crew members scurried about below. The police would soon arrive. Witnesses would be questioned, rumours would run rampant. The passengers aboard the motorcycle cruise at the next pier would naturally fall suspect.

A crew member appeared, walking briskly along the deck. "Everyone inside please!" she said as she approached Lily and two other passengers gawking at the scene below. "Stay off the deck until further notice."

Lily went back into the lounge. She removed Ben's phone from her bag and, legs still trembling, tried to collect her thoughts. There would be an investigation, but it would be difficult for authorities to round up and account for the three thousand plus passengers aboard this ship. Just maybe she could cruise her way out of Antigua. She had a phone, a credit card, some cash, and a few items of clothing. No cabin, but unlimited free food. She wasn't sure how she was going to disembark, but if she were to be apprehended, it would be far better to be in US territory.

An announcement by the captain informed everyone that there had been an incident on the pier involving an armed individual and that the situation was under investigation. He asked that no one use the balconies or open decks. He assured everyone that the situation was under control and that the ship would leave port at the earliest opportunity.

Picking up the phone, Lily entered Clair's cell number. The land line was off limits now that the police were aware of Mark's connection to the Youngs.

"Lily!" Kate said when she heard her voice. "Mark's here. He wanted to call earlier, but I convinced him to wait."

Mark's voice joined Kate's. "Lily, this is crazy. You need to get on the next plane home."

"Listen, you two. There's been a development and I don't have a lot of time to explain, so save the lecture." She related the events that had transpired that day. "Do *not* alert the police," she warned them. "If I don't get out of the country, I could be implicated in Jenson's murder and I have no reason to believe that would end well. I don't know if calls can be made while we're at sea, so if you don't hear from me between ports, don't assume there's a problem."

"How are you going to get off the ship?" Mark asked. "Don't you need to show them your cruise card and go through Customs and Immigration?"

"I'm sure I do," Lily sighed. "I don't want to drain this battery, because I have no charger for the phone. I'll try to call tomorrow when we reach the next port, but the phone will be off until then."

She ended the call and placed another to the Heritage Hotel. Her absence there would be noticed so she cancelled her room, explaining that she was visiting Half Moon Bay and had decided to stay there, but would return in two or three days to pick up her carryon bag and settle her bill. Her request was accepted without question.

Lily turned off the phone and tried to collect her thoughts. Realizing she'd escaped, Ben had probably put his briefcase in the storage compartment of his motorcycle and given chase. He'd be on his way to the airport now with a passport in some other name and would most likely be far away using yet another identity by the time Jenson's body was found. *Jenson's body.* A dark sense of guilt descended on her. She hadn't actually killed him herself, but she'd poked the snake that did.

As predicted, police arrived and secured the area around the ship. An announcement soon followed, summoning all passengers who'd been on the pier or at the checkpoints at the time of the incident, to report to their Muster Stations with their electronic cruise cards. The ship's departure was to be delayed for an unspecified length of time.

People were gravitating to the dining rooms for dinner, but Lily wasn't hungry. She'd gone from terrified to edgy. She made her way up to the Lido deck, stretched out on a lounger and closed her eyes. At some point, she became aware that the sun was no longer warming her skin. It was fully dark when the captain finally announced that the ship would be leaving port momentarily. He apologized for the delay and assured passengers that they would soon have access to all areas of the ship, but gave no update on the investigation.

Once they'd left port and the lights of Antigua began to shrink into the distance, Lily picked up a slice of pizza and a bottle of juice from one of the poolside grills and went up to the Sun Deck where a few people were gathering for *Movies Under the Stars.* She pulled on her jeans and jacket and settled in on a lounge chair. An attendant gave her a blanket and she managed to catch a little sleep during the double feature. When the movies finally ended she strolled the massive ship, resting for short periods of time on various decks.

One by one, the venues closed until, around four a.m., she found herself mostly alone on the open decks. At last the sky slowly brightened. She made her way to the forward part of the Sun Deck, leaned against the railing and gazed out at the water. The ship was approaching its next port, the quay just coming into view in the soft light. The land, with its lush green mountains sloping into the sea, reminded her of St. Kitts and suddenly time compressed and her ill-fated honeymoon seemed as present as the rising sun and the salty air. The ship was beginning to stir and a few early risers were up and about. The dining rooms would be busy soon. Lily's stomach rumbled as she headed for the stairs.

CHAPTER

28

March 20

The mountain of food in the Michelangelo Dining Room was staggering. Lily perused it all and settled on Eggs Benedict, pineapple slices and coffee.

As she was leaving, she found a discarded copy of *Princess Patter*, the daily newsletter, on one of the tables, and from that she was able to glean information about the cruise schedule. Currently, they were in Tortola in the British Virgin Islands. During the night, they would embark on the final leg of the cruise that would put them in San Juan, Puerto Rico at six the next morning.

From the dining room, Lily went up to the Promenade Deck and stared down at the clear, pale water of the harbour below. It seemed friendly enough, even inviting, but it was a significant drop from deck seven. The water looked shallow, but the draft of a ship this size had to be considerable. From somewhere in her brain's repository of information, she remembered a figure of twenty-five to thirty feet for a vessel of this size. The depth of the harbour would be in excess of that. *Enough to keep me from hitting bottom when I jump,*

Lily thought. *When I jump?* She'd caught herself plotting her next feat of escape, even as sound reasoning told her Puerto Rico would have to be the end of her run.

She considered the idea. She was comfortable in the water and a controlled fall would probably be safe. It would still be mostly dark when the ship docked and there wouldn't be many passengers around. Although there were surveillance cameras aimed at all parts of the deck, they were not likely to be monitored. She remembered once reading that they had been used on occasion to pinpoint the time someone had gone overboard *after* it had been reported by other passengers and that man overboard alarms were not commonly used.

In addition to the physical risk involved in jumping, there was a huge drawback. Someone could see her. There would be crew on the pier; a few early risers on their balconies watching as the boat arrived at its last port. Another ship could be tied up close by. There may even be customs officials milling around.

There was another option. She could jump before the ship reached the harbour, soon enough that she still had the cover of darkness, but not so soon that she had to swim a great distance. That presented a whole different set of problems, all involving danger. Rough seas, sharks, and rip currents came to mind. Lily shook off the thought and went inside to call Kate.

Once again, Mark was there when she answered the phone and Lily wondered if he'd stayed the night. "You're on speakerphone," he said.

"I have to keep this short, but any news about Antigua?" she asked.

"Yes," Mark said. "This much we found out through the internet. That Jenson guy who worked for Ben was rushed to hospital. He wasn't dead, as you'd thought, but he's in a coma."

"What? I was sure he was dead! I should have called for help."

"He'd been struck on the head. It's still under investigation. Apparently, a woman friend came looking for him when he didn't respond to her calls. And there's more. A man identified as Oliver Tate was also found on the premises, shot dead with his own gun."

"No!" Lily shouted and she quickly lowered her voice as a woman passing through the lounge area looked her way. "But who–"

"That's all I know, Lil. Dad thinks we should go to the OPP commander in Oakville, to tell him what we know about Oliver's true identity."

"Make him wait, Mark. I need one more day to get off this ship. Was it murder or suicide?"

"We don't know."

"Ben was shooting at me at the pier, so that means he had to go back home and shoot himself or get shot before the police arrived. Did it say what time that was?"

"No."

"*Mona.*"

"Who?"

"The crazy girlfriend, Mona. Maybe she was waiting for him when he got back. I don't know her last name, but there's an American couple in St. John's who probably do. Dennis Windle and his wife, Cece."

"Swindle?" Kate asked.

"*Windle.* It would have to be an anonymous tip, but–" Suddenly she was struck by a different thought. "Damn! Your phone, Kate! If it was on Ben when his body was found, then they'll connect him with you. Or if it's in his house, they'll find it."

There was silence and then Mark said, "Could be Ben ditched it somewhere because he wouldn't want to be linked to any of us, either. The police would have contacted Kate by now if they'd found her phone."

"Maybe." Lily sighed. "Listen, just wait for me to get off the ship. It's arriving in Puerto Rico – US territory – tomorrow morning and I have a plan."

"What kind of plan?" Kate's voice was full of apprehension.

"I have to go now," Lily said. "Give me until late afternoon tomorrow. Love you guys. Bye." Turning off the phone, Lily sank back into her chair and stared at the ceiling. Ben was dead. His true identity could soon be confirmed, but that wouldn't necessarily clear her of Brent's murder and if Ben's death was not a suicide, she could find herself in deeper trouble. Coming forward now was not an option.

A loud screech followed by a cold spray of water jolted Lily from her nap. She sat up and looked around. Several people were gathered at the pool and the sun was high overhead. Her skin had turned an alarming shade of pink. Standing up, she retrieved her tote bag from beneath the lounger and pulled her black shorts and pink shirt on over her bikini.

She made her way to the Botticelli dining room near the stern on deck six. She was running from the law, but how very different this was from her last experience. Instead of a blizzard, there was now scorching sun. And instead of the meager food supply that had fit into a single pocket, long rows of gourmet offerings now surrounded her on every side.

Lily filled a plate and found a table. A woman sitting alone at the table across from her did a double take.

"Oh, my! Looks like you got some sun today."

"I fell asleep by the pool," Lily confessed. "Thankfully, my face was covered at the time."

The woman fished around in her shoulder bag and pulled out a tube. "Try some Aftersun," she said. "It may help."

Lily thanked her and smeared some of the lotion over the front of her arms and legs.

"I'm Jeanette," the woman said. "That's my husband over there at the salad bar. We're from Winnipeg."

Great, Lily thought dismally. *Someone who's probably well acquainted with what's going on in the news in Canada.* "I'm Kate. My husband and I are from Baltimore. He's not feeling well so he's skipping lunch today." She hated lying to nice people like Jeanette.

"Oh, that's a shame. I hope he's better soon."

Jeanette's husband arrived at the table with a towering plate of food. Lily finished, bid the couple goodbye and took an elevator up to the Lido deck where she could find some shade.

Jeff was back at the station in Oakville, sitting next to Mark and staring at a monitor. They'd hit pay dirt with a digital recording of a silver Ford Focus entering a park in Oakville. This image was in colour and clear enough for them to make out the license number.

"That's the same car," Mark said. "The plates match and there's that cuff or triangle of clothing caught in the door."

They watched the screen as the car drove out of camera range, but twelve minutes later, it reappeared.

"Look!" Jeff said. "Same car, same cuff, different plate number!"

Mark leaned in and a smile slowly spread across his face. "Yep. Are you thinking what I'm thinking?"

"Whoever was in this vehicle pulled in here to switch the plates back."

"That's probably what he intended to do when they stopped at that school earlier. Either someone saw him or he spotted a surveillance camera, so he left." Mark squinted at the screen. "I say 'he' because I think that's a man but it's kind of hard to tell from this angle. Think you can get your OPP buddy to run this plate number?"

"He'll do it," Jeff said. "Keep in mind, the car may have nothing to do with Brent. There had been some break-ins in the area around that time. As soon as we get Lily home, we'll have to talk to someone and I think it should be Bob Gaynor."

Mark stood up and stretched, and Jeff eyed the printed message on his shirt. Come to the nerd side. We have Pi.

"Clever shirt."

Mark grinned. "My girlfriend gave it to me."

"Kate?"

"Who else?"

"I guess congratulations are in order."

"Thanks. I just have to keep her now. She's not entirely sure I'm a good idea. Can you imagine that?"

"Smart girl," Jeff laughed.

As they left the building, patchy clouds scudded across the sky, casting moving shadows over the landscape. "Today is the first day of spring," Jeff said. "Things are beginning to change. At long last."

Jemma was wearing the same powder blue fedora and pink sunglasses that she'd used to disguise her appearance at Phil's Room. "I don't know the music from your show yet," she said to the group gathered in the audition room, "but Mr. James said it would be alright if I sang *Without You.* It's really old, like from the seventies, but Mariah Carey recorded it and, um… "

"We know the song," Georgia said, smiling. "Go ahead."

Dean took his seat at the piano and, giving Jemma a smile and a nod of reassurance, played the introduction.

Jemma began singing, pitch perfect and at first, subdued. Her voice began to climb and swell with emotion as the lyrics carried her deeper into the song. Her body moved in eloquent gesticulation with the music. As she launched into the chorus, Georgia felt the hairs on her arms stand on end. She glanced at the others who seemed equally enthralled. When Jemma hit the last chorus, she was soaring.

Dean grinned as the song drew to an end, Jemma's voice softening as his fingers lightly sounded the final notes.

Her small audience applauded, something they customarily did not do. "That was wonderful, Jemma!" Michael exclaimed.

Dean hustled Jemma into the waiting area in the hall before they could begin firing questions at her. "Give us two minutes," he told her.

When the door closed, Georgia sprang. "I can't believe those pipes!"

"She's phenomenal," Spencer said. "You sure she's only fourteen?"

"Fifteen in July. What do you think? Can we consider her for the part?"

"I say we sign her on right now," Spencer said. "We still have a few call backs to see, but we need two alternates, anyway."

"I agree," Georgia said. "Okay, now talk. Where on earth did you find her?"

Dean pulled a handful of cigars from his pocket and began handing them out. "This is merely a symbolic gesture."

"Dean, what the hell–" Georgia stared at the object in her hand.

Turning to face them, Dean paused. "Georgia, don't be mad that I didn't tell you first." He opened the door and beckoned for Jemma to enter. She'd removed her hat and glasses, and her face was beautifully framed by her flowing hair.

Dean took her hand. "This is my daughter, Jemma James."

Lily leaned against the railing of the aft deck as the *Grand Princess* began to pick up speed. Other passengers had similarly gathered to watch the departure from Tortola. Lily's focus shifted from the coast to the churning water below. It looked opaque and foreboding now. In darkness, even with the wake illuminated by the ship's lights, it would be downright terrifying. In a few hours, she'd have to take the plunge and she was beginning to doubt her courage. She stretched as far forward as the railing would permit and bent her head over the side. *Will I get knocked out when I hit the water? Will I get sucked into the ship's giant propellers?* She searched her memory for accounts of passengers going overboard. The only ones she came up with involved foul play or drunken antics. Some lived, some didn't. What sane person would jump intentionally? Lily wasn't sure which was worse – the dreadful fear or the despair that was creeping in as she began to realize she wasn't up for this challenge.

"Hey! Kate!"

Jarred from her thoughts, Lily abruptly straightened and turned to find Jeanette, approaching with a drink in her hand.

"I spotted your pink shirt from up there at the bar," Jeanette said, gesturing behind them. She laughed. "Not thinking of jumping, are you?"

"Just watching the sea roll by. It's kind of humbling."

"A little scary, if you ask me. How's the sunburn?"

"Not too bad."

"And your husband? Is he feeling any better?"

"Yes, but he's in our stateroom, keeping his germs to himself."

Jeanette leaned into the railing. "I'm going to miss this. It's the first day of spring, though. Nicer weather is on the way. What's it like in Baltimore right now?"

"Quite nice. Turning green. What's it like in Winnipeg?"

"Winterpeg you mean? Still frightfully cold."

Lily smiled at the old joke.

They stood side by side in silence for a few moments as the sound of voices and laughter rose and fell behind them, and the warm wind washed over their skin. Lily gazed at the horizon and Abby's premonition came rushing at her. *You'll be going on a cruise. I see you leaning on the railing of a large ship and looking out over the water. Lots of people and laughter.*

"Oh!" Lily exclaimed; and involuntarily she clapped a hand over her mouth. She looked into Jeanette's startled face. "Sorry, it's just… well, you'll think this is crazy, but I went to see a psychic a while ago, before we planned this trip, and she said I'd be going on a cruise. I'd forgotten, but her words just popped into my head."

"Oh, I don't think it's crazy," Jeanette said, "I believe in premonitions and all that stuff."

"I'm more of a skeptic, but I have to admit, this is… strange."

Jeanette scrutinized her face and Lily was glad she was wearing her sunglasses this time. "You might think this is even crazier, but sometimes my dreams have messages for me. Like, I'll dream about someone I haven't seen in years and then out of the blue, they'll call me. It's bizarre."

Lily smiled and nodded.

"But then, sometimes my dreams make absolutely no sense," Jeanette continued. "Like this morning. I had this weird dream just before waking. The ship was approaching San Juan and I was running from something – I don't know what – I just knew I had to get away. I grabbed some water wings and jumped overboard. Me of all people, who can't even swim." She laughed.

A tingle crept up Lily's spine. "What happened then?"

"I swam. It was dark and scary, but I just kept dog paddling until I got to shore and then I saw this road and I followed it into San Juan. Then I woke up."

"Did you see sharks or anything dangerous in this dream?"

"No. I think I might have died in my sleep if that had happened."

"Strange what the unconscious mind can produce."

"It sure is," Jeanette said. "Well, I'd better find Greg. It was nice chatting with you."

"Same here. Enjoy the rest of your vacation, Jeanette."

"You, too, Kate."

As Jeanette left, Lily turned to face the sea once again. It looked just as uninviting as it had minutes before, but a calm had descended. She'd been given the little push she needed to get overboard. The idea that Jeanette's dream augured a positive outcome was something she would have rejected mere days ago, before Clair and Kate and Abby, before the miraculous string of events that had set her on this path. Was it luck or fate? Coincidence or divination? She pictured the colourful illustrations of characters on Clair's Tarot cards. Magician or Fool, Lily would go over that railing.

CHAPTER

29

March 21

The lights of San Juan twinkled in the distance, a distance Lily found difficult to judge across the darkened sea, but based on the time, she estimated the ship was about fifteen minutes from the mouth of the harbour. It was scheduled to dock at six. Given a speed of between twenty to twenty-five knots it was probably six miles out. Still too early to jump.

She'd picked her spot on the Promenade deck, port side, just below the lifeboats. Earlier, she'd scooped up a pool noodle that had been abandoned next to one of the hot tubs. She'd emptied her wallet, placing the remainder of her cash in her Ziploc bag, along with her credit card, passport, phone, and the extra set of brown contact lenses.

Lily was wearing her jeans and jacket over top of her shorts and T-shirt. The plastic bag was in her jacket, stuffed into one of the side pockets that had a zipper closure. All that remained was of no use to her. She'd rolled up her nearly empty tote and tied it snugly with her bikini top. Looking carefully around her, she stepped closer to the railing and let the bundle drop. It hit the water without a sound and disappeared. She swallowed. *Don't think about it.*

All too soon, the lights of the city loomed close and Lily discerned some of its features in the dim, predawn light. She saw the mouth of the harbour and the headlights of a vehicle moving along the shore to the left. The ship had slowed, but all was still and quiet onboard. Lily cautiously climbed over the railing and positioned herself on the other side. She pressed the pool noodle to her chest with one arm and looked down at the turbulent water, luminous green and frothy-white under the ship's lights. *Just do it. Before you lose your nerve.*

Concentrating, Lily took a deep breath and jumped neatly backwards, out and away from the ship. She plugged her nose as she descended and tried to hold her body straight so she would enter the water cleanly. The impact was harder than she'd expected and when she came to her senses the pool noodle was gone, both arms were above her head, and her jacket, shirt and bra were shoved up under her chin. She immediately began scissor kicking and stroking with her arms, struggling against her tangled clothing. The black water was blinding. She was on the verge of panic when her head finally broke the surface and she sucked fresh air into her lungs.

The ship had passed, but still loomed large, the stern and port side clearly visible. She scanned the balconies and decks for signs of activity, but not a soul was in sight. Coughing and spitting and bobbing in the wake, she adjusted her clothing. One sandal was gone, wrenched from her foot by the impact. She pulled the other one off and treaded water, recovering her composure and assessing her condition. There were no apparent injuries, just the lingering shock of her splashdown.

In the darkness, there was no sign of the pool noodle but Lily wasn't concerned. She was a strong swimmer. If necessary, she could turn her jeans into a floatation device by knotting them at the ankles and inflating them, a technique she'd learned in her lifesaving course of long ago. Fat waves were rolling toward land and soon she was moving with them, alternating a strong side stroke with a more restful breast stroke.

The shore was farther away than she'd anticipated and she guessed that a half hour had passed when she was close enough to hear the waves breaking on the beach. By then the sun had cleared the horizon and the ship had disappeared into the harbour. She could clearly see a number of flat-roofed buildings and some larger structures with turrets and stone walls. Old San Juan. A small strip of beach lay in the foreground and she angled her approach in that direction. As she drew closer, the surf began to drive her toward shore and she scanned the area ahead of her for hazards. Finally, Lily's feet touched bottom, and she was able to take a few steps before she was sucked off balance and then carried forward on another surge of sea water. At last she waded to the beach and surveyed her surroundings. Straight ahead and up a short incline were some small houses and a clump of bushes. To her left, a stony bank sloped up to a road. She made her way to a section of beach where the foliage screened her from view.

It was early, but the sun would soon take away the chill of the sea. Lily took off her jacket and removed the Ziploc bag. It had survived the entire ordeal, still sealed tight. She turned on Ben's phone and checked the time. Six thirty-two.

"You did what?" Kate exclaimed when Lily got through a few minutes later.

"I'm drying out on the beach as we speak." Lily replied, her voice remarkably light and casual. She laughed. "Yes, it was scary, but it's done. I'll be on the next flight to Toronto. I need to get a hotel room first so I can clean up and make the arrangements."

When Lily's clothes were mostly dry, she climbed up the bank to the road and began walking toward the centre of Old San Juan. She was wearing her extra set of brown contact lenses and she'd fluffed her hair into something reasonably presentable. Within an hour of her arrival in the business sector, she'd made purchases in three stores and had booked herself into a hotel. The clerk at Payless Shoes had accepted her "lost my shoes on the beach" without batting an eye.

In her hotel room, Lily made a reservation on an afternoon flight. By noon she was standing before a Customs and Immigration official at the Luis Munos Marin International Airport. The makeup helped immensely, but she and Kate were not identical. She held her breath as the official examined the photo and glanced at her face. And then she was through.

During her flight, Lily had plenty of time to think. Ben's death raised many questions, but she'd found him. Was there, as Clair believed, a benevolent force helping her? It seemed wrong to assume that she would be singled out for assistance by some kind of higher power when so many others, just as deserving, were left to suffer. Of one thing she was certain. She would do everything in her own power to determine her fate.

Jeff was waiting at the airport with open arms. The tension of the past few days and of squeaking through Customs yet again was finally released. Lily's emotional dam leaked and then burst wide open as she approached her father.

"Have the police questioned Kate about her phone yet?" Lily asked, wiping her eyes.

"It looks like no phone was found. Ben probably tossed it."

"Any word from Jemma? Or has she totally erased me from her life?"

"Jemma would never do that. Just give her some time."

Jeff was driving Clair's white Mercedes, a precaution against any measures police might have taken to track his whereabouts. Once they were on their way, heading for Rosedale, Lily related the details of her recent experiences.

"You could have died," Jeff said.

"Or got my life back."

"Well, I hope the high wire act is over."

"I'm not looking for any more excitement, that's for sure."

"Good. Okay, here's the plan," Jeff said. "Tomorrow I'm going to contact Commander Gaynor and tell him that I received an anonymous tip that Ben is alive and living in Antigua under the alias, Oliver Tate. Gaynor will then contact St. John's police and find out about the murder. From there, Ben's identity will be confirmed and, hopefully, the money he's got stashed away will be traced."

"And in what form will this anonymous tip come?"

"Phone. Tomorrow morning Mark is going to drive to a remote location and call our home phone. He's going to play a recording of one of those text-to-speech computer voices. He's also going to call 2 District with the same message. Your mother will then call me and I'll report it to Commander Gaynor. That way, when police check phone records, the round of calls, along with where and when they were placed, will show up. Our home phone is probably being tapped. It would be considered lawful interception."

"Gaynor will be suspicious. He's going to press you to tell him where I am," Lily said.

"He may press, but there's no proof. I have a feeling he's being deliberately lax about this. I hope some firm evidence against Ben surfaces, but either way, you'll have to turn yourself in soon. There are certainly enough new facts in the case to win an appeal. In the meantime, we'll have to concoct some kind of story about where you've been all this time. For now, though, you're going to be staying in Sue's cottage on Loon Lake. Kate will drive you there and stay with you for however long this takes."

It was almost midnight when they finally entered the house, but everyone was waiting up for them, even Jinx. A few excited minutes of barking and hugging and talking followed before it was agreed that everyone needed some sleep and Mark departed with Jeff.

"We should be out of here early," Kate said.

"The earlier, the better," Lily agreed.

Beryl was out on bail with strict orders to behave herself while awaiting her court date. The charges against her now included vandalism, resisting arrest, and misconduct. She had entered the grounds of Clair's house late that evening with the intention of planting another GPS tracking device inside the bumper of Kate's car. It had worked once. Well, almost. Kate usually left her Prius the driveway and Beryl figured that sooner or later Lily would be travelling somewhere in it.

The restraining order and the warnings scared her at first, but after three days of fuming, she'd had enough. She'd replayed the scene in Clair's driveway over and over and was certain that it was Lily she'd seen. Now all she had to do was prove it. She'd be smarter this time.

Beryl crept up behind the Prius and secured the tracker to the inner side of the bumper. She lingered, hiding beside a white spruce near the side fence to observe the windows. In spite of the late hour, the lights were on. She edged closer, hoping to catch a glimpse of Lily.

Half an hour passed with no signs of movement inside the house. Beryl was thinking about leaving when the headlights of a car approached and slowed as it turned into the driveway. She scrambled back to the spruce tree, hardly daring to breathe as a white Mercedes passed her and entered the carriage house. Motion sensor lights came on as a man and a woman neared the house. At this distance, it was difficult to identify the man, but he roughly matched photos she'd seen of Lily's father. The woman, it appeared, was either Kate or Lily. Minutes later, a taxi arrived and picked up Mark and the older man. She watched as, one by one, the lights inside the house went off.

Something was up and she'd be back to find out what that something was in a few hours.

CHAPTER

30

March 22

Beryl jerked to attention when her target began to move. She'd been careful about where she parked and she'd packed food too, prepared for a long stakeout. Pulling away from the curb, she pursued the moving speck on the screen of her phone until she zeroed in on Kate's Prius. When she drew close enough, she recognized the two "Kates". Laughing out loud, she backed off, allowing the car to lead the way, far ahead.

A dark feeling of dread had descended on Clair in the half hour since Lily and Kate had left. It had started as a vague sense of uneasiness, a nagging tickle in her scalp, as she'd watched them pull out of the driveway. Though she didn't share her mother's psychic gifts, there had been times in her life when she'd experienced a suggestion of those abilities. A twinge or a nudge, a soft voice in a corner of her mind. It was there now, persistent and growing louder.

Clair juggled two thoughts. Either something was amiss, or she was being a foolish old woman allowing recent events stir her imagination. "Oh, hell," she muttered and she picked her phone up from the counter and tapped in a number. "You'll think I'm kooky," Clair said when Meredith answered, "but I've got a bad feeling about this trip Lily and Kate are taking to the Muskokas."

"They're fine, Clair. I just spoke to Lily and we'll be keeping in touch."

"Well, I'm glad to hear that, but I've made a decision. I'm going to take Jinx and join them there, at least for one night. I just wanted to let everyone know."

"Hang on, Clair. Let me talk to Eric. He's right here."

Meredith covered the phone, her voice rising and falling in muffled tones at the other end.

"Clair," she said, "That's at least a two hour drive. Eric and I will take you there. We'll stay the night, make sure everything's okay, and then come back in the morning, either with or without you. And we'll get Mark to come over to stay with Jinx. Okay?"

"Oh, would you? Oh, my dear, I so appreciate this."

"To be honest, Clair, I'm dying to see Lily and show her that video of Jemma. She was spirited away before I had a chance. We can be at your place in about thirty minutes."

"I'll be ready," Clair said. "Oh, bless you, Meredith."

Clair whistled for Jinx so she could break the news to him and take him outside to do his business before she left. She felt better. The black feeling still hung in the background, but at least she was doing something about it. That sweet girl, Meredith, would change the course of her day. Just how, Clair could not have known.

Jeff was sitting in Mark's office when his son returned from his mission.

"Good job," he said, giving Mark a thumbs-up. "I've called 2 District and Bob Gaynor and, although they both want to talk to me, they've accepted the anonymous tip story, at least for now. Oh, and you just missed Eric. He dropped off Clair's key and the alarm code."

"Yeah, I'm a dog sitter now. And poor Eric is in for a ride."

"I also talked to Ryan Cross and arranged for us to have a chat and go through Brent's house tomorrow. I just levelled with him, told him the investigation will be reopened and I need to find that letter. I didn't tell him that we know about the five thousand dollars he offered the caretaker to find it."

"By now Leo and his girlfriend could have most of Brent's belongings packed up," Mark said. "We should talk to them."

"Actually, Ryan said he quit a few days ago. Apparently, Leo hurt his back or something so he's gone to his girlfriend's place in Newmarket."

Jemma listened in silence as Dean repeated the conversation he'd had with Meredith, an hour earlier. They were sequestered in a small room off the rehearsal studio, Jemma's half eaten lunch on the table between them.

"She's okay, now, though. She's on her way to her publisher's cottage up north with Kate. They'll stay there for a while and then she'll be turning herself in," Dean finished.

"She came close to dying and I let her think I didn't love her anymore," Jemma said, a sob caught in her throat. "I didn't know… I thought she'd be safe while I… I don't know what I was doing. Punishing her, I guess."

Dean reached across the table and pressed Jemma's hands between his own. "But she *didn't* die and you can still tell her how you feel."

"How could she just go off like that and risk everything?"

"Here's what I think. She loves you so much, she felt that she had to risk everything to get out of prison and back to you. And she's determined and stubborn just like you."

A fat tear splash-landed in Jemma's spoon.

"I'll take you to her if you want," Dean said.

"What about the show?"

"The show will be waiting for us when we get back. And if you never come back to it, that's okay, as long as you still want me in your life."

Jemma's chin quivered. "Can we go right now?"

"As fast as you can grab a toothbrush and a change of clothes," Dean said. "Glad I didn't turn in the rental. Have daughter, will travel."

Mark listened on speakerphone as his father feigned astonishment at Commander Gaynor's news. The body of Oliver Tate had been discovered by Antigua police and an investigation was underway to determine if, in fact, it was Ben Baines.

"Okay, I have another interesting piece of news," Gaynor said. "The Ford Focus you spotted on the surveillance video was rented at the Toronto airport by a man named Leonard Shaw. He's a resident of Chicago."

"Chicago!" Jeff scribbled the information on a note pad. "That's where Ben's biological brother, Richard Hogan, was arrested."

"It may not be a coincidence, Jeff. I don't know what to make of it, though. Hogan was serving time when Brent was murdered."

"Yes, but there has to be a connection."

Mark suddenly stabbed the paper with his finger. "Leonard… Leo! Leo is Leonard!"

Jeff stared at the name. "You could be right. Bob, there's a fellow named Leo that Brent's lawyer hired to be the caretaker of the Baines house. And he quit, just a few days ago. I'll give Mr. Cross another call and see what else I can find out."

"And I'll see what I can find out about Leonard Shaw's background."

"Thanks, Bob. Talk soon."

In seconds, Jeff was talking to Ryan Cross.

"What can I do for you?" Ryan asked.

"Solve a mystery, I hope. Your caretaker, Leo. Is his actual name Leonard Shaw?"

"Yes, Leo, or Buzz, as he was known to Brent and his buddies."

"Is he a buddy of yours?"

"More of an acquaintance. After Ben's memorial, he stayed in the area and became friends with Brent. I spent some time with them.

Watched a couple of games, went to the bar once. But I wasn't one of the gang. And I refused to use the stupid nickname."

"How did you happen to hire him?"

"Look, he didn't have a work visa, but–"

"It's not about that," Jeff said. "He may have been at the scene of the murder and police will want to question you about him."

"What?"

"I think it has something to do with the Lakeshore scam, but we haven't connected the dots yet. Do you know where Leo is right now?"

"No! He said he would be in touch, but I haven't heard from him."

"Do you know about anything that may have linked him to the Hogans?"

"Other than Ben, no. I mean, I assume that if he knew Ben in Chicago, he may have at least met Richard Hogan and Nicole Fleischer."

"Wait a minute. Fleischer? You mean Richard's wife?"

"Yes. After the conviction, she legally changed her name back to Fleischer, her maiden name."

"Do you know where she's serving her sentence?" Jeff asked.

"She's not."

"But I read that she got five years."

"You must have read an old article. Her sentence was based on the testimony of one witness, Guzman's lover, who later recanted. She claimed the prosecution had pressured her to testify against Nicole, even though she had no knowledge of her involvement. She was promised immunity. Richard had already testified that Nicole was unaware of the fraud. She admitted only to a suspicion that he'd 'borrowed' funds against future income. She got time served and was released."

"When?"

"Not sure. Several months after the conviction."

"Hmm. Okay, back to Leo. How did he get the job?" Jeff asked.

"Leo worked as a handyman. He'd met a woman here and was staying in the area picking up odd jobs and working for cash. Sometime after Brent died, he broke up with his girlfriend and moved back to Chicago, but he called me a few months ago and said he wanted to come back. He offered his services as a caretaker and said he could do repairs, clean up, anything I wanted. Later, when I needed the help, I hired him."

"Okay, Ryan. I'll pass this information on to the police. Thanks."

"Right. Keep me updated." Ryan disconnected and Jeff scrolled through his contact list.

"I'm calling the police," he said to Mark. "Meanwhile, you can talk to Lily."

Fifty minutes into their trip, traffic slowed to a crawl and then came to a standstill on the 400. "What the hell?" Eric grumbled.

"Oh, dear, I wonder if there's been an accident up ahead," Clair fretted.

Meredith, who'd been unnaturally quiet for the past several minutes, lowered her window. "Check the traffic report on your phone. Maybe something has been posted." She closed her eyes. "It's so hot in here."

Eric turned off the van's engine. "Feeling okay, honey?"

"I just told you. I'm hot and not in a good way. I had a stomach ache, but it's pretty much gone now."

"When did that start?" Clair asked from the back.

"About twenty minutes ago. I was going to mention it, but it passed."

"Remind me again when your baby is due," Clair asked.

Eric took on an alarmed expression. "The baby? You think it's the baby?"

"I'm not due for three weeks. It's that burrito I had for lunch."

Clair and Eric exchanged worried looks.

"I feel like the Goodyear blimp. And now, this backache."

Clair leaned into the front. "I think perhaps it wouldn't hurt to give your doctor a call."

Eric had his phone out in a flash.

"Don't bother. It's just–" Meredith clutched her belly and squeezed her eyes shut. "Okay, yeah, that didn't feel like a burrito."

Eric fumbled through the contact list and punched the wrong

name twice before getting through. He stepped out of the car and talked with whoever was on the other end. Two minutes later, he was back. "That was his office. He's going to call us right back. For now, we're supposed to time the contractions and get off at the next exit. The nurse said it might be false labour."

"Looks like the shoulder's blocked, too, Eric," Clair said. "Oh, I shouldn't have let you drive me. The stress may have brought this on."

"Not your fault," Meredith panted. "Ohhh, aren't these contractions supposed to come and go? This one has been constant." She made a little gasping sound and looked down. "My water just broke!"

"What does that mean? What does that mean? Is the baby coming?" Eric's voice was shrill.

"I'm calling 911!" He tapped in the number and spoke in a stuttering rush to the dispatcher. Then he listened and seemed to calm down a little as he repeated the message and described his location. He listened some more. "It's a beige Dodge Caravan. Yes… thank you. Please hurry."

"I think we should put her in the back and get her to lie down," Clair said when he'd ended the call.

"Right. The back seats fold down into the floor. They're sending an air ambulance. There's a pileup blocking all lanes this side of the next exit so nothing will be moving for a while."

Clair climbed out of the van and watched as Eric lowered the seats and moved aside some pieces of film equipment and a large folded tarp that had been stored in the back. They helped Meredith lie down with her feet facing the rear doors.

She emitted a long, loud wail. "This pain is relentless!"

Clair flew into action. "Eric, I want you to find a way to fix that tarp around the back of the van with the rear door open so it forms a roof over my head. When the ambulance arrives, they can take her straight out the back, but we don't need an audience."

Eric set about tying the tarp to the van, creating a makeshift cubicle. When he finished Clair told him to canvas nearby cars, searching for a doctor or a nurse and collecting items she might need – a knife or scissors, a first aid kit, towels, a blanket, water.

"My bag!" Meredith shouted. "Look in my bag!"

Eric grabbed her tote from the front seat and pawed through it. "Scissors, tissues, hand wipes…" He began tossing items into the back alongside his wife. "Hand sanitizer, one bottle of water…" A tiny smile played on his lips. "And a lighter."

"Okay, leave it with us. Now go see what else you can find."

When Eric returned with a blanket, three towels and several more bottles of water, Clair was standing at the back, leaning in. Meredith's stretch pants were off and a jacket had been draped over her from waist to knees. Her lower legs protruded from the van. Clair ripped one of the towels into strips.

"Did you find anyone with medical training?" she asked.

"Not yet."

"I think Meredith could be in precipital labour."

Eric stared at Clair, wide-eyed. "What's that?"

"It's when the contractions are continuous, or nearly continuous and extremely long and intense. It can be a very fast labour."

"How do you know about this stuff?"

"Before I married Bill, I was training to be a midwife," Clair said.

"Really? Have you ever actually delivered a baby?"

"Well, yes, I assisted in some deliveries."

"Thank God," Eric said.

"Of course, that was sixty years ago," Clair mumbled under her breath as he disappeared around the side of the van.

By this time, people in the surrounding cars knew what was going on and were helping to round up anything they thought might be useful. Ice, a plastic pail, more water, a ball of string, even some codeine-laced cough syrup.

"We're praying for you," a woman said, poking her head through the tarp. Eric had to do some crowd control. He looked frazzled when he returned to the cubicle.

Clair was placing a bunched-up piece of towel in a garbage bag. "Her mucus plug has become dislodged from her cervix."

Eric's hand flew to his mouth as a sour taste rose in his throat.

"Labour could kick in hard now, but there's no telling how long it will take."

The parking lot of the restaurant where Kate and Lily had stopped for lunch offered Beryl a clear view of the Prius. As she watched, one of the women got out of the car, returning a short time later with a container of takeout. Beryl focussed her binoculars on them from her parking spot at the side of the street. She glanced around and was surprised to see that a woman in a black Toyota Corolla parked two spaces ahead of her, also had a pair of binoculars trained on the parking lot. The man beside her was staring in the direction of Kate's car.

Interesting. Cops? Or something entirely different?

Kate recognized the number on her phone's display and passed it to Lily. "Mrrf," she said, a bit of shredded lettuce dangling from the corner of her mouth.

Lily chuckled and put down her wrap. "Hey, what's up, Mark?"

"Big news. Leo, the caretaker, is also known as Buzz, that mystery guy who showed up at Ben's memorial service. And Leo's full name is Leonard Shaw. And Leonard Shaw is the name of the person who rented the silver car that was parked near Brent's place."

"Shut up!"

"You sound like Jemma," Mark laughed. "Know what else? He's from Chicago and we're wondering if he knew Richard and Nicole Hogan who, incidentally, goes by the name Nicole Fleischer and is *not* in prison. She was released when her conviction was overturned sometime before Brent's death."

"This is a huge break! Fleischer – that's German. Leo's fiancé, Hannah, has a slight German accent. It wouldn't be a big leap to assume that Nicole somehow hooked up with Leo and became Hannah."

"That's brilliant, Lil. It ties her to the murder. We'll see what else we can find out, but I think your troubles may soon be over."

"We're not far from Sue's cottage and I think I should keep out of sight for now."

"Agreed. I'm thinking Leo and Hannah, whoever she turns out to be, have left the area, possibly gone back to Chicago by now. Either way, they'll be apprehended soon. We'll keep you posted. Give us a call when you get to the cottage."

"I will," Lily said. "Call you back soon." She repeated Mark's side of the conversation to a flabbergasted Kate.

"Leo and Nicole killed Brent?"

"It looks that way. I think they suspected Ben was still alive and living off the money from the scam. They tried to get information from Brent and, in the process, he ended up dead."

"I assume Leo wanted the caretaking job so they could look for Brent's letter," Kate said.

"Hoping it would tell them where to find Ben." Lily tapped away on Kate's phone and before long she was looking at a photo of Nicole Fleischer. "That's her," she said. "The woman I met at Brent's house." She passed the phone to Kate.

"Vanna White?"

"I thought so, too!"

"Except she's younger," Kate said, "and miserable."

"Well, this is a mug shot. My own wasn't exactly glamorous."

Lily shifted her gaze to a gull soaring above the trees. Soon she would be free. In the meantime, she could finally relax. The cottage was the perfect place.

"Where the hell is that helicopter?" Eric's face was face damp and creased with anxiety. Clair pulled him aside and spoke softly. "It's possible the accident up ahead has taken priority. Stay calm for your wife's sake."

"Eric!" Meredith screeched. "Come here!"

Eric crawled into the back of the van and stroked Meredith's head. "Yes, my love?"

"I need something for the pain," she moaned.

"Honey, let's just do those relaxation techniques we practised."

Meredith grabbed the front of his shirt and yanked him so hard, their noses touched. "Give me the damn cough syrup!"

Eric wrenched her hand free and backed off. "Opiates could harm the baby. Just breathe, love."

Meredith began to sob, called Eric an unflattering name, then uttered a guttural groan as the pain peaked again.

"It won't be long now," Clair informed them. "Start pushing, Meredith."

There was a long half grunt, half scream as Meredith bore down.

"Good girl. Again."

Eric held her hand and continued to stroke her hair as Meredith dug her nails into his wrist and pushed.

"Quick, Eric! Here comes your baby!" Clair called out.

Eric slid out of the van and bent to watch at the tailgate as Clair cradled the head and shoulders of the tiny, slimy form entering the world. She cleared the airway and a cry broke the stillness as the infant took its first breaths. In the background, a chorus of cheers rose from the motorists who had continued to monitor the situation through lowered windows.

"It's a girl!" Clair exclaimed, placing her on a towel. "She's small, but she looks healthy." She tied off and cut the cord as Meredith simultaneously laughed and sobbed. Clair gently wiped the baby down, wrapped her in a clean towel, and handed her to Eric who, by then, had scrambled back into the van to kiss his wife's face.

The thwacking sound of rotor blades greeted them and grew louder as Meredith and Eric gazed at their daughter, who continued to wail at the top of her tiny lungs.

"She's so beautiful," Meredith marveled. "And strong. Listen to her!

"She's perfect."

Clair stood at the back of the van cleaning herself with bottled water and towels, her face aglow. Next to her, the floor of the van was liberally soaked with the blood and gore of childbirth and Eric had to look away to fight his gag reflex. He briefly reflected, with some regret, on his choice of the sandstorm interior, rather than black, when he'd purchased the van. Wisely, he kept this thought to himself.

The paramedics ferried Meredith and the baby to the chopper, Eric trailing unsteadily behind. Shortly, a female police officer who had arrived with the chopper approached Clair.

"I'll drive you home, Mrs. Young," she said.

"Oh, what about Eric?"

"He'll accompany his wife. We'll take his van to the next exit and go back to Toronto. Traffic should be moving again soon."

Clair watched the helicopter lift off. "I hope Meredith and the baby will be okay."

"They're doing fine. The father's a little shaky, though. They were giving him oxygen when I left," the officer chuckled. "You delivered the baby?"

Clair nodded. "Seeing that baby come into the world was exhilarating."

"You are amazing."

"Oh, you're so very kind, my dear," Clair said, allowing herself, at last, to feel relief and gratification. It wasn't until she was belted into her seat in the van that the uneasy feeling from which she'd been so thoroughly distracted, returned.

CHAPTER 31

March 23

"It's a keypad entry system," Kate said, punching buttons above the handle. "Sue told me the door locks automatically, so memorize this code."

A hydro truck and a Toyota sedan rolled by and the roar of a four-wheeler sounded from across the lake. "Busier than I expected," Lily observed.

The cottage door opened with a squawk and memories of being here with Brent came flooding back to her. So much in her life had changed, but the room looked exactly the same. She and Kate set their luggage and bags of groceries on the floor and walked over to the patio doors to gaze out at the lake.

"No swimming today?" Lily said.

Kate laughed. "Sue said it would be mostly frozen. Spring breakup doesn't happen here until late March or April." She looked around. "This is charming."

"Three bedrooms and a nice bunkie," Lily said, throwing open the curtains. "And it's insulated. Most of the cottages here are seasonal." She turned the thermostat up. "Did Sue tell you how to turn on the water?"

"Yes. She also said there's no landline."

"Well, at least we have your cellphone... if I can manage not to lose this one. And speaking of phone, I'd better touch base with Mark," Lily said. She picked up the bags of food and carried them into the kitchen.

"I'll bring in the rest of the groceries," Kate said, turning to go out.

Lily called Mark.

"I forgot to mention that you have visitors on the way," he said.

"Who?"

"Clair was worried. She said she had a bad feeling about you being at the cottage. I think she was just feeling left out."

Lily felt a pang of apprehension.

"Eric and Meredith are driving her and yours truly is looking after the mutt. Try to act pleasantly surprised when they show up."

"Okay. Thanks for the heads up."

They chatted a few minutes longer then Lily said goodbye, pocketed the phone and called out to Kate as she began unpacking the groceries. When there was no answer, she peered out the window above the sink. A sudden knock at the front door startled her. Kate having trouble with the keypad? Lily went into the living area and peeked through the sidelight next to the door. A slender woman wearing a tweed bucket hat, and large, dark sunglasses was looking back at her.

"I'm the neighbour," the woman mouthed, smiling and pointing in the direction of the next cottage. It seemed strange to Lily that anyone would be at their cottage this time of the year, especially the deserted looking one next door. Then she spotted the woman's shoes. They were two tone grey runners with pink laces. These were the same shoes she'd noticed on the feet of the woman she'd surprised in Brent's attic.

There was no time to think it over. Nicole Fleischer was here, and probably Leo, too. And Kate was missing. Lily ran into the kitchen and frantically searched the countertops. Where had she put the damn phone? The sound of shattering glass jarred her. Someone was breaking in through the window in one of the bedrooms. She yanked open a drawer and grabbed the first thing she saw, a paring knife. Then she raced to the sliding doors at the back of the cottage and released the lock. The door refused to budge. Lily shoved the small knife into the back pocket of her jeans and tugged with both hands. It finally broke free and rolled along its track.

As Lily emerged, an intense pain shot through her body. She screamed as her muscles contracted involuntarily and, totally incapacitated, she dropped to the deck. In the next instant, her hands were behind her and a thin rope was binding them. The phone she had absently thrust into the front pocket of her jeans pressed against her thigh and dimly registered beneath the subsiding pain. She felt herself being yanked to her feet and pushed roughly into the house. Her legs were trembling and weak as she staggered inside. Lily locked eyes with Leo. Still gripping her arm, he shoved her across the room. He opened the front door for Nicole. She removed her sunglasses and hat, shaking free the blonde hair that had been tucked out of sight.

Leo jerked Lily toward an armchair and twisted her around. "Sit," he ordered, shoving her backward with one of his steel-toed work boots.

Nicole jumped. "Take it easy, Leo!"

"Where's Kate?" Lily gasped, wincing. Her hands were working to slip the paring knife out of her pocket.

Leo answered calmly. "Hog-tied and blindfolded in the back of her car. Couldn't have you hearing a gun go off. She didn't get a look at us, so maybe she'll be luckier than you." He pulled a pistol from the waistband of his pants. "Good of you to choose such a remote location."

Lily tried to contain her panic as she turned the knife in her fingers and began to discreetly saw at the cord binding her wrists. "Why are you doing this?"

Nicole was holding a Taser like the one she assumed Leo had just used on her. "You're the only one who's seen my face," she said. "Eventually, you would have figured out who I am and why I was in that house. As far as anyone else is concerned, there's no connection between me and Leo at all."

Leo advanced toward Lily, arms still relaxed at his sides. He watched her eyes drop to the Beretta in his right hand as he stopped in front of her.

"Why didn't you just shoot me outside?" Lily asked and she wondered if they intended to question her first.

"Too loud. And the Taser is so much more fun." Leo smiled. "Most people don't get to know the details of their death in advance." He held the gun, palm up, beneath her nose. "March twenty-second, Loon Lake, nine millimetre semi-automatic."

Nicole was jittery. "Don't make this any harder than it is, Leo."

"Do you really think I didn't know who Hannah was before you showed up here… Nicole?" Lily turned her face away from the pistol and glared at her.

Nicole frowned and motioned for Leo to stop. She stepped closer. The move was meant to appear threatening, but it allowed Lily to sense her agitation. "If you'd known who I was before now, the police would have come after us already. What else did you just figure out?"

Lily held her eyes. "Leo got the caretaking job so you could look for the letter that you hoped would lead you to Ben. And probably spelled out your part in the Lakeshore Investment scam.

Leo smirked. "Thanks, by the way, for that little tip. The jury didn't buy your story about the letter, but we did."

"Did you realize who I was in the attic?" Lily asked, remaining focussed on Nicole.

"Of course. You introduced yourself as a writer doing research on Brent. As soon I got a look at your face, I knew. You'd been all over the news every day."

"Well, I guess you were a little more invested in the story than the general public, right?"

"Come on," Leo growled. "She's stalling."

"Just wait!" Nicole snapped. Her face looked strained as she brought it close to Lily's. "What else do you *think* you know?"

"I know that if you kill me, you'll be caught. The police are looking for you on both sides of the border."

Nicole stared at her.

"You could have just disappeared like Ben," Lily said. "Why would it matter if I figured out who you were?"

"First of all, that would have implicated Leo. And also, unlike

Ben, I have no desire to surgically change my appearance and live in a foreign country. I'm rather fond of this face."

"So, you and Leo managed to get your hands on the missing money?"

"Ben and the money are not a problem anymore," Leo blurted. "You're the problem."

Nicole was pacing now, eyes on the floor. She was thinking. She was worried.

Leo was getting impatient. "No one else knows anything," he said.

"I don't like this," Nicole fretted. "We shouldn't have come here." She turned to Lily. "I never wanted it to play out this way. But you saw me, and Leo thinks…"

At this, Leo grabbed her arm and pulled her toward him. "What the hell are you doing? There's no other way. You can't go soft on me after everything we've been through."

"Just… let's slow down a minute and–"

"No, let's get this over with." Leo released her arm and moved toward Lily.

"Please, Leo. Come over here," Nicole said, tugging on Leo's leather jacket.

Leo followed her across the room, where Nicole spoke to him in hushed tones.

Lily continued to work the small knife awkwardly over the cord behind her back. The blade was dull, but soon she'd be through. If the pistol came within her range, a well-aimed kick could send it flying and maybe she'd be the first to grab it. There was a better chance she'd get shocked again or shot, but she had no other ideas.

A faint *clunking* sound broke the silence and Leo whipped his head in the direction of the back of the house. "Did you hear that?"

They both listened, focussed on the patio doors, and Lily adjusted her position as she continued to saw.

"If she moves, zap her!" Leo said, racing toward the deck.

Nicole scurried over and pointed the Taser at Lily. "What are you doing?"

"Just trying to get comfortable," Lily said.

"Stop moving!"

They glared at each other in the wordless wait that followed.

Nicole stood close to Lily, holding the Taser straight out in front, her face pinched with anxiety.

Suddenly the patio doors opened and Beryl appeared, walking just ahead of Leo. He held the gun to her back. At the same moment, Lily sawed through the last threads of the cord and wriggled her hands free to get a good grip on her little knife.

"We have company," Leo announced and Nicole swung the Taser in their direction.

Beryl wore an expression of confusion as her eyes travelled from Lily to Nicole.

"Who are you?" Nicole demanded, so pumped she was shaking.

Lily could see Beryl trying to make sense of the scene – her quarry sitting in a comfortable chair with her hands tucked strangely behind her back, facing a very jumpy and armed woman who looked remarkably like Vanna White. Minus the cheerful smile. She didn't know if what happened next was intentional or the result of Nicole's tense grip on the Taser. The weapon fired, and the electrodes, their wires trailing behind, shot out and connected to Beryl's belly. A ragged wail erupted as Beryl fell forward and vibrated uncontrollably on the floor for a full five seconds. At last, she slowly pushed herself to her knees and stared up at Nicole.

"Answer the question!" Leo barked.

"I'm a… I'm a correctional officer," Beryl stammered. "Beryl… Sweeney." She yanked the barbed ends of the wires from her shirt.

"Put your hands behind your back, Sweeney. I don't know what the hell you're doing here, but you're gonna talk in a minute." Leo handed Nicole the gun and told her to keep it trained on Lily and Beryl, then took another piece of cord from his pocket.

Nicole stood two paces away, the Taser still in her right hand, the Beretta trembling in her left. She glanced nervously from Lily to Leo, who was crouched with one knee on the floor. When Nicole's attention lingered on him, Lily made her move. Bracing herself on the arms of the chair, she kicked hard at her target. She was right behind the gun as it sailed through the air, hit the pine floor and slid out of sight beneath an antique oak cabinet. She changed her course and ran toward the back deck. Beryl and Leo were both on their feet. In her peripheral vision, Lily saw Beryl's bulky form moving toward Nicole. The thud of Leo's boots followed her as she charged out the patio door.

Lily leapt over the three steps off the deck and sped toward the lake. The blue denim shirt she was wearing over her T-shirt billowed behind her. Leo was on her heels, his larger stride gaining on her as she neared the ice. She felt his fingers graze her back as he grasped the fabric of her shirt. She angled her arms and let it peel away. Leaping off the low bank, she skidded on the rough ice. It was thick near shore, but out on the lake, some areas were beginning to open up. Here and there, small pools of water glistened in the sun.

Lily scanned the opposite shore. The cottages there were likely also vacant, but there was a good chance she could outrun Leo once she reached the road. He was fast, but she had endurance on her side. At the moment, neither was moving at top speed as their feet slipped and slid on the ice. As she ran farther out onto the lake, its texture began to soften, becoming rubbery in places. Lily glanced back to see Leo, now several metres behind, picking his way toward her. Water seeped into the spot where she'd just stepped. She moved forward quickly, then stopped, her eyes darting to the ice ahead. The dark area straight in front looked thin and there was a patch of open water to the left. Leo saw that she was hesitating and made a charge at her. She turned and ran, veering to the right.

He was almost on top of her when they broke through. A shock ran through Lily as the freezing water enfolded her. She kicked hard and popped to the surface. Leo came up, gasping and spluttering and clawing frantically at the water. He grabbed at the edge of the ice and it broke away under the weight of his arms. The cold was stinging and numbing. Lily knew she'd have to get out quickly.

To her surprise, she realized she was still clutching the paring knife in her right hand. She swam to the edge of the big hole, then plunged the knife into the ice and tried to haul herself up. It gave way but she kept trying until she found a solid spot that could support her weight. She had managed to pull her upper body out of the water when Leo grabbed on and tried to climb over her. The ice broke away, but, in his panic to stay afloat, Leo remained clamped to her. Struggling to keep her head above water, Lily tried to break his hold by stabbing her knife repeatedly at his arm.

The memory came to her in a sensory flash of colour and smell and sound.

Her royal blue swimsuit. Chlorine. Her lifesaving instructor's voice projecting across the pool. "If the victim will not release his hold on you, submerge yourself. A drowning person wants to be at the surface and will let go if you go under."

Taking a deep breath, Lily stopped struggling and began to descend. Her hands were numb, but she maintained her hold on the knife. As anticipated, Leo released her and clawed frantically toward the light. Quickly Lily surfaced, swam to the opposite side of the hole and smashed at the ice until she found another solid edge. She stabbed the knife into the crusty ice, but her numb fingers couldn't grip the handle and it slipped from her grasp and lay on the ice. Slinging her left arm over the edge, Lily put the fingers of her right hand in her mouth and held them there for a few seconds to restore some circulation.

Behind her, Leo was floundering, pressing at edges of ice that continued to break beneath his weight. His leather jacket and heavy work boots, laced high and double tied, were weighing him down and the cold was quickly defeating him. Lily picked up the knife and, holding it as firmly as she could, thrust it into the ice. She pulled her body up and forward until her rib cage rested on the frozen surface, then repositioned the knife farther away and kicked furiously to elevate her legs. Clapping her left hand around her right, she strained and wiggled until her hips were out, then stabbed at the ice one last time and heaved her body forward, lifting her legs clear.

The splashing sounds had all but ceased. Lily turned her head to see Leo clinging to a chunk of floating ice. "Help," he pleaded. His voice was desperate.

Lily couldn't stand, much less help. Lungs still heaving, she met his eyes and spoke the last words he'd ever hear. "March twenty-second, Loon Lake, drowning."

She rolled away from the hole and slithered to safer territory. Behind her, a paroxysm of splashing, gasping and choking broke the stillness and then, just as suddenly, there was silence. Lily rested her head on her arms and breathed deeply. Her pounding heart drove blood to her limbs and began to restore sensation. When she looked up again, fragments of slowly spinning ice were the only traces of Leo's struggle.

Pulling herself along like a wounded soldier, Lily crept toward shore. When she thought it was safe, she rose to her hands and knees and slowly stood. Sunlight caressed her bare arms, rosy from the biting cold water.

She was a few steps from shore when Kate burst through the open patio door and ran toward her. "Lily!"

"Kate! Oh, thank God!" Lily took faltering steps across the last of the ice and dropped to her knees on the lowest stone step that led up the bank. And then Kate was at her side, an arm around her waist, lifting her to her feet.

"Nicole?" Lily panted.

"Handcuffed on the floor. Come on."

Beryl stood at the door holding a blanket and as Lily stepped inside, she wrapped it around her.

"Thanks," Lily mumbled, still numbed by her ordeal.

"No need to thank me," Beryl said. "I'm sure you hate me and I don't blame you."

Lily was too overwhelmed to respond. She noticed then that one of Kate's wrists looked red and raw. She reached out and turned her hand over and her eyes looked questioningly into Kate's.

"I'd worked one hand free and was tackling the knots when Beryl found me," she said.

Lily nodded slowly. Her eyes filled and her throat tightened. She'd almost cost her friend her life. Kate wrapped her arms around Lily and they clung to each other as Beryl stood behind them, observing awkwardly.

"What happened out there?" Kate asked at last, gripping Lily's arms.

"The ice broke. I got out. He didn't."

A muffled cry drew her eyes to the floor in front of the fireplace. Nicole lay face down, her head turned to the side. Her feet were tied with the same cord that had bound Lily's wrists, and her arms were pinned behind her back with handcuffs Beryl had intended to use on someone else.

Beryl hauled Nicole up by one arm and sat her down on the hearth.

"We should call the police," Kate said.

Lily patted the front pockets of her jeans. "I'm afraid your brand new phone is at the bottom of the lake."

"As long as *you* are not."

"Use mine," Beryl said.

Kate took the phone and stepped into the kitchen.

Lily changed into dry clothes and returned to the living room. She sat on the edge of the coffee table and rubbed a towel over her wet hair as she glared at Nicole. "Okay, your turn to answer some questions. Ben's dead. What do you know about that?"

Nicole lifted her head, glared back and clamped her lips together.

Beryl picked something up from a nearby end table and Lily saw the Taser in her hand just before she pressed it into Nicole's ribs. Nicole writhed in pain and cried out.

"How do you like it, bitch?"

"No, Beryl! No Tasers!" Lily shouted.

Smirking, Beryl pulled the weapon away. "This particular model works as a stun gun when the cartridge is spent," she said. "Not as incapacitating, but it still hurts like hell. I found an extra cartridge in her pocket, though." She put her face right in front of Nicole's. "Now answer the nice lady's questions or I'll load it and give you the full monty."

Wincing, Nicole turned her head away. "Leo killed Ben. Call her off and I'll talk."

Beryl pulled a footstool in close and sat down.

"That was Leo chasing you on the motorcycle in Antigua. You led him to Ben and he caught him off guard. Shot him with Ben's own gun. He had to kill that black guy, first, the one who came along in the truck," Nicole said, her voice dull.

"Jenson," Lily told her. "And he's not dead."

Nicole's expression remained flat.

"Were you in Antigua with Leo?"

"No, I stayed in Toronto."

"How did Leo find out about Antigua?"

"I knew you'd seen something in those photos on the office wall. When you went downstairs and told your friend about the map coordinates, I listened in on the monitor. There were still hidden cameras in the house."

Lily's mind flashed back to the monitor on Brent's desk. In her excitement, she'd forgotten about it as she spoke to Sue. "And so you examined the photo and figured out the coordinates."

Nicole nodded. "But first I followed you in my car."

"I didn't see another car when we were there."

"It was hidden in the garage so Ryan wouldn't know I was there. I called Leo from my car and told him what was going on. I lost you in Toronto traffic, but Leo did a reverse lookup for the landline phone number you'd given me and found the address. I got there in time to see your friend drop you off."

"Then what?"

"By the time I got back to Oakville, Leo had examined the photos, figured it out and booked a flight to Antigua. We wanted to track Ben down before anyone else did. I went back and staked out the Young house. We figured something was going to happen soon."

"You were there when I left for the airport in the morning?"

"I followed you there, then I called Leo and he was waiting at the airport when you arrived."

"And I led him straight to Ben."

"Leo didn't find him at the exact coordinates on those photos, but he guessed that you had more information. He was able to track you to the boat and then to Ben's house the second morning you were there."

Kate came back into the room. "The police are on their way," she said.

Beryl leaned forward, elbows on her knees, the Taser still poised in her hand as she stared ominously at Nicole. Nicole's eyes darted to the message printed on Kate's shirt. The last thing I want to do is hurt you, but it's still on the list.

Lily resumed her interrogation. "Now tell me about the letter, the confession Brent told me he'd written. Did you ever find it?"

"Yes. It was handwritten and sealed inside the back of one of the photos with the coordinates on it. The police didn't cut the backing. We did."

"Then why were you still there?"

"The letter didn't tell us where Ben had gone. And it's not like we had anything better to do. We were looking for more clues. Then when you escaped, there was renewed interest in the case and we wanted to see how that would play out.

"Which one of you killed Brent?" Lily asked.

There was silence and Beryl leaned closer.

"It was an accident," Nicole said. "We suspected Ben had faked his own death and made off with our money. Leo tapped his phone and bugged Brent's house, hoping to find out where he'd gone. Then you came along and he was about to confess everything. When we got there that day, he was sitting in the kitchen with a bottle of scotch in front of him. He wouldn't talk. We tried to bargain with him and we threatened him with blackmail. Leo threatened to harm his son. Then I picked up a knife from the block on the counter and flashed it at him. It was just meant to scare him, but he lunged at me and I slashed him. I never intended to kill him."

Not right then, anyway, Lily thought. "How did the hoodie get splattered?"

"It was draped, front side out, over the back of one of those swivel chairs at the island and that's where we were standing when I grabbed the knife. The blood sprayed all over me and everything around me.

"Then what?"

Nicole closed her eyes. "He just dropped. There was nothing we could do for him. I freaked, but Leo calmed me down. He said we had to get out, but first he needed to remove the wiretap."

"When had he tapped the phone?"

"After he befriended Brent and spent time at his house. He'd spotted a phone jack in the garage, so one night he broke in there and installed an in-line tap and some kind of device that recorded and transmitted calls. He hid it under a workbench. Anyway, he ripped all that stuff out and waited for me in the car. I was wiping away prints when my phone rang and Leo told me there was a car pulling into the driveway."

"You were still in the house when I went in?"

"I'd gone out the side door. After you went in, I ran past your car and tossed in the jacket. Then I saw another car turning in –

like suddenly it was Grand fucking Central Station – so I ducked behind the bushes. That car pulled into the side driveway and then Leo came along in the rental and I got into the back seat. Kept my head down till we were out of Oakville." Nicole's chin quivered and a tear trailed down her face. "And now he's dead."

"So are Ben and Brent, because of you," Kate said. "And Leo would still be alive if he hadn't been trying to kill Lily. Did it ever occur to you that Leo was just using you to get to the money? She probably just saved your life, too."

Nicole sniffed and stared off into space as the first faint sounds of sirens reached them.

"How did you hook up with Leo? Was he involved with Lakeshore Investors?" Lily asked.

"No," Nicole muttered. "He was in our social circle. To Richard, he was just Buzz from San Diego. He introduced him to Ben because they both liked to sail."

"And let me guess. You and Leo had been having an affair, but Richard didn't know. He thought you'd recover the money and be waiting for him when he got out."

Nicole was silent.

"Did Ben have access to the money?"

"We were trying to cover our tracks when the police showed up. Richard sent Ben out the back door with the bank records and one of our computers. He was supposed to safeguard everything and then he'd get a big payout when our sentences were up. Richard stupidly believed that because Ben was his blood brother, he could trust him. I told him from the start not to bring him into the business, but he never listened to me. He was a fool."

"Certainly a fool to trust you," Kate said.

"I didn't love Richard. I had planned to take my cut, divorce him, and marry Leo."

The sirens were close now and Nicole looked almost relieved. Lily and Kate got up and walked over to the front window. Beryl rose to her full height. She brought the Taser to Nicole's face and rubbed it lightly along her cheek. Nicole flinched and squeezed her eyes shut.

"Thank you for your cooperation, sweetheart," Beryl purred. "Maybe I'll see you in prison." She bent down and breathed into

Nicole's ear. "You can be my special pet." Then she picked up the damp towel, wiped down the Taser and tossed it onto the floor.

Kate opened the door as two police cruisers stopped in front of the cottage. Nicole was arrested and placed in the back of a cruiser, and Lily and Kate poured out their stories. Two more OPP cruisers and an ambulance from Gravenhurst arrived. Crime scene photographs were taken and two of the investigators ventured a short distance onto the ice to scan the water. Mark and Jeff were called. Lily drank hot tea at the kitchen table as she continued to answer the questions put to her by a detective.

Beryl leaned against one of the cruisers under the watchful eye of Sergeant Buckley, a tall, talkative fellow with a broad chest, a boyish face and a high, Herman Munster kind of forehead.

"That was a nice bit of detective work you did, tracking them here," Buckley said.

Beryl scuffed at a bit of gravel. "I wasn't even on the right track."

"You were only acting on the information you had at the time and it was more than the police were able to do." He stuck out his hand. "I'm Roland," he said, "Roly to friends."

He was four inches taller and Beryl had to look up. She took in the kind, hazel eyes and the full, dark hair, just beginning to grey at the temples. She glanced at his hands. His ring finger was bare. *Roland, eh? Roland… Roly… Roly and Beryl. Not the best pairing of names. But it couldn't hurt to be friendly.* By the time Beryl tentatively reached for his hand, Roland was withdrawing his. She gave him a half-hearted smile, then looked down and resumed her scuffing.

"You know, if it weren't for you, this could've ended very differently. You may have saved their lives."

"Nah, that one, Lily, she's got an angel on her shoulder."

Roland was thinking this was a rather sweet sentiment until Beryl completed the thought.

"Or a horseshoe up her ass."

The sergeant's smile evaporated and he turned his attention to the lake. "The ice is breaking up fast. Maybe the dive team will get a boat in the water tomorrow."

An officer poked his head into the kitchen where Lily was still talking to the detective. "There's someone out front waiting to see Lily," he said. The detective nodded his approval and she went to the door.

"Jemma!" Lily cried, clamping her daughter in her arms.

"They wouldn't let us in. Mum, what happened?" Jemma asked, her voice choked.

Dean stood just behind Jemma and Lily pulled him into the hug, too. "Thank you," she murmured into his ear. "I'll tell you all about it, but right now, I'm just so happy you're here. It's all over. I'm free!"

"Sorry I was so mean. You know how much I love you, right?" Jemma wiped tears from her face as Lily, kissing her forehead, finally broke the hug.

"Always, without question."

"We got stuck in traffic on the 400 or we'd have been here sooner." Dean looked around anxiously. "Are you and Kate okay?"

"We are now," Lily said. She lifted her face to the sky. The world felt different: safe, friendly, and warm. She knew it was just as mysterious and complicated, and as wonderful and magnificent, and tragic and disgusting as it had ever been. But in that moment – it was beautiful.

CHAPTER 32

March 24

A large group of family and friends were crammed in Meredith's room at the Toronto General Hospital. The nursing staff, well aware of the identity of the visitors and the dramatic events of the previous day, had turned a blind eye to the rules. Had they not, Lily would have ignored them anyway. She was a seasoned outlaw now.

Meredith was propped up in her bed looking very pleased with herself. Eric stepped into the room, a bundle cradled close to his chest. Laying their baby gently in Meredith's arms, amid a swell of oohs and ahs, he announced, "Everyone, we'd like to present to you, our precious daughter, Clair."

There was a delighted, collective gasp. Clair, the elder, clapped her hands to her face, wearing in an expression of shock that rapidly melted into a wide smile.

"We owe you so much Clair," Eric continued. "This is our tribute to you."

"We love the name and we love *you*," Meredith added.

"I am so deeply honoured," Clair gushed, and with that, the room came alive as family members jostled for position, softly touching baby Clair's tiny round cheeks and fine hair, and fawning over Meredith.

Lily had her turn, then kissed her sister's cheek and slipped to the back of the room. Surrounded by family, she felt content. Sunshine beamed in through the windows, casting her in a spotlight of warmth as clouds passing over the city drifted by. She gazed at the scene beyond the window. Thirty days ago, a savage storm had roared in across the landscape and she had run, not away from it, but with it. She thought of the Strength card Clair had shown her and how the lion could be tamed, not with force, but with love. Without that love, she never would have found the courage and determination to conquer her beasts. But she had. She, Lillian Alice Mullaly. LAM.

EPILOGUE

March 31

It was unseasonably warm on the last day of March at Jeff and Emma Mullaly's home on the St. Lawrence River. The lawn had begun to turn green and along the riverbank the first hints of yellow appeared at the tops of daffodil shoots. Purple crocuses were scattered throughout the flowerbeds. The trees and bushes were still bare, but their buds were beginning to swell.

Family and friends were gathered to celebrate Lily's official declaration of freedom. Much had happened in a few short days. The story was everywhere on both sides of the border. The press was clamouring for interviews and Lily's fan base had gone through the roof, shooting sales of her previous books sky high.

Nicole, having confessed everything, was awaiting her trial. Divers had recovered Leo's body from the lake and released it to his brother in San Diego. Although he'd had no prior convictions, Leo had been previously investigated in connection with a number of crimes, including some questionable insurance claims and the suspicious death of his wife.

The documents relating to the money Ben had stashed away in foreign accounts had been found among Leo and Nicole's possessions and just over six million dollars had been recovered. This, along with the proceeds from the sale of Ben's assets was to be returned to the victims of the Ponzi scheme.

Jenson was expected to make a full recovery. His last memory of the day he'd been attacked was of Lily calling to him from behind the office door.

Back at Grand Valley Institution for Women, Rayne was no longer queen bee. She'd pulled her tough girl routine on a young inmate who had then returned with a posse of allies and confronted her behind one of the bungalows. Whatever had transpired there had effectively put an end to Rayne's reign. When Lily's conviction had been overturned and her story flooded the news, Rayne had sat soberly in the common room, watching the broadcast without her usual malice. She was destined to serve out her time without the entourage she needed to fuel her ego.

Beryl had been persuaded to resign from her job when it was suggested that she might be fired if she didn't. She was exploring opportunities in the securities field while she considered a future in private investigation. The media was courting her and her accounts of her experiences, though not entirely accurate, were entertaining. She'd struggled to write Lily a letter, but words were not her forte. Instead, to Lily's amusement, she'd sent her a dozen ten-ounce cartons of Milk Duds and a note that said, "Sorry for being such an ass. Beryl".

Lily and the rest of the family had finally heard Jemma sing at an impromptu performance organized at the audition studio. Jemma had laughingly described her mother as being "completely flipped out" midway through the first song. Lily had agreed to share custody and hire a tutor so that Jemma could sign on with the cast of *Thin Air.*

Lily had also agreed to continue living at Clair's home in Toronto while she and Kate worked on the book on the condition that she would be allowed to cook from time to time. This had been a tough negotiation, but Lily had prevailed.

There had been much discussion within the ranks of the legal system as to what should be done about the "accessories after the fact" who had come to Lily's aid following her escape. In the end, in light of her innocence, the mishandling of evidence that contributed to her wrongful conviction, and the overwhelming public support for all concerned, charges were not laid.

Lily, happily brunette again, leaned on the railing of the narrow deck and looked out over the guests clustered on the patio and the lawn below her. Sue and her husband were there, as were Kate's parents who, upon hearing the news, had returned from Florida. Jinx was there, too, barking ferociously at a squirrel that scolded him from the overhead branches of a tree. "Kate 'n Mark," whose joined names now had the familiar ring of an established couple, laughed from the sidelines. Clair sat in animated conversation with Jemma and Dean on the patio. Whatever she was saying had a wide-eyed Jemma on the edge of her seat.

Lily inhaled deeply. The air had the fresh, clean scent of renewal, the returning of life. The door behind her slid open and her parents joined her at the railing.

"I hope you don't mind, but I invited Bob Gaynor to join us. He's very anxious to talk to you and hear your story," Jeff said.

"Tell him to buy the book." Lily grinned. "Is he the tall, balding gentleman down there by the water? The one Georgia is flirting shamelessly with?"

"That's him and he's flirting right back."

Emma was beaming. "Just think of it. Thirty days ago, you were running through a blizzard and now here we are, basking in the sun!

Lily smiled and waited. She knew what was coming.

"But that's March for you. In like a lion, out like a lamb."

ACKNOWLEDGEMENTS

I am grateful to the following people:

The earliest readers who gave me valuable feedback on the evolving manuscript: Linda Mason, Shelagh Mathers, Tara Marion, Melody Lawrence.

Bev Humphrey who patiently listened, read and shared her thoughts at every stage of the process. Her enthusiasm and support kept me on track.

My agent, Bill Hannah and associate agent, Kathy Olenski who saw the merit in this story from its beginnings and who gave guidance and encouragement that helped me continue to pursue my goal.

David "J.D." Carpenter and Peter Blendell who generously helped to steer me along this new road. How fortunate I am to have the support and advice of these accomplished authors.

An extra thank you to Peter Blendell. I could not have asked for a more dedicated or brilliant editor.